Book 2
of the
Cornish Chronicles Series

Waiting for the

Harvest Moon

Ann E Brockbank

**Front cover by © R W Floyd, from an original oil
painting**

ISBN-13: 9798687885270

For my very special friends,

Angie and Alan

.

ACKNOWLEDGMENTS AND THANKS

My grateful thanks go to all you lovely people who buy and read my books. I so appreciate your continual support. You are all wonderful I am enormously privileged that you believe in me and chose my books to read.

There is always a long list of people to thank for helping me get this book to publication and here they are. As always, I couldn't have written this book without the editorial help and support of some very special people. My upmost thanks go to Angie, for her historical guidance and reining in my creative spelling and to Cathy for her sensitive editorial suggestions and for putting the stray apostrophes in the right place. You both improve the book no end. Also, to Wendy who is the first to read the finished manuscript. I cannot thank you all enough for your generous time, friendship and expertise.

Once again, my heartfelt gratitude goes to Sarah and Martin Caton and their lovely family for allowing me to use their beautiful home Bochym Manor as a setting for 'Waiting for the Harvest Moon' and my previous novel 'A Gift from the Sea'. I don't think I have ever found a more inspirational place to write about.

To my beloved partner Rob for your love and encouragement. As always, your beautiful artwork adds a special quality to my novels.

To the amazing staff at Poldhu Café, I thank you for your continued support by selling my books locally.

If you enjoyed this book, please could you leave a short review on Amazon? You can do this even if you didn't buy the book on Amazon! If you loved this book, please spread the love and tell your friends, hopefully they too will support me by buying the book.

ABOUT THE AUTHOR

Ann E Brockbank was born in Yorkshire, but has lived in Cornwall for many years. Waiting for the Harvest Moon is Ann's sixth book and the second in the Cornish Chronicles series. Her inspiration comes from holidays and retreats in stunning locations in Greece, Italy, Portugal, France and Cornwall. When she's not travelling, Ann lives with her artist partner on the beautiful banks of the Helford River in Cornwall, which has been an integral setting for all of her novels. Ann is currently writing her seventh novel. Ann loves to chat with her readers so please visit her Facebook Author page and follow her on Twitter and Instagram

Facebook: @AnnEBrockbank.Author
Twitter: @AnnEBrockbank1
Instagram: annebrockbank

Waiting for the Harvest Moon

.

Chapter 1

Cornwall - 17th March 1907

The wind blowing up the Helford River was as sharp and cold as a knife. Sophie Treloar paused from black-leading the range and sat back on her haunches. Despite the icy draught from beneath the front door, Sophie was hot, and beads of perspiration stippled her brow. She pushed a stray hair from her face with her sleeve and rolled her head to ease the stiffness from her neck. She glanced dismally at her hands - her fingers, once nimble at her needlework, were now rough and pitted with grime, tipped with ragged nails. Alas, this had been her lot for eight long years. There was no time for vanity - as soon as the black-lead was done, she'd have to burnish the steel rims and trim edges, along with the top plate of the range with thick wire wool to prevent rust building up.

The sound of heavy footsteps advancing to her door made her heart falter, Jowan - her husband was due back any day from his fishing trip. A curl of anxiety wormed into her stomach at the thought of him - she had hoped for at least another day of peace. As always, he'd arrive home, stinking of fish, with a raging thirst for both ale and his marital rights, and, without doubt another disgusting infection to pass on to her. Taking a deep quavering breath to steady her nerves, she turned to meet her adversary as the door opened. Her relief was palpable when the tall, cumbersome frame of her mother-in-law, Ria, lumbered into the house.

Sophie noted the curl of Ria's lip and resented the fact that she revelled at her unease.

Ria shed her hat and coat, lowered her sizable bulk into the fireside chair and folded her arms on her ample bosom.

'I saw you day-dreaming. It's a good job my Jowan didn't catch you, my girl and that's the truth!'

1

Silently, Sophie turned her attention back to the job in hand. She'd perfected the art of dumb insolence towards Ria's domineering ways - mainly because she had neither the will nor the energy to retaliate.

The 'daydreams' Ria so sarcastically spoke of, were Sophie's way of coping with the disillusionment of her empty, oppressive life.

Sophie had been eighteen when Jowan breezed into her life. He was tall, strong, quite good-looking, and at the time, generous with his money. He offered her marriage, a life away from gutting fish in Newlyn, and a cottage, situated in the lush and leafy vale of Gweek at the very top of the Helford River. His description of Alpha Cottage at the bottom of a lane surrounded by green, fertile hills blinded her for a while - the reality quickly disenchanted her. She'd arrived as a new bride in Gweek, bundled unceremoniously into the tiny cottage to meet her disapproving mother-in-law, and from that moment, never allowed to venture out alone. Ria became her keeper when Jowan was away, and the hills and lanes Jowan had so enticed her with remained totally out of reach. Her insular world was observed - either from the small square windows of the cottage which overlooked the harbour, or from the wagon which took them to Helston and back on market days. Desperately lonely, the lack of a baby in the cradle to love, only added to her sorrow and soured Jowan's temper towards her.

The wind was rising from the south-west and rattled ferociously at the cottage windows. That morning, Sophie had observed that several cutters had moored against the Custom House Quay - a clear indication a storm was imminent. She cast her eyes heavenward. *Please let the storm hinder Jowan's journey home.*

*

Around four nautical miles from Cadgwith, the howling gale and high seas tossed the fishing boat like a cork. The boat *Marnie* was registered to skipper, Jack Tehidy. It worked out from Gweek on a regular, three days off, four days on rota. All five men aboard were used to shocking weather, but this storm felt particularly vicious, especially as they were hindered with the thick fog blanketing the Lizard peninsula.

Their progression past the Maenheere Reef — a famously treacherous rocky outcrop of half-submerged rocks a mile off the Lizard - took all the skill and expertise of this experienced crew to navigate. Jack had been heading for Coverack harbour, though the last time they made port there two days ago, one of his fishing mates, Jowan Treloar, met with an unfortunate incident. It was a strange event - they often put to port there to offload fish and take a libation in The Paris Inn and had never met with any hostility before. There had been no altercation in the Inn as far as any of them knew — but when Jowan, a six-foot-four hulk of a man, returned from relieving himself outside with a cut eyebrow and a bloody nose, everyone wondered who'd been brave enough to take him on. Jowan claimed he'd fallen, but Jack was not so sure - Jowan had been unusually subdued for the rest of the trip. With that in mind, Jack Tehidy made a decision.

'We'll head for safe harbour in Cadgwith, mates, and sit this out there until the morning,' he shouted.

There was a general grunt of agreement. There were worse places than The Cadgwith Cove Inn, to shelter from a storm.

It was shortly after ten when they finally navigated into the cove, soon to be joined by three other fishing boats with the same idea. As they anchored off, to wait in line to be winched ashore by the women of the village, the fog was pierced by the red glow of a distress rocket, swiftly accompanied by the eerie sound of a ship's long drawn out whoo-op horn rising above the noise of the storm.

'Oh, Christ!' Jack Tehidy said gravely. 'Something's happened, and by the look of it it's near Lizard Point.'

The red glow lit the cove and the faces of the waiting

fishermen. Winching began in earnest then, in order to get the fishing boats and crew ashore so they could man the lifeboat. The men knew the flare would have been spotted by villagers in the surrounding fishing communities on the Lizard and beyond, but that did not deter them from readying themselves for the rescue.

While the crew of the *Marnie* waited to be winched in, they watched the first lifeboat launch from Cadgwith. The *Minnie Moon,* a thirty-nine foot open wooden boat, along with the fifteen-strong crew, dressed in oilskins and cumbersome cork life-belts, set out into the stormy ocean. It was being rowed ferociously by six oarsmen, though barely stemming the tide as they pulled against the prevailing conditions.

Jack knitted his brows. 'Christ, they're going to be knackered by the time they get there in this weather! When we're aground I'll see if they need volunteers to go overland to help. I've no doubt they'll bring the survivors into Polpeor Cove on the Lizard. Who's with me?'

Most of his loyal crew nodded, although Jowan Treloar did so reluctantly. It was one thing to fish for a living - that was a dangerous enough occupation in itself, but heroics were definitely not his thing. All he wanted was to sit down somewhere warm with a glass of ale. He had things on his mind - serious things he needed to think on.

Once the *Marnie* was safely winched ashore, the crew made for The Cadgwith Cove Inn. Brandy seemed to be the order of the day, so the landlord set a row of glasses on the bar.

'Get this down you lads,' he said, dishing out the amber liquid. 'This'll take the chill off.' He raised his glass. 'I've seen the flair go up. Here's hoping there'll be no lives lost tonight.'

Everyone in the bar raised a glass to that.

'Did I see our vicar, the Rev. Harry Vyvyan on the *Minnie Moon*?' One local asked the landlord.

'Aye, tis so. I was surprised, to say the least. Vyvyan is

not one to take to the open seas normally, but on this occasion, I reckon the urge to help overtook all else.'

There was a collective nod of admiration - Vyvyan was a good soul.

A sudden gust of wind at hurricane speed thumped the side of the Inn, making everyone flinch. There was nothing else to do for the moment but settle down to wait for news.

*

It took hours for the *Minnie Moon* to reach its destination. Drenched and exhausted from being battered relentlessly, the Cadgwith lifeboat arrived at the scene, simultaneously with the Lizard lifeboat. They quickly learned to their relief that more were on their way from the surrounding villages.

The Coxswain of the *Minnie Moon* struggled at first to see the stricken vessel - such was the density of the fog and the difficulties caused by a strong south-westerly gale. It was only by chance the crew knew they had reached the *SS Suevic* when they smashed into the liner's hull, which knocked one of the crew overboard. He was quickly heaved back on board and the rescue commenced.

They found the vessel to be a huge 12,000-ton ship owned by the White Star Line. To their dismay, two of the ship's lifeboats had been launched with women and children aboard, and were in utmost peril upon the dangerous rocks. So before doing anything else, the *Minnie Moon* pulled up alongside the ship's lifeboats so a crew member could go aboard.

Vyvyan was the first to volunteer. 'Try to steady it,' he yelled to the oarsman as he stood precariously in the gale ready to jump into the first boat. He was swiftly followed by another crew member who jumped into the other. 'We'll safely guide these back to land,' Vyvyan shouted. 'I'll bring the boat back if I can.'

They headed just left of the Lizard Lighthouse to the nearest beach at Polpeor on the Lizard where Vyvyan, unloaded his grateful passengers. His immediate thought was to try to return to the *SS Suevic* with the boat. Unfortunately, and to his dismay, the vessel was unable to cope and it was smashed on the rocks. Unperturbed, he valiantly swam back to shore and waited for the Lizard lifeboat so he could return to the wreck to assist where he could.

'This is going to be a long night,' Vyvyan shouted to the growing crowd that had gathered on the beach. 'By all accounts there are about 500 passengers aboard. We're going to need some help to man these lifeboats!'

Within minutes, several young lads were despatched either on foot or horseback to fetch willing volunteers from the neighbouring villages.

*

The Cadgwith Cove Inn stayed open all that night as the wives of the lifeboat crew huddled around the fireside with their children, their faces etched with worry, waiting for their men to return safe to them. When word finally got through to Cadgwith of the magnitude of the rescue, it was via an exhausted lad who had run all the way from the Lizard.

The lad shivered in a blanket by the Inn's fireside with a mug of tea. 'They say the ship was on the final leg of a voyage from Australia to Southampton before it run aground on the Maenheere Reef,' he said. 'It has no less than 500 passengers and crew on board!' There are four lifeboats helping, but it's going to take hours to get everyone off, so I've been sent to get volunteers.'

One man stood up. 'I'm in. Who else is up for it?' Several men stepped forward, as did Jack Tehidy. 'Count me and my crew in,' he said as Jowan glowered behind them.

*

Polpeor Cove on the Lizard was awash with women and children, when Jack and his crew arrived over an hour later. The vicar met the volunteers at the water's edge. He was soaked through to the skin, exhausted but very relieved to see them.

'Good men,' he cried trying to make himself heard over the storm. 'What a night! The liner is stuck fast, but in all my days, I have never seen a captain keep such a calm head as that of Captain Jones of the SS *Suevic*. Would you believe - he is conducting the evacuation of his crew and passengers whilst calmly smoking his cigar! I'll tell you. If anyone could stop a panic, it would be a man who can keep the ash on the end of his cigar in a gale!' He grinned.

*

During the ensuing sixteen hours, the 60 crewmen of the four wooden lifeboats from Cadgwith, Coverack, The Lizard and Porthleven, along with several volunteers, made multiple journeys, rowing back and forth in dense fog and towering seas to rescue and bring to safety 456 men, women and children from the stricken liner. Each time they grounded at Polpeor Cove the villagers waded into the icy waves, in darkness to bring children to shore.

Jowan was drenched, terrified, bone-tired and thoroughly disgruntled at having to leave the warm public house. He was on his second trip back from the ship, but almost as soon as Polpeor Cove came into sight, an almighty wave tipped the boat, upending all aboard into the freezing foamy water. Screams of panic rang out in the cove as villages ran out in to the waist deep water to help the floundering passengers. Jowan's fatigued body was screaming in pain as he tumbled helplessly into the retreating waves. This, he knew now, was definitely going to be the last journey on a lifeboat.

*

It was midday when the last passengers were brought to safety. Every man and woman at the cove slumped drenched, exhausted, but elated, at such a good outcome. The carts from Cadgwith had made two journeys back to the village, loaded with women and children to be housed and fed by the locals there. Jack Tehidy, his crew, plus several other volunteers that set out with them, joined the wagons on their final journey back.

'Has anyone seen Jowan?' Jack asked his fatigued crew who were slumped against the sides of the wagon. Everyone shook their head.

'He was with me in the lifeboat that came in about nine this morning,' Jim Drew said. 'If you remember we got caught in a wave which upended us into the surf, but I thought he swam to safety - I believe everyone else did because it happened quite close to the beach.'

'And no one has seen him since?' Jack scratched at his beard.

Everyone shook their heads.

'Perhaps he was hurt and took an earlier wagon back to Cadgwith,' someone offered up. But on their return to Cadgwith, there was no sign of him. They waited the rest of the day to see if he showed up, but he never came.

Jack stood on Cadgwith's shingle beach at first light, anxiously twisting his salt-laden hat in his hands as he waited for the *Marnie* to be rolled back into the water. What the hell was he going to tell Ria and Sophie?

Chapter 2

It was a scene of perfect, albeit noisy domesticity in the Blackthorn's kitchen at Poldhu Cove. Guy and Ellie Blackthorn, who owned the Poldhu Tea Rooms had been married for five years and were still very much in love. They had just spent their first night in their newly built cottage, a stone's throw from Poldhu Beach. Their move to a larger cottage would free up their old house for Guy's brother Silas, and his soon-to-be bride, Jessie, due to marry in a week's time. It had been a problematic night trying to settle everyone into their new sleeping arrangements - the ongoing storm had not helped. Their two children, Agnes aged four and Zack aged three, were given rooms of their own for the first time, but neither were enamoured with the prospect. Needless to say, Ellie and Guy had inevitably found them together in Zack's bed that morning.

Guy wrapped his arms around Ellie as she prepared breakfast. 'How did *you* sleep my love?' he said placing a loving hand on her swollen tummy.

'Uncomfortably, and I still have four more months to go!' She set the table and ushered the children to their places.

Brandy, one of their three dogs, sat up from her basket, her ears pricked in anticipation. Ellie grinned. 'I think the postman is imminent. I swear Brandy can sense Archie coming from two hundred yards away.'

Sure enough he walked into the kitchen a minute later.

'Morning all.' Archie handed two letters over in exchange for a welcome mug of tea, which he drank with relish. 'I see you've settled in here then!'

Guy laughed. 'We have, though everything is a little chaotic at the moment, especially as we have the arrangements for Silas and Jessie's wedding on Saturday too!'

'It looks like the weather is improving for it. That wind has dropped, thank goodness.'

'Amen to that.' Ellie and Guy said in unison. Ellie in particular had fretted during the storm. The tea room had been completely wrecked after a previous storm five years ago – she did not want a repeat of that!

As Guy handed a letter to Ellie, he inspected the writing on the one addressed to him.

'Have you heard the news?' Archie said.

They both looked at him with interest.

'A massive liner ran aground on the Menaeahr Rocks late on Sunday night. It was en route from Australia to Southampton when it was caught in that storm – I don't suppose that damn fog helped either. Apparently, the rescue went on for over 16 hours, but all 456 passengers and crew were saved, and not a single life was lost.'

'Goodness me, where are they all?' Ellie asked as she helped Zack take the top off his boiled egg.

'Almost every house on the Lizard peninsula has taken at least one person in. I believe the liner's owners are making arrangements for their ongoing journey.'

'That must have been terrifying for them,' Guy said.

'Aye, it must have! Anyway, I must be off. Thank you for the tea.' Archie winked.

Ellie wiped the egg off Zack's mouth and watched the consternation on Guy's face as he read his letter.

'Bad news?'

'Worrying news, actually. It's from Amelia Pascoe. She asks if I can put Bert Laity up temporarily in my cottage in Gweek. She says he's been sacked from his job at the Corn Mill - for attending his wife's funeral would you believe!'

Ellie took a sharp intake of breath. 'But that is shocking! Poor, Bert.'

'Indeed!' Guy folded the letter into his pocket. 'I need to go and see what's happened. Hopefully I'll be back before supper.' He got up and shrugged his coat on.

'Send my condolences to Bert won't you, and if you have time, call on Eric and Lydia Williams to say hello.'

'I will,' he said kissing her goodbye.

*

The residents of Gweek had also suffered sleepless nights due to the storm. The wind had roared around Alpha Cottage like a hungry beast, rattling the windows until Sophie feared they would break. When darkness loosened its grip that morning, Sophie rose and dressed warmly against the chill of the dreary March morning. She grabbed her mane of golden curls, which long ago had lost their sheen, and twisted it into a tight bun. She needed no mirror and was glad of the lack of one in the bedroom - vanity was a thing of the past. Silently she stood for a while at her bedroom window to watch the village waking up. The wind had eased, but the rain came in squalls, as low dank clouds raced across the village, pouring down upon the already drenched harbour. Several people were milling around the village inspecting their roofs for damage. Resignedly she turned from the view and went downstairs to build a fire. Jowan would inevitably be home that day.

Four hours into her daily chores and with her head inside the range busily scrubbing at a stubborn mark, the sound of a fist hammering on the front door startled her, causing her to bang her head. Grimacing, she inched back onto her haunches and rubbed her head with her wrist so as not to soil her hair with her filthy hands. The hammering started again and Sophie glanced hopefully towards Ria.

'There is someone at the door,' Sophie stated.

Ria shrugged. 'Answer it then. I'm resting my legs.'

Sophie shot her a sharp look. *Why a fifty-year-old woman would feel the need to rest her legs only an hour after rousing herself from her bed - she did not know.*

Sophie eased herself off her knees, wiped her hands on a cloth, and tidied her hair. The icy gust of wind almost took her breath away when she opened the door.

'Who is it, for god's sake?' Ria shouted. 'Hurry up and shut that door. You're letting the cold air in.'

Choosing to ignore her demands, Sophie looked down

at the young boy standing before her.

'Captain Jack says you're to come quick,' the red-faced boy spluttered.

'Why?' Sophie puzzled

'Come on! The *Marnie* has just docked.'

Sophie had never been beckoned to meet the *Marnie* before, and with Jowan aboard, had no desire to do so now.

The boy reached out his hand. 'Come on, Mrs! I can't go back without you, Jack'll brain me.'

Sophie sighed - perhaps they'd caught something unusual in their net. 'All right, I'm coming.' As she grabbed her shawl from the back of the door, Ria stirred in her chair.

'Hey! Where do you think you're going?'

'Out!' Sophie snapped.

'You are not, my girl,' she proclaimed as she struggled to get to her feet. 'Jowan will be back on the tide and he'll scat you if you're off gallivanting.'

Sophie shot her a derisive look. *Gallivanting indeed! When had she had the freedom to gallivant?*

The river was high and the seagulls circled hungrily as the boat unloaded its catch when Sophie walked onto the quay. Without the restraints of Ria by her side she nodded a courteous greeting to Kit Trevellick, who was stood outside his carpentry workshop adjoining the Custom House.

Sophie stood with her hands on her hips as she searched for Jowan - everyone on the fishing boat seemed busy with the baskets and nets.

'Captain Jack? I've fetched her!' the boy shouted holding out his hand for a penny.

Jack Tehidy looked up and nodded gravely. He barked some orders at the crew and then disembarked.

As he neared Sophie, he took off his hat and cleared his throat – she noted that his normal ruddy features looked pale and pinched.

'Mrs Treloar.'

Sophie arched an eyebrow - Jack normally addressed her by her Christian name. 'Morning Jack, I suspect you've had a rough journey? That storm was dreadful, wasn't it?'

'Aye 'twas so.' Jack nodded. He took a deep measured breath.

A sudden sense of disquiet hit her when she realised that she was being watched by the rest of the crew.

'I've grave news, I'm afraid.'

Sophie's world stilled. As her mind raced with all eventualities, she suddenly realised that Jack was still talking to her. 'Sorry, what was that you said?'

'Tis Jowan, Sophie. He was…well, we were all involved with the rescue of a ship off the Lizard yesterday…'

Jack's Adam's apple rose and fell as he swallowed hard and for a moment that was all Sophie could focus on, which was just as well, because Jack could barely make eye contact with her.

'The thing is, Sophie, Jowan went overboard whilst saving others.'

An unexpected flush of adrenalin seared through her veins and she unconsciously shot her hand out to Jack. 'Is he dead?'

He grabbed her arm to steady her. 'Yes,' he said darkly. 'We believe he is. We searched and waited, but we couldn't find him. I'm that sorry, Sophie. If it's any consolation, your man died a hero.'

Her hand fanned out across her breastbone. *Jowan was dead!* Suddenly feeling very detached from her surroundings, she stepped back from Jack, a fraction before her knees gave way.

'Oh, god, Sophie!' Jack tried to catch her as she collapsed at his feet.

*

Kit had been watching the exchange with curiosity - he simply couldn't recall ever seeing Sophie Treloar out alone before. It was a shock when he saw her collapse. He dropped what he was doing and was knelt at her side cradling her head in his arms in an instant.

'What the hell happened?' Kit looked up at Jack wildly.

'Jowan has drowned.'

Kit's eyes widened.

'He went overboard during a rescue.'

'Did you get him out? Have you got his body aboard?'

'No,' Jack grimaced, 'the sea hasn't given it up yet.'

They both looked up and exchanged a worried glance as Ria came blazing onto the quay like a steam ship in full sail.

'What the hell is going on here?' she yelled, grabbing Kit's jacket. 'Unhand my daughter-in-law immediately.'

Deeply aware of the impropriety of having his arms around a newly widowed woman, Kit helped Sophie to her feet - though she was clearly still unsteady on them. 'Sophie's had a shock, Mrs Treloar, she fainted,' Kit gave his faltering explanation.

'Shock! What shock?' Ria demanded, as she dragged Sophie from Kit's hold.

Kit looked on helplessly as Sophie winced when Ria's great hand pinched her arm.

'My Jowan will hear of this, Kit Trevellick! Where is Jowan anyway? Jowan,' she shouted up to the fishing boat.

'Ria!' Jack reached out to quieten her. 'Ria! Listen to me. I need to tell you…'

'Just a minute, Jack,' she snapped impatiently as she shoved Sophie away from the group. 'You, get back home before Jowan sees you. You're a disgrace!' But much to Ria's consternation, Sophie remained exactly where she stood.

'Ria.' Jack attempted again.

'What?' she snapped, whilst glowering at Sophie.

'I'm afraid I've bad news. Jowan has drowned,' he said meekly.

'He's what?' she breathed. Her great bulk appeared to shrink before them.

'He drowned, while saving others.'

She narrowed her eyes. 'No! It's not true. You're lying, Jack Tehidy.'

Jack shook his head. 'It's true, Ria. He died a hero.'

Ria began to shake uncontrollably until her knees gave way and she hit the ground with a thump. She began to moan like a cow missing her calf. The moan turned into a pitiful cry, increasing in volume until she emitted the most appalling, heart-breaking wail. Neither Jack nor Kit could lift her from where she lay, so Dr Eddy was sent for.

Sophie crouched beside Ria, but she pushed her away, so she stood back while the doctor, Jack, Kit and Jim Drew hoisted Ria onto her feet and walked her unsteadily back to Alpha Cottage.

While they heaved her upstairs so Dr Eddy could administer a sleeping draft, Sophie cupped her elbows in her hands and cast her eyes around the sparse uncomfortable cottage. *Jowan was dead!* The words rang around her head.

Jim and Jack came back downstairs and Jack placed a comforting hand on Sophie's shoulder. 'I'll bring Jowan's wage round to you later when I've doled it out.'

She glanced at him and nodded. 'Thank you.'

'Am that sorry for you - truly I am.'

Sophie nodded again, and he left.

Kit was the next to come down the stairs.

She gave him a grateful nod. 'Thank you for your kind attendance on me earlier,' she said shyly.

'I'm happy I could be of assistance. Do you need me to do anything else?'

Sophie couldn't remember the last time someone had offered to do something for her. 'No, thank you, Mr Trevellick. Please, let me see you out.' He seemed to hesitate, almost reluctant to go and Sophie noted the sudden intensity in his blue eyes, as though he wanted to say more, but instead, he smiled gently and left.

Sophie made her way upstairs, and after what seemed

like an age, Ria's wailing ceased as the sleeping draft took hold. Dr Eddy put his hand into the small of Sophie's back and ushered her back downstairs.

'She'll sleep for hours, now. Can I get *you* anything, Sophie?'

'No, I'm fine doctor, thank you.'

His eyes crinkled sympathetically. 'Very well, my dear. Let me offer my condolences for your loss.'

As she closed the door behind him, she spread her hands upon the rough wood with mounting anticipation. This door, this bloody door which let in the draught and kept her firmly locked behind it, was open! Sliding her fingers down to the lock they rested on the shiny brass key which normally resided in Ria's pocket. She curled her fingers around the cold metal - a turn to the left, locked it, and then the glorious click to the right released her from her prison.

Chapter 3

A shiver of anticipation ran down Sophie's spine as she stepped back outside the front door. The storm had left an air of decay in its wake, but the watery sun was trying its best to prevail. At the bridge, she glanced at Jack's fishing boat, but there was no movement on it now, the crew were probably home with their families. The tide was ebbing back to the sea – to where Jowan rested in his watery grave!

With an overwhelming urge to just walk, Sophie set off with no direction in mind - she just needed to be somewhere other than Alpha Cottage.

After observing the normally bustling village from the confines of her window, the place seemed unusually void of life today. Strangely enough she was grateful for the solitude. She needed to be alone with her thoughts.

The sunny yellow stems of primulas growing in abundance in the grassy bank called out to be plucked. With a posy tucked into her skirt waistband, she walked past Barnfield, Farmer Ferris's farm, where the rooks high above her in the great sycamore trees hawked and fought as they built their nests. Walking down to the second bridge she took the lane to the right. Passing the neat row of mill houses adjacent to the Corn Mill, she walked a few yards further until she came to an ancient flat stone bridge which spanned the stream. Struck by its tranquil beauty, this seemed the right sort of place to stop for a moment.

The trees, bare except for their swelling buds, cast shade from the emerging spring sunshine from their great canopy of branches. The stream, swollen from the storm, delighted her senses as she watched and listened to the water rushing over the stones. A cloud of midges surrounded her and as she flapped them away a movement caught her attention. Was someone watching her? She waited a moment but saw nothing but an empty lane. Turning back, she settled her eyes back on the stream. A huge sense of calm prevailed, she could not remember the last time she had felt so settled in her mind. Taking a deep breath, she closed her eyes and unpinned her hair from the bun she'd been made to wear since the wedding band had been put on her finger. Feeling the air on her scalp as she ran her fingers through her hair, she shook her curls loose until they tumbled down in a golden waterfall. She wrapped her arms lovingly around herself. *I'm free! At last, I'm free!* She turned again to stare down at the empty lane - was someone there watching her? *Of course there's no one there, Sophie. I'm free now to do as I please, without being watched.* It felt so liberating.

*

Kit sat back on his haunches as Sophie walked back along the lane. With her hair loose and colour in her cheeks she had never looked so beautiful. He was hiding behind a blackthorn hedge and had been stung several times by the nettles. He had no ulterior motive to follow her, other than to see she was safe - after all, she'd had quite a shock! It was so good to see her walk out alone. Ria had been her constant, and Kit suspected, unwanted companion these last eight years.

He recalled the first time he'd set eyes on Sophie - her loveliness had ruined him for all other women. His heart had been lost to her when she'd glanced at him as Jowan ushered her into Alpha Cottage the day he'd brought her home. He knew it was wrong of him, but from then on, he'd yearned for her from afar. Under the watch of her domineering husband and mother-in-law, Kit had dismally observed Sophie's vitality wither before his eyes. He'd made it his mission to always smile at her whenever their paths crossed, hoping that he could make her feel special, even if it was just for a fleeting moment.

*

Once Sophie was out of sight, Kit left his hiding place, ruefully rubbing dock leaves on his nettle stings. As he pulled the gate closed and leant over to lock it, a voice behind him made him jump.

'What's this, Kit? Did you get caught short or something?'

Kit turned and grinned as his old friend Guy Blackthorn jumped down from his wagon, swiftly followed by a little terrier dog.

'Hello, Guy, I'm just making sure this gate is locked,' Kit said, too embarrassed to admit he was spying on Sophie. 'I see you've adopted Harry's little dog - I wondered what had happened to him.' He bent down to scratch its ears.

'I promised Harry on his death-bed that I would,' Guy answered.

'Talking of Harry, I think this is the first I've seen of you since his funeral back in October. Is business good? Are you well?'

Guy nodded. 'I am, thank you, and business is good - there's always work for a thatcher. I've also been busy finishing the new cottage we've built to accommodate our growing family, but I'm here today on a mission of mercy, so to speak.'

'Oh?' Kit raised an eyebrow.

'Amelia Pascoe wrote to me, asking if Bert Laity could live in my cottage. It's been empty since Harry died, so I was happy to oblige. Apparently, the mill owner, Gilbert Penvear sacked Bert when he took a day off to bury his wife Mabel!'

'I know, it's shocking! We've all been trying to help him. You're a good man, Guy.'

'Well, I simply can't stand injustice. I've just been teaching Bert how to make willow spurs for thatching roofs - I thought it would give him a small income. Harry made them for me until he died, so Bert's doing me a favour.'

'So how are Ellie and Silas?' Kit asked, nimbly side-stepping the terrier's cocked leg.

'They're well. We have another baby on the way and

Silas is to marry his sweetheart Jessie this weekend.'

'Goodness, little Silas getting married, eh?'

'I know! It makes me feel old. You're very welcome to come to the wedding - I know Silas would like to see you. It's at midday on Saturday - you could stay over. We have plenty of room now.'

'Thank you, I will. It's been ages since I visited Poldhu.'

'It's fortunate that I came across you actually. We were talking about you the other day. It's a wonder your ears weren't burning.' He grinned.

Kit grimaced. 'Nothing bad I hope?'

'No, it was all good. Ellie and I are friends with Peter and Sarah Dunstan – the Earl and Countess de Bochym, you know, from the Bochym Estate in Cury.'

Kit nodded. 'Well, Peter might have some work for you in a couple of months. They have a boating lake and the boats need some repair.'

'I'd welcome the work, thank you.'

'Look, Kit, it's been good to see you but I must be off. If you see Eric and Lydia Williams at the dairy farm, send them my regards and tell them they too are welcome at the wedding. I was going to call on them, but I'm running late now.'

'I'll tell them. Oh, by the way. We've just had word that Jowan Treloar has drowned.'

Guy eyes widened. 'Has he now?'

'Apparently drowned helping with the rescue of a ship that ran aground a couple of days ago.'

'*Jowan* - helping in a rescue?' Guy asked incredulously.

'I know! The only person Jowan normally helps is himself.'

Guy gave a snuffled laugh. 'I should think he'll not be missed by many, especially that poor wife of his. I always felt sorry for her – it can't have been an easy life.' He cocked his head. 'I suspect this is good news to you. I know you've always held a candle for her.'

Kit gave a raffish grin. 'It's true, I have.'

'Well, my friend, I wish you well for what might happen in the future. I'll see you on Saturday.'

They shook hands and Kit waved him off.

*

Gilbert Penvear watched the exchange between Kit and Guy from his Manager's office window at the Gweek Corn Mill. He narrowed his eyes. *Bloody, Guy Blackthorn, damn his eyes!* He'd just found out that he'd offered up his cottage to that wastrel Bert Laity. Laity could easily have buried his wife on a Sunday, but no, he'd gone ahead and taken time off! How were people meant to learn that there were consequences to taking a lax view of work? There was always some do-gooder ready to step in to help.

He straightened up indignantly, well as straight as he could despite the slight hump to his back caused by a curvature of the spine. He was fifty-two-years-old and although his hair and eyebrows were prematurely white, he rather thought himself as still handsome. As always, he was groomed to perfection and demanded that his downtrodden manservant made sure that his clothes were always immaculate. Whenever he ventured out, he wore a bowler hat and leather gloves, and carried a gold handled walking stick – useful to hit stray dogs and free-range children with. He enjoyed the power he held over people and marvelled at how his authority grew daily.

The news of Jowan Treloar's death was an interesting development to Gilbert. His latest wife had recently, and most inconveniently, died on him. She was no great loss as a companion - but then he hadn't kept her for that reason. Granted, her noncompliance in the bedroom and ongoing malaise when he forced her to do her duty - coupled with her refusal to eat, until her skeletal body had repulsed and angered him – but now, he was left wanting. Not many things made him smile, but the thought of a young widow in need, especially one as ripe and comely as Sophie Treloar between his thighs - made his groin tingle.

*

Kit walked slowly back to the centre of the village. The rooks were flying in unison making a great black cloud flitting to and fro as they prepared to settle for the evening. It was nothing like the starlings murmuration but it was spectacular in its own way.

He paused before he turned into the boatyard and glanced over at Alpha Cottage. The curtains were closed as was the way with a death in the family. Jowan had been a bad-tempered, often drunk member of the community - he'd not be missed by many, with the exception of Ria. Kit smiled inwardly – with the news of Jowan's demise, and seeing Guy today, all in all it had been a good day.

*

Sophie stood at her bedroom window, the curtains parted slightly so she could see out, but not, she thought, so that she could be seen. The effervescent fizz of excitement had not left her since first hearing the news of Jowan's demise, and she was quietly contemplating her future. Her eyes glittered with happy tears, momentarily blurring her vision. She blinked furiously and it was then that she saw Kit Trevellick standing at the far end of the bridge. Was he looking at her cottage? Could he see her? She stepped back slightly. Kit's smiling handsome face was the first person she'd seen as she stepped down from the wagon as Jowan's bride. She'd been struck by the intensity of his gaze, as though he could see right through to her soul. From that day forward Kit was the only man, who despite Ria's scowls, would offer up a smile and a cheery hello to Sophie whenever their paths crossed. As the years of drudgery took its toll, Kit's attention to her made her believe that she wasn't as worthless as Jowan had deemed her. Kit made her feel…. less invisible. Sophie had hardly dared to look at him properly before today, and had certainly never been in such close proximity. The sight of his dark glossy curls hanging over her face, and his eyes gazing down at her when she'd come to from her faint in his arms, had sent a frisson through her body. His eyes were the bluest, kindest eyes she had ever seen. But wait, Jowan too had had blue eyes, and she remembered being attracted to them once, but his had turned cold and steely grey when he was angry, which of late had been his trait. Shuddering at the thought, she wrapped her arms around herself. *But he's gone, Sophie, Jowan has gone forever,* and her mind bubbled with possibilities, and an independence she could only ever have dreamt of before.

Chapter 4

Sophie lay awake listening to the sounds of the night. The owl hooting, a wily fox snuffling in the hedgerows and the rustling of rooks disturbed by a squirrel, punctuated the many thoughts whirring around in her head. The sweet fragrance from the posy of primulas she'd picked earlier wafted in the soft breeze coming from the window – she'd never been allowed flowers beside her bed before. Free now from the restraints of her domineering husband, Sophie could hardly sleep for the exciting possibilities she now faced. Gone were Jowan's drunken advances and dreadful infections his philandering brought her. Her priority was to find her own place to live - to be completely independent from Ria. She would skivvy for her no longer than it took to get away from Alpha Cottage. This was not uncharitable of her - Ria was only fifty and could well run this cottage if she just moved herself. Firstly, she needed money, and for that she needed a job, but she'd think about that on the morrow.

*

Kit had been hard at work in his carpentry shop since first light. As well as boatbuilding, and being a master furniture maker, Kit was also the local coffin maker. He was fashioning a foot stool today, a calming occupation which settled his thoughts. The death of Jowan had given him hope - hope that in a respectable amount of time, he would find the courage to declare his heart to Sophie. To be with her was all he'd yearned for these last eight years - just to be with her, to show her how wonderful life could be was all he wanted. It was unfortunate that Jowan's body had not been found. Until it was, Sophie's future was in limbo. She'd have to wait a full seven years before she could remarry. He smiled inwardly. *Now I'm getting ahead of myself.* Kit was not an arrogant man, but felt confident that the fleeting glances they'd exchanged over the years, told him his feelings were reciprocated.

Kit put down his tools to take a breath of fresh air when he noticed the sun breaking through the early morning mist. The gentle breeze ruffled his hair slightly as he walked to the riverbank where his boat *Harvest Moon* was moored. She was a Falmouth Cutter and he'd salvaged her seven years ago from further down the river. She'd been no more than a rotting hull, but years of blood, sweat and a few 'choice' swear words had seen her lovingly restored to her former glory. Soon she would be ready to sail down the river again. Would Sophie be with him at the helm? They could sail off and live together as man and wife until he could slip his own band of gold around her finger. *There you go again, getting ahead of yourself!* Oh, but it was nice to dream, but it was a dream he'd have to wait for and he was good at waiting. He climbed onto the deck of the boat and looked over to Alpha Cottage. The urge to go to her now, to take her in his arms and hold her close to his heart for eternity was powerful, but he knew all he could do today was courteously call on her and offer his help should she need anything.

*

Sophie woke from the best night's sleep she'd had for a long time. Her euphoria was such that she felt as though she could bounce off the ceiling with excitement. This was not however appropriate behaviour for a widow, and she knew she'd have to curb her eagerness to start her new life - for now there were chores to be done.

Sophie had been up for hours and was just preparing to do the washing in the back yard when Ria emerged from her bedroom, grief stricken and suitably attired in mourning clothes.

Shooting a contemptuous look at Sophie, she said, 'I can see by the look on your face that you've shed not a single tear for my poor son! Nor do you have the decency to wear black for his passing.' She fumbled in her pocket for a handkerchief to dab her eyes.

Sophie glanced down at her attire – Ria had a point.

She hadn't given a second thought to her choice of clothing when she'd dressed so buoyantly that morning. 'I've dirty chores to do,' she said to appease. 'I'll dress accordingly once they are done.'

'You'll go and change *immediately*. What if someone had called and found you dressed inappropriately?'

Glancing at the clock, she replied tersely, 'I've been up since six! It's still only nine. I should think it highly unlikely we would receive callers yet!'

'You wilful girl, don't take that tone with me - Jowan will not tolerate insolence in this house! Now go and change immediately. Folks will think you don't care about what has happened - and they would be right, wouldn't they?' A loud rap on the door silenced Ria.

They exchanged a swift glance before Sophie smoothed down her apron and made for the door.

'Stop! You can't answer the door without proper mourning clothes on. I *told* you this would happen!' Ria said contemptuously. 'Put that black shawl around your head and tell whoever it is that we are not at home to visitors yet.'

Sophie opened the door to find Gilbert Penvear on the doorstep. She stepped back, nauseous at the overwhelming smell of cologne that emanated from him. He wore a dark wool coat over his starched white shirt and grey necktie. His trousers were pressed and fell neatly onto highly polished shoes – his attire looked quite out of place in this busy port.

'Good morning,' he said removing his bowler hat.

His eyes seemed to travel the length of Sophie's body as though he was undressing her. Deeply uncomfortable under his gaze, she pulled her shawl closer.

'May I offer my sincere condolences for your loss?'

Sophie nodded, but said nothing.

'I wish to speak to your mother-in-law.' He began to step over the threshold without being invited.

'I'm sorry, Mr Penvear.' Sophie halted his

advancement. 'Please forgive us, but we are not at home to visitors at the moment.'

'My business is with your mother-in-law and rather important.' He pushed the door open and walked past her.

Ria had sat down at the table and was darting questioning eyes towards Sophie, as Gilbert entered the room.

'Mr Penvear,' Sophie said firmly. 'I beg you, but we are not ready to.....'

Gilbert held his hand up to Sophie to rudely halt her mid-sentence.

He turned to Ria, 'If I might have a private word with you, Madam?'

'Oh!' Ria flustered. 'Very well.' She glanced at Sophie. 'Get on with what you were doing,' she instructed.

'With pleasure,' Sophie said sotto voce. Glad to be away from Gilbert's cloying cologne, she willingly returned to her washing.

Once she was gone, Gilbert sat down without an invite and pulled at his shirt cuffs to reveal shiny cufflinks. A short silence ensued except for the ticking of the clock, as he looked disdainfully around the cottage.

'I am here to offer you help, Madam.'

Ria cleared her throat. 'Help?'

'With your son gone, I expect his widow, and yourself, his grieving mother, are now in dire need of finances.'

Ria shifted uncomfortably. 'We have no need for charity, thank you very much. My daughter-in-law will find work!'

Gilbert snorted derisively. 'This is not charity, Madam. I don't do charitable things. This is a proposition!'

Ria arched an eyebrow - was he about to propose marriage to her? After all he was only two years her senior and widowed himself not long ago. She patted her hair under her black bonnet.

'Your daughter-in-law will come and live in Quay House, as my housekeeper.'

'Oh!' Deflated momentarily, she pursed her lips. 'No, Mr Penvear, Jowan would not approve.'

'I beg to differ, Madam. I'm confident your son and I share the same sentiments. I take it you wish to maintain your daughter-in-law's reputation by protecting her from unwanted suitors? As you know she's a very young attractive widow, and will inevitably be a source of interest to the single men of the village.'

She suddenly thought about Kit's unsolicited advances to Sophie and nodded.

'I do not encourage my staff to socialise. Nor would I allow anyone to call on her. Under my close protection you will have the satisfaction that she will be shielded from these undesirables, while you reside here in the comfort of your own home, and your rent will be taken care of by the wages she'll receive.'

Ria frowned - thinking of all the housework she'd have to do herself. 'It's a kind offer and I thank you for it, but I can't manage this cottage without her.'

'That will be taken care of. You'll have the services of Mrs Drew my present housekeeper - I have no need for her once your daughter-in-law is in residence.'

Ria smiled as she digested his offer. 'Well, thank you. That would be a perfect solution, Mr Penvear. Jowan would, I think, rest in peace at your kind proposition.'

Gilbert gave a curt nod. 'I shall expect her to start Monday week. See that she presents herself at Quay House on April 1st at eight prompt.' He replaced his hat. 'I bid you good day. I shall see myself out.'

*

Sophie heard the door bang – she surmised that Penvear must have gone. Curious as to what he wanted with Ria, she put the next load of sheets in to soak and went indoors to find Ria looking rather pleased with herself.

'What did he want?'

'He came to offer you work!' she said.

Sophie folded her arms angrily. 'Then why did he not

speak to *me* about this?'

'Because,' Ria lifted her chin haughtily. 'as Jowan's mother and the most senior member of this household, it was only right that he should arrange this with me. You're to be his live-in housekeeper as from Monday week.'

Sophie's mouth dropped incredulously. 'I *beg* your pardon?'

'You're to present yourself at Quay House at eight, prompt!'

Livid, Sophie said, 'I will do *no* such thing, and if he comes anywhere near this door again, with his offers of work, I'll send him packing!'

Ria smacked her palm on the table. 'I will not have this insolence, Sophie. You *will* do as you're told.'

That was it, Sophie rounded on her. 'Can we just get one thing clear now, Ria. As Jowan's widow, I am now my own person and I'm not answerable to anyone - *least* of all you!' She turned on her heel and returned to the back yard. Angry and liberated in equal measure, Sophie slammed the washing against her washboard. *Bloody Penvear, horrible, odious man that he was! How dare he think he can organise my life?* She was done with being ordered about.

*

By the time Sophie had pounded her rage out on the washing, pegged it out on the line and cleared the tub and washboard back into the outhouse, her anger had abated slightly. She inspected her hands, which were red raw from the soap and water and dabbed on a little lanolin to sooth them. It was the only little pot of luxury product she owned, and she kept it in the outhouse away from beady eyes.

When Sophie entered the front room, Ria was stood by the fireplace, her arms folded. It was clear by her stance, and lack of tears, that her grief had taken on a different tack. She was clearly ready for another quarrel which Sophie was not prepared to partake in.

'It was your fault!' Ria's voice was low and filled with

the bitterest contempt.

Sophie ignored her and put the kettle on the stove.

'It was your fault my Jowan died!' she reiterated.

Sophie reached for the tea caddy but chose not to answer. Anger and aggression was just another expression of grief. Sophie knew that herself. She'd been orphaned at the age of ten and remembered the anger and injustice of losing her mother so soon after her father had died. It had been such an alien emotion to her, but her kind Italian neighbour, Beatrice Bottino, who had taken her in, assured her that it was normal to feel that way and it was all part of the grieving process.

Ria took her silence for guilt. 'Nothing to say to that, have you?'

Sophie turned and calmly said, 'What do you want me to say to such a statement? How could it possibly be my fault that Jowan died?'

'Because you were a useless wife to him - a wife who couldn't hold onto his seed and produce a live baby, that's why!' she spat savagely.

Sophie faltered, remembering the heartbreak of losing every one of her four babies - she reached for the chair when a sudden need to sit down overwhelmed her.

Oblivious to Sophie's distress, or perhaps because of it, Ria continued, 'All Jowan wanted was to be a father! It was all he thought about day and night. I have no doubt it was on his mind when he fell overboard and lost his life. The poor man was distraught, so it *is* your fault, and don't you deny it.'

Sophie's distress turned to fury. She flew at Ria. 'How dare you, …' She was so angry she could hardly speak for a moment.

Ria shrank back from her, surprised at Sophie's unprecedented vehemence.

'You have gone too far, Ria!' she said in deep authoritative voice. 'That is a despicable thing to say to me!' She ripped off her apron and walked to the front door. 'Jowan wasn't the only one heartbroken at the loss of those babies!'

Ria recovered her stance. 'Where are you going?' she demanded, but Sophie did not answer. 'You come back here - you hear me? Jowan does not permit you to go ....' But the door had slammed before Ria finished the sentence.

*

For a good few seconds, Ria felt completely disorientated, she was not used to being disobeyed. A curl of fear formed in her stomach - Jowan would be so angry with her for letting Sophie out of her sight. He had charged her to keep Sophie in check when he was away from home and she had failed him. Great fat tears welled as she reached unsteadily for the chair.

Chapter 5

Sophie ran sobbing from the cottage. With no idea where she was going, she crossed the bridge and ran up Chapel Hill as fast as her feet would carry her.

The local midwife, Amelia Pascoe was in her hen coop when Sophie fled past. Hearing her distress, she put down her bucket and shouted after her. But by the time she reached the bottom of Chapel Hill, she was disappearing into the distance.

Sophie paused exhaustedly a hundred yards up the hill. Unused to running, she leant heavily over an ornate iron gate to catch her breath. She ran her arms along the length of the gate and hung her head low as she wept openly for the four babies she had miscarried through no fault of her own. Those dark, penetrating, sorrowful memories never left her. The nausea and breast tenderness suddenly ceasing, and then that awful wait for the first cramps before a show of blood.

Pulling away from the gate, she cradled her stomach. Ria's accusations cut deeper than any knife, for she knew Jowan blamed, and even accused her of doing something to end the pregnancies! With each subsequent miscarriage he had grown more irate with her. Amelia Pascoe had tried to reason with Jowan, saying that Sophie worked too hard, was chronically underweight and lacking in the benefits of fresh air and sunshine, but her arguments fell on stony ground. All Sophie had ever wanted was to hold her own baby in her arms – it would have been a source of happiness in her miserable existence. But it was not to be. Eventually Sophie rejoiced each time her monthly cycle appeared - it was the lesser of the two heartbreaks.

Finding no handkerchief in her pocket, she wiped her tears with her sleeve, and tried to focus on the gentle hum of a bumblebee, flitting across the hedgerow flowers, its pollen baskets bulging. When the hum suddenly intensified, Sophie realised it had become caught in the gossamer threads of a spider's web. 'Oh no you don't!' she said as the spider ran across its silvery trap, and began to wrap its thread around the bee. She snapped a twig from the hawthorn bush, lifted the bee from the web, and placed it carefully onto the ground. She knew not to interfere anymore - the bee would clean the web from its body if left well alone. Yes, she'd deprived the spider of a meal, but she knew what it was like to be caught in a web.

She jumped when she heard a voice behind her.

'Are you all right, Sophie? I saw you run past.' Amelia Pascoe, rosy-faced, breathing heavily was holding a handkerchief out to her.

Gratefully taking it off her, Sophie dabbed her eyes. 'I will be, thank you.'

Amelia smiled sympathetically. 'Is there anything I can do to help?'

'No, thank you. I just need a little time on my own to think,' she said, hoping that she didn't sound too rude.

Amelia nodded. 'Well, you know where I am if you need a friend.'

Sophie nodded with a broken sigh.

'I'll leave you to your thoughts then. Come and have a cup of tea one day, my door is always open for you.'

Sophie's lip trembled at her kindness. As Amelia walked away, Sophie felt her emotions settle a little and she turned back to face the field. The small path winding its way along the hedgerows towards the stile at the top seemed to beckon her. The path was steeper than it looked, and she had to rest a moment before she climbed onto the stile to look down to the vista across Gweek. An enormous sense of ease settled on her breast as she finally looked down on this long sought-after view.

Taking a deep breath of warm spring air, clean but for the slight tang of saltiness, she watched the river slowly meander up over the mud beds. Bird song filled the afternoon sky, black and white cows grazed the upper reaches of Gweek Wollas Farm, and in the woods to the right, a woodpecker's tatter-tat-tat could be heard. All this was hers now to enjoy – just as soon as she could get away from Ria. The battle she had ahead of her, depressed her - Ria clearly assumed a hold over her.

'Well, Ria, you are very wrong in your assumption!' Sophie shouted down the field, grinning at her outburst.

She made herself as comfortable as possible on the stone wall, bathing in the beautiful solitude of the afternoon, relishing the joy of having time to sit and think. This would be *her* stile from now on – a place of calm to enable her to form a catalyst of how she would now live her life. As the sun moved through the sky, the shadows lengthened and she became aware of the cold stone seeping through her thick serge skirt. Reluctant as she was, it was time to go back. Descending the path, Sophie wondered if Ria had seen the error of her cruel words, but knowing Ria, she thought perhaps not.

A familiar anxious sensation curled in her stomach as Sophie reached out to open the door of Alpha Cottage. She took a deep, measured breath, ready for the inevitable verbal onslaught from Ria, only to be stopped at the door by Jack Tehidy calling out.

'Sorry to bother you, Sophie. But may I come in?'

'Of course, you can, Jack.'

Sophie stepped through the door and glanced at Ria, who by her angry stance was waiting to berate her.

'So! There you are! Where the *hell* have you been? The minister from the Mission church has been here and you …..' Ria stopped mid-sentence as Jack followed Sophie in.

Sophie relished the fact that Jack had quite taken the wind out of Ria's sails.

Bowing his head respectfully, Jack clutched his hat tightly in his hands. 'I do beg your pardon for the intrusion, Ria.'

'That's quite all right,' said Ria with an exaggerated sob. 'I'm afraid I'm a little overwrought. I've been left all alone to deal with my grief.' Ria glanced scornfully at

Sophie.

Jack nodded. 'It must be very difficult for you both.' He turned to Sophie, and handed over a bag of money. 'This is Jowan's wage. Don't take this the wrong way– it's not charity, but the others have put a bit in as well, just to tide you over. It's what they all wanted to do.'

'Thank you, Jack.' Sophie curled her hand around the last bag of coins she would be handed. Unlike her mother-in-law, she was not averse to a little charity. By the weight of the bag there wasn't much in it, but then the catch was not always huge - as she knew to her cost. Jowan often came home in a foul mood from a poor fishing trip to take his frustration out on her, after drowning his sorrows in the pub with money they could ill afford to spend.

'I know you don't have his body to bury, but will there be a service for Jowan?' He glanced between Sophie and Ria.

'Of *course,* there'll be a service!' Ria sniffed. 'It will be noon this Sunday at the Mission Church! I've had to arrange it all by myself, because Sophie here saw fit to wander off for the *whole* afternoon!' She shot a derisive glance at Sophie. 'Everyone will be welcome back here afterwards.'

'For a cup of tea,' Sophie was quick to add.

'For a full *wake!*' Ria parried. 'Just because I can't bury my son, doesn't mean we can't give him a good send off.'

Noting the evident hostility in the room, Jack shifted uncomfortably. 'Righty o, I'll be off then. I'll let everyone know.'

'I'll see you out, Jack,' Sophie said anxiously. She stepped outside with him and pulled the door shut behind her. 'Thank everyone won't you?' She shook the bag. 'And Jack, I'm afraid it *will* just be a cup of tea after the service. Despite what Ria wants, we simply can't afford a full wake.'

'I understand, Sophie.' He smiled sympathetically. 'I'll see you on Sunday.'

As Jack turned to leave, Sophie's heart stilled when she saw Kit walking towards her. When his face lit up on seeing her, she felt a sudden unexpected frisson soar through her body.

He whipped off his hat, leaving an imprint where the brim had been on his dark glossy hair. 'Hello, Mrs Treloar,' he said softly.

Sophie inclined her head shyly. 'Mr Trevellick.'

He twisted the hat in his hands. 'I just thought I'd call, to see if you needed any help with anything.' He smiled. 'Anything at all?'

Unless you have some idea of how to get rid of my mother-in-law, I think not, she thought. 'Thank you. That's very kind of you, but no, I need nothing.'

'Well,' his eyes twinkled, 'I'm just over there.' He pointed to his workshop on the river bank. 'If you should need anything.'

A smile curled her lips. 'I know,' she replied softly. 'Thank you, Mr Trevellick.'

'Right....I'll... bid you good day then?'

They stood there for a moment motionless, until Sophie said, 'Good day then.' She noted his shoulders droop slightly, as though he wanted to stay, but then he turned reluctantly and walked away. Her eyes followed him with interest as he made for The Black Swan. It was then that she saw the group of faces grinning at her from the Inn's window. Sophie flushed furiously - they were clearly entertained by her interaction with Kit. Her eyes narrowed. *Oh, so that's your game is it, Kit Trevellick? First Penvear comes here with his roving eyes and offer of work, and now Kit's on my doorsteps with a mischievous twinkle in his eye!* She set her jaw hard. *Well, you can both just leave me alone. I am done with men!* She flounced back into the cottage, slammed the door and looked up to find Ria holding her hand out. Defiantly Sophie wrapped her fingers tighter around the bag of coins.

Ria snapped her fingers. 'Hand the money over.'

Devoid of expression, Sophie pushed the bag into her skirt pocket.

Ria's lips quivered angrily. 'How dare you *disrespect* my position in this house? I am the housekeeper! I hold the purse strings.'

Without another word, Sophie walked upstairs, ignoring the barrage of protest. Closing her bedroom door, she wedged a chair behind it, smiling at her small triumph. She counted the coins out on the bed – there was barely enough for the rent and food. If there was to be a wake, then it *would* be done on a shoestring budget and not the lavish send-off Ria had in mind - they simply could not afford it. The thought of food made her stomach rumble - she'd had nothing since breakfast. Despite knowing there was a pot of stew in the range oven, she had no intention of going back downstairs that evening to listen to Ria's wrath.

*

When Kit stepped into The Black Swan's bar, everyone nodded at him knowingly.

'*What?*' Kit said, to no one in particular.

'We saw you.' John Drago the landlord grinned as he wiped a glass. Kit shrugged. 'We saw you paying the pretty widow some attention.'

'And?' he said defensively.

'Jowan's not been dead these past two days and you're in there like a rat up a drainpipe.'

Kit clenched his jaw. 'I went to see if she needed anything!'

'And, does she?' John winked at his other customers.

'No!' he said losing patience. 'Now can I have a drink or not?'

'It's not often that we get a young widow in our midst,' John said as he poured a glass of ale. 'If Kit isn't interested, you need to step in there, Jory. Perhaps give it a month or two though, but she'd make a fine and good mother for young Jenna. She won't do *you* any harm either,' he grinned and everyone laughed.

Jory Trevone, who had been tragically widowed five years previously, scowled darkly at John. 'I'll thank you not to match-make me! No one can replace my lovely Elizabeth, and Jenna has no need for another mother, so you can stop your prattling,' he grumbled into his ale.

'Suit yourself.' John shrugged, 'So, what about you, George? That forge of yours could do with a woman's touch, and she'd keep your bed warm at night!'

George Blewett curled his lip. 'Nah! I want a chick ready for plucking if I'm going to take one to my bed. I'd not go for an old broiler like her - she must be twenty-six if she's a day.'

Kit slammed his glass on the bar. 'Stop this at once! How dare you speak like that? Sophie's a fine-looking woman, so stop discussing her like she's cattle, ready to go to market.'

'Oh, aye.' John nodded. 'It seems to me that you *do* have your eye on her! As I say, "like a rat up a drain pipe."'

Kit thumped the bar again, making several glasses bounce alarmingly. 'For Christ's sake! The poor woman is probably having to cope with that battle-axe of a mother-in-law, and the worry of where the money to feed themselves is coming from, now there's no wage coming in. You'd all do better to put your heads together to come up with a solution of how we can help her to fend for herself.'

The landlord looked suitably admonished. 'Well, I need someone to launder the sheets, if she's a mind to do them.'

Kit nodded. 'Thank you, John, I'll let her know.'

Eric Williams added. 'She can try her hand at milking if she wants. I've need of a new dairy hand.'

'I thank you too, Eric.'

Jack Tehidy spoke up. 'Ria's just told me there's to be a memorial service for Jowan on Sunday. Now I know they're not flush for money at the moment - we had a rubbish catch what with the storm and all, so I reckon we should ask our wives to contribute to the wake. What do you say?'

Kit nodded. 'Thank you, Jack, that's a good idea. I think Sophie would appreciate that.'

Chapter 6

There had been an air of frosty discontent in Alpha Cottage all morning - mainly due to Sophie's attire. She'd risen early to break her fast, and though resigned to dress in mourning, when she unearthed her black skirt and blouse from her clothes trunk, the pungent musty smell of mildew made her nose wrinkle in distaste. With no plans to go out anywhere for a few hours, and the day being fine and dry, she pegged her 'widow's weeds' on the washing line to air. She quickly dressed in her normal attire, knowing this would induce an onslaught of abuse from Ria – the first of many that day, no doubt. She ate a meagre breakfast, before donning an apron to carry out her normal duties. It was Thursday - Pig-Swill Man day and by the high odour the slop bucket in the kitchen was emitting, it was not a day too soon. The weekly visit to the village's main swill bin was Sophie's most hated job. Thankfully it was situated fifty-yards up the lane because it stank to high heaven. The clouds of bluebottles around it would inevitably dive onto her bucket and buzz around her head as she frantically emptied it, put the lid back on and escaped while holding her breath. To her dismay she found the remains of yesterday's stew - which would have easily made another meal - had been wastefully and quite deliberately dumped in the swill bucket by Ria. They could ill afford to waste food at the moment. She picked the bucket up and carried it to the front door only to find the key had gone and the door was well and truly locked. *So, Ria! You plan to keep me prisoner, do you?* Patting the bag of money tucked safely in her skirt pocket, she awarded herself a knowing smile. *We'll see about that.*

*

There was still a slight odour emitting from her black skirt as Sophie smoothed the creases out of it, but she needed to go out to the shop. Although she had no desire to dress as a widow or to grieve Jowan's passing, she would, for decency's sake. But underneath her skirt, she defiantly wore the whitest, brightest petticoats she possessed.

When Sophie came down the stairs, Ria was in her favourite chair by the fire resting her stockinged feet on a small stool, a look of self-righteousness on her face.

'At *last,* you show some respect for my poor son.'

Sophie wrapped her shawl around her shoulders and picked up her shopping basket.

'Where do you think you're going? You can't get out - I have the key!' Ria patted her apron pocket.

'And *I* have the money in my pocket,' Sophie answered calmly, 'so I suggest you open the door if you want me to go out and buy some food for this wake.'

Ria flustered. 'I haven't made a list of things we'll need yet.'

'There's no need for a list, Ria. I'll buy a ham to boil and press, and enough flour to make bread for sandwiches - *that* will have to do.' She watched Ria's nostrils flare.

'If you think I'm sending my Jowan off with a few ham sandwiches, you are very much mistaken! Jowan will have a lavish wake befitting a beloved son.'

'*Ria,* we have barely enough money to cover the rent and put food on the table for the next two weeks. A lavish wake is completely out of the question - you must see that?' She watched as Ria's eyes filled with tears, so she said in a softer voice, 'Jowan would not want us to waste money and see us go without. A ham tea will be quite adequate and people will understand our circumstances. Just remember, people have put a little more into Jowan's wage bag for us this week and they won't be pleased to see it was spent extravagantly.' Seeing Ria's shoulders droop in defeat she added, 'Unlock the door, Ria so I can go and buy the ham.'

*

Kit had been keen to pass the job offers onto Sophie, but so far, his attempts to speak to her had failed. He'd seen Sophie that morning walking across the bridge towards home with her shopping basket. He'd waved and called out, but she appeared not to have noticed him. Setting off in hot pursuit, he called her name twice, and though he thought she hesitated for a moment, she carried on walking home. By the time he reached Alpha Cottage, the door had been closed and by the sound of it, locked. Unsure as to what to do for a moment, he decided to knock. There was a marked delay and the sound of high voices before it was unlocked and opened by Ria.

'Good day, Mrs Treloar. Would it be possible to speak with Sophie?' Although expecting a hostile response from her – because there had never been any love lost between them - he'd not expected Ria to pick up the broom and jab him with it, in order to clear him from her doorstep! Stepping back in alarm he brushed the dust from his trousers as the door slammed shut in his face and the lock once again engaged.

Walking back to his workshop undeterred, he thought perhaps it would be better to wait until after the service on Sunday before trying again. He'd have a better chance of speaking to Sophie alone at the wake, without Ria's hostile intervention. Besides he needed to finish making a coffin for an unfortunate gentleman in Seaworgan before he headed off to Poldhu the next day. He planned to stay over at Poldhu on Friday, attend Silas's wedding on Saturday, and then return home in time for the memorial service for Jowan on Sunday. It was important that Sophie knew she had his support.

*

With a flourish of his hand, Kit stood back and admired his work, congratulating himself on a job well done. Kit was, by trade, a skilled furniture maker, fashioning the most beautiful pieces of oak furniture which all sported a very intricately carved seahorse –his signature mark. He'd been influenced by the Arts and Craft movement and had travelled to meet with some of the finest bespoke furniture makers in the movement. His appreciation of wood was apparent in the care and attention paid to his coffins. Kit had learned his basic carpentry trade from his grandfather, Rory Trevellick, a jolly fellow, liked and respected by all who knew him. Rory had also been the local funeral director, but when he passed away, Kit had continued to make coffins. He drew the line however at having dead bodies in his workshop! His job now was only to supply Mr Greaves, the funeral director. Kit left him to do all the grim necessities for the unfortunates!

With the coffin finished, Kit glanced at the clock as it chimed six. He knew where to find Clem Greaves at this time of day. Though not much of a drinker himself, he would occasionally pop into The Black Swan for a sociable glass of ale after work.

*

With the ham on to boil, the oppressiveness of Alpha Cottage once again fell like a low weather depression on Sophie. She stood at the window, wringing her hands in frustration. The need to break out and run to her stile was almost unbearable, but the door had been locked as soon as she returned from Moyles shop. Just as soon as this damn memorial service was over, things would be very different. Like the pupa of a butterfly encased in its sack, Sophie felt she was undergoing a remarkable transformation – a metamorphosis. Very soon she would become a butterfly and with her new wings she *would* fly.

*

Ria sat in her chair observing Sophie's body language. She looked strange and agitated, like a coiled spring, and knew she must act to quell her restlessness – for Jowan's sake.

'Come away from the window. If you're looking for Kit Trevellick, I scat him away with the broom. That man has always had an eye for you and it's disgraceful of you to encourage him. How could you flirt with other men when my boy's not cold in his grave?'

Sophie shot her a sharp incredulous look.

'You can take that look off your face, and show some

43

respect to me too. There will be no more gallivanting about the countryside. I have allowed you to flit about these last few days, what with the upset and wake to sort out and such, but after Sunday you will act appropriately as a widow and honour your dead husband's wishes and not go out alone. The sooner you're settled into Quay House, under Gilbert Penvear's watchful eye, the better.' For a moment Ria thought Sophie was going to turn on her, but obviously thought better of it, because instead she flounced upstairs without uttering a word. 'And on the subject of Gilbert Penvear,' Ria shouted up after her, 'you need to buckle down and get this place spick and span. If I'm going to have Mrs Drew housekeeping for me, I'll not have her telling all and sundry that we were mucky.'

*

Sophie leant her head back against the bedroom door, her hands over her ears to drown out Ria's voice. *Oh, shut up, you stupid woman.* She shivered - it was cold up here in the bedroom, but she simply couldn't stand to be in the same room as Ria a moment longer. Pulling her shawl about her shoulders she stood at the bedroom window, but pulled back when Kit walked into view. She'd heard him call out her name that morning, but pretended not to hear him. She had nothing against Kit - he seemed to be a kind, considerate man and she had never heard a bad word said against him, but she was determined not to give him any encouragement – despite Ria's accusations.

*

When Kit entered the Black Swan, sure enough Clem Greaves was propping up the bar with several other men, including Eric Williams the dairyman, who was taking a swift libation before supper.

'Look here, Kit,' Clem said. 'There's an article in the Cornishman about that sea rescue of the *SS Suevic*. You know, the one Jack Tehidy and his crew were involved in when Jowan Treloar drowned!'

Kit stood over the newspaper which was spread out

over the bar top.

'It says here the incredible courage and perseverance of the four lifeboats involved saved 456 lives that day, and not a single life was lost! Not a single life, except for Jowan's, eh?' Clem stated.

'Yes.' *And he was no loss to anyone.*

Clem scratched the stubble on his chin. 'It's strange they didn't mention that Jowan was lost, presumed drowned though. After all, Jack Tehidy said he died a hero trying to help the stricken passengers.'

Kit took a sip of ale. *Having Jowan and hero in the same sentence didn't quite ring true.* 'Perhaps they'll mention it next week, after the wake.'

'Aye, maybe. It seems that the wreck has become something of an attraction down on the Lizard. Hundreds of people have been down there to look at the stricken vessel while they try to salvage its cargo and the passenger's belongings.'

Kit nodded. 'I would think that'll take some doing. Jack Tehidy said the ship was huge. Apparently, it's full of meat and wool!'

'It's a bloody shame it didn't break up then.'

A glass was raised in agreement.

*

Sophie glanced around the sparse soulless bedroom, settling her eyes on the hard bed with its lumpy mattress. She hated that bed - even now, when there was no threat of sharing it or fighting off Jowan's drunken advances. If Alpha Cottage was her prison, then this was her cell. When she had her own home, she'd have the softest sheets she could afford and perhaps a feather pillow, and books! She'd have books and flowers by her bed ... she glanced at the vase of wilting primroses and made herself a promise that she would always have flowers by her bed during the warm months. With that happy thought, she pulled her chair up to the open window to watch the world go by. Soon her attention was diverted when an elderly gentleman came into view. He was stood near the water pump, his head darting this way and that, as though he was lost. As he moved closer to the door of the Inn, Sophie realised the man was wearing a bowler hat, a collar, tie, jacket and boots but no trousers …

'Oh!' She realised he was bare legged, and so obviously not wearing his union suit. She saw the door of the Inn burst open and Eric Williams ran out to grab the gentleman by the arm.

'Come on, Pa,' Eric said, 'you know you're not meant to be out.'

Sophie watched as Eric marched him back towards Gweek Wollas Farm, whilst trying in vain to pull his shirt tails down over his exposed buttocks.

Poor old lad, Sophie sighed. She'd heard that Jim Williams had lost his mind. He had been such a nice gentleman as well - always doffing his hat to everyone he met. It was so sad to see his life deteriorate like that.

Chapter 7

It was late Friday afternoon when Kit steered Willow down the steep hill to Poldhu Cove. The vast golden beach was a sight to behold and offered up the most spectacular vista. The cove sat in a deep inlet flanked by cliffs to either side. The Poldhu Tea Room was nestled cosily between sand dunes and reed-beds, but it was an exposed coast, often battered by wind and waves. The mist and unsettled weather after the storm had abated for now, and he hoped, for the sake of everyone, tomorrow would be fine for Silas's wedding.

Kit found Guy relaxing on the tea room terrace with a glass of ale and a newspaper.

'Kit, my friend,' he grinned. 'I'm so happy you could join us. Are Eric and Lydia with you?'

'Unfortunately, not - but they send their apologies. Eric's poor old pa has completely lost his mind. They're having trouble keeping him safe indoors and didn't want to leave Charlie to deal with him. Lydia sent a cheese over as a gift though - it's a ripe one too.' He wrinkled his nose.

'Ah, well, at least you're here. Come and meet the family. Ellie, our guest is here,' he called out.

Kit looked down at the small girl at Guy's feet.

'This is Agnes.' He pulled her into his arms and brushed the sand off her face. 'Agnes is four, and she is a little monster. Aren't you?' The child giggled and wriggled back out of his arms. 'And this is Zack.' He pointed to the boy sitting quietly on the sand playing with a toy. 'Zack is almost three and as good as gold, and then as I told you the other day, my lovely Ellie has another on the way.'

Genuinely happy for Guy's good fortune, he said quite enviously, 'What a lovely little family.'

Guy grinned broadly. 'I am blessed. Ellie has given me everything a man could ask for.'

'Are my ears burning?' Ellie came out, shielding her eyes from the bright afternoon sunshine.

'It's all good things, Ellie. Come - meet my old school friend, Kit Trevellick.'

'I'm very pleased to meet you at last. Guy has told me all about you.'

Kit was dazzled by her warmth - Ellie was beautiful and positively radiant in her pregnancy. 'I'm pleased to meet you too, Ellie, and I've heard much about you. Guy is a very lucky man.'

'Oh,' she winked at Guy, 'I think I'm the lucky one.'

'What a wonderful place this is.' Kit gestured to the spectacular view.

'Yes, it is rather nice - especially at this time of year. The summer gets very busy though with the Poldhu Hotel guests, but it's all good for business.'

'Ellie is a fine business woman. She juggles this place and looks after these two monkeys.'

'Now, Guy. You know I don't do it alone. I have Jessie to help.'

'Is that Silas's bride-to-be?' Kit asked.

Ellie nodded. 'It is, yes. You'll meet her tomorrow. I've sent her off to her cottage before Silas gets back from work. It's bad luck to see each other before the wedding. Now if you'll excuse me, I must finish the baking for tomorrow.'

'Can I get you a glass of ale, Kit?' Guy asked. 'I think we are better out of the way. Ellie will have everything sorted in there.'

'If it's no trouble, thank you.'

Kit was helping young Zack build a sandcastle, when Guy returned with his drink. 'You'll make a rod for your own back, now, Kit. Zack will pester you to make more.'

'I don't mind. I love children,' he answered wistfully.

'So, how is Jowan's young widow fairing?'

Kit gave a crooked smile. 'I think she'll be all right.'

'I should say so. I think she'll be heartily glad to be rid of him. I reckon she had a poor life with him. I've seen him stinking drunk after a fishing trip, heading off home to her.'

'So have I,' Kit grimaced. 'She still has to contend with that battle-axe of a mother-in-law though.'

'Ria! Ugh! A terrible woman!' They chinked glasses in unison.

*

Sore heads and a cold swim to sober up were the order of the day the next morning for Guy, Kit and Silas. Ellie had left them on the terrace the previous evening, drinking to health, wealth and happiness, and had no sympathy for any of them as she noisily prepared breakfast when they returned from the beach.

'Come on, eat up. I've lots to do,' Ellie said slightly louder than was perhaps necessary. 'Sarah will arrive from Bochym soon to help get the girls ready.'

*

The day, which had promised a little sunshine at first, was lowering by the time they all arrived at Cury Church.

Jessie, once a maid at Bochym Manor, before having the good fortune to be offered a job with Ellie at the tea room, wore a dress of fine white linen edged with exquisite lace. Her long glossy chestnut hair was pinned up at the sides, and adorned with a coronet of spring flowers. The lace on her dress was hand-made by Ellie, a craft that seemed to be dying out due to manufactured lace. Then Sarah Dunstan had set up the Arts and Craft Association at Bochym Manor and Ellie's work now graced the gowns of the well-heeled society throughout the country. Jessie had in attendance her friend, Betsy, the head maid from Bochym, and Agnes, who to Ellie's dismay, had already soiled her dress with mud.

Silas, resplendent in his new suit, though uncomfortable in his stiff collar, stood nervously at the altar waiting. He was just nineteen-years-old, a year younger than his bride of twenty. They had met and fallen in love when they were fifteen and sixteen respectively but instead of marrying as soon as they could, Silas wanted to give Jessie the very best a man could offer. So, they had enjoyed a long, happy courtship, while Silas earned enough money and helped Guy build another cottage, so that he and Jessie could start their married life in their own home. This was their time now!

As the congregation of twenty watched Silas marry the love of his life, the rain which had held off all morning began to drum on the church roof. Nothing could dampen their happiness though.

*

The wedding breakfast was held at the tea room. Ellie and Jessie had laid on a buffet to rival any society wedding, and everyone was able to toast the happy couple with bottles of fine vintage champagne sent down from Bochym.

There was much talk of the *SS Suevic* amongst the guests, as many of them had been down to the Lizard to take a look at the stricken vessel.

'I don't know what they are going to do with it,' Guy said. 'It seems to be stuck fast. They've been ferrying goods and passenger's belongings off it all week.'

'Perhaps the next high tide will float it,' Kit said.

'Perhaps. Those lifeboat men deserve a medal for their bravery.'

'I'll drink to that,' Kit said feeling woozy from the champagne.

'Guy?' They looked up as Ellie approached with Sarah. 'Silas and Jessie are about to set off on honeymoon and Sarah and Betsy are leaving now. Forgive me Kit, but have you been introduced to Sarah Dunstan the Countess de Bochym?'

Kit was struck by Sarah's delicate, patrician beauty. 'No, I haven't had the pleasure.' He placed his hand on his chest and bowed. 'I'm very pleased to meet you, your ladyship.'

'Mr Trevellick.' Sarah reached out her soft hand to shake his.' 'I believe you are a master carpenter?'

Kit shook her hand, embarrassed at the roughness of

his to hers. 'Yes, my lady.'

'I understand my husband is about to send word to you regarding some work he would like you to do? You come with a high recommendation.' She smiled at Guy. 'I do hope you can find the time to come to us?'

'It will be a pleasure. I shall look forward to hearing from him.'

'I'll bid you all goodbye then. Thank you for a lovely day, Elise, Guy.' She kissed them both warmly on the cheek and set off with Betsy back to her carriage.

'Gosh! She's lovely, isn't she?' Kit said.

'She's lovely both inside and out, as you will find out, Kit. Won't he, "Elise".' Guy grinned, teasing her with Sarah's use of Ellie's proper name.

Ellie laughed. 'She really is the kindest person you will ever meet. Now can we get you another drink, Kit?'

'No, thank you. I have really enjoyed myself, but I think it's probably time I left too. I'd like to get home before dark.'

Ellie's attention was caught by Agnes who had just taken her third piece of cake. 'Excuse me. I need to stop her before she is sick!'

Guy laughed as he watched Ellie prise the cake out of her daughter's sticky hand. 'It's a shame you have to go home tonight, Kit, I see you so rarely now.'

'Well, I want to attend this memorial service for Jowan. *Not* that I hold him in any esteem! It's just…,' he paused for a moment, 'I want to be there for Sophie.'

Guy nodded. 'Good man.'

*

As the bride and groom set off to spend a couple of nights in the luxury of The Poldhu Hotel, Kit hitched his pony to his cart and bid a fond farewell to Guy and Ellie.

As they watched him go, Ellie said, 'I must say, I like Kit a lot. He's a good-looking man! Why hasn't he ever married?'

'Ah, well, he's been in love with the same woman for

many years.'

'Oh?' There was a sudden intensity in her eyes.

'She was married to someone else, but she's been recently widowed.'

'Oh! I see,' she breathed. 'Is that the service he's going to tomorrow?'

'Yes.'

'And, does this newly widowed woman know that Kit loves her?'

Guy shrugged.

'Well.' She slipped her arm through his. 'Hopefully they will find a way to each other.' She smiled up at him. 'Like we did!'

*

When Sunday morning dawned, Sophie began to prepare for the wake and a memorial service she had no desire to attend. It was going to be a trying day. She'd felt so grateful that Amelia had offered her help, and that several of her neighbours had pushed notes under their door offering to make pasties and cakes - it seemed it wouldn't be such a strain on her financial resources after all.

Sophie began to make the ham sandwiches, whilst Ria sat in the chair dabbing her eyes. At ten, as promised, Amelia Pascoe turned up, with a massive tea pot and a box containing several cups and saucers she had sourced from various people.

'I guessed that you wouldn't have enough cups, Ria, so I brought you some,' Amelia said brightly.

'That's kind of you, Amelia.' Ria snuffled into her handkerchief.

'Right, Sophie. What can I do to help?'

'Sophie's fine, don't bother yourself, Amelia,' Ria intervened.

Amelia winked at Sophie. 'It's no bother. I'll set the table for you.'

Sophie smiled gratefully. Soon the promised pasties and cakes began to arrive and the table groaned under the weight of food.

'Oh, my!' Ria declared looking at the spread. 'This just shows how respected my Jowan was!'

Sophie exchanged a doubtful glance with Amelia.

As Amelia took her leave, Sophie glanced at the table. Her eyes watered at everyone's kindness.

'Huh! I don't suppose those tears are for my boy,' Ria scoffed.

Making a conscious effort not to retaliate today, Sophie made her way upstairs to get ready.

'No, I didn't think so,' Ria shouted after her. 'But it's time you showed Jowan some respect. You're a disgrace to his memory. Things are going to change dramatically after this service. So you'd better buck your ideas up and begin to act like a widow. I'll not have any more of your hysterics or disobedience. This is still Jowan's house and you will obey by his rules.'

Sophie listened to her ravings as she pinned on her hat. She smiled inwardly. *I think not.*

*

Gilbert Penvear stood at his mirror and straightened his tie, turning his face to make sure his manservant had shaved him correctly. He hated shoddy work and if one whisker showed, he would dock his manservant's wage by a halfpenny. He didn't normally attend a funeral service of anyone in the village, but this would be an exception.

His thoughts were of Sophie Treloar, as they had been for several days and nights now. Confident that people always did what he told them to do, he assured himself that she *would* attend him, as requested, a week tomorrow.

She was a fine, comely looking woman, though a little thin perhaps, but on the rare occasions he'd spoken to her, he'd found her manner and countenance a little sour - he'd soon eradicate that! She would live with him under the pretence of housekeeper, but... he licked his thin lips, he had other plans for her. He needed a woman in his bed, and Sophie, being an impoverished widow with a dependent mother-in-law, could not afford to turn him down. The personal arrangement would of course be kept secret from everyone, but once a full seven years had passed, and if he was still alive, he'd marry the woman and all would be right and correct. In the meantime, Mrs Drew, his present housekeeper, an old and not at all aesthetically pleasing woman, would, as promised, and at considerable financial inconvenience to him, be sent to appease Ria Treloar. It was a perfect plan and he congratulated himself on it.

He smiled as he dabbed his cologne onto his clean-shaven chin and glanced at his neat bed - very soon Sophie Treloar would be attending to all his needs. The thought made him adjust a stirring in his underclothes.

Chapter 8

Dr Eddy escorted Sophie and Ria out of their cottage to the waiting mourners, for the procession up to the Mission Church. Sophie had been surprised and slightly unnerved to see Gilbert Penvear standing at the back of the church when she'd entered — he'd never been known to attend anyone's funeral in the village before! She hoped he would not attend the wake - she had no wish to engage in any conversation with that odious man. While the vicar droned on, Sophie felt quite detached from the proceedings and had to stop herself from yawning several times. She'd have thought the absence of Jowan in her bed would have made sleep easier, but money worries had made sleep problematic these past couple of days - she had no idea how she was going to make ends meet. One thing for certain though, she was *not* going to take up Gilbert Penvear's offer. Her mind drifted as to what she could do. She knew how to gut fish, but it was not a job she relished if she could help it. Her needlework skills used to be good too, having been taught by Beatrice, the Italian neighbour who had taken Sophie under her wing when she'd been orphaned. Beatrice had shown her how to make clothes, embroider and perfect the art of Italian quilting. It was a skill she loved, but Jowan had put a stop to that "frivolity" as he'd called it. She was allowed to make her own clothes and shirts for him, but he said, "Quilting and embroidery were for the gentry, not for the likes of us." She was heart sore whenever she thought of Beatrice. She had no idea if she was still alive or not. They had corresponded regularly when Sophie first came to live in Gweek but then the letters stopped abruptly and she'd never found out why. Perhaps she would make some enquiries now.

When everyone bowed their head in prayer, Sophie could see from the corner of her eye that Kit Trevellick hadn't bowed his - instead he was watching her. *Well, he could just stop that malarkey. As kind as he was, she was not, and*

never would be, on the market to entertain another man in her life!
*

While Sophie poured tea and Amelia handed out the food, Kit stood alone, puzzled by Sophie's avoidance of him. Twice he'd tried to engage her in conversation, but twice she had apologised, stating that she was busy and walked away from him. He had the distinct impression that she was annoyed with him for some reason, though he knew not what he had done! He turned his attention to Amelia Pascoe for a moment - a widow herself for over twenty-five years. As a midwife and nurse, she selflessly gave her time to others - if anyone could help him, *she* could.

'Amelia?' Kit beckoned her to one side as she passed with a plate of sandwiches. 'I wonder,' he said taking one, 'if you could do me a favour?'

'If it is something in my power, of course I will. What is it?'

'I've asked around and a couple of people have offered work for Sophie, but I've been unable to tell her. She seems a little reluctant to speak or even look at me.'

Amelia glanced at Sophie. 'I suspect she is probably a little overwhelmed by the events of the last few days. Don't take it personally. She's unused to interacting with people - Jowan and Ria saw to that! I fear the poor girl has become institutionalised.'

'You're right. Perhaps she won't think too kindly if it looks like I am trying to organise her life for her. It would be nice for her to think that she was able to sort some work out for herself - without the intervention of a man.'

Amelia smiled at his thoughtfulness. 'Tell me what you know and I'll drop some hints to her – it'll be up to her then if she takes them up.'

He smiled gratefully and told her the job offers.

'So, how is that boat of yours coming along? We're all waiting for the *Harvest Moon* to launch.'

Kit beamed. 'She's almost ready. I'll take her for sea trials soon.'

'And then you'll leave us all for sunny climes?'

Kit shrugged. 'Maybe.'

She quirked an eyebrow. 'I thought that was always the plan?'

'It was…is.'

Until a certain young woman found herself widowed perhaps?

'Maybe it would be nice just to sail her up and down the Helford. There is no place better!'

'Perhaps,' he said evasively.

*

When the last mourners left the cottage, and with no sign of Ria getting up from her chair, Amelia kindly offered to stay back and help clear the debris from the table.

'Come and see me tomorrow, Sophie,' Amelia said, 'We can have a chat and share a nice cup of tea. Shall we say about eleven?'

Genuinely touched, she said, 'Thank you. I shall look forward to that.'

'What are you two whispering about?' Ria demanded.

Amelia winked at Sophie. 'We are talking about a nice cup of tea.'

'Chance of one would be a fine thing. I could die of thirst for all Sophie cares about me.'

Sophie looked at Amelia and rolled her eyes wearily.

*

With a spring in her step Sophie completed her regular chores the next morning, washed her hands and tidied her hair ready to take tea with Amelia.

'And where do you think you're going?' Ria's arms folded in disapproval.

'To see Amelia!'

'No! You're not. You'll stay indoors and behave like a decent widow should. The key is in my pocket and *that* is where it will stay.'

Through the narrow aperture of her lips, Sophie hissed, 'You think you've won, don't you? Well, you're mistaken. I will *not* be kept indoors by you a moment longer than I have to.' She turned and ran back upstairs.

*

With a cake baked and the kitchen tidied, Amelia glanced at the clock - Sophie was ten minutes late. Wiping her hands down her apron she pulled her shawl around her shoulders and walked the few paces across the bridge until Alpha Cottage came into view. Sophie was waving from the upstairs window.

'Ria's locked me in!' she shouted.

'What the devil is she playing at? Come downstairs, Sophie, I'll sort this out.' Amelia thumped on the front door.

'Who is it?' Ria shouted though the door.

'It's Amelia. Open the door.'

'No, go away. We're in mourning and not accepting visitors.'

'Ria!' Amelia snapped. 'Stop this nonsense now and unlock the door so that Sophie can come out!'

'*Amelia Pascoe*, what gives you the right to tell *me* what to do? I am following Jowan's orders. Sophie must not go out alone!'

'You are being totally unreasonable. Sophie's not alone - she's with me! And with respect, Jowan is dead! *Now* unlock this door.'

'If you had any respect, you would not speak like that of Jowan!'

Ignoring Ria, Amelia shouted, 'Sophie, what do you suggest we do?'

'Perhaps you could go to The Black Swan and tell the landlord that we're locked in and need someone to break the door down, please?' Sophie said gleefully.

'Righty-oh!'

Ria blanched. 'You'll do no such thing, Amelia. I'll not have anyone vandalising my front door! Do you hear me?'

'I hear you, but if you do not unlock it in the next ten seconds, rest assured, I *will* get someone to break it down.'

Outnumbered, Ria fumbled in her pocket for the key.

She pushed Sophie sideways and unlocked the door and poked her head through the gap. 'Now, you look here Amelia Pascoe,' Ria snarled - she was so angry she could hardly speak

Sophie saw the opportunity and took it. Grabbing her bag and shawl she pulled the key from the lock and wrenched the door wide open. Ria shrieked and reeled back as Sophie stepped triumphantly out into the morning sunshine, and in a state of euphoria, practically skipped away from Alpha Cottage.

'I demand you come back, you wilful girl,' Ria screamed. 'And you've not heard the last of this, Amelia Pascoe.'

They heard the door slam behind them.

'Did you get the key, Sophie?'

'Yes, it's in my pocket.'

'We need to get another made, then. You can't be doing with that nonsense.'

When they stopped outside the forge, Sophie hesitated. She knew few people in the village, but she knew George Blewett the blacksmith to be an uncouth, disagreeable man. He'd been a friend of Jowan's and spent many evenings at Alpha Cottage drinking and gambling with him. 'I...I daren't go in there, Amelia.'

'Ah don't worry, his bullying ways don't frighten me. Give the key to me and wait here.'

As she waited, Sophie glanced up at the terrace cottages adjacent to The Black Swan Inn. One in particular had stood empty since the occupier had died a month ago. How she wished she could afford to put up a month's rent in advance so she could get away from Ria, but it would take months before she could do that.

Amelia emerged from the forge, dusting herself down as though she'd been soiled. 'It'll be ready in an hour, and don't worry I'll pick it up for you.'

'Thank you.'

Amelia squeezed her arm. 'Come on, let's have that tea

and chat now.'

Excited and nervous in equal measure to be invited to tea, Sophie wondered what they would chat about. Unused to small talk, the only interaction she'd had with Amelia before was when she'd been summoned to Alpha Cottage to deal with Sophie's miscarriages or infections, and that had been under Ria's watchful eye.

Amelia's kitchen was warm and tidy, and Sophie felt immediately at home there. A cake stood proudly in the centre of her scrubbed wooden table, along with fancy tea cups and saucers. As she took in these new surroundings, she admired several rather good drawings which were on the wall. 'Who is the artist?'

'Young Jenna Trevone, next door,' Amelia said bringing the tea pot to the table. 'She's talented, isn't she? And she's only thirteen! I always buy her drawing materials for her birthday in September, and she shows her gratitude by drawing these for me. She inherited her talent from her mother, Elizabeth, who was a beautiful artist. That's one of hers there.' Amelia pointed to a painting depicting Gweek from the hills surrounding it. It was a scene of pure tranquillity and had been painted from the stile Sophie had sat on recently. 'They used to go out and draw together in the fields up yonder. I'll wager Jenna could be a fine artist too one day, *if* she gets the chance.'

Sophie heard the suggestion of doubt in Amelia's voice. 'It would be a shame if her talent goes to waste.'

'Aye!' Amelia sighed. 'Unfortunately, Jory, her father, finds these things frivolous and I don't think for one minute he encourages her. The man is so wrapped up in his grief the only thing he thinks of is losing himself in his cups with George Blewett! It was a crying shame it Elizabeth died so young, and for the poor little mite to lose her mother. It's been five years now and I miss Elizabeth every single day,' she said pouring the tea.

'I'm afraid I didn't know Elizabeth very well, but I remember she always had a smile for me - as did you.'

Amelia reached over to place her hand on Sophie's sleeve. 'We all felt for you, but things can only get better now. How are you in yourself? You looked a little distressed up by Farmer Ferris's field.'

'Oh, you know - elated, frightened, annoyed....free!'

Amelia smiled. 'Well there are two positives there. What are you frightened of?'

'Starvation - if I don't find some way of getting work.'

'Have you tried?'

She shook her head sadly. 'I've been held back for so long - I've lost all confidence in myself. I don't know how to start or who to approach.'

'That's understandable.' Amelia nodded. 'And annoyed, you said?' She raised her eyebrows.

'Well, you saw how obstinate Ria is. I'm sick of her, Amelia. I actually hate her. I don't like the word, but she's made my life intolerable over the years and she thinks she can continue to do it now, even though Jowan's gone. Well, I'm not putting up with it any longer!'

'Well said!'

'I need to find somewhere to live away from her and her controlling ways.'

'Well, I might just be able to help you on the job front. Would you like a slice of cake?'

*

Sophie felt as though the weight of the world had been lifted. She and Amelia had been to see Eric Williams and she'd secured a job in the milking parlour of Gweek Wollas Farm. She also had in her possession a spare key tucked safely in her pocket and an arm full of smelly bed linen she'd just collected from The Black Swan Inn.

'Do you want me to come in with you to see Ria?' Amelia asked.

'No, thank you. I'd rather like to do this myself. I can't tell you how grateful I am for your help, and for being a friend to me. I so desperately need a friend at this moment in time.'

Amelia wrinkled her nose. 'Well, you know where you can always get a friendly cuppa now, and when you have your own house, you can return the compliment.'

She felt her shoulders droop. 'I fear that will be a long time off. But as soon as I do, I promise you'll be my first guest.

*

Kit smiled warmly when Amelia appeared at the door of his carpenter's shop.

'Goodness gracious, who's died?' Amelia nodded at the coffin.

'Don't worry, it's nobody from the village. It's for a gentleman from Constantine. Would you like some tea? I'm just about to make one.'

'No, thank you, Kit. I just wanted to tell you that Sophie is to start at Williams's farm as from tomorrow. She's going to have a go at milking this afternoon.'

'Thank you, Amelia. I appreciate your help.'

Amelia could see the relief in his eyes. 'The pleasure is mine. It's nice to know Sophie has someone like you looking out for her.'

'Well, she's had a rotten life with Jowan. I've seen her go from a vivacious young woman to…well, a shell of her former self. I'd love to help more, but I get the impression she doesn't want it.'

'With good reason - she'll be a little wary of men now. Give her time to find her feet and she'll emerge like a butterfly once she has her wings back.'

'I'll look forward to that day. Let's hope this job will give her some independence from Ria.'

'Oh, I think by the way Sophie was talking, she'll stand up for herself now.'

Chapter 9

When Sophie entered Alpha Cottage, she walked into an atmosphere she could have cut with a knife.

'Key.' Ria held out her hand.

Sophie dumped the pile of dirty laundry at Ria's feet and handed the key over, happy in the knowledge the spare one was in her pocket.

Ria sniffed disdainfully at the laundry. 'What's all this, and where have you been?'

'Securing work, if you must know,' Sophie said primly. 'I've a job at Williams's farm - I'm to milk there morning and evening.'

Ria retracted her neck. 'What on *earth* have you done that for? Gilbert Penvear is expecting you to start at Quay House as his housekeeper next Monday!'

'Well, he'll just have to keep expecting me, won't he? Because I'm not interested in that horrible little man's offer.'

'You silly, ungrateful girl! If you don't take Penvear's offer, what of *me*? We'd arranged that his present housekeeper would come and keep house for me! Besides, you'll need to earn much more than Mr Williams will give you to keep us both!'

'No truer word said, Ria. *That* is where you come in.' She gestured to the pile of washing. 'The Black Swan needs this back in three days' time, washed and ironed.'

Ria's lip quivered. 'You're not suggesting, that I.., you can't expect me to do such work?'

'Oh, but I do!'

'Well,' she said deeply affronted, 'You are very much mistaken. I can't be doing that at my age!'

'You are only fifty, Ria - it's not beyond you. You'll soon get the hang of it.'

'I'll do no such thing. Now get that disgusting pile of washing out of my front room, it stinks.'

'No, Ria! This is going to be *your* job, until you find

something else you want to do. We cannot live on fresh air, and I am certainly not skivvying for you any longer. I will earn my own money at the farm. That money will be mine. I shall eat what I wish from now on and I'll put half the money up towards the rent every week. *If* you want to stay here too, and *if* you want to eat, you will have to earn your own money! I suggest you make a start on that *disgusting pile*, quite soon. John Drago says there will be a pile to collect every three days - that will give you enough time to launder and iron them.'

'How *dare* you do this to me? After all we've done for you. You had nothing when Jowan brought you home.'

'And now I'm his widow - with even less,' she parried calmly. 'The only thing you and your son did for me was to make my life a misery.' Sophie watched Ria swell with rage and feared at one point she might break out of her stays.

'You should be ashamed of yourself - speaking ill of the dead like that.'

'No Ria, I'm not ashamed, in fact I'm proud to have found myself a job, and *you* should be grateful that I have secured a job for you as well. I could have left you to find one for yourself, you know, but I *didn't*. I'm going to get changed now - I have my first milking lesson this afternoon.'

*

Ria was scowling from her chair when Sophie was ready to leave for her milking lesson. The pile of dirty linen had been kicked into the middle of the room. When she tried the door, it was locked again, but with a little nonchalant shrug, she unlocked it with her own key and stepped out of the cottage, ignoring Ria's protests.

As arranged, she met Lydia Williams in the dairy so they could both walk up to the milking parlour. As they rounded the courtyard, a well-built lad with bright orange curly hair and freckles covering his face and forearms, ambled amiably up towards them.

'This is Stan, Sophie, a valued member of our farming

family here. He's also part of the milking team.' Lydia turned to face Stan full on and mouthed the words, 'New girl!' She brushed her right hand up in front of her left palm and drew her left index finger from her ear to her mouth.

Sophie watched open-mouthed at the strange interaction, and smiled warmly as she held her hand out to Stan.

Stan shook it furiously, as a strange garbled sound came from his lips.

Sophie cast an anxious glance at Lydia.

'Don't be alarmed. You're privileged. Stan isn't often vocal, for chance he is laughed at. But he clearly likes you.' Lydia grinned. 'Stan is deaf, but he will communicate with you if you're patient enough to listen and watch what he is trying to enunciate.'

'Oh, I see.' She turned to Stan and shouted. 'Hello. I'm pleased to meet you.'

Stan frowned.

'He can't hear, but he can lip read to a certain degree. So don't shout your words at him, because your face will distort, making it more difficult for him to understand you.'

'Oh!' Sophie's cheeks pinked.

'Just wave and mouth the words, "Hello."'

Stan grinned and nodded and then gestured something to Lydia with his hands.

'Her name is Sophie,' she mouthed, making several finger movements on her hand.

Stan grinned widely and walked off.

'Thank you for taking time with him, Sophie, not a lot of people do. Some people are frightened of him, and some think because he can't hear that he's daft in the head, but he isn't. He has a lot more sense than a lot of lads his age.'

'How did you learn to communicate with him using your hands?'

Lydia laughed gently. 'I only know the simple hand signs that Edith, Stan's ma taught me. When Edith realised Stan was different from other children, she raised her concerns with Mr Jenkins as to whether Stan would be able to go to school. By extraordinary good fortune, Mr Jenkins had a brother with the same impediment, so he patiently taught both Stan and Edith the basic sign language. It was an absolute god send because it meant Stan was able to go to school and learn with all the other children. Mr Jenkins was a saint!'

'Will you teach me?' Sophie asked.

'Of course, I will.' Lydia smiled warmly at Sophie. 'So, come on and I'll take you to my Eric and you can meet the other dairy hands.'

*

In her crisp, white cotton apron and her sleeves rolled up to her elbows exposing her creamy skin unused to the sun, Sophie stood nervously in the farmyard. With great trepidation she watched the herd make their way through the gate towards the milking parlour. One by one the beasts lumbered towards her - their great swaying udders heavy with milk. They brought with them an overwhelming smell of dung and sour grass as they walked into the milking shed and stood patiently for someone to see to them.

'Which one do you do first, Mr Williams?' Sophie asked nervously.

Eric grinned. 'Which ever one presents itself first. Though Glenda here,' he pointed to the biggest cow, 'she's a bully, and if another gets in her way, she'll show her disapproval.'

Eric saw Sophie swallow hard at the size of the beasts. 'Nay now, don't be afraid. They're gentle giants. Now let me introduce you to everyone. You'll perhaps know our Charlie of course.'

Sophie nodded.

'This here is Stan.'

'Yes,' Sophie smiled. 'We've already met.'

'Excellent. The maid over there is Dora.' Dora looked up from her work and smiled. 'And this is Lizzy Pike, the Mrs calls her the daughter we never had,' he grinned. 'Lizzy lives with us. Her ma lives down river so it's easier for her to stay. She's one of our best milkmaids, so she'll show you the ropes and you'll be up and running afore you know it. We have thirty cows and six of us including me and we all do our fair share of difficult cows - you know, the cows that will hold the milk up, and the ones that kick like hell. You'll get to know which ones I mean. I'll not tolerate any dairy hand that takes a deliberately long time at an easy cow, hoping to bypass the naughty ones until another easy cow comes in line. We used to have a hand that did that all the time, it fair riled everyone, so he got his marching orders - hence the opening for you, my dear.' Noting the consternation on Sophie's face, Eric said, 'Oh, now, don't ee worry about the kickers, we only have two naughty ones and we put a special leather strap on their legs to stop 'em kicking the pail over.'

Sophie glanced up as a man appeared in the doorway. He was as round as he was high, with a smattering of white hair across his otherwise bald head. His legs were bandy and he wore a great wooden yoke similar to what oxen would wear.

'This here is Ely Symonds. Once you've filled your pail, Ely will carry them off to our Lydia in the dairy. Right now, my beauty, I'll put you into the safe hands of Lizzy here. You'll be milking like a good 'un in no time.'

'Have you got a scarf with you?' Lizzy asked.

'No.' Sophie frowned.

'Here, I've a spare one. Put it on. It'll save you having to wash your hair if the cow shits on you!' She grimaced. 'It does happen on occasions, I'm afraid.'

'Aye, and bloody red hot it is if it hits you!' Charlie quipped from where he sat in one of the other stalls.

Lizzy grinned as she pulled the three-leg stool over to

the cow.

'Now watch carefully. Before you begin milking, secure the cow's head so that she can't wander off. Speak to her softly and gently pat her side so that she knows where you are. Don't make any sudden movements. If you surprise her, she may panic and kick you or step on you. Grab one of the buckets of warm water over there please.'

Sophie did as she was bid.

'Right, you have to wash her teats with the cloth before you begin milking her. This prevents any muck she's picked up out in the fields from contaminating the milk. Washing with warm water helps to bring down the milk.' She winked. 'So, I make sure I do a good job.' She pulled at the towel draped over her shoulder. 'Always dry her teats before you start to milk.' Lizzy beckoned Sophie to sit on the stool. She then grasped the cow's tail, pulled it round and told Sophie to lean her forehead on it. 'It'll stop it swishing in your face. First, we always strip the teats of muck by squeezing each teat downwards. Be careful and make sure the mucky milk goes onto the ground and not in the pail. Right, now gently clamp each teat between your extended thumb and first finger. Can you feel the teat fill in the palm of your hand?'

Sophie did as she was told. 'No, I can't feel anything.'

'She knows you're new to this so you may need to nudge her udder to help stimulate it, just like a calf would do, that should let the milk down.'

Sophie did this and tried again to milk her, this time the teat swelled in her palm.

'Right, good, it's coming. So, as you press down on the teat, maintain your grip on the base of the teat so that the milk doesn't flow back up into the udder. *Don't* yank her teats! Just squeeze your fingers from the middle to your pinky to force the milk out. Be gentle yet firm.'

With a satisfied squirt, the milk came, unfortunately it soaked Sophie's apron.

Lizzy snuffled with laughter. 'You need a better aim

than that or Eric will scat you. Milk that teat until the udder above it looks saggy and wrinkled. If you're not sure have a feel, it'll feel much softer. When that happens, we move to the diagonal teat and start again. Most of us prefer to alternate our hands to stop the fingers from aching.'

After a few attempts Sophie sighed with relief when she began to fill her pail with ease.

'All right, I'll leave you to it. I'll be in the next stall. So, shout if you need me.'

'Thank you, Lizzy,' Sophie said with nervous gratitude.

It was a slow laborious task that first milking session and Sophie only milked two cows out of the thirty, but she felt a huge sense of achievement.

Once the cows were milked and sent back out into the field, Eric winked at her. 'Good work, maid. So, do you want to do it tomorrow?'

'Yes please, Mr Williams.'

'Six-o-clock sharp then - the cows won't wait you know!'

'I'll be here.'

*

The sun was setting in the western sky as Sophie walked back along the riverside towards Alpha Cottage. The thought of going back home to Ria's unpleasantness began to strip the euphoria she'd felt while milking.

'How did it go then?'

Sophie spun around to find Amelia behind her. 'Oh, Amelia, I really enjoyed it! Another few months and I'll have enough to put up some rent. I hope this is still available then.' She nodded to the empty house on Rose Terrace.

Amelia glanced at the house in question and smiled. 'I hope it is too.'

*

After popping into the post office to buy herself a muffin, Sophie returned to Alpha Cottage to find the pile of washing was still where it had been kicked, and Ria in the armchair with her arms folded over her ample bosom.

'You think you're clever, don't you? Well, I'm having John Rowe the locksmith here tomorrow to change the locks. So that spare key you've acquired will have been a waste of money. I've decided you can keep that silly farm job until you take up Mr Penvear's offer - we could do with the extra money. But *I* will accompany you to and from the Williams's Farm and that is my final word on the subject.'

Sophie curled her lip slightly as she took off her hat and coat.

'And you can move that lot before you dish supper out, it stinks!'

Without another word, Sophie went upstairs, pushed a chair against her bedroom door, lit a fire and toasted a muffin for her tea. Afterwards she lay on her bed, reading a book Amelia had lent her, ignoring the shouts and protests coming from the other side of the door.

Chapter 10

Sophie was up with the lark the next morning, and as expected, Ria's threat to accompany her to the farm had not materialised - Ria was never one to rise before nine. Sophie enjoyed her morning cup of tea in relative peace and quiet, but before she left, she stoked up the range and brought two buckets of water in, ready for Ria to boil for the washing – it would be up to Ria then to get on with it.

For the first time she was able to take in the beauty of the early morning village as she walked along the riverbank. The branches of the blackthorn hedges edging the Williams's fields filled her senses with the clean sweet fragrance of the frothiest white flowers – it was as though the hedges were coated with a hoar-frost following a crisp cold starry night. With the tide out, a rich earthy smell filled the air as the swans and ducks feasted hungrily on the mudflats. She stood at the edge of the riverbank, quite unconcerned that the dew-covered grass was dampening her skirt and petticoats. Crouching down, she scooped the droplets into her palms to bathe her face – a luxury never experienced before. As the morning sun climbed into the Cornish sky, it swept away the night shadows and warmed the damp dew on her skin. She felt refreshed, alive and, dare she say, born again.

*

Kit stood at his window with a mug of strong tea in his hand. By chance he'd seen Sophie walking along the riverbank, and could hardly peel his eyes from her. Although still dressed in black, her demeanour was as bright as the spring morning. He marvelled at the skip in her step - it seemed that the caged bird was learning to fly.

*

Sophie presented herself at the milk parlour just before six in her headscarf and crisp white apron, ready and waiting for Charlie and Stan to bring in the cows.

She greeted everyone and made a point of signing hello

to Stan and was awarded with a grin which reached from ear to ear!

Slightly quicker today, Sophie managed to milk three cows. She also found that if she sang softly to the cow, it stood quiet and contented while she milked it. Her melodic voice soothed every man, woman and beast in the milking parlour, making her a popular addition to their fold.

Once the cows were milked, Charlie and Lizzy led them back out to the fields while Stan showed Sophie how to feed the pigs. Nothing was ever wasted and because they made their own cheese and butter to sell in their dairy, the large quantities of whey, a by-product of the cheese making process, was fed to the pigs. Sophie smiled as they guzzled hungrily, thus making her own stomach rumble.

Eric came to see how they were getting along and draped a friendly arm around them both.

'All done?' he asked Sophie.

'Yes. What's next?'

'Breakfast, so look sharp, Lydia's waiting for us all.'

Breakfast was an unexpected part of the job, so when Sophie stepped into the farm's massive kitchen, the warm smell of bacon frying made her stomach rumble more. Her eyes were drawn to the high beam ceiling from which a ham carcass hung curing from a great hook. Further along an array of pots and pans hung from a rack, some blackened with only patches of the original copper showing through. A roaring fire blazed in the grate, next to which a fat cat stretched, lazily toasting its paws. Sophie felt her cheeks pink with the warmth of the room.

'Hello, Sophie. How was your first morning? I bet you're famished! Sit down, breakfast won't be a tick.'

'Can I help at all?'

'Aye, if you've a mind to.' Lydia grinned thankfully. 'Set the table, there's cutlery in the table drawer and put that there loaf in the middle - folks will cut off what they want. There's butter in the larder, you could bring that in for me, but keep the lid on it otherwise the cat will lick it.' She nodded to the slumbering tortoiseshell cat. 'Prudy might look like she's sleeping, but one whiff of butter and she'll be up on that table like a kitten.'

Sophie grinned as she set the table and then picked her way over the various pairs of shoes strewn across the floor leading to the larder.

'Just kick your way through, Sophie. They're a bloody untidy lot who live here,' Lydia said, pushing a stray hair from her face while she moved the bacon around the frying pan.

Breakfast was hearty and the chatter around the table lively. Everyone made Sophie welcome. She felt so grateful and very lucky to be part of this happy group. Charlie and Lizzy were both thirteen, but their playful banter, despite their youth, made it apparent that these two cared for each other deeply. And from the kind and tender way Eric and Lydia interacted with each other, there was no doubt of their love. Dora was a quiet little thing, and kept smiling lovingly at Stan. He however, seemed to be constantly looking and smiling at Sophie – it was clear she'd made a special friend in him.

'Right, you lot back to work. I've cheese and butter to make and customers waiting.' Lydia was swapping her breakfast apron for a clean one. 'Charlie, Lizzy get off to school or you'll be late.'

Eric kissed Lydia on her plump rosy cheek and beckoned Sophie to follow him back to the milking parlour. There she was given a stiff broom and tasked to sweep and swill the milking parlour with Dora. It was ten by the time Sophie made her way back home, conscious that each step took her closer to losing her buoyant mood.

'Sophie.' Amelia was walking briskly over the bridge to meet her. 'How was your morning?'

'Wonderful, just wonderful.'

Amelia grinned. 'I can see in your face you mean that. Now Sophie, don't take this the wrong way – and don't frown - it's not charity but I just want to help you find your independence from Ria. She was complaining in Moyles shop earlier today to anyone who'd listen, about you expecting her to do The Black Swan's laundry. Apparently, she hasn't touched the bundle you took home yesterday and has no intention of doing so, and nor will she until you leave her.'

Sophie sighed. 'I know.'

'So, I've put up the rent for the house you were interested in.' She gestured to the house in Rose Terrace, 'It's paid until May 1st.'

Sophie's mouth dropped.

Resting her hand on Sophie's. 'It's going to take you too long to earn enough to rent your own place, and I have some money which I am quite willing to lend to you.'

Sophie's eye's blurred with tears. 'Oh, Amelia, thank you, but....'

'No buts. I am not in any need of the money back soon. So, you can pay me back whenever you feel able. I trust you implicitly, and know you'll pay it back. Anyhow it's too late to say no.' She dangled the keys in front of her eyes.

Sophie covered her mouth in disbelief.

'Shall we take a look?' She grinned. 'Apparently, Glenda Riley who lived there was terribly house-proud. I suspect you won't find a speck of dust except for what has accumulated since her death. The range is in good working order and I could lend you some blankets and a pillow. You could just move in today if you wish.'

'Thank you so much, Amelia.' Then her face dropped. 'I just hope that I can get back out of Alpha Cottage after collecting my things! Ria has John Rowe the locksmith coming round to change the locks. He might have already been. I might need your help, to get me out again.'

'You've no need to worry about the locksmith.' Amelia winked. 'Ria was telling Mr Moyle that she was getting a new lock fitted today, because - and she looked at me when she said it - her key had been tampered with! So, I went to see John and explained the situation. He is very happy to conveniently forget about the job for the time being. You may not know many people in this village, Sophie, but a lot of us have your best interests at heart.'

Sophie laughed joyously as Amelia grabbed her arm and pulled her towards the house.

*

Ria looked up, clearly anticipating the locksmith, but her face fell when she saw Sophie coming through the door.

'Oh, it's you, is it? This will be the last time you flit in and out of this house, Madam.' Ria nodded her head.

Sophie smiled and went straight upstairs. It was eleven-thirty - she needed to be back at the farm by four. She had plenty of time to gather her belongings, of which there were few, and move into her new home. With her bag in hand and the leather purse of money tucked into her pocket, Sophie came back downstairs.

Ria frowned at the sight of the bag, but turned her attention to the pile of coins Sophie was placing on the table.

'It's about time you gave that money back to me. Now I suggest you get on with this stinking pile of washing, before you make dinner, otherwise you'll lose that job.'

With a wry smile, Sophie said, 'The job is yours to lose - not mine. I suggest you do it, and do it quickly. This is half of Jowan's last wage — it should pay your rent with a little over for food. I'm leaving now, and I'm not coming back. You'll need to earn the money to pay for this place on your own. John Drago at The Black Swan will not look too kindly if you're late with the first lot of laundry. Perhaps he'll give the job to someone more willing to do it.'

Ria's mouth whitened. 'You can't leave! Jowan would be angry if you left me all alone.'

'Jowan is dead, Ria,' Sophie said softly. 'It's time for us both to move on.'

'You ungrateful woman! Is this all the gratitude I get

for welcoming you into my home?'

'With respect, Ria, the only welcome I received was your cold, unyielding hatred towards me.'

'Damn your insolence.' Ria flared her nostrils. 'I do not wish you any luck in this world - you deserve none! Do you hear me?'

'I hear you. I however, wish you all the luck in the world – you'll need it.' She nodded to the pile of washing, picked up her bag, cast a derisory look around the room and left.

*

Ria heaved herself up out of the chair and kicked the pile of laundry around the room. Yes, it was true, she'd not welcomed Sophie. The girl had stolen the affections of her beloved son from her, and expected to breeze in here with her books and needlecraft, thinking she was going to be mistress of this cottage! But no sooner had she stepped down from the wagon, still in her Sunday best from her wedding, she was attracting the attention of Kit Trevellick. It had been a constant trial for them to have to watch her like a hawk from that moment on. A baby would have settled her flighty ways but...... she turned to the window and shouted after Sophie, 'Good riddance to you and your barren body. You're nothing but an embarrassment to womankind and the memory of my son!'

Ely Symonds toothless grin appeared at the window and made her jump. 'Are you all right in there, Ria?'

'I'm fine, Ely, just bloody fine,' she snapped.

Ria felt dread like she had never felt before. This was the first time she'd been left completely on her own. Her lip trembled and the first frustrated tears began to fall.

Chapter 11

Sophie had fallen into a deep, satisfied sleep, having cleaned her new cottage from top to tail the previous evening. She woke at dawn to the sound of silence and a bowl of primroses beside her makeshift bed.

Pushing the covers from her legs, she stretched luxuriously and walked barefoot to the window. Flinging it wide open, she took a deep breath of spring air as the first sounds of birdsong punctured the morning light. Turning back to survey the room, she glanced at her bed. She had slept on several blankets and though it was uncomfortable, she wouldn't change this bed for the mattress she'd left behind at Alpha Cottage.

Thankfully though, Eric had promised her some sacks of straw and Lydia had offered her a bolt of ticking and the use of her sewing machine. So, just as soon as she finished her morning milking chores, she would set to and make herself a comfortable mattress to lie on.

*

Ria it seemed, had been quick to denounce her wayward daughter-in-law to all and sundry, so when Lydia opened the dairy that day, she found herself inundated with village women wanting to know if it was true - that Sophie had so cruelly and mercilessly left an old grieving woman to fend for herself.

Bristling with indignation, Lydia punched her fists into her sides. 'Excuse me! What's with this 'old woman' malarkey? Ria is only fifty. If she just got off her lazy behind, she could fend very well for herself! You all know her, and how she's kept Sophie under her thumb all these years and don't deny it!' She paused and glared at everyone while they murmured inaudibly. 'It's time for Sophie to branch out and make a life for herself now her husband has passed away.'

There was a collective murmur of disapproval.

'And if you don't like it, you can go and find

somewhere else to get your milk and cheese! Because if I hear another ill word said against Sophie, I will not serve you, *ever* again!'

They lowered their heads meekly and did their daily shopping without another complaint. When they all left, Eric popped his head around the doorway.

'That's my girl.' He grinned at his wife.

*

Lydia had set up her Singer sewing machine in the back parlour for Sophie to use. Sophie flexed her fingers - it had been so long since she had used a machine like this, but her fingers remembered how to thread and spool it. Running her hands over the wheel, she settled her foot on the treadle and worked well into the afternoon sewing the mattress bag. With a couple of hours before afternoon milking, Eric took her to the barn so she could stuff the bag.

It took her a lot longer than anticipated, and when she'd finally hand sewn the last seam, she sat down, hot, exhausted and covered in straw dust.

Taking a drink of milk from the ladle in the dairy to quench her thirst, she donned her scarf and apron and settled down to milk. Her limbs felt like lead and she felt almost fit to drop when she walked her last pail of milk over to Ely.

'Right then, Sophie,' Eric said, 'I'll let you and Dora swill and sweep the parlour, while I load your mattress onto the cart.'

'Thank you, Eric, I'm so grateful.' An hour later she wiped her forehead with the back of her hand and yawned noisily as she stepped out into the late afternoon sun. Pulling the scarf from her head she ran her fingers through her hair to let the cool spring breeze to her scalp. Barely able to put one foot in front of the other, her heart lifted as she approached the waiting cart. As well as her mattress, it was loaded with two chairs, a table and an iron bedstead! Sophie bit her lip to stem the tears.

'Lydia found this lot in the loft when she went searching for the ticking. They've been there years gathering dust, so we thought you could make use of them, if you want them? There's a box of china crockery, a tea pot and kettle and some old curtains as well.'

'Oh, Eric, Lydia.' Sophie hugged them both in turn. 'Thank you, you're both so kind.'

'Come on.' Eric grinned as he pulled away from her hug. 'Let's get you settled in with your new things, and I say that word 'new' loosely.'

That night, thoroughly exhausted, Sophie lay down on her new mattress, barely noticing the sweet smell and rustle of the straw it contained. She was asleep in seconds and for the first time her dreams were peaceful.

*

A pool of yellow light spilled down from the gas lamp on the bridge, but Gilbert Penvear stood away from its illumination. He wore a tailored midnight blue wool coat over his crisp white shirt and pressed flannel trousers. A brushed bowler hat covered his pomaded white hair and he lent heavily on his cane.

He'd heard from a third party that day that the young widow had left her mother-in-law and moved into her own cottage. Not only that, but she'd clearly spurned his offer of work and secured herself a job on the dairy farm. He snorted - well, she shouldn't get too settled. *No one, but no one, defies me!*

He eased the strain in his neck - he'd been watching Sophie's silhouette through her thin curtains as she'd moved slowly around her bedroom. Once her candlelight extinguished, he had to adjust his clothing to accommodate his growing excitement. His hair might be as white as driven snow, but there was still a red-hot fire below – a fire which needed stoking. He groaned at the thought of possibilities to come. His breath quickened while his heart beat out a thumping rhythm - until something moved in his peripheral vision. Alarmed, he stiffened his stance and pulled back into the shadows as Kit Trevellick came down the steps of The Black Swan with Amelia Pascoe. As they neared Sophie's gate at Rose Terrace, they stopped for a moment and glanced up. Gilbert could hear them murmuring softly, before they proceeded over the bridge to their respective homes.

With his ardour quelled, Gilbert returned to Quay House, poured himself a generous glass of fine cognac and snipped the end from a Havana cigar. Angry that it was going to take longer for his plan to come to fruition, he had no doubt in his mind he could still bring it about. Taking a drag of his cigar, he rested it on the ashtray to curl a spiral of smoke up to the ceiling. The slug of brandy burned as it travelled down his throat. He closed his eyes as his mind wandered back to Sophie's silhouette. Soon there would be no thin curtains to block his view he mused, as he unbuttoned the fly on his trousers.

*

Two days after moving in, Sophie took great pleasure in inviting Amelia to tea. She had produced a scrumptious cake and though her crockery was mismatched, the tea table with its posy of flowers in the centre was a sight to behold.

'Well Sophie.' Amelia looked around the cottage with delight. 'It looks like you have made yourself a lovely home here.'

'All thanks to you, Amelia.' She hugged her warmly.

'I've been to see Ria. The stubborn woman wouldn't let me in at first, but she yielded in the end. You'll be pleased to know she finally succumbed and did the laundry. In fact,' she quirked an eyebrow, 'she's taken on doing John Drago's personal laundry too. It'll do her good to do some manual work! I think some good will come from you leaving her - not that Ria will ever admit it.'

'I'm relieved. I did worry that she wouldn't be able to run her own household. This has put my mind at rest.'

'You're a good woman, Sophie. Ria doesn't deserve

your concern.'

Sophie shrugged indifferently and then poured the tea.

Amelia took a bite of cake. 'Gosh this is good. Did I tell you I have guests coming? Well, I'm saying guests - it's my sister and husband. They're staying for a couple of weeks until they finalise buying a cottage in Gunwalloe. Have you ever been there? No, of course you haven't, silly me, but if you have a chance go and visit the village. It has the most wonderful cove with a church snuggled into the dunes.'

'It sounds lovely.' Sophie smiled.

'My sister has wanted to live there for so long and very soon she will have the chance. They can hardly wait. You will have to come and have tea with us all. She'd like to meet you.'

'Thank you, I will.'

*

By mid-April, Sophie had been happily working at the farm for three weeks. The cows had got used to her now and she felt part of the dairy team. Her efforts to learn sign language from Lydia sometimes brought strange looks from Stan when she got it wrong, but he was clearly grateful and had started to present her with a tiny posy of wild flowers every morning before work.

Sophie had just fed the pigs when she heard Lizzy shouting.

'I've heard it, I've heard it!'

Sophie shielded her eyes from the sunshine as Lizzy ran up to them.

Stan looked totally bemused at Lizzy's excitement, but when she cupped her hand to her ear and then made a beak shape with her index finger and thumb, Stan's eyes widened, as did his smile. He dropped his swill pail, and they both plunged their hands into their pockets and then spat on the ground.

'Ugh!' Sophie jumped back from them. 'What are you two doing?'

'It's the 14th April - St Tiburtius Day.' Lizzy grinned excitedly.

'So?' Sophie shrugged.

'Well, I've heard a cuckoo call!'

Sophie was still bemused.

'Don't you know about St Tiburtius Day?' Lizzy laughed. 'If you hear a cuckoo today, you should turn over all the money you have in your pockets and then spit on the ground for good luck? But don't look at the ground while you're doing it!' she warned. 'And you're only to do it if you're standing on soft turf. If the ground beneath you feels hard, you'll be due bad luck!'

'Oh, I see. Shall I do it then?'

'Why, did you hear the cuckoo too, then?'

'No.'

'Well, you absolutely best not do it! Not unless you hear it yourself!'

Sophie frowned. 'What about Stan? He did the spitting, but he can't hear.'

'Ah well,' Lizzy said confidently, 'I like to think that I'm Stan's ears. He's had enough bad luck in his life. If I can pass a bit of good luck to him, then I reckon that's allowed.'

'You *are* funny, Lizzy.'

'Ah well I always say, never pass up a chance of good luck.'

Sophie walked back to the farmhouse kitchen, consciously listening out for the sound of a cuckoo. Although she felt very lucky to have a job and a house of her own, a little more good luck wouldn't go amiss.

*

Sophie was the first to enter the farmhouse kitchen. As always, she set the table while Lydia cooked the breakfast.

'Who was shouting out there, Sophie?'

'Lizzy. She'd heard a cuckoo and was telling me about St Tiburtius Day.'

Lydia laughed. 'She's a one for superstitious nonsense,

that's for sure. Are *you* superstitious?'

'A little I suppose, but I believe 'what will be will be."

'That's my girl, now before that hungry lot get here, I want to ask a favour.' She wiped her damp hands down her apron.

Sophie took off her milking bonnet. 'If it's in my power, I'll do it.'

'I watched you make that mattress bag the other week and I reckon you're a dab hand with that sewing machine.'

Sophie gave a wistful sigh. 'I enjoyed using the machine. I haven't used one for such a long time. I was taught to sew first by hand and then machine by my good friend Beatrice. In fact, I have just received a letter from her after eight years! We lost touch shortly after I came here, but it seems our correspondence was intercepted by a certain someone.'

Lydia tsked.

'She's very old now, but it's good to be back in touch. I owe her so much. She taught me the art of Italian quilting as well, but of course Jowan wouldn't let me do anything like that. I'd dearly love to sew again.'

'That is music to my ears. Eric bought the machine at an auction years ago for me to make my own clothes - I can't get them to fit you see.' She patted her ample body. 'I tried to make them, but I'm just hopeless. Give me a ball of wool any day and I'll make something with it, but sewing anything, with the exception of darning socks, is absolutely not my forte.'

'I'll gladly make some clothes for you, if you want?'

Lydia pulled her chair up to Sophie excitedly. 'Would you?'

'Of course. Just get the material and I'll do it for you.'

Lydia squeezed her hand. 'Why don't we go on a little shopping spree to Helston to get some material?'

Sophie laughed joyously. 'I'd love to.'

'Oh, come here and give me a hug.' Lydia pulled Sophie into her ample bosoms. 'We'll go tomorrow. Eric will drive us in on the cart.' She clasped her hands gleefully. 'I haven't had a new dress in years.'

Chapter 12

When the pony and cart pulled up the next morning after breakfast at Williams's farm, Sophie faltered slightly - Kit was at the reins!

'Oh, good, here's Kit!' Lydia said. 'Eric has to wait for the vet. Gertrude has a gammy foot - I don't know if you noticed this morning during milking?'

Sophie nodded that she did.

'I've left Dora in charge of the dairy, so I'm glad Eric is staying behind. Not that I'm saying she isn't capable, she is, but I don't like to leave her to fend for herself. So, Sophie, we have the pleasure of Kit's company.'

Kit had jumped down to help them aboard.

'Thank you, Kit.' Lydia took his hand. 'My knees are playing up today.'

When Lydia was settled, Kit turned to Sophie, but she was determined to try and climb aboard without his help - unfortunately her skirt got in the way and she slipped.

'Please, Mrs Treloar, allow me.' Kit held his hand out for her to take.

Sophie smiled reticently as she placed her hand in his, and despite her resolve, was shocked at the sudden frisson she felt. Their eyes met for a second before she looked away in embarrassment - feeling quite unsettled with what had just happened.

*

The journey passed quickly and Sophie found Kit to be fine, entertaining company. After an hour in Mrs Tonkin's haberdashery, the ladies were in possession of several yards of material, cotton for sewing and braiding to edge. Lydia had also insisted on buying enough material for Sophie to make two new garments, saying it was the least she could do. She also bought Sophie several large scraps of satin, so she could try her hand at Italian quilting again - so intrigued was Lydia to see it done.

'Now then, I do believe it's time for tea and cake,

Sophie, otherwise I shall waste away,' she said with a wink, as they stepped out into the busy high street. 'Let's find Kit and then go to Mrs Bumbles - her cakes are delicious.'

Kit was waiting a little way down the high street and was watching an organ grinder and his monkey. The poor creature was pushing a cup for money into people's faces as they crowded around to watch the spectacle. Kit looked on disapprovingly - he hated to see wild animals like this and was amused when the monkey bit someone who tried to grab its tail. His attention was diverted when Lydia and Sophie approached with their goods.

'Hello, Kit. I hope we haven't been too long.'

'Not at all, I had some shopping to do myself.'

'Come, join us for tea. You must be ready for a cuppa,' Lydia insisted.

Kit hesitated. 'Well, as long as Mrs Treloar is happy for me to join you as well?'

'Sophie doesn't mind, do you, Sophie? We're all friends together, aren't we?'

Sophie smiled shyly. 'I'd be happy for you to join us.'

Mrs Bumbles tea shop was situated opposite the Blue Anchor public house, which dated back to the 15th century and was home to the famous and very potent Spingo ale. They were shown to the window seat and watched in amusement as a customer from the Blue Anchor staggered out of its door, only to land face down in the deep gutter that flanked the High Street.

'It looks like someone's been Spingo'd,' Kit nodded.

Lydia gasped. 'Goodness, how much has he consumed to get into that state? It's only midday!'

'You don't need much Spingo for your legs to turn to jelly, as I know to my cost!'

'Surely you have not been in that state, Kit! I always thought you to be a moderate drinker.'

'I am now. I was very young when I had my first taste of that stuff. I was so poorly it was a full year before I drank another drop of ale again. Everyone thought I had turned temperance.' He grinned.

Lydia and Sophie chuckled.

As Kit spoke animatedly, his knee accidently brushed against Sophie's, sending that same shock wave through her body as before. He retracted it immediately, but she could still feel where he'd touched her.

'So, Kit, how is the boat coming along?'

'It's almost finished actually.'

'So, you'll be sailing away soon?'

'Well, that depends if I can persuade someone to come with me. Adventures are always better shared - it's a lonely life at sea.' His eyes flickered slightly towards Sophie.

'And do you have anyone in mind to share this adventure with?' Lydia teased.

Kit raised a warning eyebrow to Lydia. He knew she meant well, but he didn't want to make it obvious where his intentions lay.

'Sophie, what do you think? Don't you think it'll be a good thing for Kit to share his life with someone? He's been a bachelor for too long.'

Sophie laughed lightly. 'You're asking the wrong person, Lydia. I have no doubt it works for some people to share their lives, but it clearly didn't work for me - as I found to my cost. Personally, I could never contemplate it again. Having said that, I do hope you find someone to share your adventure, Mr Trevellick.'

Kit smiled sadly and turned slightly to gaze outside.

Lydia watched his reaction – she could have bitten her tongue off for her insensitivity. 'Never say never, Sophie. Not all relationships are unhappy. Look at me and my Eric. We've been married for fifteen years and not a sharp word has ever passed between us. So, I'll say only one more thing. I wish you both a good life whether you spend it with someone or not. Now, who wants another slice of cake?'

Kit picked at his cake and said little unless spoken to for the duration of the tea. Lydia thought he looked like a man who had lost a pound and found a sixpence.

The journey home was noticeably lacking in the vitality Kit had shown on the journey out, and everyone was relieved to get off the cart at the Williams's Farm. Sophie was not insensitive to the fact that she'd been the cause of Kit's melancholia and was sorry. It was clearly obvious that it was she he wanted to share his life with, Lydia had also implied as much, but as much as she found Kit to be incredibly kind and sociable, she simply could not entertain the thought of another man again. It had been only fair to tell him how she felt, but oh, why did she feel so awful?

As he held out his hand to help her step down from the cart she smiled and gave his hand an apologetic squeeze. The blueness in his eyes seemed to intensify as he returned her smile.

'Thank you, Mr Trevellick.' She wanted so much to say something else to him - but knew that if she did - she'd give him hope and that would be cruel.

*

While Sophie made her way home to change before afternoon milking, Kit fed and watered the Williams horse, and then carried the goods they had bought and placed them on Lydia's kitchen table. He was not prone to low moods, but today the troubles of the world were on his shoulders and it showed in his face.

Lydia could see he was disheartened and she was heart sore for him. 'Kit, I'm sorry I…'

'No, don't Lydia.' He stopped her. 'I know what you're going to say and in truth I'm glad you brought it up. At least now I know where I stand with Sophie.' He sighed deeply. 'You know I've always liked her, but I understand her sentiments, I do. She's had a hard life with Jowan - no one can blame her for not wanting another man.'

Lydia rested her hand on his. 'All I'm going to say is – do *not* give up hope. I've seen Sophie's reaction when you are near her. Say it's a woman's intuition but you clearly provoke something in her. Believe me when I say that.

Give her time to heal and find herself again. It may take months, even a year, but be patient.' She squeezed his hand. 'I have every confidence that the *Harvest Moon* will sail into the sunset with you both on it.'

*

Lydia was deep in thought as she churned the butter a few days later. Eric's father's health had worsened during the night and when the doctor had examined him that morning, she and Eric were told to expect the worst. Jim Williams was not a great age - he'd been sixty-one last birthday, but he'd begun to lose his mind some three years ago. It was nothing specific at first, the odd forgetful moment, leaving the cattle gates open, forgetting people's names and such, but alarm bells started to ring when he started to think that Lydia was his long dead wife. From then on, his mind deteriorated rapidly and they would often find him wandering about the village in his shirt tails and very little else. In order for Eric and Lydia to get on with their daily business, he'd been confined to his locked bedroom since he'd been found outside The Black Swan with no trousers on a few weeks ago. He was thoroughly cared for and visited every hour by Lydia to keep him comfortable. It was hard work, but Lydia would miss the old man. He'd always possessed the same sunny happy disposition which Eric had inherited. As a young bride, Jim had welcomed Lydia with open arms onto the farm where four generations of Williams had worked.

Her reverie was disturbed when Edith Mumford, Stan's mother, stormed in, like a ship in full sail. Lydia arched an inquisitive eyebrow - Edith was wearing her Sunday best hat on a Tuesday - she meant business!

Edith stood for a moment, to catch her breath, glanced around to make sure there was no one else in the dairy and said through pursed lips, 'All right, who is this Sophie?'

Lydia tipped her head. 'You mean our Sophie?'

'Yes!' She flared her nostrils. 'The new maid!'

'It's Sophie Treloar,' she answered cautiously,

wondering what on earth Sophie had done to upset Edith.

'What?' Edith was horrified. 'You mean Jowan's widow!'

Lydia stopped churning the butter and wiped her hands down her apron. 'Yes.'

'Oh, for god's sake.' Edith started to pace the dairy.

'For goodness' sake, Edith, stop moving about you're making me dizzy. What's the problem?'

'I'll tell you what the problem is! My Stan talks about her non-stop. It's Sophie this and Sophie that.'

Lydia smiled inwardly at the mental image of Stan frantically hand signing Sophie's name, but she could see Edith was in earnest.

'Stan's clearly in love with her!' She stamped her foot angrily. 'I mean, what the devil is Sophie thinking? He's ten years her junior. It's not right, I tell you…it's, it's just not right!'

'Whoa now, Edith.' Lydia held her palm up. 'Are you implying what I think you're implying?'

'Yes, that she's after my boy. He has no money you know!.' She lifted her chin indignantly. 'He can't support her!'

Lydia snuffled with laughter. 'I can assure you that Sophie has no design whatsoever on your Stan.'

'Well, you say that, but why is he so excited about her? Come on, tell me that?'

'It's because Sophie has taken the time to learn some hand signs so they can communicate with each other. She's just being friendly that's all. Has he said he's in love with her?'

'No! But what if Stan takes her friendliness the wrong way? Everyone thinks that just because he can't hear and speak, that he is just a big daft bugger, but he's not! He's an intelligent boy with.,' she could hardly say the words, 'the sort of urges a boy gets at his age - if you know what I mean.' She began to fan herself furiously. 'Is it hot in here?'

Lydia understood Edith's concern. She'd brought Stan up singlehandedly since losing her husband ten years ago. They shared an incredibly close mother and son bond because of the way he was, and how people shied away from him. Lydia suspected that Edith assumed that she would never have to share her son's love with another woman.

'Edith.' Lydia walked around the counter towards her. 'You're getting yourself worked up over nothing. When Sophie came to work with us, I sat everyone down, including your Stan, and told them that Sophie was trying to find her independence after an unhappy marriage. I told them that all Sophie wants is to earn her own money and enjoy a life that has been denied her up until now. I can categorically say she has absolutely no designs on *any* man. Sophie is a wonderful person - kind and friendly to everyone. Now if I were you, Edith, I'd be grateful to Sophie for investing time with Stan. You know yourself that people shy away from him because they don't understand his limitations. If Stan is happy and talking, well, that has to be a good thing.'

Edith's bottom lip quivered. 'Well, if you're sure.'

'I am. Sophie Treloar is not, and never will be, romantically interested in your Stan.' As she spoke, Edith looked indignant. 'Not, I might add, that Stan isn't a handsome chap, he is, but not for Sophie.' She crossed her fingers behind her back, hoping with all her heart that Stan wasn't romantically interested in Sophie.

Chapter 13

Lydia turned this way and that, to admire herself in her new olive-green dress and matching jacket, her eyes watering with gratitude.

'Sophie, this is lovely, and such a good fit.' She ran her hand over the bodice. It was a classic design, pinched in at the waist, but with an ample bodice to accommodate Lydia's frame. The hem skirted the top of her boots and Sophie had sewn a light green piping along the bottom of the skirt and again two inches up. The same piping decorated the cuffs of the jacket. 'I'm overwhelmed. I can't wait to wear it. Did you make something for yourself with that lovely material I bought you?'

'I did, look.' She held the apple green and white striped skirt and white high-necked blouse to her body and swung to and fro.

'Put them on then so I can see,' Lydia insisted.

'But I'm meant to be sweeping the cow shed out!'

'Oh, fiddlesticks. This is way more important. It's not every day we get new clothes, is it? Anyway, I told Eric you were needed in the house. So, Stan's swilling the cow shed for you.'

'That's kind of him.' Sophie began to take off her work clothes. The posy of wild flowers she wore in her belt was placed carefully on the table.

'They're pretty!' Lydia commented.

'Mmm, Stan gave me them.'

'Be careful with Stan, I don't want him falling sweet on you,' Lydia said seriously.

As she buttoned up her blouse she said, 'I know what you mean. I do feel a little bit awkward about him giving me them - especially as Dora is sweet on him, although she wouldn't admit it. Bless her she looks so downhearted when he gives me the flowers every day. I wish he wouldn't do it actually.'

'His ma is worried about him – she doesn't want him to

get hurt.'

Sophie stopped buttoning momentarily. 'You're not seriously saying that she thinks I'm encouraging him? Are you?'

Lydia wrinkled her nose. 'It's all right, I've put her straight. I might just have another word with Stan though. In the meantime, don't give him any encouragement.' It was said heartfelt and not as a warning.

'But you know that's not likely to happen, don't you?' Sophie said seriously.

'I know, but *he* doesn't.'

She stepped into her new skirt and twirled to show her new outfit off. 'What do you think?'

'I think you look lovely in that. I've never seen you in anything other than dark clothes before.' *God help Stan when he sees you in this though,* she mused. *In fact, God help Kit if he sees you in it too.*

'It's good to be out of mourning clothes, though I suspect Ria will berate me to all and sundry for not wearing them longer than a month.' She started to undress again.

'Pay no attention to her. Wait a moment, why are you taking off your new clothes?'

'I'm keeping them for best, of course!'

'No, I won't hear of it. This is just the first of many dresses you'll be making for me and yourself - that's if you don't mind,' she added. 'So, you'd better get ready to accompany me on my shopping sprees, especially if you want to choose your own fabric design.'

'Lydia, you know I've the rent on my cottage due on May 1st and I need to pay Amelia back as soon as possible. I simply don't have spare money for material!'

Lydia clasped her hand on Sophie's. 'I'll be buying it for you - as payment for making my new clothes. I've never had a new summer wardrobe before, and one dress is *certainly* not going to be enough!' She grinned.

*

Kit was on the deck of his boat, reading the letter he'd received from Bochym Manor, when he spotted Sophie across the riverbank. The sight of her dressed in bright clothes, with her hair tumbling loose down her back, caught his breath. *Oh, lord, give me strength to wait for her.* Despite Sophie's declaration to live an independent life, Lydia had given Kit a smattering of hope that she may one day change her mind. He'd loved her so long - he couldn't give up on his dream of being with her now. She dominated his thoughts from morning to night. She was even in his dreams. The urge to get up and follow her was almost too strong to ignore, but he knew he must not. He would heed Lydia's words and wait. He closed his eyes – oh, but the wait was killing him.

*

Ria picked her iron off the range and spat on it to check the temperature - it hissed pleasantly. She rather enjoyed the job of washing and ironing the linen from The Black Swan – not that she'd admit that to anyone! She kept up the pretence that she'd been mistreated by her wayward daughter-in-law's abandonment of her. In truth though, it kept her busy, put money in her pocket, and gave her a sense of pride that she was making her own way. It pleased her that she'd also lost a little bit of weight recently if the elastic in her bloomers was anything to go by. Twice she'd had to tighten them for chance they would fall down!

She was flourishing the iron over a sheet she was about to press, when she spotted Sophie walking across the bridge. She gasped – the girl was dressed up like a turkey! The sight made her blood boil. Had she no shame? What sort of widow walks about in bright clothes! She clasped her hands to her face - Jowan was going to be so angry with her that she'd let his wife break her leash. But what could she do? The girl had become wilful. Even though she knew Jowan was dead, she feared what would happen on that awful Day of Judgment when she stood not only before God, but before Jowan too - she quickly crossed her heart. He'd be waiting for her when that time came to guide her into the next world. How would she face him, knowing that she'd failed him so spectacularly?

*

Taking Lydia's advice, Sophie wore her new clothes to take her regular afternoon walk. With a spring in her step, she filled her lungs with fresh air and felt as though she was walking on a cloud without the cumbersome black mourning clothes.

Over the past weeks, she'd explored many of the lanes surrounding Gweek, but a couple of particular walks were her favourite. As she turned into the lane running alongside the mill, the heady fragrance from the sunshine yellow gorse growing among the hedgerows filled the air. On reaching the stile at the top of the lane, she sat for a while taking in the view. The buds on the sycamore trees were about to burst open, but for now, the lane was adorned with the snowiness of the blackthorn. A hare caught her attention as it stood proud on its hind legs, sniffing the air. It was unusual to see a hare, though rabbits were in abundance. Since working at the Williams's Farm, she'd had her fair share of rabbit for the pot. Stan and Charlie were absolute crack shots. It was a necessary evil, as they could be 'destructive little buggers' as Eric called them. They'd strip a cabbage field in days if allowed. Sophie mentally willed the hare to stay well away from the Williams Farm. She eased herself off the stile and made her way back down the lane, passing Bramble Cottage. She stopped to admire the perfectly situated whitewashed 'roses round the door' cottage. Although she loved her own little house, this was her favourite cottage, although Lydia had told her that disturbing things had happened there to the owner, Guy Blackthorn. He'd suffered an attempt on his life from the previous mill owner, and lost his mother in a devastating fire there. All was well now though. She understood Guy was happily married, living at Poldhu with his little family.

Sophie stopped, as she always did, at the stone bridge spanning the stream. This was where she'd first walked to, on hearing of Jowan's death. The stream bubbling over the rocks beneath her had filled her with calmness that day, and did so today, until she was unexpectedly joined by Gilbert Penvear.

'Good day to you, Mrs Treloar.'

Sophie stepped back a pace, as Penvear, dapper in his fine suit and polished shoes, took off his hat to her.

'Good day,' she said shortly. Having no desire to speak with this man, she began to walk past him, but he held his gold topped cane up to halt her progress.

'What fine weather for the time of year! Do you not think?'

Sophie looked down at the cane which he'd now lowered to the ground. Even in the fresh air his cologne caught the back of her throat. She looked askance at him. 'It's the weather one would expect at the end of April,' she replied crisply.

His eye twitched in annoyance of her quip. He moistened his lips with the tip of his tongue and took an unhurried salacious look from the hem of her skirt right up to meet her eyes. 'And I see you've dressed for it.'

Sophie remained silent, but shifted uncomfortably under his gaze - his cold grey eyes seemed to chill her bones.

'I'm glad to see you've discarded your widow's weeds. Black does not suit you.'

'Mourning suits nobody,' she replied tersely.

Unperturbed, he carried on. 'I hadn't realised that you walked this way. It's my favourite walk too. I'm unlikely to see any of my tenants up here, you see. They're always moaning about this and that.' He sighed. 'Such a tedious lot - present company accepted of course. I trust you've settled into Rose Terrace.'

Sophie's stomach flipped. She had no idea he owned her cottage. She'd been told that Rick Bray would collect her rent! Fighting to conceal the shock, she answered flatly, 'Yes, thank you.'

He gave a baleful smile. 'Now you're out of mourning, I'll expect you to attend tea with me at Quay House. I'll send my man with an invitation.'

Sophie cleared her throat. 'Thank you, but I really don't have time to make social visits. I am very busy at the Williams Farm.' She tried to disengage herself from his company, but he stopped her again with his cane.

'Yes, you disappointed me when you spurned my generous offer of the position of housekeeper to go and work in that midden, nevertheless.' He gave a tight smile. 'I *shall* forgive you, *this* once. I'm sure you'll see sense very soon.'

Sophie was taken aback - this conversation had the unreal quality of a bad dream.

'Well.' He gave her another salacious look before replacing his hat. 'I'll bid you good day. When you come to tea, we'll set another date for you to take up the position of my housekeeper.'

'I already have a job - I have no need for your position, thank you very much,' she answered tartly.

'Yet!'

'I beg your pardon?'

His lip curled. 'You have no need for it, *yet!*'

What the hell does that mean? Chilled by his manner, Sophie pushed past him vowing never to take this walk again.

*

Still unsettled by the encounter with Penvear and being a little early for milking that afternoon, Sophie stopped by the riverbank. With the tide full in, there was wildlife a plenty. A heron stood tall, proud and elegant on the bank by the bridge, waiting and watching for its catch. A kingfisher darted to and fro, the flash of iridescent colours never failed to catch Sophie's breath. There were several swans and ducks residing on the banks of the upper reaches of the Helford River, and if Sophie had a stale crust of bread, she'd often feed it to them. This particular day, she was delighted to see that one of the ducks was marching her little ducklings towards the river. Sophie did a double take when the last in line was a little bright yellow chick awkwardly trying to keep up. 'Oh, no!' One of the farm hens must have laid an egg in the duck's nest! Fearful that the mother duck would encourage the chick into the water with the other baby ducklings, Sophie scrambled down the bank to save it, only to find the chick happily pecking at bugs around the water's edge, clearly not at all tempted to take a dip. The mother duck was making quite a racket calling for the chick to follow, so unsure of whether to intervene or not, Sophie sought Lydia's advice.

'You best go and fetch it then.' Lydia said, 'It'll be Rosie's no doubt - she's been laying eggs everywhere this week. In fact, I bloody sat on one this morning that she'd deposited on the armchair by the fire.' She turned and showed Sophie the offending eggy patch on her rear end. 'I've not known that lazy hen to sit on any of her eggs to hatching stage. I'm sure she thinks she's a bloody cuckoo. Thank god for Big Bertha, I say, she's hatched all of Rosie's eggs, so she'll adopt it.' Lydia grinned and then glanced at the clock. 'If you're swift, you'll have time to get it now. I can't leave the dairy, I'm about to skim the milk.'

The chick was where she last saw it, and the mother duck was still calling for it to enter the water. With one eye on the duck, Sophie picked her way down the river bank, carefully avoiding the muddy residue the receding tide was leaving. Fortunately, the tiny chick put up little or no fight for being caught, unlike the mother duck, which started quacking furiously at Sophie. With the feathery bundle cupped in her hand, Sophie scrambled back up the riverbank, only to be dive-bombed by the now airborne duck. She tumbled but held onto the trembling chick, as the duck pursued her. Scrambling to her feet, she tripped again as the duck came at her from the side. Her squeals attracted the attention of Charlie who came running along the riverbank with his shotgun. She saw Charlie take aim. 'No, Charlie!' she yelled. 'She has ducklings.' But it was too late - the gun went off, making every single bird in the village take flight squawking and screaming in the air. Sophie squeezed her eyes shut, horrified at the prospect of all those orphaned ducklings, only to open them again when Charlie started shouting.

His shotgun abandoned on the grass - he was running towards the cow field flapping his arms furiously about his head. 'Get off, you silly bugger,' he yelled as the duck dive bombed him.

Taking her chance, Sophie retrieved the gun and ran like the wind up to the farm with the chick clutched to her chest, only to find Stan, Dora and Lizzy laughing heartily at the scene before them. When they saw Charlie turn and run towards them, with the duck in hot pursuit, they all screamed with mirth and ran to the shed to hide. Charlie was the last to enter. He slammed the door shut and stood panting with his back to it. His straw-coloured hair was stood on end and his face was covered in mud. Outside, the duck was quacking furiously.

'Christ, Sophie. What the hell did you do to that bloody duck?'

Sophie, equally dishevelled, held out her hand to reveal the chick. 'She hatched this.'

'Well, give it back to her - otherwise we'll be stuck in here all day!'

'Oh, no, Charlie - it'll die, or drown!'

'Aye and Pa will scat us if we don't start milking soon.'

They could all hear the cows mooing outside.

Sophie frowned and appealed to Charlie's better judgment, but he would not be swayed. She put the chick on the floor and opened the door. The duck ran to greet it, quacked loudly to make her displeasure known to everyone and waddled off with the chick to find her other young.

Chapter 14

The morning after her encounter with Gilbert Penvear, Sophie came home from work to find the dreaded invitation to tea from him waiting on her doormat. Well, invitation was too polite a word for it - it was more of a command for her to attend him at Quay House at two-thirty on 30th April. The sight of it quite dampened her high spirits. By the salacious way that deeply unsavoury man had looked at her yesterday, she had no doubt what his real intentions were. The thought made her skin crawl. Screwing the invitation into a ball she threw it on the fire to be burnt later that evening. After finishing her cottage chores, she grabbed her hat and shawl to take her daily walk. Determined to avoid yesterday's route, for chance she happened to bump into Penvear again, she set off up Chapel Hill to her favourite stile, in the hope of picking some bluebells and campion for her bedside table.

*

Following the Earl de Bochym's request to mend some of the lake boats, Kit found himself steering his pony and cart down the long drive towards Bochym Manor at the latter end of April. He'd never been here before but had heard about it. It was reputed to be the best laid gardens on the Lizard, and although not a gardener himself, it was somewhere he was looking forward to visiting. Half way down the drive, he saw a sign advising tradesmen to take a right turn, which he did. He smiled when he saw peacocks wandering about the grounds and one was even on the chimney top calling at his approach. He followed the long winding road which skirted the back of the manor, and came upon a row of six thatched cottages. He carried on until he came to a series of outbuildings, one of which, by the smell of it, housed a piggery. He pulled his pony to a halt and wrapped the reins around a gatepost. As he walked, a gaggle of geese and hens scattered from where they were pecking at the ground for tasty morsels. He'd been told to make himself known to the estate steward, located in the cottage opposite the magnificent bell tower. He didn't have to knock - the steward had seen him approach and was waiting with his hand held out in welcome.

'Hello there, Kit Trevellick I presume?'

Kit nodded and shook his hand.

'James Parson, the estate steward, good to meet you. His lordship is expecting you. He's up the tower at the moment winding the clock.' He grinned. 'He won't be a moment.'

When Peter Dunstan, the Earl de Bochym appeared, blinking into the bright sunlight, he looked every inch a country gentleman. He was dressed in tweed, despite the warmth of the day and by the look of the perspiration on his forehead, he was feeling the effects.

'You should have let me do that, my lord,' Parson said.

'Nonsense, the stairs keep me fit.' He smiled amiably at Kit. 'I take it this is Mr Trevellick.'

Kit nodded and bowed.

'Splendid. You come highly recommended as a master carpenter by Mr Blackthorn.'

Kit smiled. 'Thank you.'

'Come, let me show you the boats, there are four of them in all.'

Kit followed the gentlemen as they walked down towards the gardens, allowing him a glance at the fresh early summer blooms emerging from the formal borders.

'Are you a gardener, Mr Trevellick? I see you are interested in our parterre.'

'I'm no gardener myself, but I love to see a well laid out garden, and I understand Bochym is renowned for its formal gardens.'

'That's all down to the countess. Hardly a day goes by when Sarah is not working side by side with Mr Hubbard our gardener. Feel free to wander about. I'm sure you will come across her, elbow deep in the borders.' He grinned.

They took the lane to the right of the manor and followed the long winding path towards the small lake. As they approached, Kit heard a strange thumping sound. He cast a questioning look to the Steward, but Peter answered his unspoken question.

'The noise you can hear is the ram – a water pump. It was part of the Regency period romantic remodelling of the Poldhu River, to create a series of ornamental ponds, rapids, ravines and waterfalls, as well as supplying the water to the manor.' As they approached the small boating lake he added, 'Here are the boats, we've pulled them ashore for you. As you see the gunwales are rotten, I should have had them seen to before the spring, but with one thing and another, time just runs away with me. One or two of the seats are loose too - if you could secure them, I would be more than obliged.'

Kit bent over to check the seats, they looked sound enough. 'There is nothing here that can't be fixed, my lord.'

'Splendid. There is wood in abundance in the outbuildings next to where you left your cart. Just take what you need. When can you do the job?'

'I can do it in a couple of weeks - if that is acceptable? I have to complete another job in Gweek first.'

'That would be perfect. I think Sarah needs them done by Midsummer, if that's a possibility?'

'Absolutely.'

*

After assessing the repairs to the boats, Kit bid farewell to the estate manager and set off to Poldhu to call on Guy and Ellie. It seemed silly not to call in, being so near to them. He found the tea room buzzing with people, even though it was early in the season. Guy had told him that since The Poldhu Hotel opened in 1901, it had brought many well-heeled people to the cove, and in turn, boosted the tea room's business.

He found Jessie and Ellie busy serving customers, and

Kit felt slightly uncomfortable to have called at such a busy time.

'Kit!' Ellie greeted him warmly. 'Take a seat. Guy and Silas aren't home yet but they'll be back within the hour.'

'Oh, perhaps I'll not stay - you look very busy.'

'Oh, you must. Guy will be happy to see you. In fact, stay the night and have supper with us. Would you like some tea, cake perhaps?'

'Please don't bother yourself with me. Perhaps I could help you. Can I do anything?'

'No,' Ellie said happily. 'We have everything under control. This is just a normal day. Let me bring you some refreshments. I have some lovely fluffy scones, and fresh cream?' She grinned.

Kit licked his lips. 'Well, if it's no trouble.'

*

When all the customers had gone and the tea room cleared and clean, Guy and Silas arrived home, hot and dusty with thatch.

'Kit my friend, what a good surprise. You're staying the night I hope?'

'Thank you, yes, Ellie has already invited me.'

Kit watched with envy as Guy wrapped his arms around Ellie to greet her - how he wished for just an ounce of their happiness.

'Do you fancy a swim, Kit before supper?' Guy suggested. 'It looks as though Silas is already down there and I'm roasting.'

Kit shielded his eyes from the sinking sun as he looked seawards. 'Count me in. Is that a dog in the sea with Silas?'

'It is. That's Blue. He was my dog until he changed his allegiance, damn his eyes.' He grinned. 'The dog follows Silas everywhere, and I mean everywhere. It's only because his wife Jessie puts her foot down that the beast doesn't sleep with them, but it sleeps right outside the bedroom door. Here.' He threw him a towel, 'Let's go and cool off before supper.'

*

With the tea room chairs stacked, Jessie and Ellie stood on the terrace and drank in the late afternoon air.

'Will you join us for supper tonight?' she asked Jessie.

'We'd love to. I've made a pie this morning - it should go around us all.'

'I'll do the vegetables and pudding then.'

'No rest for us, eh?' Jessie watched Kit run down the beach shedding his clothes alongside of Guy. 'Don't you wish we could be so free and easy and swim naked like nobody's watching, Ellie?'

'Hey,' Ellie pulled her away. 'Stop watching, you're a married woman.'

Jessie sighed. 'Men have all the fun!'

'There is nothing to stop you taking a swim in your birthday suit,' Ellie said seriously.

'What? With all those guests up at the Poldhu Hotel watching!'

'Well, go over to Church Cove - no one will see you there.'

'I did last summer, and the vicar caught me! Don't you remember?' she grinned.

Jessie chuckled. 'He still blushes when he sees you now.'

They laughed as they set off to pull together a shared meal.

*

Supper with the Blackthorns consisted of a simple meal of fish pie and samphire, followed by an apple turnover, all washed down with a jug of ale. It was good for Kit to have some company as he ate alone normally. They reminisced about school in Gweek, although Silas was a few years younger than both Guy and Kit, and laughed at stories of growing up in Gweek. They'd been good times, but it seemed to Kit, they had a much better life down here on the coast.

As the table was cleared, Guy stretched his long legs

out. 'Did you take a look at the workshops at Bochym while you were there, Kit?'

'No, I just looked at the boats.'

'They've set up an Arts and Craft Association in the workshops. Ellie is part of it, although she doesn't reside there, but she makes hand-made lace in her spare time. You should take a look when you go back to do the work on the boats – I think it would interest you. Sarah doesn't mind if you wander around - in fact she positively encourages it.'

Kit smiled at how familiar Guy was with the local gentry. 'It does sound interesting.' Kit said, thinking about the bespoke furniture he himself made. 'I'm due back there in a couple of weeks - I'll take a look then.'

'Well, Silas and I will be there as well. We're about to start re-thatching the workshops.'

As the clock chimed ten, Silas and Jessie took their leave.

Kit also stood up. 'Thank you for supper.'

'You're always very welcome,' Ellie said.

Kit shook Guy's hand. 'I'm envious of your lovely little family, Guy - I'm not ashamed to admit it.'

'Well, maybe a certain someone in Gweek might have missed you while you've been away.'

Kit wrinkled his nose. 'I don't think so. She's understandably wary of men.'

'Well, if I were you, I'd go and make a wish at Bochym's holy well when you go back there.'

Kit grinned. 'You don't believe in all that nonsense, do you?'

'Believe it or not it *has* been known to bring about something you wish for.' He winked. 'There is no harm in visiting. I'll see you in the morning.'

*

In their bedroom Guy kissed Ellie passionately.

'Oh, Mr Blackthorn, what was *that* for?' Ellie wrapped her arms around his waist.

'Just for being a wonderful wife,' he said kissing her again.

Ellie's heart filled with love for this man. Five years married and through the trials and tribulations of pregnancies and childbirth, she still marvelled that he found her fascinating.

'What are you smiling at?'

'You.' She grinned happily.

Chapter 15

May Day was a joyful celebration of the coming of summer after a long winter. Helston had its Flora Day, which everyone, who could, flocked to watch, but Gweek always held this May Day celebration on the village green – come rain or shine. Thankfully today was dry, although the sun seemed a little reluctant to show its face. The village green was situated almost at the bottom of Sophie's garden path, so she watched with interest as the maypole, festooned with flowers and multicoloured ribbons was hoisted up into position. It was still early – six-thirty, but people were already up setting their food and drink stalls out. There would be an archery competition, dancing, tug of war and musicians, and of course the crowning of the May Queen.

Lots of people had been up before sunrise in order to gather flowers and greenery to decorate their houses, in the belief that the vegetation would bring good fortune. Sophie had to admit, she'd never seen the village look so pretty. Ria and Jowan had never entered into the spirit of May Day, so this was the first time Sophie had seen it all come together.

As she set off to the farm to milk, she hung a bunch of laurel and bluebells on her gate, and in her skirt waistband she tucked a posy of Lily of the Valley.

At the edge of the cow field, Sophie found Lizzy knelt down scooping dew onto her face. 'Lizzy! You'll get your skirt soaked.'

'I know, but it's the 1st of May today. I'm washing my face in the dew, to make my skin clear and my freckles disappear, and then Charlie will think I'm beautiful,' she said coyly.

'I'm sure he thinks *that* anyway.'

'Oh!' Lizzy's eyes widened with interest. 'Do you really?' She clasped her hands together. 'He's the most handsome boy in the world and I want him to marry me one day.'

'Lizzy. You're only thirteen!'

'I know but I have to make him fall in love with me now, before anyone else catches his eye. I'm performing every ritual I can to make him fall in love with me!' Lizzie checked to see if anyone was in earshot. 'I even did the ritual that unmarried girls perform on the 20th January - the eve of St Agnes, so that they can dream of their future husbands. First, I transferred all the pins, one by one, from my pincushion to my sleeve, whilst reciting the Lord's Prayer. I didn't eat a thing all day, and then I walked backwards upstairs to bed.'

Sophie snuffled a laugh. 'Did it work?'

'Oh, yes! I dreamt of Charlie that night - mind you.' She grinned. 'I dream of Charlie every night anyway.'

'You *are* nutty.'

Lizzy sighed. 'I'm nutty about Charlie. I don't suppose you'll need to do anything barmy like that, being that you are so pretty and Kit loves you anyway.'

Sophie's world stilled, as Lizzy skipped off towards the gate.

'Come on,' Lizzy shouted, 'Let's get the work done so we can get down to the village green.'

Flushing up to the roots of her hair, Sophie wondered what on earth had Kit been saying to people?

*

Milking went by in a flash - so preoccupied was Sophie with what Lizzy had said! *Had Kit boldly declared his love for her to all and sundry? If he had, he had no right to speak so freely.* She was still in high dudgeon when she broached the subject with Lydia after breakfast.

'Sophie, sit down and stop getting in a tizzy about this,' Lydia said, 'Kit has never verbally declared his love for you, but,' She smiled openly, 'everyone in the village knows that he's held a candle for you since the day Jowan brought you here. Kit wears his heart on his sleeve you see. From the moment he set eyes on you, there wasn't another woman who could take your place in his heart.'

Sophie blanched. 'But I…'

Lydia halted Sophie's protests. 'Now I know what you're going to say, that you've never given him any encouragement, but he was infatuated the moment he saw you. I know, you see, because I asked him once why he hadn't got a sweetheart. You know what he replied?'

Sophie shook her head.

'He said, "There is only one woman for me and she's married to someone else."'

'Oh!' Sophie said shakily. 'What am I to do?'

'Nothing, you don't have to do anything.' Lydia reached over and placed her hand on hers. 'Rest assured, Sophie, Kit will never move on this matter, unless *you* decide to reciprocate his feelings.'

*

The irony was not lost on Sophie that she was excited about the May Day celebrations – a day of love and romance and new beginnings, especially as she was so reluctant to let another man into her life. As she walked home, the words, "There is only one woman for me," made her feel slightly heady. She glanced towards Kit's boat – apparently, he was away looking at a job on the Bochym Estate and visiting friends at Poldhu. She was glad she wouldn't bump into him today – she was unsure about how she'd manage a meeting, knowing now how he really felt about her.

*

May Day proved to be a delight for Sophie. There was music and dancing and everyone seemed to be enjoying the day. After the May pole dance, where to many of the mothers' consternation, the children had got their steps wrong, leaving the ribbons in a twisted muddle at the top of the pole, the highlight of the day was the crowning of the May Queen. The accolade this year went to fifteen-year-old Loveday Killigrew, who sat in a flower-decked chair to preside over her 'subjects' and clearly enjoyed every single moment of her special day.

Sophie parted company briefly with Eric and Lydia to buy a glass of elderberry cordial. When she returned, she found they had joined Lizzy and Charlie to dance a jig. Sophie smiled at the latter - there was no doubt that they would be happily married when they were older.

She pondered, not for the first time that day, on what Lydia had said about Kit. Though astounded, she was quite heartened by his devotion, but it worried and saddened her to think he would waste his life on a dream that would not, could not, come true. She *must* dismiss all thoughts of Kit and love from her mind, and then smiled ironically as she scanned the crowds for a sighting of him, just in case he'd returned home.

As the music played, Sophie happily tapped her foot in rhythm, until, that was, Gilbert Penvear stepped in front of her. She felt a cold chill run through her.

'A word.' He flicked his head for her to follow.

Sophie regarded him reproachfully and turned to walk away, but Penvear grabbed her arm, pinching her skin as he yanked her back.

'I *said* I want a word with you.'

'Unhand me at once!' She tried to pull her arm free, but Penvear dug his finger deep into the fleshy part of her arm and pulled harder. She flinched when another hand reached in between them.

'I believe the lady does *not* wish to speak to you,' Kit said, twisting Penvear's arm so that he was forced to let go.

Sophie reeled back in shock, watching Penvear wince as Kit twisted his arm up his back before pushing him away.

Penvear staggered backwards, staying upright only with the aid of his cane. He brushed his sleeve as though Kit's hands had soiled him, shot a venomous look at Sophie before turning to Kit. 'You'll be sorry you did that.'

'I very much doubt it,' Kit said tersely.

'We'll see about that.' Penvear walked away, and as he neared the village green gate, he knocked a small child out of the way with his stick. The child howled into his mother's skirts, but because it was Gilbert Penvear, the woman was sensible enough not to reprimand his actions.

Sophie covered her face with her trembling hands, deeply embarrassed to be the centre of such an altercation - she prayed that no one had witnessed it.

'Are you all right?'

She looked up into his eyes, and found them full of concern. 'Yes, thank you - a little bruised perhaps, but I'm truly grateful to you.' Her heart accelerated - for a moment she thought he was about to embrace her, but quickly retracted his hands and awkwardly raked his fingers through his hair.

'What on earth was that about?'

'I think he took umbrage that I ignored his invitation to tea yesterday,' she said dryly.

Kit narrowed his eyes. 'I wonder what he's after.'

'Whatever it is, I won't give him the satisfaction!' Sophie said angrily. Knowing how Kit felt about her, she thought it best if she now took her leave. 'Thank you again for your help, Mr Trevellick.'

'I'm happy to assist anytime you might need me, Mrs Treloar,' he said meaningfully.

She met his gaze and his blue eyes seemed to look deep into her soul. 'Thank you,' she said shakily, suddenly aware of the tingle in every fibre of her body.

*

Kit watched her walk away, his heart aching with love for her. If only he could put his arms around her, to keep her safe from predators like Penvear. He must be more vigilant from now on and keep a look out for her.

He cursed that he'd spent the past half an hour watching her from the wall, trying to build up courage to ask her to dance. *Damn it, Kit, go and ask her now - It might take her mind off what has just happened.*

'Mrs Treloar?' He caught her up by the gate to the green.

As she turned to face him, her hair lifted in the breeze and fell gently onto her shoulders – the sight made his heart miss a beat.

'I wondered. Would you like to dance?'

She smiled, but her eyes were full of unshed tears. 'I think I would rather like to go home, thank you. Gilbert Penvear has quite ruined my day.'

'Of course, forgive me.' Kit watched despondently as she walked away.

*

The music and merriment had gone on until well after dark, but Sophie didn't venture out again. Instead, she took herself off to bed after supper to try and read, but she was troubled, and continually berated herself for not having danced with Kit. It was the least she could have done, after he'd saved her from Penvear's clutches. She sighed. If only he'd asked her to dance before the incident - she believed she'd have said "yes".

*

After a fitful night, Sophie rose unable to shake the disquiet she felt. Penvear would not let up on his pursuit of her, of that, she was sure. It angered her that she was not allowed to enjoy her first spell of freedom without that dreadful old man making life miserable for her. She knew she must disengage herself from her plight somehow – perhaps she would speak to Eric about him.

As she stepped out into the morning light, several people were out on the green collecting the debris left from yesterday. Screwing her nose up, she detected that the rank smell of stale sweat was emitting from a fat-bellied drunk with a large bulbous nose, snoring by the wall. Side stepping to give him a wide berth, she walked along the riverbank, and glanced towards Kit's boat, feeling a little tingle of delight to find him aboard and waving at her. She tentatively waved back, and that tiny gesture made her feel so much better – perhaps he didn't feel any ill will against her for not dancing with him.

112

Eric met her at the farm yard entrance - a look of disappointment in his eyes. 'We'll be *that* sorry to see you go, Sophie.' He waved a letter in his hand.

Sophie halted. 'Go where?'

'To Penvear's - to be his housekeeper.' He waved the letter again. 'It was on my doormat first thing this morning. I must say, Sophie, I thought you'd have told us yourself.'

'What?' She grabbed the letter and gasped.

I hereby give notice for Sophie Treloar to quit her milking job with immediate effect. She has taken up the position of housekeeper at Quay House.

Gilbert Penvear.

Her mouth formed an 'O'. '*How dare he?*' She trembled angrily. 'I am certainly *not* going to that man's house to be his housekeeper!'

Eric blew his cheeks out. 'Well, that's a relief. We did wonder why you hadn't told us face to face.'

'Oooh, that man!' She stamped her foot, splashing cow dung up her petticoat. 'How *dare* he do this?' Her eyes filled with frustrated tears.

'Now, now, Sophie, don't cry.' Eric pulled her into a great bear hug.

'Eric, I don't know what to do,' she cried. 'That revolting man seems determined to take control of my life. He confronted me yesterday at the celebrations, but thankfully Kit stepped in to help. Penvear is frightening me now.'

'Shush, now, dry your eyes and all will be well. Let's get the milking done. Then I'll go and speak to him later today. I'm not having my Sophie upset.'

Chapter 16

When Sophie arrived back home, she found to her dismay a Notice of Eviction on her doormat. She glanced at the rent money on the table, which should have been collected yesterday, and set off to Rick Bray's, the rent collector's house with the letter and money firmly in her grasp.

'I'm really sorry, Mrs Treloar,' Rick said, 'I'm only following orders.'

'Whose orders?'

'Gilbert Penvear's.'

Sophie's stomach flipped. 'But the rent was paid up until yesterday and this month was waiting to be collected. I've done nothing to merit eviction!' She was acutely aware of the desperate whine in her voice.

'I'm so sorry, but your house is needed for a family of four. It has three bedrooms you see,' he added lamely.

She shook her head in disbelief. 'Do you have something else I can rent then?'

Rick pulled his lips tight. 'I'm afraid not.' He did, but was under strict orders not to offer it up.

Panic ensued. 'So, how much notice do I get?'

'None. Mr Penvear wants you out today.'

'What?' Sophie felt her knees soften. 'But, but where am I to go?'

Rick shrugged. 'I'm really sorry.' His heart ached for her, but to disobey orders would mean he too would be evicted from his home and he had a family of five to look out for.

She walked away dazed and confused, and as reluctant as she was to knock on Amelia's door, knowing she had visitors, she didn't know what else to do.

Alarmed at her distress, Amelia pulled her into an embrace. 'Whatever is the matter? Come in quickly, but excuse the mess. My sister and husband have gone to Helston, so I'm in the middle of washing.' She led Sophie to the kitchen. 'Sit down and I'll make us some tea. I could do with one too.'

Sophie slumped at Amelia's kitchen table, leant her head on her arms and wept openly for a good couple of minutes. When she felt Amelia push the teacup gently against her arm, she lifted her teary face. 'I'm to be evicted today.' A sob shuddered in her throat.

Amelia paled and sat down heavily. 'What, without warning? Haven't you paid your rent?'

'He never collected it. I thought perhaps it was because of May Day.'

'Well have you been to see Rick Bray? What explanation did he give?'

Sophie rubbed her eyes with her knuckles. 'Apparently a family or four is in need of my cottage.'

Amelia's brow furrowed. 'I know of no family needing such a thing. Did you ask him for another cottage?'

'I have but he hasn't got one,' she sobbed.

'Surely he has.' Amelia frowned. 'There is something fishy about this. You haven't by any chance annoyed Gilbert Penvear, have you?'

Sophie looked up mournfully and told her all that had happened. 'I have an awful feeling he has set his sights on me, Amelia, but he makes my skin creep.'

Amelia's jaw tightened. 'This is too much - that man thinks he can do, or have, anything he wants! What the hell is he playing at? Right then.' She slapped the table with her hands. 'There is nothing else for it – you'll have to leave Rose Terrace.'

'But where will I go?' Sophie's eyes filled again with tears. 'I loved my little house.'

'I know you did, Sophie. We *will* soon find you another. Do you think the Williams could put you up for a while?'

Sophie shrugged. 'They don't have a spare room, but I'm sure they will let me sleep on the settee for a few nights, but I don't like to put on them like this, with Eric's pa being so ill.'

'Now Sophie, don't fret.' Amelia plunged her hands

into her apron pockets. 'Damn it, you could have stayed here, but for my sister and husband. Look, you go and pack your things and I'll see what can be done. If all else fails, the Williams's settee will be your best bet, until we sort out something more permanent.'

Sophie pulled herself up to stand. 'What about my furniture?'

'I'm sure Eric will store it in the barn for you. Now go quick.' She gave Sophie a little push. 'Get your belongings together and wait for me. I think I've had an idea.'

As soon as Sophie left, Amelia set off to Custom Quay.

*

When Sophie returned home, she found another letter waiting for her – this time from Penvear.

You are expected to present yourself at Quay House this afternoon. A cart will arrive for you and your personal things at 4.30 p.m.. Leave your furniture in situ - you will not need it. You'll start work as my housekeeper tomorrow under the original terms. I have terminated your mother-in-law's employment for The Black Swan, so she will depend on you to obey me. Gilbert Penvear.

Sophie's knees trembled as her distress increased tenfold. Blinded by uncontrollable tears, she quickly packed her belongings, of which there were few. She wrestled her new mattress into the front room and dragged the two chairs and the table to stand by the door. The bedstead would have to wait until she could engage some help. A knock on the door made her start – *Oh, please don't let that be the Two Quays cart before I have a chance to sort this out myself.* With great trepidation she opened the door only to find Kit, Eric, Charlie and Amelia standing there smiling.

Kit stepped forward and removed his hat. 'Mrs Treloar, Amelia has brought it to our attention that you're in need of a room rather urgently.'

'Not only that! But my situation has just worsened.' She held Gilbert's letter out for them all to read.

If Eric could have breathed fire, he would have done. He growled audibly. 'I'm going to have some serious words with *that* man about this later.'

'But Eric,' Sophie cried, 'what'll I do about Ria? She'll be destitute without employment. Despite everything, I can't let her starve.'

Amelia smiled. 'Your loyalty to Ria does you credit, but don't worry, leave John Drago to me. Ria will *not* lose her job,' she said confidently.

'Good, now with that sorted,' Eric said, 'Kit here has an offer for you.'

Kit smiled softly. 'I have a room for you.' He must have seen her eyes widen because he put his hand up in his defence. 'No, now, don't fret. It's not in my cottage. It's in the sail loft above. It's clean and tidy and yours, if you've a mind to take it. We can move you over there now. Just say the word.'

She bit her bottom lip and smiled. 'Thank you, Mr Trevellick .That's, that's very kind of you.' The words caught in the back of her throat.

'Right, come on.' Eric rubbed his hands together. 'Let's get this lady moved to her new abode, while Amelia deals with John Drago at The Black Swan.'

*

John Drago eyed Amelia with a degree of caution - he'd seen that look in her eyes before and hadn't come away unscathed from it.

'I understand Ria has lost her job?'

Drago's mouth dropped. 'How the hell do you know? Because *Ria* doesn't yet!'

Amelia dug her fists in her hips. 'I know!'

Drago swallowed hard. 'Penvear offered the services of Mrs Drew at a 1p a week less than I am paying Ria.'

'Did he now? You do know that Penvear has done that to make Ria dependent on Sophie so that she has to work for him against her will?'

'Oh!'

'Oh, indeed! You must revoke his offer now!'

'Well, I, I don't know if I can revoke it. Penvear isn't

someone to cross, you know?'

'Neither am I! If you terminate Ria's employment, I might have to have a word in Mrs Drago's ear, about you calling on the widow, Mrs Trig.'

John Drago's eyes widened. 'Consider it done!'

'Good! It was nice doing business with you,' she said brushing her hands together.

*

While the men humped her furniture up the stone steps to the sail loft, Sophie sat in Kit's front room, still wearing her hat and coat, nervously clutching her bag of clothing on her knee. Amelia had called to tell her that Ria's employment was no longer in jeopardy. Sophie had no idea how she'd done it, but was very grateful - there was still a part of her which felt a little obligated to Ria's wellbeing.

Her eyes scanned the room. It was clear only a man lived here, for there were no frivolous fancy soft furnishings adorning the room, no rugs nor pictures on the walls. The furniture however was of high quality and consisted of a bookcase groaning under the strain of many books, two armchairs, a foot stool, a table and two dining chairs. A clock ticked above the mantelpiece and in the layer of sooty dust which covered it, stood two candlesticks, a pile of letters and a teapot. There were curtains at the windows and shielding the bedroom area but all had seen better days. Sophie wondered what state her room was going to be in, "it's clean and tidy," Kit had said. She tried to clear her head of uncharitable thoughts. Kit had come to her rescue again and no matter what state the room was in, she would be eternally grateful to him for doing this.

As she sat and listened to the scraping of feet and furniture upstairs, her fingers traced something unusual on the underside arm of the chair. She put her bag down and got on her knees to investigate.

Sophie heard Kit thanking Eric and Charlie for their

muscle power before a thunder of footsteps descended the granite steps. She tried to scramble back from where she had crouched down the side of the chair, but it was too late, she felt her body stiffen as Kit entered the room.

'Are you all right down there?' Kit grinned.

'Yes, thank you. Forgive me, Mr Trevellick,' she said pulling herself off her knees. She lowered her head and brushed down her skirt, embarrassed to be found in such a strange position.

'Kit.' He smiled and threw his hat on the table. 'Please, as we're to be neighbours, call me Kit.'

Sophie lowered her head. 'As you wish, it's just that I....' She gestured towards the seat she'd been investigating.

'You felt something under the armrest?' Kit finished her sentence.

Sophie relaxed and smiled. 'Yes, I was trying to see what it was.'

'Allow me.' He tipped the chair on its side to reveal a small carved seahorse under the arm rest.

Sophie crouched again and ran her fingers delicately over the tiny creature. 'It's beautiful.'

'Thank you.'

She looked up at Kit. 'Have you carved this?'

He nodded with a grin. 'And hand-made all the furniture you can see, although there isn't much of it admittedly.'

Sophie looked around her. She reached under the arm rest of the other chair and smiled when she felt the shape of the seahorse.

'There is one on the foot stool and bookcase as well, and under the table by the window there.'

'May I?' She lifted the foot stool, satisfied to find it on the inside of the leg and then knelt to run her fingers under the table. 'I can't find it on here.' She looked up to find Kit grinning at her, and realised how bizarre she must look crawling about on his floor. But before she could redress the situation, he'd knelt beside her and taken her hand in his to guide her fingers towards the underside of the table leaf. She inhaled sharply - his touch felt like a bolt of lightning searing through her.

Sitting back on their haunches now they faced each other and smiled. Sophie tried to steady her voice to ask, 'But why do you hide them - they're so beautiful?'

'I like to keep them secret, so it's a surprise when anyone finds them. I just love seahorses. They're fascinating little creatures. I found one once when Grandpa took me to Porthleven when I was a child. It was washed up on the beach, so I kept it and studied it. I drew it umpteen times and then I thought I'd carve one into a piece of wood my Grandpa gave me. He was a master furniture maker and would carve Tudor Roses into his pieces. I, with my love for the sea and its special little gifts, decided this was going to be my signature on all the furniture I made, and so it is.'

'But you went into boatbuilding?'

'Yes.' He laughed. 'And coffin making.' He got to his feet and held his hand out to help Sophie up. 'It pays more. I've only just started making furniture for myself. I needed naturally seasoned English oak you see, and since moving into the workshop I found it in abundance on the banks of this river - hence the furnishing.'

'But it seems such a shame that nobody sees your work.'

'Yes, they do - you've seen it!' He leaned closer and whispered. 'I don't show it to just anyone you know.'

Sophie smiled at the tease. 'Well, you should, they're beautiful pieces.' She looked at Kit with fresh eyes. It was lovely to speak to someone who had such passion for their work.

'Shall I make us a pot of tea? Though you'll have to forgive my array of cracked cups, I don't usually have visitors.'

'Thank you, Kit that would be lovely.' Although she

had always referred to him as Kit in her head, it felt strange to be saying it out loud.

'Shall I show you to your room now while the kettle is boiling?'

'Yes please.' She followed him outside and carefully up the steep granite steps, for there was no handrail.

He opened the door with a flourish. 'Ta-da.'

She smiled at his cheeriness and she stepped through the door. 'Oh!' She held her hand to her chest. The room was light and airy and…. clean. Her furniture had been placed in the middle of the room ready for her to push into their final resting place. 'It's *really* lovely. Thank you.'

'I've not lit your fire yet. I just need to put a light under the kindling.'

'Please don't put yourself to any more trouble on my account.'

'It's no trouble, Mrs Treloar. I'm happy to help.'

'Sophie,' she said, almost inaudibly.

Kit leaned forward. 'I beg your pardon?'

They met each other's eyes. Sophie cleared her throat. 'If I'm to call you Kit, then you must call me Sophie.' *Oh, god! Have those few short words just sealed my fate?*

Kit's smile made his eyes twinkle. 'I'm honoured, Sophie.'

When his rich voice said her name, she knew then she was lost to him.

'Sophie?'

Deep in her reverie she suddenly realised Kit was speaking to her. 'Sorry I…..' She tipped her head back to ease the tension in her neck and shoulders. 'I was lost in thought for a moment. It's been quite a day.'

'I can imagine, but everything is settled now though.'

She smiled inwardly. *Not everything.*

'I was saying, you have water and a fireplace, but should you need to bake, you'll have to use the range downstairs. It's lit all the time and my door is always open.'

'Oh!' She hesitated. 'That's very kind of you.' She

wouldn't dream of intruding.

He must have sensed her unease because he added, 'Please don't feel troubled about the arrangement - I am often out working, and bread *must* be baked.' he grinned. 'I promise it will not be an intrusion.'

'Your kindness overwhelms me. I really don't know what I would have done today without you, or yesterday afternoon for that matter.'

Kit wrinkled his nose. 'Well, we can't let Penvear win, can we? Come – let's have that tea now.'

*

At Quay House, Eric Williams pushed past the manservant, stormed into the library, grabbed Gilbert Penvear by his coat lapels and pinned him to the wall by his neck. With his legs dangling an inch from the floor, Penvear coughed and choked, but Eric held tight.

'The only thing preventing me from punching your bloody lights out is your age. Because that's what you deserve.' He banged his head against the wall, 'I'll just give you fair warning. If you so much as speak to, or approach Sophie, *ever* again, you'll find yourself face down in my midden, you lecherous old bugger.' Eric let him loose and Gilbert's knees crumpled as he fell to the floor gasping for breath.

'Are you threatening me?' he croaked.

Eric stamped forward, making Gilbert cower. 'Too bloody right I am! Others in this village will take great pleasure in helping me carrying it out as well.'

Gilbert sat on the floor trembling. 'Get out of my house, Williams.'

'And *you.*,' Eric jabbed a finger at him, 'stay out of Sophie's life!' As Eric slammed the door after him, several pictures fell from the wall with the reverberation.

As Eric swept through the house, Jeremy Nancarrow, Penvear's manservant, pushed himself into the shadows of the hallway, stifling a laugh into his hands.

Chapter 17

Sophie had been living in Kit's sail loft for two weeks, and by the looks and halted conversations whenever she passed anyone, it had been a topic of conversation amongst the villagers ever since.

It had taken a while for her to settle and get over her embarrassment of using Kit's range downstairs. Even though he assured her that it wasn't a problem, it unsettled her to intrude on his privacy. The fire she lit in her quarters was adequate to cook most things, but in order to make bread, which she did every other day, she simply had to use the range.

By observing the pattern of Kit's working day, she normally timed her bread baking when he was out at work, but this particular day, he'd retired early for his dinner. He was busy cooking when she stepped into his front room.

'I beg your pardon, Kit.' She faltered on the doorstep. 'Do you mind if I get my bread out?'

'Be my guest.' He moved to the side to give her access.

Grabbing her oven cloths, a beautiful herby aroma teased her nostrils. 'Mmm something smells good.' She peered into the cauldron.

'It's watercress soup'

Her stomach made an involuntary rumble. 'Oh! She placed her hand on her tummy. 'Forgive me. The combination of aromas is making me hungry.'

'Share a bowl with me if you like - in return for a slice of your fresh bread.' He flashed a cheeky grin.

A curl of anticipation stirred within her. To sit and eat at his table, just the two of them, felt uncomfortably intimate.

Noting the consternation on her face, he added, 'Or you can take a bowl upstairs if you'd rather.'

'No, it's fine, thank you. I'll share your table - it will be easier.'

He held out a chair for her and set two places. Sophie

settled, albeit awkwardly. The table was located just under the window and she was convinced the world outside was watching in outrage.

He sat beside her and rolled his sleeves up revealing silky dark hairs on his forearms. Her mind strayed as she wondered at the rest of his body, then blushed furiously realising what she was doing.

Kit looked at her curiously. 'Are you all right, is it too warm in here?'

'I'm fine, thank you.' She lowered her eyes and broke a piece of bread and then took a sip of the steaming soup.

'My goodness, this is delicious.' She flourished her spoon over her meal. 'I don't believe I have ever had …what did you call it?

'Watercress soup.'

'I've never had it before.'

'It's in abundance at the moment. It's in the stream, just under the bridge by the Corn Mill. I picked it fresh this morning, along with some wild garlic, mixed it with an onion and a potato and that's all there is to it really.'

Knowing what was poured into the river every day, she gasped. 'You picked it out of the *stream*!'

He grinned. 'Don't look so mortified, it's been washed well in fresh water, I assure you. In fact, I don't believe we eat a single vegetable that hasn't been peed on or worse, at some time.' He winked.

Sophie laughed at Kit's 'down to earth' attitude. 'Mill lane is not somewhere I walk now, since the day I came across Penvear. I'd rather I never set eyes on him again.' Sophie shivered involuntarily at the mention of his name.

'Strangely enough, I saw him today while I was gathering the cress.' He grinned boyishly. 'He gave me such a filthy look. I reckon he's seething because you're living above me.'

'I really don't know who that man thinks he is - evicting people because they don't bend to his will!'

'Well, one thing is for sure, he doesn't own this

building, thank goodness. He can't do anything about you being here, and from what I heard, Eric frightened the living daylights out of him. So I reckon you'll have no more trouble from him.'

'I can't tell you how relieved that makes me feel.'

When they had finished their meal, Kit sat back and stretched his legs out under the table.

Sophie marvelled at how easy it was to be with him. 'Where did you learn to cook so well?'

'Mother taught me. We had little money so she and I would forage for food and herbs in the fields, streams and hedgerows - she could make any dish delicious.'

'Are your parents still alive?'

He shook his head. 'Mother's been gone these last ten years. She was a large strapping woman, who ailed nothing, but then suddenly over the course of a year she shrank to skin and bone. The doctor purged her for a tape worm to no avail, in the end he believed there was a cancer eating her from the inside.'

'Was that Dr Eddy?'

'No, it was a doctor in Helston.'

'How awful,' Sophie rested her hand on his sleeve. 'And your father?'

Kit sighed. 'He was a fisherman. He had an accident at sea and died when I was five, so Mother had to bring me up. We lived here with my grandparents – in the room upstairs where you live. The carpentry workshop was my grandpa's and while Mother went out to work, grandpa taught me all I know about carpentry.'

'Where did she work?'

'She was a cook in the workhouse at Helston.' He smiled. 'She prided herself on making tasty food to give the poor souls working there a treat.'

They both smiled and looked out of the window. The warmth of the day made the midges gather in the afternoon sun.

'Eric says we can milk the cows outside this afternoon,

with the weather being so nice.'

'Is that better than indoors?'

'I don't know - I've never milked outside before, but I should think it won't be as smelly.' She grinned. 'And the bonus is, we don't have to sweep and swill the cowshed afterwards.'

'I'll look out for you in the field then, to see how you're getting along.'

'Talking of work, I should go. I have some washing to do before I go back. Thank you for dinner, Kit,' Sophie stood to clear the bowls.

'It's all right, I'll do that.' Kit pushed his hands against his knees and stood up, reluctant that their meal had come to an end. 'I'll let you know when I make another batch of watercress soup so you can join me again for dinner.'

She smiled warmly. 'I'll look forward to that.'

'It won't be for a while though. I'm off to Bochym Manor in a few days. I have four rowing boats to mend.'

'Oh!' Her buoyant mood deflated slightly at his impending absence. 'Will you be gone long?'

'I'll be back in two maybe three weeks, hopefully.'

'But who will make the coffins should anyone die?'

'I have four in lieu. If more are needed, god forbid, I'll return briefly to make them.'

*

Gilbert Penvear had been in a foul mood for the last two weeks, much to the detriment of his employees at the Corn Mill. Dan Wilton the foreman normally oversaw their work, and they were happy when that happened, but every now and then their boss Penvear would come in to put the cat amongst the pigeons and manage to upset his whole workforce.

He was a disagreeable, domineering boss - stingy with his wages and sharp of tongue. Nothing was ever right in his eyes. If he found one thing out of place or not to his liking, everyone would have their wages docked. Life at the mill was normally dreadful, but had become unbearable over the last fortnight, and no one, except his manservant, Jeremy Nancarrow, knew why his temper was so vile.

Jeremy knew that the young widow had slipped the net his master had cast and had gone off to live with Kit Trevellick – and for that reason, everyone was suffering. Jeremy was glad that she was safe from his clutches - he'd seen how Penvear's late wife had suffered under his inhumane treatment of her and did not wish that for the lovely young widow Sophie.

After the altercation between Penvear and Eric Williams, Jeremy had very nearly lost his job for allowing Eric to enter Quay House. He'd lied of course, and said that he'd been on an errand for the duration of Eric's visit, but Penvear still took his anger out on him at every opportunity.

'Damn his eyes,' Gilbert spat his venom at Jeremy as he tried to help him dress for luncheon. 'That bastard Trevellick was scavenging under the bridge today for watercress - no doubt to take home to serve up to his new wench! Well, we'll see who wins that game. Sophie Treloar is mine!' He knocked the comb out of Jeremy's hand and sent it flying across the room.

'Pick it up, you clumsy oaf,' he yelled. 'And go and scald it. I don't want you scratching my scalp with the teeth of that filthy thing.'

Jeremy did as he bid. He hated his job and his master, but there was little hope of getting another position if he left Penvear's employment. He was a powerful man and would blacken his name to another potential employer if he ever tried to leave.

As for Kit, Jeremy had been to school with him and liked him a lot - he would make a point of warning him that Penvear was on the war path.

*

It was an unusual experience for Sophie to be out in the sunshine milking. Puffs of dandelion seeds floated in the late afternoon sun as they all tethered the cows they were milking to a large stake and settled their stools in the meadow, knee deep in wild flowers. It was certainly easier outside! The cows were happy in their field - more relaxed, in fact they were so relaxed Charlie got shat on by his cow Sunflower while he was trying to make her stand still! Everyone stopped what they were doing, to watch with amusement as Charlie danced about cursing like a navvy whilst scooping great handfuls of red-hot shit from his hair. Lizzy physically wet herself laughing and had to run back to the farm to change her drawers!

'All right, settle down everyone,' Eric said with a grin. 'Charlie, get on with the job in hand otherwise you'll upset Sunflower.'

'*Me,* upset *her*! Look what she's done to me! I stink!' The dung was dripping down his face now, so he wiped it with the only clean piece of sleeve he had.

'Oh, stop your moaning. It's not the first time you've been shat on and it certainly won't be the last. It'll soon dry in this sun.' He winked at Sophie.

Sophie turned gleefully back to her job, edging the milking stool a little further away from the business end of her cow, Daisy. She grasped her tail to stop it swishing in her face and trapped it against the cow's side with her forehead, but as she milked, she had the strangest sensation that she was being watched. She glanced towards Kit's boat, and sure enough he was stood there. Her heart gave an involuntary leap, but her head sent out alarm bells. *Stop it, Sophie. You must not let him into your heart.* But she could not help but watch him watching her.

*

Seeing Lizzy running towards the farmhouse to change her drawers, Lydia shot a questioning look towards Eric. When he'd smothered his mirth enough to explain what had happened, Lydia closed the dairy door and huffed and puffed up the field to relieve Charlie so he could go and change his shirt. She very rarely milked nowadays - it made her back ache too much, but from the sound of what had happened, she thought she had better step in. It did not go unnoticed that Sophie's attention was on the boatyard rather than her milking. Lydia followed her gaze towards where the *Harvest Moon* was moored and Kit was standing. Her smile grew - there was definitely a spark of interest going on between them.

*

When Sophie brought the last of the milk pails down with Ely, Lydia waited until Ely had gone, and said, 'You could do a lot worse than Kit you know.'

Sophie put the pail of milk on the table top and looked hard at Lydia. 'I did do a lot worse, and I've already told you, I've no intention of letting another man into my life.'

'But Kit is a very different person to Jowan.'

Sophie folded her arms. 'I know he is.'

Lydia mirrored her stance. 'Don't let your anger of Jowan's treatment towards you put you off men, otherwise you'll cut off your nose to spite your face. Kit will love and adore you, if you let him.'

Sophie felt frustrated tears forming. 'I know he would, and if I was looking for another man - and I'm *not*, we....' She sighed and looked away.

'What?'

'We could not marry. Theoretically I'm still married, Jowan's body was never found. It'll be seven years before I can ever think of marrying again, *if* I wanted to.'

Lydia's lips curled. 'I know of two couples in this village alone who live together as man and wife, though they still have a spouse somewhere who has deserted them.'

'But everyone knows I am newly widowed here and,' the tears that had threatened began to fall, 'I wouldn't be able to give Kit children.'

Lydia pulled her into a hug. 'Kit wants *you*, not someone to mother his children. If he'd wanted to be a father, he would have chosen a wife long ago, but he is waiting for *you*. As for living here in this village, well, you could always go and set up home elsewhere.'

Sophie dried her eyes. 'I thought you were my friend?'

Punching her fists into her hips Lydia said, 'I *am*!'

'Then why do you want me to leave?'

Lydia shook her. 'I want you to be happy for once in your life. Though, lord help me, Eric would kill me if he heard me telling you to leave with Kit. You're one of the best dairymaids we've had!' She grinned.

'He has nothing to worry about. I'll never leave.'

'Just you think on what I've said and *don't* lose this chance of happiness. Enjoy your independence for now if you must, but remember companionship is a far happier situation to be in. Please don't lose Kit by constantly pushing him away. He might completely give up on you.'

Sophie lowered her eyes. 'I hear you Lydia, I hear you.'

Chapter 18

It was with a certain degree of reluctance that Kit set off for Bochym Manor a few days later. The meal he'd shared with Sophie, and the sadness in her eyes when he'd told her he was going away, made him think that perhaps there was just a modicum of hope that she would change her mind about opening her heart to love again. He steered his pony and cart down the long dusty drive at Bochym, took the lane to the tradesmen's entrance and made himself known to James Parson, the estate steward.

'Hello, Kit,' James greeted him warmly. 'Let me show you the cottage we've allocated for you first. You can stable your pony or put her in the field down by the front garden, with the sheep, whatever is best for you. Once you've settled, his lordship said to tell you, that you're free to walk around to familiarise yourself with the grounds and the gardens if you wish.'

'Thank you, I will.'

The cottage, located opposite the stables, was neat and comfortable. Kit quickly settled his pony in the bottom meadow, before going in search of the wood shed. He wanted to make a start on the boats as soon as possible - there would be time enough in the evenings to stroll around the gardens. He'd only been away from Gweek and Sophie for a few hours and already felt the separation keenly.

He opened the door to the woodshed and the warm, earthy fragrance of bark and moss filled his nostrils - some would call it musty, but to a carpenter it was perfume. He selected, and cut, several pieces of seasoned wood for the gunwales and placed two of them in the lake to soak for a few hours. He would normally steam the wood to bend it if he'd been in the boatyard, but here soaking would be the answer. While he was waiting for the wood to become malleable, he began making good the seats on the boats. It really was the most perfect setting to work. The sun was warm on the back of his neck and the slight breeze ruffled through his hair to keep him cool. Occasionally a group of moorhens paddled noisily across the lake in front of him and the odd frog would sit and eye him curiously. Around the side of the lake, nature had put on a glorious show of spring flowers. Cowslips and wood sorrel pushed their heads through the moss and rocks and in the distance a purple hue of bluebells carpeted the woodland floor. After working solidly for three hours, Kit laid a cloth on the ground and took out his luncheon of bread and cheese.

'You've settled in then?' Guy Blackthorn came walking up to him.

Kit rose to shake his hand. 'I have and very nicely too. What a place to work! I'm obliged that you recommended me to the Dunstans.'

'Well, I know no better Boatwright than you.' He grinned.

'So, are you working here now, Guy?'

'I will be next week. I'm just on a social visit to speak to Peter.'

'How is everyone at home?'

'They're well thank you. Listen, Peter and some of the crafters are meeting at the Wheel Inn for a glass of ale tonight if you want to join us.'

'Sounds good to me.'

'We'll see you around six-thirty then, but if you want to go early to eat, they do a fine pot of stew.'

*

Having worked solidly through the afternoon, Kit did indeed enjoy the delights of a meal at The Wheel Inn. When the others joined him, Guy introduced Kit to some of them.

'I believe I told you that Bochym was the home of the Bochym Arts and Craft Association. It's a subsidiary of The Arts and Craft movement. It was set up by Sarah, two years ago for talented craftsmen who made beautiful objects to sell. It's just the men here this evening - the ladies are enjoying a soirée of their own at home,' Guy said. 'It's quite a community now. Sarah herself is a fine artist and she has some important connections, so everyone does really well selling their wares. There are six people living and working on the estate, three men and four women, her ladyship included, and of course, Ellie is part of it, though she works from home. They have a very nice lifestyle indeed.'

As he listened, Kit felt quite excited at the prospect of taking a look around. 'This is music to my ears. I've been influenced by the Arts and Craft movement myself. In fact, I travelled up country to meet with some of the finest bespoke furniture makers in the movement. It spurred me on to master my craft.'

'Well then you will fit right in here.' Guy chinked glasses with Kit.

The public house was buzzing with excitement that evening, regarding the surrounding beaches on the Lizard being strewn knee deep in wool. It was only when Peter arrived to partake in his evening glass of ale, that the real story came out.

'Have you heard about the wool, my lord?' James the estate steward asked.

'I have, yes,' he answered, gratefully taking the glass of ale from the landlord. 'Hopefully it will be used wisely to make clothes to keep the villagers warm this coming winter.'

'Where's it come from then?' the landlord asked.

'It's from the *Suevic* which ran aground in March,' Peter answered.

'So has she broken up then, my lord?'

'In a fashion, yes. I heard that the Liverpool & Glasgow Salvage Association - acting on behalf of the White Star Line who own her, recommended that as the rear 400 feet of the ship's length was undamaged – that was the portion that contained the boilers, engines and passenger accommodation - they could attempt to save the stern half of the ship by separating it from the impaled bow.'

'How have they done that then without it sinking?' the landlord asked.

Peter smiled – as everyone listened agog.

'It appears that the *Suevic* was divided into watertight compartments by airtight bulkheads, which could, if they held their integrity, allow the ship to remain afloat even if divided.'

'So, they blew part of it up?' James asked incredibly.

'They did, yes, on the 2nd April, and it was successful. The aft half of the ship floated free and fortunately the exposed watertight bulkhead held its integrity. The *Suevic* has been able to steam under her own power, albeit in reverse and guided by tugs, up to Southampton.'

'And the rest of it?'

'The damaged bow was left on the rocks. By all accounts it broke up by the pounding waves on the night of the 9th and 10th of May. I believe it contained 2000 bales of wool.' He gave a little smile.

'Good pickings then?' someone said and a great cheer went up.

'I heard a lot of it has come in at Polurrian,' Guy said to Kit. 'Apparently you can't move for the stuff. It'll be in quite a state, but I'm going down tomorrow afternoon to bag myself some - do you want to come? I know Lydia would be thrilled to get some free wool.'

'Good idea. I wonder if we'll find Jowan Treloar's body underneath it.'

He grimaced. 'Well part of me hopes not, but on the other hand if we do, Sophie would be free to marry again….if she pleases.'

'Is she still with that battleaxe of a mother-in-law?'

'No, she walked out on Ria almost as soon as she heard about Jowan's demise. She got herself her own cottage and a job at the Williams Farm.'

'Good for her!'

'Ah but, Sophie fell foul of her landlord, so, she is currently residing in my sail loft.'

'An interesting development.' Guy grinned. 'So, I take it all plans of sailing into the sunset on the *Harvest Moon* are off then?'

'For the moment, yes.'

'Is there hope for you and her to get together then?'

'I don't know. After life with Jowan, she is heartily sick of men. I know its early days, but having spoken to her, Sophie is adamant that she does not want to be with another man. She values her independence and I don't blame her. She's been under Ria and Jowan's thumb for so long, she's forgotten who she used to be.'

'Ah, I'm sorry, Kit.' Guy patted his arm. 'Well, perhaps now she lives near you, she'll realise what a fine fellow you are and that you are *nothing* like Jowan.' He slapped him on his back. 'Anyway,' he drained his glass, 'I must be going. Supper will be waiting. I'll see you tomorrow afternoon then, say at four?'

'All right, I'll collect you with the pony and cart if you like?'

*

As predicted, Polurrian Cove was knee deep in a tangled mess of stinking wet wool. It seemed that everyone else had had the same idea, because the beach was packed with people dragging great wet lumps of wool up the beach.

Kit and Guy set to and filled ten sacks before they left, exhausted and aching but very pleased with themselves. They looked back at the others still picking wool off the beach. It was clear it would take days for it to be gathered up. They both knew not a scrap would be left and there would be no one on the Lizard this winter without a warm jumper to wear.

*

When they arrived back at Poldhu, Kit fed, watered and hobbled his pony while Jessie and Ellie excitedly inspected the pickings despite it being covered in kelp and sand.

'Look at them!' Guy laughed. 'The well-heeled society enjoys gifts of diamonds. My Ellie is thrilled with sacks of stinking wet wool.'

They both watched the girls laughing together as they stuffed the wool back into the sacks.

Ellie walked back to the cottage, grinning broadly. 'Thank you for collecting the wool,' she hugged both Guy and Kit. 'We've decided to sort it out later. We're going to dig a well in the stream and let the clean water wash it for a while. I must say there's a lot of wool - it should keep us in jumpers for a few years.' She smiled at Kit, 'How do you like working at Bochym then?'

'Very much, I'm obliged to Guy for putting in a good word.'

'That's what friends are for. You'll stay for supper I hope?'

'Well, if it's no bother.'

'Of course not, I always cook too much. Make yourself at home.'

'Ellie, darling,' Guy said, 'Kit too has four sacks of wool on his cart. He's taking it back to Lydia Williams. He'll be at Bochym for a couple of weeks at least and it'll perish if he leaves it in the sack, could you put his with yours in the well?'

'Of course. If you take it all down to the stream, I'll soak it and get it ready. You can pick it up next time you come for supper.'

'I'm obliged to you too now,' Kit said bowing gallantly.

*

Sarah arrived just as Kit had finished his lunch the next day. She wore a straw hat and a large brown apron, which covered very ordinary clothes for a lady. Her gloves were covered in grass stains and dried mud, and she carried with her a wicker basket full of flowers and small garden implements.

'Good day, Mr Trevellick. Forgive me for not welcoming you to the estate yesterday. I was in Truro most of the day. I do hope you have everything you require.'

Kit bowed. 'Thank you, my lady, yes.'

'And you've settled into your accommodation, I trust.'

'It's very comfortable, thank you. You look as though you have been busy?'

'Yes, there is always a lot to do in the garden. I'll leave you now to your luncheon. Please, feel free to take a look around the formal gardens. You are free to wander anywhere.' She smiled, 'I do like to show off my beautiful borders.'

'Thank you, my lady, I'd rather like to see the holy well too if I may.'

Sarah smiled knowingly. 'Of course, it's just down the steps to the right, before you come to the parterre.'

'Thank you. Perhaps I'll take a wander down there now.'

*

Kit opened the wrought iron gate which led into the formal gardens, and as he stepped down into the garden his senses were bombarded by the smell and beauty of the flower borders. He walked down the middle gravel path to where the love seats were located and down more steps to the parterre. He looked to the right to where Sarah said the holy well was located. Carefully making his way down the slippery stepping stones, he crouched down near the small bubbling pond. He took in the ambience of the lush vegetation surrounding it, before closing his eyes and making his wish.

'Are you here to help Papa?' A female voice startled him.

Kit stood up to address the young girl standing above him. She looked about thirteen and was dressed in a rather elaborate pink satin. For the world, she looked like someone who had stepped out of a 17th century painting.

'Yes, I am, Miss.'

'Good. We have been waiting a long time for help to come,' she said petulantly. 'Are you a lawyer then?'

Kit frowned. 'No, Miss, I'm a carpenter.'

She stamped her foot in exasperation. 'Well, *you'll* be no help to him then! Will you?' She turned abruptly and flounced off towards the house.

Kit stood stock still, wondering what on earth that was all about. He craned his neck to see where she had stomped off to, but she had vanished from sight.

Chapter 19

Sophie let herself into Kit's quarters to take the bread out of the range. The room felt strange and empty without him. It almost echoed as she walked back to the door with the bread wrapped in a clean tea towel. He'd only been away a couple of days and despite herself, she felt his absence keenly. It wasn't as if they were in each other's pockets, but he was always somewhere in the near vicinity, with a ready smile and wave of hand - she missed that. She glanced around the room, which was stark and without any sort of comfortable furnishing. In her own room upstairs, she'd made a rag rug and several cushions and was in the process of making a fresh pair of curtains. It all looked very homely. She'd have loved to have a free hand at putting just a few soft touches to Kit's room - he certainly needed new curtains, but decided that it was not her place to do that. Her eyes rested on the armchairs Kit had so lovingly made and she tapped her lip in thought. Sophie had spent a few hours in Helston that afternoon with Lydia and was now in possession of several large scraps of good quality material, including some satin which she was going to Italian quilt and make into a bag. Before she did that though, she thought perhaps there was something she could do to make things cosier for Kit.

Lydia had sent the sewing machine over to Sophie - her accommodation being so much lighter to work in than Lydia's front room. It now took pride of place under the window so she could sew and enjoy the view over the fields of Gweek Wollas Farm. Putting her bread on the table, Sophie glanced at the clock - she had an hour before she was due to milk. With her fingers itching to make a start, she laid her material on the floor and began to cut out some shapes.

The tide had come in while Sophie sat by the window sewing, and a large steamer ship sailed into view and docked. A ship in port meant that the peace and quiet of the afternoon would soon be shattered. With that she put down her sewing, picked up her milking apron and bonnet, and stepped out into the afternoon sun.

*

At Bochym Manor, Kit was laid at a strange angle with his head under the boat's seat as he adjusted the tenon to fit snugly into the mortise, when he heard someone delicately clearing their throat to catch his attention. He shuffled out from where he lay and was startled to find his visitor was a rather beautiful red-headed woman.

'Well, hello there,' she said rather jauntily as she held out her hand.

'Good day to you, Miss,' Kit said wiping his hands down his shirt before he shook her hand. She had the greenest eyes he'd ever seen. A fiery red tail of curls hung down her bodice and was tied with a bright green ribbon. The clothes she was wearing under her long serge apron looked good quality, as did her suede boots. This woman was not without money.

'Georgina Blake darling, but everyone calls me Georgie.' Her perfectly painted lips parted to show a row of small white teeth. 'And you are?' she said with a sparkle in her eyes.

'Kit Trevellick.'

'Well, Kit Trevellick.' She pouted and moved closer. 'I am *very*, *very* pleased to meet you.'

Kit laughed at her forward manner and was shocked at how deep she was looking into his eyes.

'I see you're getting the boats ready for our summer soirées on the lake,' she said, running her fingers across the newly fitted rowlocks.

'As you see,' Kit murmured.

'It's divine down here by the lake – the parties - the picnics,' she purred. 'In fact the whole set up here at Bochym is divine, don't you think?' Her fingers had left the rowlocks and were now walking seductively up the front of his shirt.

Quite taken aback, Kit stepped away from her. 'Set up?'

'Why the Bochym Arts and Craft Association of course!' she breathed.

'Oh, I see.' He took a large intake of breath and his nose filled with her scent which reminded him of a rose garden. 'You're part of the association I take it?'

'I am, yes.' She fluttered her eyelashes. 'We're a rather talented lot, even if I say so myself. Tell me, darling, why have you not been to see us?'

Kit smiled nervously. 'Maybe I will when I get a moment.'

'Oh, but you must come now.' Her hand was caressing his arm. 'Come - let me introduce you to everyone.'

'But..' Kit looked down at his half-finished job.

'No buts, darling. I'm simply dying to show you what we do here. Oh, damn! her ladyship is coming now.' She let go of his arm and Kit noted the tedium in her voice.

'Good morning, Georgina, Mr Trevellick. How are you both this morning?' Sarah was again dressed for gardening.

'Good morning to you, my lady.' Kit bowed.

'I can see the work you have done so far is of the upmost quality,' Sarah said glancing down at the boats. 'Have you taken a look at our workshops yet? You may be interested to meet with the craftsmen and women working here.'

'No not yet. Miss Blake was just about to escort me there.'

'Splendid, then let me accompany you both.'

Kit saw Georgie's face fall slightly, but in truth he was rather glad of Sarah's intervention - Georgie unnerved him somewhat.

Conscious that he was in his old work clothes, he wiped his hands down his shirt again and raked his fingers through his hair as he followed Sarah up the drive towards the back of the manor. As they rounded the building, Kit spotted Guy and Silas on the first workshop's roof and waved. 'My goodness, is that a dog on the roof with them?' Kit was astounded.

'It is indeed,' Sarah laughed. 'Wherever young Mr Blackthorn is, so too is the dog. I admit I've never seen a dog climb a ladder before! Have you Mr Trevellick?'

'I can't say as I have.' He laughed.

The postman joined them at that moment with mail for both Sarah and Georgie. While the ladies exchanged pleasantries with him, Guy climbed down the ladder to speak to Kit.

'I see you've met Georgie?' Guy whispered.

Kit grimaced. 'Is she for real?'

'Oh, yes!' He grinned. 'She's good fun though - when you get to know her.'

'I'm sure she is.' Kit quipped.

'I knew she'd take a shine to you.'

'God help me. You could have warned me. She was practically making love to me down by the lake!'

Guy snuffled a laugh. 'God won't help you if Georgie gets her nails into you. Tell her you are spoken for or she'll never leave you be.'

'But I'm not, am I?' Kit's eyes flashed with concern.

'Well, I'll leave it to you to explain that to her.'

'Sorry about that, Mr Trevellick,' Sarah said beckoning him forward. 'Shall we get on with the tour? As you can see we're a very sociable group here. Many share meals together in each other's homes and of course socialise at the Wheel Inn,' Sarah said casually.

'Yes,' Kit said. 'Miss Blake was also telling me about the picnics.'

Georgie wrinkled her nose.

'Yes, Georgina certainly knows how to party,' Sarah said candidly. 'I must admit though the picnics are rather special. As we walk around to meet everyone, they will show you in turn what they do. We have six people at the moment living and working on the estate, who make and sell their wares. I myself paint, so being part of a group like this has its benefits. As you can imagine, Peter and I have a vast network of clients who are very interested in this sort of specialist workmanship.'

As Kit walked around, he was amazed at the wonderful array of things that people were making, and he found everyone to be very friendly and accommodating.

'Well now,' Sarah said after the tour, 'I must leave you now, my garden beckons.' As she made to leave, she turned and smiled. 'I forgot to ask, did you visit the holy well, Mr Trevellick?'

'I did, thank you.' He wondered if he should mention that he'd upset her daughter there, but having thought about it, the girl in pink looked too old to be Sarah's child, so he kept the little exchange to himself.

'Oooh, what did you wish for?' Georgie breathed.

Kit laughed nervously and shook his head.

'Your ladyship, Kit doesn't have to return to work straight away, does he? He could stay and take a cup of tea with me if he'd like to,' Georgie pleaded.

With a hint of a smile, Sarah said, 'Mr Trevellick can do as he wishes.'

'Thank you, but, perhaps another day - I'd like to get back to work.'

Georgie looked quite put out. 'Well, Kit, you know where I am,' she pouted seductively.

*

It was almost six and the port of Gweek had been busy all day. Cargo was being unloaded, shouts and cursing reverberated around the village and carts trundled to and fro with goods loaded from the steamer ship. Ria watched it all happening from her front doorstep. No doubt the crew of the ship would descend on The Black Swan later, and her sleep would inevitably be disturbed as they made their way back to the ship with bellies full of ale.

As she stood watching, she bristled slightly at the sight of Sophie walking along the riverbank with a skip in her step. *No doubt making her way back to Kit Trevellick's house —the girl had no shame!* An automatic scowl set on her face. Her living there with him was the talk of the village, and Ria dreaded to think what Jowan would say about it.

'Your face will stay like that if the wind changes, Ria.'

Ria shot a sharp look at Amelia who was making her way back home with her pails of water from the pump. 'She's a disgrace to Jowan's memory.'

'She is not! And one day you'll find out how much you owe to Sophie.' Amelia said evenly as she walked away from her.

'What do you mean?' She shouted after Amelia. *How can I be indebted to that…that…hussy.*

*

Sophie rounded the bridge into the boatyard to find it buzzing with activity. Customs men were all over the steamer, checking the cargo as crates of brandy, and other goods were being unloaded from Europe. She acknowledged Jeremy Nancarrow, Penvear's manservant who was sat upon a cart waiting to take the goods away once they'd been checked and passed by customs. He nodded back, ever courteous whenever he saw her. Sophie felt sorry for the man, having to work for such an ogre.

Sophie watched the comings and goings while she sat on the bench outside Kit's cottage enjoying a glass of homemade elderberry cordial in the early evening sun. She saw four barrels of the finest French brandy loaded onto Gilbert Penvear's cart. They were all marked with Penvear's name along with a large red cross on the underside.

One of the boatyard men, Ken Trefusis, was stood nearby watching - his face looked thunderous.

'Gosh that's a lot of brandy, Mr Trefusis! Is that all going to Penvear?' Sophie asked him.

'Aye and not a penny paid in tax!'

Sophie frowned. 'How come?'

'It's possibly something to do with Ian Crocker the Customs Officer, living rent free in one of Penvear's property.' He tapped his nose.

Sophie's eyes widened. 'Shush! Won't you get into trouble if you're heard telling me that?'

'I couldn't care less who knows. I've just been sacked by Crocker. All I did was to question this transaction – because there is something fishy about it you see. They're all the same these bloody people with money - they still want something for nothing. I hope Penvear chokes on his brandy.'

So do I, Sophie thought.

*

After sewing late into the night, Sophie fell into a deep sleep almost as soon as her head touched the pillow. *She dreamt of the ship workers unloading the cargo and watched as one of them started to climb the granite steps to her sail loft holding a case of brandy. She tried to call and stop him, but he continued to climb.* Suddenly Sophie woke with a start. A deeply disturbing sensation curled inside her - someone *was* walking up her granite steps! Was Kit back? No, he'd never frighten her in the middle of the night. So, who was it? She took a sharp intake of breath when a silhouette appeared at the window of her door, the shape a shade darker than the night. The handle squeaked as it was being turned. Every nerve end in her body stood alert. Her heart began to thump wildly against her chest. Had she secured the door before retiring last evening? She couldn't remember - she didn't always. Oh, why didn't she do it every night? With every one of her senses heightened she knew she must move quickly. Pushing the covers away she ran to the door as fast as her leaden legs would carry her. With a swift turn of the key, the door locked and the shadow moved back slightly.

Pressing herself against the wall, a film of sweat drenched her shaking body. Her clock struck three. Who the hell was that at this time of night? It could only be one of the crew from the steamer ship, chancing his luck. She would not sleep again tonight that was for certain.

*

Gilbert Penvear retreated down the steps, rejoicing at his

torment of Sophie. She would soon learn that nobody defied him and got away scot free. He knew Trevellick was away from home and couldn't come to her rescue, so it was a perfect time to play a little game with her. He had no intention of entering her room, no, he just wanted to frighten her, and from the audible cry of fear he'd heard through the door, he'd accomplished his goal. He sighed in satisfaction - the sound of her fear caused an excited stir in his groin. He sucked the air between his teeth, imagining her trembling in her nightdress, naked underneath the thin material.

With great stealth he moved into the shadows. His urge was such he knew he must succumb to his building lust and relieve himself. He stepped behind Dr Eddy's camellia bush until the deed was done.

*

Gilbert sneaked back into Quay House through the kitchen entrance, so as not to alert anyone. Discarding his soiled damp underclothes, he left them on the floor of his dressing room for his manservant to deal with. He crawled between his bed sheets and then, not for the last time that night relieved himself while he thought of Sophie.

Chapter 20

Eric frowned as he watched Sophie usher her next cow in to milk. She looked pale and wan that morning - not her usual rosy persona. Dark circles shadowed her eyes and she was unusually quiet as she got on with her work.

'Everything all right there, Sophie?' he asked.

She just nodded and got down to business.

Eric scratched his head. He'd have a quiet chat with her once this lot were milked, just to make sure Penvear wasn't bothering her again.

'Oh, Eric, Eric, come quickly,' Lydia's voice shattered the harmony of the milking parlour.

Eric released the teats from his fingers and stood up. 'What's wrong, my luvver?' He rushed quickly to her side.

Lydia had bent double to try and catch her breath. 'I've just looked in on your father and he is very ill,' she gasped.

Eric's shoulders dropped. 'Oh, god! I've been dreading this moment. Has the doctor been called?'

'Yes,' she cried. 'I've sent Ely for him, you must come, now.'

Eric shot a worried look around the milking parlour - everyone had stood up from their stools.

'Go,' Sophie urged, 'Charlie, you need to go with your pa as well. I'm sure the rest of us can manage the milking, can't we?' She looked around and everyone nodded in unison.

'Thank you,' Eric said gratefully - he knew everything would be in good hands as he set off to follow Lydia down the yard.

*

After milking, Sophie and Lizzy made the breakfast, but as Lizzy had to go to school, the rest of the farm workload was shared between herself, Dora and Stan. After taking breakfast trays upstairs for everyone, Sophie opened the dairy, while Stan and Dora set off to swill the milk parlour. Sophie smiled at Stan and Dora walking amiably together.

Thankfully Stan had stopped giving Sophie flowers every day, but he still gazed at her with adoring eyes. She hoped now that Dora too had begun to learn how to communicate with Stan – he would perhaps turn those adoring eyes towards a more willing recipient.

Sophie pulled open the heavy wooden doors to the dairy, and although the building was kept scrupulously clean, there was always a distinct odour of sour milk on first entering. She donned a crisp, clean, white apron, but realising that her milking cap was soiled, she fumbled in her skirt pocket for a ribbon to tie her hair back. The only one she had was a scarlet one – it would have to do.

After wiping down the surfaces ready for the influx of customers, she began to prepare to turn the butter and set the cheese while she waited. This job was not part of Sophie's remit, but she'd asked Lydia to instruct her in all the jobs in the dairy, for no other reason than to give Lydia the odd day off occasionally.

It was by great misfortune that the first customer to enter the dairy was Ria. Sophie stiffened - this had been the first time she'd come face to face with her since leaving Alpha Cottage.

On seeing Sophie, Ria pulled herself up to her full size and looked derisively at her daughter-in-law.

'Why are you here? Where is Lydia?' she demanded. But before allowing Sophie to answer, she added, 'Look at you, stood there in your bright clothes, dressed up like a Christmas turkey. You should be ashamed of yourself. My boy is not cold in his grave and you strut around like a spring chicken. Shame on you, by rights you should still be in mourning for him!'

Ignoring Ria's many references to poultry, Sophie smiled. 'Good morning, Ria, I do hope you're keeping well?'

'Bah! No doubt you're dressed like that with your ribbons in your hair for your fancy man! Oh, yes, I *know* you've moved in with him. Shame on you, the whole village is in uproar about it,' she snarled, turned on her heel and left without buying anything.

Sophie looked down at her plain white apron covering her brown skirt and the ribbon in her hair. Hurt by the inference, she pulled the ribbon off, turned her milking cap inside out and tucked her mass of curls into it.

Fortunately, the comments Ria made were not given any credence by any of the other customers visiting the dairy that day. Everyone else had greeted her courteously - first asking about her health and wellbeing, and then as to the reason for Lydia's absence.

When Sophie closed the dairy at the end of the morning, she prepared a cold luncheon for everyone. As no news was forthcoming from old Jim's bedroom, Sophie helped with the other chores about the farm before the quartet set to once again to milk the herd in the late afternoon.

Sophie found Lydia in the kitchen after milking, teary eyed and weary, attempting to make supper for everyone.

'The old lad is still hanging on, Sophie, but he's not long for this world now. I'm sorry you've all been left to cope.'

'Don't be sorry - we are managing fine. Now come away from the range and I'll cook. She sat her down with a cup of tea and prepared a meal of ham, eggs and sliced fried potatoes for everyone.

The steamer was still in port when she finally reached home, so she secured all her doors and windows when she retired – she didn't want to take any chances of being murdered or molested in her bed. It had been an incredibly busy day, and she was exhausted, but it still took her until after two before fatigue overtook anxiety allowing her to fall asleep.

*

Sophie woke at dawn to the bright, sunny day, so all felt right with the world, until she remembered about Jim Williams and then the day did not seem as sunny. Grateful that there had been no nocturnal visits to her door, she would certainly be on her guard until the steamer left port.

Once again there were only four of them to milk that morning. The parlour wore a mournful air and all was quiet except for the general noise of milk squirting into iron buckets and the swish of tails and moos of the cows.

The inevitable news of Jim's death broke just before noon that day, and the village of Gweek closed their curtains and mourned for one of their eldest and most respected residents.

*

On Tuesday the 28th of May, Kit was surprised, delighted and saddened in equal measure when he received a letter from Sophie. The postman offered the letter up to him with an apology that it had been stuck at the bottom of his sack and should have been delivered the other day.

Saturday 25th May 1907

Dear Kit,

On behalf of Eric and Lydia, I have been asked to write to you with the very sad news of Jim Williams's death today. The news came some eighteen hours from the start of his deterioration in health. Although feelings are raw at the moment, it is perhaps a blessing for the old man and indeed for Lydia and Eric, who have diligently cared for him during his long ill health. The burial is to be on Tuesday 28th at 1:00 p.m. at Constantine Church.

Kit drew a deep breath and pulled the fob watch from his waistcoat to check the time - it was already eleven! He collected his tools and went in search of the estate steward to beg a leave of absence. If he didn't make it to the church, at least he could be there to show his respects at the wake. He glanced down to read the rest of the letter as he walked back to his cottage.

Mr Greaves, the funeral director, visited your workshop with Eric and they have selected and taken the best coffin you had pre-made, so all is in order on that score. Eric hopes you can attend the funeral, but understands fully if not.

I am sorry this letter holds only sad news but I hope you are enjoying your time working in a different location. If we don't see you on Tuesday, we all look forward to your return after completing your work there.

With good wishes.

Sophie

*

Gilbert Penvear's walk was marred by the sight of Kit's pony and cart as it trotted over mill bridge. He narrowed his eyes - he was seriously displeased. He'd gleaned from several sources that Kit would be working away for at least two weeks! He could only imagine that he'd returned for the Williams's wake. Most of his workers had requested to attend, but they had all been given the same answer. Anyone taking time off to attend a wake would not have a job to come back to. He'd have to curb his nocturnal visits to the boatyard until Kit had gone again. He'd taken to hiding under the tarpaulin covering Kit's boat, so that he could watch Sophie at her window where she sewed by candlelight. He moistened his thin lips at the thought - he'd like to have got closer, but just a glimpse of her was all he needed to feed his lust.

*

The delight on Sophie's face when she saw him waiting at the Williams's Farm made Kit's heart sing. He first gave his apologies and reason for not attending the burial to Eric and Lydia, and then made his way towards Sophie.

He smiled tentatively. 'How are you?' He could have no idea how glad she was to see him.

'I'm well, thank you, Kit. By the look of your tanned face, I can see you're brimming with health!'

'Yes, the benefits of working outdoors.' *Oh, Sophie, I miss you.* 'Is all well at home?' *Please say you're missing me.*

'Yes…Everything is fine.'

Detecting a falter in her voice he said, 'I should…'

'I just…'

151

They both spoke in unison and laughed.

'Please, you first,' Kit said.

She smiled and her whole countenance changed. 'I just wondered, how much longer you will be away for?'

Oh, god! She does miss me! 'I was just going to say, I should be back home soon. The boats should be finished in a couple of weeks.'

'We all miss you, Kit,' she said shyly.

'That's nice to hear.'

'Are you staying home for the night?'

He detected the concern again in her voice. 'I was going to return straight away, but perhaps I'll leave first thing tomorrow.' He watched as she visibly relaxed. Something was definitely bothering her.

'That would be better for you too perhaps,' she said in earnest.

'It would, yes. I shall definitely stay. Tell me, Sophie, you haven't had any more trouble from Penvear have you?' he enquired cautiously.

She shuddered 'No, I haven't seen him, thank goodness.'

He touched her arm for the briefest moment. 'Because if he does bother you, you're to speak to Eric immediately, do you promise to do that?'

She looked deeply into his concerned eyes. 'I promise, Kit, thank you.'

*

The wake carried on late, to accommodate the mill workers wanting to show their respects. Sophie left with the others to milk, leaving the Williams family with the gathering. Her stomach fluttered, realising Kit had waited to walk her home.

The evening sun still had some warmth so they chose to sit outside, but before they sat, Kit checked on his boat and found to his dismay that the tarpaulin had been untied.

'Have you seen anyone around my boat, Sophie?'

'No, why?'

He furrowed his brow. 'The tarpaulin ties have been undone.'

'Perhaps the wind caught it?'

'Perhaps, but they were quite secure. I'll pop a note through Constable Treen's door before I go. Maybe he'll keep a check on it at night.'

'Good idea,' Sophie said, hoping that would also keep her nocturnal visitor away.

They chatted amiably as the sun sank and bathed the village in a warm glow. He told her of the Arts and Craft Association at Bochym and all the people involved. They sounded a lively lot and Sophie envied him the company. It seemed that the women involved in the association also gathered in the local Inn with the men, to socialise - a scandalous idea that would probably be frowned on in Gweek. The only woman to frequent The Black Swan was Amelia Pascoe. The men folk accepted her, because she was a force to be reckoned with. There were few things in this village that could not be solved by asking Amelia to intervene. She feared no one and did not suffer fools gladly. So, she sat quietly in the corner of the snug, observing all and saying little, while partaking in a gill of ale. It was a shame there weren't more ways for women to socialise in this village apart from the odd social chat over tea and cake.

As the sun set and twilight fell, the birds began to roost in the surrounding trees. The evening air filled with clouds of midges, splitting in fright at the emergence of bats from the Customs House eaves. All felt right with the world as they sat in silence and drank in the evening ambiance.

Sophie found the companionship of Kit to have a soothing effect on her ragged nerves. However, she had no intention of telling him about what happened the other night - she did not want him to go back to Bochym with an uneasy mind, fearing he would not be able to concentrate on his work if he was constantly worrying about her. She suspected he knew something had unsettled her though, as he'd been very attentive to her. One thing was for sure, she would sleep easy in her bed tonight knowing he was close.

She glanced up at Kit and marvelled at his still, peaceful persona. He was a man at one with his surroundings. He didn't speak when words were not needed - he was just there for her and she was so grateful.

Despite being told by Lydia, Sophie could see for herself now that he cared for her deeply. If she was truthful to herself, she cared for him too. It was all well and good wanting freedom, but Lydia had been right, the need for companionship far outweighed the novelty of independence. But …

'A penny for your thoughts?' Kit broke the silence.

'I was just thinking how lovely it was to sit out on a warm evening.' She smiled softly at him. 'It was something I always wanted to do. I had to watch from an open window at Alpha Cottage as people strolled through the village. I'd hear the laughter of children on the green and see the men spill out of The Black Swan to drink their ale in the evening air.'

Kit nodded. 'Your new life must be a welcome relief after living in *that* house.'

She clasped her hands together on her lap and sighed. 'I relish it with every fibre in my body.'

'I know. Your happiness shines from within.'

'It's…' She faltered slightly. 'It's nice to spend the evening in good company too.' She lowered her eyes shyly.

'Why, thank you for that compliment.' His eyes sparkled. 'I've never had better company myself.'

She laughed softly.

'But alas our evening must end.' He placed his hands on his thighs and stood up, 'I need to be up with the lark, but hopefully,' he smiled warmly at her, 'we'll enjoy many more evenings like this, if you wish.'

So it was with great reluctance that they parted to go their separate ways that night. As Sophie made her way to the granite steps, he touched her gently on the sleeve.

'Sophie, will you write to me? I know I won't be away that long, but it was so lovely to get your letter the other day, despite its sad contents. I miss *everything* in Gweek, you see.'

Without thinking she curled her hand over his. 'Of course, I will, if you want me to - though I should think little will happen between now and you returning.'

He lifted his eyes from where they had settled on her hand. 'Just let me know how you are then.'

'I will.'

'I shall probably be gone in the morning before you wake.'

'Well, have a safe trip back, won't you?'

'I will.'

Sophie could feel something was pulling them together and felt powerless to stop it.

Chapter 21

Gilbert Penvear had spent the day in a pleasant state of agitation and excitement as he anticipated his night time trip to the boatyard. On his morning walk he'd been delighted to see that Kit Trevellick's pony had gone from its field. That could only mean one thing – he'd gone back to where he was working.

As he readied himself in his dark unassuming clothes, it did not escape him that for someone so normally fastidiously clean and well-dressed, scuffling under a dirty tarpaulin and acting like a vagrant went quite against the grain. Needs must though - to enable him to grasp whatever morsel of pleasure Sophie's image allowed him. Unfortunately, the lengthening of the days meant that he saw less of her image. Her ridiculous farm job hours made her retire before it was full dark. Damn these summer evenings – they were spoiling his pleasure.

It was almost ten-o-clock when he walked with conviction across the bridge, past Barnfield Farm towards the boatyard. A trembling thrill of ecstasy came, as each step brought a flush of excitement searing through his veins.

'Halt! Who goes there?'

Gilbert stopped so quickly he almost stumbled.

'I said, who goes there?'

Gilbert prickled with annoyance as Constable Treen advanced on him. 'What the devil do you mean by shouting at me like that? Can a man not take a walk without being detained by the police now?' Gilbert said authoritatively.

Although his vision was impaired by the twilight, Treen knew this voice was Penvear's, but this did not perturb him. 'What pray is your business in the boatyard at this hour?'

'The business is mine to know and none of yours.'

'I beg to differ on that account, and ask you to adjust

your tone when speaking to an officer of the law.'

Gilbert realised that it was perhaps unwise to bring attention to himself with the police, as they were not to be trifled with. 'I was about to relieve myself somewhere private - if you must know.' He snuffled inwardly at the irony.

'Is it not strange that you should walk, what, 200 yards from your own home to urinate?'

'I think you will find one day, that the bladder of a man of advancing years, cares nothing for distance or location.'

Treen's lip curled into a smile as he gestured Gilbert to do as he must.

Gilbert snorted irritably as he turned and aimed, but the lusty excitement that had gathered in his groin rendered it almost impossible for him to urinate.

'Having trouble?' Treen sniggered.

Gilbert covered himself and without another word stormed off back towards Quay House. He stripped off the clothes he was wearing and rolled them into a ball, throwing them angrily into the corner of his dressing room. This was Trevellick's doing! Sophie must have told him she'd been frightened, and he'd put Treen on watch of his property. One way or other he'd make Kit pay for interfering in his plans.

*

Kit had noted whilst in Gweek, the trees there were still displaying their spring branches - the leaf buds just waiting to burst fully open any moment. Here at Bochym though in this sheltered valley, Kit was surrounded by trees displaying their new tender leaves, swathing the valley in hues of every colour green.

He worked happily knowing that there had been a marked shift in his relationship with Sophie during his visit, and he was keen to get this job done and return. Something or someone had unnerved her - it was plain to see, but she hadn't been forthcoming with any worries. He had taken the liberty of posting a short missive through

Constable Treen's door before he left, mainly for him to check on his boat, but also to make sure that no one was bothering Sophie.

He'd been back at Bochym three days, another week should see him finish.

'Letter for you here, Kit,' James Parson said. 'It came to the steward's cottage.'

He recognised Sophie's handwriting immediately. He put down his tools and ripped it open.

My dear Kit, He sighed at the endearment.

The swans on the river have hatched five cygnets no less. The proud family are gliding majestically up and down the river for all to see. The tree buds are opening now, and Gweek is swathed in a lovely fresh green hue.

I've been to Helston with Lydia for more material, and as always, she pays me for making her clothes, which is hardly a chore, by insisting on buying me material of my choice. I'm sure I shall have to move to larger premises if I make any more clothes for myself. I jest of course. I am very happy where I am and have no wish to move from my surroundings.

Eric is understandably quiet. The death of his father - even though in truth he lost him a long time ago, has hit him hard, but as always, he rallies and has a smile for everyone, even through his grief. Life goes on though, and the cows need milking no matter what state of mind we are in. We milked again outside, without Charlie befalling into any dirty mishaps this time. He gives the rear of any cow a wide berth now just in case!

Lydia asks for your swift return, as do we all, and says to remind you that we will be having a midsummer picnic supper and you're not to miss it.

I hope we will see you sooner than midsummer. Mr Greaves has taken another coffin this morning. You now have two more left for the next couple of unfortunates, so your swift return is essential.

Amelia still enjoys the company of her sister and brother-in-law. The cottage they had set their heart on, with the rather lovely name of Toy Cottage, has unfortunately fallen through their hands to another buyer. It's a Mr Compton Mackenzie, an actor and budding writer, who has made a favourable offer to the vendors, even though he has no intention of taking up residence there until next year. Apparently, he doesn't stay long in any one place and may soon sell again in a couple of years. Amelia's brother-in-law has decided now to rent in Gunwalloe until Toy Cottage comes up for sale again.

Well, that is all the newst. I hope that keeps you up to date with our life here in Gweek.

I hope you're well, and as I said, we look forward to your return. With best wishes

Sophie

Kit read and re-read the letter and smiled warmly. He was just about to kiss her name when Georgie appeared at his side.

'Oh!' She pulled at the letter in his hand. 'Do I detect a love letter from your high colour?'

Her voice jarred him, and he snatched the letter back from her grasp. Forcing a smile from somewhere, he said, 'News from home.'

'Ugh - how droll! I am sure nothing exciting happens in those river backwaters. Not like here, Kit. Eh?' She pawed at his sleeve.

He pulled his arm from her touch and she laughed at his coyness.

'Oh, don't be displeased, I'm only jesting. I'm here to tell you we're having supper at the Wheel Inn tonight. Are you joining us?' She ran the tip of her tongue across her top lip.

Kit watched her act of flirtation with dismay. He had no idea how to respond or deal with her continuing attendance on him. When he'd first met her, he'd been courteous and chatted amiably with her - as he had done with the others involved with the association. He'd told her of the boat he'd built in Gweek and his work as a furniture maker. He should have known when it was clear she was hanging on his every word that she had a taking for him. He must make her understand that he was not for her. 'No, thank you. I've made my own supper,' he said firmly.

'Oh, Kit,' she purred as she moved closer. 'Just a little drinky poo then.'

'No! Thank you.'

'We could have a drink at mine if you don't want to be social at the inn. In fact, that would be sooo much better.' She took a deep sensual breath.

'*No*, thank you,' he said firmly.

She stepped away, pouting as though wounded. 'Oh, darling, I understand. You'll be tired after making up time after your tedious trip home, so I'll forgive you for your lack of humour today.' She curled her lips seductively. 'I'll call by tomorrow, and hope you are in better humour.' She stepped away and turned her back to him waving her hand as she walked. 'Goodbye my darling, Kit,' she called out. 'Just remember, little Georgie here has the patience of a saint.'

Kit watched her walk away, shook his head in dismay and then spent the next few hours arduously working so as to get this job done.

When Guy arrived later that afternoon to see if he wanted to join him for a drink, he said, 'Only if we go into the main bar where the ladies are not allowed.'

Guy grinned knowingly. 'Georgie?'

'Yes, Georgie!'

'You need to put her straight about Sophie. Tell her how things stand.'

'But *where* do things stand? I can't make a false claim on Sophie. What if it got back to her? I don't want to do anything to mar any relationship that may develop in the future by speaking out of turn now.'

'Then we'll have to keep Georgie from you somehow.'

'That is not easy working down here alone.'

'Well, I might just have a solution to that. Come on, Peter wants a word with you over a mug of cider.'

*

With his tools cleared and a quick swill of his face, Kit met up with Guy. They took the road which skirted the front of the manor, so as not to alert Georgie where they were going. It was as they passed the front garden, that Kit saw the strange girl he'd encountered in the garden again. She was dressed in pink, looking out at them from the upstairs windows.

'Any idea as to who that girl might be, Guy?' Kit nodded up to the window.

'Which girl.'

'The girl in pink, three windows from the gable end.'

Guy looked up. 'I see nobody.'

'Third window along,' Kit reiterated.

Guy shook his head. 'I think you've been in the sun too long. I see no one.'

'But, oh! She *has* gone now, but I met her a few weeks ago, by the holy well. She asked if I was a lawyer and if I had come to help her father.'

'Possibly a visitor to the manor,' Guy said dismissively. 'So, you made your wish? What did you wish for?'

'I refuse to say - in case it doesn't come true.' His broken sigh spoke volumes.

'It will, my friend.' Guy patted him on his shoulder. 'If you want something enough, it will happen.'

*

As May blended into June, the weather was glorious. Sophie delayed her return home after the morning on the farm and chose instead to sit in the apple orchard adjoining the Williams's Farm. The soft blush of the apple blossom, which had provided a glorious optimism of warmer months to come, had now all but vanished. All that was left was a carpet of fluffy petals browning slightly as they settled into the earth. Now it was the turn of the elderflower bushes to adorn the valley with clusters of cream flowers. This beautiful display was a sight to behold after spending so many years only catching a glimpse of this spectacle. Every single bud, shoot, flower and baby bird or animal was a symbol of new life and Sophie relished every moment.

With her heart full of early summer hopefulness and her skirt waistband holding a posy of elderflower, she made her way happily back home to find a letter waiting under her door.

Disappointment was an absolute understatement as she read the letter Kit sent. She was actually quite shocked at the mix of tumbling emotions it created.

My dear Sophie,

I trust you are well. I must say your letter filled me with such joy to hear news of home. It makes me quite homesick. Unfortunately, I must endure it for another two weeks, as I am to be detained here at Bochym. His lordship has asked if I can make good the rotting eaves in one of the cottages Guy is thatching. As much as I am missing everyone there, the earl pays me a great compliment in his continued confidence in my carpentry skills, and as Guy proposed me to him, I believe it would be impolite to refuse this job. Rest assured, I will be home for Midsummer.

I'll take my leave and close this short letter now. It was but to inform you of my situation. I'll write a more worthy response to your lovely letter just as soon as I get a moment to myself.

With all good wishes to you.

Kit

Sophie folded the letter and tucked it into her skirt pocket as the sudden intensity of tears began to form. It was clear now that with this emotional response, her heart had quite taken over her head in her quest for an independent life.

Chapter 22

Although Kit had thoroughly enjoyed his time at Bochym, home and Sophie were where he wanted to be. He glanced at his fob watch in consternation, it was nine-thirty - he was a lot later home than intended. He'd had to make a late adjustment to the joists he'd been replacing, and feared that Sophie, Eric and Lydia would think he wasn't coming to their midsummer picnic.

He'd been invited to the Bochym midsummer party on the lake with the other members of the Bochym set, but declined, needing instead to be home with the people he had grown up with. He'd endured quite a struggle to prise Georgie from his arm as he was trying to leave. No matter how much she had pleaded and pawed at him, urging him to stay and enjoy her company, he resolutely shook his head. He was so glad to be away from her – it had become a real battle to keep her at arm's length these past few weeks. Never had he come across a woman so intent on getting her own way. No matter what he said, or how many times he politely refused her many, many suggestive invitations, her obstinate pursuit of him had been consistent.

As he pulled up in the boatyard, he jumped wearily from his cart to stretch the stiffness from his back. It was then he spotted Sophie walking along the opposite bank towards Gweek Wollas Farm with a blanket over her arm. Releasing a deep emotional sigh, all the trials and tribulations of having to deal with Georgie these past few weeks melted away, knowing that in the next half hour he would be back beside the woman he loved.

He unhitched Willow from her harness and walked her back to her field, gave her a feed and a pat, tickled her ears then let her go. She whinnied happily then trotted off to the trough for a drink. With a spring in his step, he set off back home taking a moment to marvel at the sky. Tonight, it was painted pale blue and pink and in the far west the clouds were shredded with vivid gold and orange streaks. It was truly an evening to behold.

After a quick wash and change of shirt, he set off to the Williams's farm, thankful he was able to take the short cut across the river as the tide was out. He was half way over when he heard what was music to his ears - Sophie had spotted him and was shouting his name. His heart filled with joy to see her waving.

'Kit, you're back!' Lydia welcomed him warmly as she, Eric, Charlie and Lizzy joined him on the incline of the field carrying various baskets of food and musical instruments. 'We were beginning to despair that you would not come.'

'I just got in half-an-hour ago. Here, let me carry something for you.' Kit took the heavy basket from Lydia and fell into step with them all. 'Guy and Ellie send their love to you both.'

'They're all well, I hope? Oh, but I would so like to see their little uns,' Lydia clasped her hands together.

'Why don't you invite them over for supper then,' Eric suggested.

'And put them where? It's too far to come for supper and then go home again!'

'You could put them in Pa's room!'

She cocked her head. 'Are you sure? It's only been a couple of weeks since we lost him. Will it not be a little too raw?'

He sighed sadly. 'Well, Pa has no need for it, now he's gone on to a better life, though it'll take a bit of clearing out!'

'I'll gladly do it if, you feel that is what you want.' Lydia squeezed his arm.

'We'll do it together, my love.' He smiled gently. 'I must say, I'd like to see Guy again and his little family as well.'

Lydia could hardly contain her excitement as a plan began to form in her head.

As they approached the others, Dora, Stan and Sophie were sitting on several large blankets. Kit was delighted to see that Sophie was making room for him next to her. As he sat, his arm brushed against hers and by the curl of her smile, the contact was not unwelcome.

'It's nice to have you back,' she whispered.

'It's nice to *be* back, Sophie, thank you for your letters, they've kept me going.'

Her smile broadened as she nodded shyly. As always, whenever he was in close proximity to her, his senses were heightened. The sight of her dressed in an apple green dress with her boots kicked off and her toes freely wiggling in the grass, made him tingle pleasantly. Her blond hair was blowing slightly in the soft evening light and he savoured the soft fresh fragrance of summer which came from the posy of elderflower she had taken to wearing in the waistband of her dress.

Kit smiled thankfully at Lydia as she handed round the flagon of cider and mugs. She rummaged in her wicker basket and produced a freshly baked pasty for everyone. She too had a new dress fashioned by Sophie, cut well to flatter her ample body. It was navy blue, trimmed with pale blue piping at the neck and cuffs, and Lydia was clearly enjoying the way it flattered her shape, as too was Eric, by the adoring looks he was giving his wife. Sophie seemed to have the knack of making everyone feel sensational. Kit's stomach rumbled loudly at the smell of food, making everyone laugh. He hadn't realised just how hungry he was.

After chatting and eating while the sun faded in the western sky, Eric, who had brought along his fiddle, began to play.

Kit stood up and held out his hand hopefully to Sophie. 'Will you dance with me tonight? I've been waiting since May Day for you to say yes, remember?' He was thrilled when she took his hand willingly.

Soon Charlie and Lizzy joined in and then Dora and Stan. For over an hour they all danced, under the lantern lights, changing partners at every new tune. When it came around to dance with Sophie again, Kit's fingers tingled with joy at her delicate touch. Never had he believed that she would be in his arms, dancing so freely and happily with him. The music soon brought other villagers and musicians to join in - many of them bringing their own flagons of cider to share.

Eventually, most of the villagers departed, leaving just the Williams party, but finally at midnight, happy and slightly intoxicated, they all made their way home. There would be a few sore heads in the morning, but nobody cared. Life was good and summer was here.

Kit and Sophie were the first to traverse down the field and across the river bed, the yellow hue of moonlight pathing their way.

In giddy high spirits Sophie stumbled slightly on a slimy stone, shrieking as she began to fall forward, but Kit was quick to save her fall, and pulled her securely into his arms.

They both gasped in unison at the close proximity they found themselves in, and Kit was heartened when Sophie made no immediate effort to pull away from him. Conscious to not hold her tight, so she knew that she was free to leave his embrace, she met his gaze in the lamplight and his heart melted.

'Gosh, Kit, I thought I was going to take a tumble there. Thank goodness you caught me.'

Kit's heart was hammering in his chest. 'Always glad to help a lady,' he whispered.

*

As the rest of the party walked back to the farmhouse, Lydia saw Stan watching the unfolding incident in the middle of the riverbed. The light of the waxing moon showed that when Sophie had shrieked and stumbled, Kit had caught her, because they were now stood in a rather compromising position for all to see.

Lydia laid her hand gently on Stan's shoulder. He turned and shrugged resignedly, took the basket from

Lydia and set off to the house, with Dora following behind like a wounded lamb.

Lydia lingered a moment, until she saw Kit and Sophie carry on with their journey across the river. She was sorry for Stan, but Sophie wasn't the right woman for him. There was only one man for Sophie - and she had just been in his arms. After watching them together this evening, and what had just happened, perhaps Sophie's aversion to starting another relationship was abating. She would see how the land lay over the next few days, but one thing was sure, Lydia was determined to get those two together properly, if it was the last thing she did.

*

Kit had slept well that night, mostly due to cider and exhaustion, but also to do with having a settled mind. The time he'd spent with Sophie the previous evening had filled his heart with delight, and given him hope for a future with her. He'd danced and laughed with her and then there was the moment at midnight when his world stilled. When at last she pulled away from his arms, she'd smiled warmly, and without any awkwardness whatsoever, had walked by his side to their respective homes and bid him goodnight with the words, 'I'm very happy that you're home, Kit.'

When he rose the next morning, he walked out of the gloom of the cottage shielding his eyes from the bright morning sunlight, and despite his sore head, the sounds and sights of summer made his heart sing.

*

Whereas Kit had slept well, Sophie however had struggled to sleep, her mind being a whirl of emotions - most of which had not been at all unpleasant. Continually reliving the moment Kit had caught her when she had slipped, she marvelled at how protected she felt, even though he'd encircled her gently with his arms. There had been no unwelcome squeeze or lust in his manner, and he had certainly not taken advantage of the situation. Like a true gentleman, he'd waited until she made whatever move she wanted, which of course was to gently move away from him. She'd never been given the choice before and that spoke volumes about Kit's character. She turned over in bed and sighed. The whole incident had caused a seismic shift in their relationship though – nothing would be the same again and that thought frightened her.

*

During morning milking, despite the sore heads, Sophie had to deflect the knowing looks and teases from her fellow dairy hands. Even though she firmly stated that she'd slipped on the riverbed and Kit had caught her, her words fell on deaf ears, and the teasing continued in good humour. It was plain to see, everyone, with the exception of Stan by the wounded look he gave her, would be happy if she should find love again, especially if it was with Kit. It was this thought that perturbed her. As she made her way home, she knew that she needed to speak candidly to Kit. Without doubt there was a place in her heart opening up for him, but she just didn't know how it was possible for her to let him step into it.

*

Her chance to speak to him came just before she was due to return to work that afternoon. He'd been out of the workshop most of the day and arrived home just as she was cooling a saffron cake fresh out of the range oven.

When he walked in, Sophie felt a lump form in her throat when she noted how his face lit when he saw her standing there.

He took a deep appreciative breath. 'I swear your baking makes my stomach somersault - it smells so delicious.'

She laughed gently. 'I'll halve it for you. I made a large one in order to do that.'

'Thank you.' He threw his hat on the table and raked his fingers through his hair until it stood on end.

They stood for a moment while they both looked at

each other.

'Kit, I....'

'Sophie if it's about last night, I'm sorry. I perhaps overstepped the mark by holding you a tad longer than was respectable.'

'Oh, no, Kit!' She moved a step closer to him. 'Please don't apologise about that - you were a real gentleman. It's just that, well...' She swallowed hard as she tried to say the right thing, so wanting him to understand the reason for her reticence, but she could not. Instead, she said, 'I've been teased mercilessly this morning, about last night.' She held her hand out to stop him from speaking. 'No, hear me out. I openly danced with you most of last evening and our little incident whilst crossing the river did not go unnoticed by all at the farm.'

'Oh, Sophie. I am sorry.'

She reached out to touch him. 'Don't be sorry. I had a lovely, happy time with you, so it's only to be expected that people will talk. It's human nature.' She gazed deeply into his eyes. 'I like you, Kit, I like you a lot and I've heard from many sources now that you like me too.' She smiled tenderly as his face softened. 'But, I can't...well...' She took a deep breath. '.... I'm not able ......' She squeezed her eyes shut for a moment. 'I had not expected to feel this way, ever, but I do feel there is something between us - I want you to know that, but I can't promise anything....... I'm sorry, I ...'

'Can I speak now?' he joked and she lowered her eyes. He gently lifted her chin to make her look at him. 'Yes, I do like you. I *love* you, Sophie. I always have and I always will. My heart was yours the day you came to Gweek, but you belonged to someone else. I vowed that no other woman would take the place in my heart that is yours and yours alone. I was prepared to spend a lifetime loving you from afar - that is still the case.' He reached for her hand and brought it to his lips. 'You have my heart, my protection and my enduring love, and *if* and when you feel ready, you will have all that a man of my position in life can give you.'

'Oh, Kit.' Overwhelmed, she clasped his hand in hers, as her eyes blurred. Never had she heard such heartfelt words spoken to her.

*

Sophie set off back to the farm, deep in thought. She pulled her shawl around her shoulders as though chilled, even though the day was warm. For someone who had just heard the most wonderful declaration of love, her face wore a sorrowful appearance. It was her conscience she was struggling with. Yes, her true affection for Kit had been building over the last few weeks – the letters to and fro, the sense of loss at him not being around, but a sob came to her throat and almost choked her. She stopped abruptly to regain her composure - her eyes darting from the village centre to down river and then her face crumpled yet again. *Oh, Kit!* More than anything else, she knew that he was the man for her, but she should *not* have given him hope. It was wrong of her, especially when she knew her awful secret might keep them apart forever.

Chapter 23

Lydia was overjoyed by the sacks of wool Kit had brought her – though despite Ellie rinsing it in the stream, it still stank to high heaven. Lydia didn't care. She immersed it in baths of soapy water, took off her skirt, petticoat and stockings and stamped on it until it was clean. Within hours, her washing lines were full of wool blowing in the wind. Once it was dry though, no one over the next few days got away from having to hold a skein of wool between their hands while Lydia rolled it into usable balls.

It was about a week after the midsummer picnic that Lydia asked Sophie in for a cup of tea, in exchange that she hold a skein for her to ball from the never-ending pile of wool. They chatted amiably about general things, and though Lydia waited for her to say anything about a shift in her relationship with Kit, she was dismayed when nothing was forthcoming.

After finishing their cuppa, Sophie set off home and Lydia took herself back to the dairy. She stood a while at the dairy doors watching until Sophie had reached home. She saw her stop at the bench where Kit was sitting, but the exchange between them was quick, and, she noted, without any romantic gestures. *What is wrong with that girl?*

'What are you frowning at, my beauty?' Eric said as he stepped into the dairy. 'If the wind changes your face will set like that.'

'Cheeky.' She kissed him on the cheek and his familiar smell of cow dung and milk filled her nostrils. 'It's Sophie and Kit. I thought after the picnic they would get together.'

Eric shook his head. 'Let them get on with it at their own pace. If it's going to happen it will. Now stop your match-making and hand me a drink of that milk, I'm fair parched.'

*

Sophie stopped when she found Kit on his outside bench

darning a hole in his sock. He looked up and grinned and she returned his smile. Since mid-summer they had fallen back into their easy relationship, both enjoying the fact of him being back working in Gweek. Sophie had noted that he'd made pans of his special watercress soup when she'd visited his kitchen, but he'd not asked her to join him again for supper. It was perhaps for the best.

'I wish I could knit as well as I can darn.' He joked. 'There is more darn than sock now.'

'I'm afraid I can't help you there. My forte is sewing. I never learned to knit. Ria knitted all the jumpers and scarves for us. I hate to give her credit for anything - but her knitting skills *were* second to none.'

'Well, I suppose everyone has to have at least one good quality,' he mused.

Sophie left him to his task, but when she saw him later, he was walking with a limp as though he had a stone in his shoe. She would ask Lydia to knit him some new socks.

*

A rather unexpected invitation came Sophie's way a couple of weeks later when she was called into the dairy after milking.

The room was dripping with muslin encased curds hanging from the hooks, and Lydia was leant over a vat of milk with her skimmer in her hand.

'Ah, Sophie, there you are. Here look, take that.' She pushed a brown package into her hands.

'What is it?'

'Four pair of socks for Kit. Hopefully that will stop him from limping.' She winked.

Sophie laughed. 'Goodness, I can't believe you've made them that quickly!'

'They take no making,' she said, leaning back to stretch the stiffness from her neck. 'Anyway, I wanted to ask - what are you doing on Sunday night?'

Sophie folded her arms. 'Very little, I should think.'

'Good, we're having a few people over for supper on

Sunday. Would you like to come?'

'You need someone to serve you mean?'

Lydia laughed heartily. 'No silly. I'm inviting you to supper.'

'Oh!' Sophie felt her face flush with excitement - she'd never been invited to supper before. 'Thank you - I'd love to come.'

'Well, it's nothing special mind, just a gathering of a few friends.' Lydia noted the look of consternation on Sophie's face. 'Now don't look so worried, you'll know some of them, well,' Lydia tipped her head knowing that Sophie had not had the chance to socialise much, 'If you don't know them, you'll know *of* them.'

'Will you need some help beforehand?'

'No, I'll have it all sorted, just turn up.'

'Thank you, I will,' she said brightly.

*

Gilbert Penvear had acquired the disposition of a caged tiger over the last few weeks, and the sight of Kit Trevellick making one of his twice weekly visits to the stream to collect watercress, made him even angrier. It was Monday today, if Gilbert's assumption was correct, he'd be along again on Thursday or Friday, though he knew not when or at what time. He tapped his fingernail on his teeth as he began to form a plan to rid himself of Trevellick once and for all.

Later that night, Gilbert slipped unnoticed out of Quay House. It wasn't a visit to feed his lust of Sophie, no - Trevellick had put paid to that. This task was hard, hot work, and his arms ached alarmingly, but it was something he had to do himself. When he finished his task, he rubbed his hands together. The first part of his plan had been put into action, now it was time for the second part.

*

The customs officers stood in the hall of Quay House the next morning while Gilbert told them what he knew.

'All right, Mr Penvear, just to get the facts straight,' one

173

of the customs men said, 'you say that you saw a small rowing boat come up the river at high tide last night and that it stopped by the bridge?'

Gilbert stood with his hands clasped behind his back. 'Correct.'

'And you believe that they left some contraband there for someone to pick up?'

'I do. There was a lot of shuffling noises going on and then the boat rowed away,' he lied.

One of the officers first glanced out of the window and then at his colleague before turning back to Gilbert, 'And, you saw all this from your house?' he asked sarcastically.

Gilbert's hackles rose at his tone. 'Don't be so ridiculous, man. Are you blind or something? Is it not plain that my house is at least thirty yards from the bridge?'

Suitably admonished, the customs officer shifted uneasily. 'I beg your pardon.'

Gilbert nodded. 'When I saw the boat row past my house I took a quiet stroll to the bridge, to see what underhand deeds were going on.' He sniffed the air. 'Someone has to keep an eye out for these excise dodgers,' he added without a hint of irony.

'Did you inspect the goods?'

'I did, the next morning. It appears to be a barrel of cognac.'

'Very well, Mr Penvear, we thank you for your vigilance. We'll take a look and have someone posted to watch. I should think they'll not leave it there long.'

Gilbert's lip curled. 'You may have to wait a few days I suspect.'

'I assure you - we'll patrol secretly until the contraband has been picked up.'

*

When Sophie stepped out of the Corn Mill clutching a stone of strong flour in her apron later that week, she noted that there were a couple of men wandering about who she knew not to be local. The day was lowering, so she quickened her step to stop her flour from getting wet. As she approached home, she could hear Kit cursing as he worked on the draft of a schooner moored at the quay.

'Having trouble?' she grinned as she shouted up to him.

Kit spun around. 'Sorry if you heard me cursing, but…' He hit the plank of wood he was working on in frustration. 'They have given me warped wood which I can't work with. I hate it when the wood yard tries to fob me off with tropical wood.'

'Tropical wood!' Sophie arched an eyebrow.

'Yes, it's bent like a banana,' he grinned.

She laughed at his joke. 'I've come to tell you, I'm making bread. Do you want some of it later?'

'I will, thank you, that's kind of you.' He hesitated for a moment and then asked, 'If you want, I'll make some more watercress soup to go with it.'

Sophie grinned. 'I was hoping you'd say that.'

'Then I'll go and collect some later. I think this job is going to take some time.'

'I'll see you for supper then,' she said running up the steps of the sail loft as great dollops of raindrops began to fall and Kit started cursing again.

*

The band of rain swept up the river, and after thoroughly drenching the village, moved away up country to leave ribbons of blue sky in its wake. Kit downed tools at five-thirty to make the soup for their supper. It was a rare treat for Sophie to instigate a meal together, so he was keen to make supper as delicious as possible.

*

Sophie put the fresh bread on the breadboard and began to set the table. Kit's soup was bubbling nicely on the range - all it needed was the addition of the main ingredients, which Kit had gone to collect. She glanced at the clock and frowned. He should have been back by now. She hoped he'd not slipped and fallen in the river. Once that thought had entered her head, she could not settle.

She threw a clean cloth over the bread, took the soup off the heat and pulled her shawl around her shoulders.

As she turned out of the boatyard, her mouth dropped. Kit was walking over the brow of the hill flanked by two customs officers - one of which was carrying a barrel.

'Kit!' Sophie ran towards them. 'What's happening?'

'Move aside, Madam,' one of the customs officers flanking Kit growled.

'Kit, tell me, what's happened?'

Kit winced in pain as the officer tightened his grip on him. 'Sophie, they think I've been smuggling cognac!'

'What! Now wait a minute. Stop, I say, stop!' She tried to halt their progress. 'This is ridiculous. Kit is no smuggler.' Her voice was a few octaves higher than normal.

A voice from behind them brought them all to a halt as Dr Eddy came out of his garden. 'Sophie, Kit, what's going on?'

'They've arrested Kit, Dr Eddy, for *smuggling,* would you believe!' Her eyes blurred at the injustice. 'He only went to collect some watercress to put in our soup! The pot is still warm on the stove,' she added weakly.

'What *is* the meaning of this?' Dr Eddy demanded as he stood in front of them all.

'As the woman here said, he's been caught handling contraband cognac.'

Dr Eddy looked at Kit who shook his head. 'As Sophie said, I was collecting watercress and they just jumped on me. I never touched the barrel! I didn't even know it was there!'

Dr Eddy narrowed his eyes. 'This is ludicrous. I've known Kit all his life - he hasn't a criminal bone in his body.'

'Dr Eddy, look!' Sophie grasped his arm and pointed to the barrel. 'This barrel belongs to Gilbert Penvear. I watched them load it on the cart a few weeks ago! If you look, it has a red cross on it!'

The customs officer flared his nostrils. 'A red cross could be anybody and more likely to be marked for smuggling,' he sneered.

'No, look!' She made the customs officer tip it so Penvear's name, although rubbed out, was still visible. 'Perhaps it's Penvear you need to speak to about illegal contraband.'

'That is a libellous allegation, Madam.'

Sophie shrugged. 'Nevertheless, you might want to check if the tax has been paid on this barrel, *I* suspect it hasn't.'

The customs officers glanced at each other and the grip on Kit's arm relaxed.

'I think you owe Mr Trevellick an apology, gentlemen?' Dr Eddy said firmly as Kit was pushed away.

'We'll look into this further. *Don't* leave the village,' the customs officer warned Kit.

'I'm hardly likely to do that, am I? I live here and my accommodation is attached to the Customs House!' Kit said rubbing his arms where they'd held him.

The trio watched as the barrel was carted away down the hill.

'Oh, Christ!' Kit rubbed his face anxiously. 'Thank you both, and thank god you recognised that barrel, Sophie, otherwise I would have been thrown into jail. It's quite obvious that Penvear had a hand in this. Jeremy Nancarrow gave me warning the other week that Penvear was on the war path against me.'

'Why?' Dr Eddy enquired. 'What have you done to Penvear?'

'I gave Sophie a room when he evicted her. He wanted to make her homeless so she'd be forced to live with him as his so-called housekeeper.'

'Did he now?' Dr Eddy twisted his mouth. There were very few people the good doctor disliked in the village, but Penvear was one of them. 'I'll speak to him, Kit.'

'Thank you, Dr Eddy, but I don't know what you'll be

able to do.' Kit said wearily.

'Oh, I have a little something up my sleeve.' *Penvear had a rather nasty gout condition, which he would refuse to treat unless this vendetta towards them was dropped.*

*

Kit sat quiet and shaken at the table while Sophie chopped some cabbage to put into the soup to replace the missing watercress. Once it was back on the stove bubbling away, she pulled up a chair and took his hands in hers.

The gesture was totally unexpected but not at all unwelcome. He looked up and gazed deep into Sophie's eyes.

'Are you all right?'

He nodded and squeezed her hands. 'Thanks to you.'

'I'm so sorry. I seem to have brought a lot of trouble to your door by residing here.'

'You haven't, Sophie, I can assure you of that. Having you as my neighbour is a joy I would not forgo.'

'It's a joy for me too.' She watched as the tension of the day fell from his face. 'Now, dinner will be ready soon. Do you have an appetite?'

'Yes, I think I do now,' he said feeling the great lump of anxiety that had settled in his throat disperse.

'Good, now I think this is the right time to give you something that I've made for you. I hope it will cheer you.' She shyly handed him the cushion embellished with a beautiful quilted seahorse.

Kit gasped. 'You've made this for me?' He ran his fingers over the intricate needlework. Sophie nodded. 'It's the most beautiful thing I've ever seen,' he breathed. 'I'm…I'm speechless. I don't believe I've ever been given such a beautiful present before. Thank you so much, Sophie.' He hugged the cushion to his chest and when he looked at her, he made her feel as though she was the only woman in the world.

'It was my pleasure to make it for you. Now, let's eat.'

As they settled down, they saw the two customs

officers flanking Ian Crocker the Custom Officer.

'Well, it seems Mr Crocker's tax and excise papers are not in order for Penvear's cognac,' Sophie said. 'With a bit of luck, Penvear will be arrested next.'

Kit turned a questioning eye on her.

She grinned widely. 'I'll tell you what I know about Penvear's contraband cognac after supper.'

Chapter 24

Sophie was busy doing the last knead of her bread. With floury hands she popped the loaf into a tin and took it down to the range.

'Oh, Kit!' she muttered when she saw the cushion she'd made for him, sitting proudly on the spare chair. She'd told him it had been made for his comfort not as an ornament, when he'd declared that it was, "Too nice to sit on."

Popping the bread in the oven, she wiped her hands down her apron, picked up the cushion and moved it back to his armchair before returning to her room to wipe down her table top. Twenty-five minutes later she went to check on her bread, but it needed another few minutes. As she was putting the loaf back into the range, she heard the front door open.

'Coo-ee, Kit darling. Surprise, surprise!'

Sophie spun around, shocked to find a beautiful red-headed woman standing before her. For a split second she didn't quite know how to respond to this interloper - who clearly knew Kit well.

'Oh!' The woman looked put out. 'And *you* are?'

Sophie placed her hands on her hips crossly. 'I might ask you the same question?'

'Georgina Blake - Georgie to my friends. Pleased to meet you, I'm sure.' She stepped further into the room without invitation. 'Your turn now?'

'Sophie Treloar,' she said, aware of the tremor in her voice.

'Oh, thank goodness for that!' Georgie fanned herself furiously. 'I thought for one awful moment, Kit had a little wife at home he'd failed to tell me about.'

Sophie felt she'd been knocked sideways. Struggling to gain some composure, she was aware this woman was watching her with amusement.

'No, I'm not his wife. I live above Kit, but we share the

range to cook on.'

Georgie pulled a face. 'Oh! How terribly inconvenient!'

Sophie eyed her suspiciously, wondering on what level of inconvenience she was referring to.

Georgie pulled off her gloves and threw them on the table before taking a long look around the room.

'How very bijou this place is.' She took a large intake of breath and settled her gaze back on Sophie. 'So, where is the darling man?'

'He's delivering a coffin.'

Georgie pursed her lips. 'Ugh! How positively dire! When will he be back?'

Sophie glanced at the clock. 'Very soon, I should think.'

'Good, then I'll wait.' She flaked down into Kit's chair and pulled the cushion Sophie had made for him from behind her. She cast a quick glance at it before placing it on the foot stool to put her feet on. 'Oh, that journey on the wagon – my goodness but I'm pooped.'

Outraged, Sophie stepped forward, pulled the cushion from under Georgie's feet and hugged it. 'This cushion is very special to Kit. It is not for resting dirty shoes on!'

Georgie threw her head back and laughed. 'Kit won't mind. He knows I like to make myself at home wherever I am.'

Disconcerted now - it was quite apparent that Kit knew this woman well. Against her better judgment she asked, 'May I get you some refreshment? Tea? Lemonade?'

Georgie tutted unconsciously before answering, 'No, don't let me keep you from whatever you were doing. In fact, you can leave me now if you wish. I am sure you have other chores to see to, upstairs.' She waved her off with a flick of the wrist. 'I promise I won't take any more liberties with the furnishings,' she teased.

Adamant that she had no intention of leaving this woman alone in Kit's front room, known to him or not, she pulled out one of the dining chairs, sat down and replied curtly, 'I can assure you I have nothing awaiting my attention *upstairs*. I'm quite happy to sit and wait for my bread to finish its bake.'

Georgie cast an unhurried look over Sophie's attire, but Sophie refused to feel disconcerted because she was wearing her honest work skirt and blouse. A long awkward silence ensued, before the words spilled out of Sophie's mouth - unable to stop them. 'How do you know Kit then?'

Georgie gave a wry smile. 'I met him at Bochym of course. He came to look around my studio there. I'm an artist, did I tell you? No, I don't think I did. Anyway, he came to visit and the rest, they say, is history.'

It took all of Sophie's resolve not to flinch. 'I see.' Sophie tried to drag a smile from the depths of somewhere. Her brain and heart were sending urgent messages to her eyes, but she knew she must not show this woman how distraught she felt.

'And you - what do *you* do, darling?'

Darling! Quite taken aback by her address, she answered proudly, 'I work on a dairy farm.'

Georgie screwed her nose up in distaste. 'Really?' she said as she reached into her handbag and brought out an ornate silver cigarette case. 'Tell me, who do you think was the first to see a cow, and think, "I wonder what will happen if I squeeze these dangly things and drink whatever comes out?" She grinned at her own joke, as she selected a cigarette to fit into her holder. 'Care to partake?' She offered the case up to Sophie.

'No, thank you, I don't smoke and I don't think Kit would want you to smoke in here.'

'Oh, darling, Kit won't mind a bit.'

'Well, I think he *will.*' Sophie answered adamantly. 'And I don't want cigarette smoke in here while I'm baking.'

Georgie sighed heavily, and then reluctantly took the cigarette out of its holder. Her eyes cooled as she looked beyond Sophie to the outside. 'So, is that the famous *Harvest Moon* moored out there I see?'

Without following her gaze, she said, 'It is, yes.'

'I thought so. Kit has told me *all* about it. I feel as though I know the boat intimately by the passionate way he speaks about sailing away into the sunset. Perhaps I'll go and take a look around it, you know, get the feel of it while I'm waiting.'

'I don't think he would wish anyone to go aboard her without him being there!'

Georgie regarded her curiously. 'For a neighbour, you appear to know a lot about what Kit would or wouldn't like.' Her lipstick mouth curled with a cold smile.

'Yes, I think I know Kit well.' *Or at least I thought I did.*

'Mmm, perhaps not as well as you thought, you obviously don't know how it is between us, do you?'

Sophie's heart was hammering with loathing for this woman, but she forced herself to keep the emotion from her face. Fortunately, a moment later she heard the familiar sound of Kit's cart as it rounded the bridge into the boatyard. She practically leapt out of her seat and moved to the range to check on her bread.

Kit stepped over the threshold. 'Hello, Sophie. I'm just going to take Willow to her field. Gosh, something smells good. I'm absolutely fam…. ished,' he finished the last part of the sentence almost inaudibly. 'Georgie! What on earth are *you* doing here?' His eyes swept from one woman to the next.

'Well, darling, if the mountain will not come to Muhammad, then Muhammad must go to the mountain.' She put her hands on his shoulders and kissed the air each side of Kit's head, glancing at Sophie as she did. 'But darling,' she looked wounded at the shock on his face, 'are you not pleased to see little old me?' She fluttered her eyelashes at him.

'I'm sorry, Georgie, but this is so unexpected. I …' Lost for words, he glanced towards Sophie who watched the scene silently by the range.

'Well, darling.' She walked her fingers up his shirt front.

'You know how much I like surprises.'

Kit took a step back and shot her a warning look. 'I see you've met Sophie,' he said, the words catching in his throat.

'Yes, I have, and charmed I am with her too.' She flicked a glance at Sophie. 'Naughty, naughty boy, you didn't tell me you had a female lodger.'

Sophie could smell the bread burning and swiftly yanked the range door open. She pulled out the loaf, which was slightly browner than she liked and put it to cool on the top of the range. Unable to stay a moment longer, she bowed her head and muttered, 'I'll leave it here to cool, Kit. You'll perhaps need some of it for tea.' She forced herself to look at Georgie. 'It was nice to meet you, Miss Blake.'

Georgie crinkled her eyes. 'Likewise, I'm sure.'

Kit started to follow Sophie, but she turned. 'No, don't see me out, Kit.' At this moment in time, she knew she could not speak to him rationally. She picked up her skirts and ran up the granite steps to the sanctuary of her quarters. As she closed and locked the door, she leant her hot forehead against the coolness of the glass in the door. Feeling both lightheaded and sickly, she almost shrank inside herself. The shock of seeing another woman so familiar with Kit, had wounded her deeply. *Hadn't Lydia warned her that Kit would look elsewhere?*

Oh, Kit! She pictured herself dancing with him at midsummer - the sound of him singing as he swung her around, the warmth of his smile and the comfort of his strong arms around her. Now look where her foolishness for not telling him the real reason she could not be with him had got her! She'd clearly lost him to another, and all the lovely times they'd shared were now spinning down a great dark vortex.

Slowly she moved to sit by the table, silently casting her eyes around the room, now adorned with homely items. Only half an hour ago she'd been happy.

The knock on her door when it came made her jump. 'Sophie! Sophie, are you still there?'

Sophie held her breath until his footsteps retreated down the steps. She waited and waited until the clock struck a quarter-past-four and she reluctantly made a move to get ready for milking. As she gathered her apron and cap, she heard Kit's door bang downstairs, followed by Georgie's tinkling laughter. She moved to the window and saw Georgie linking her arm with Kit's. Georgie was flourishing a lighted cigarette, and as she walked, she turned and glanced up at Sophie with an air of self-satisfaction.

Distraught but impelled to continue watching, Kit took Georgie by the hand, as he helped her up aboard the cart. She pretended to stumble and fell against him laughing. The cart moved off without a backward glance from Kit, and all that Sophie was aware of was a vast cavern of emptiness engulfing her.

*

On the other side of the riverbank, Stan was taking a quick break before the afternoon milking session. He was in a reflective mood. He'd been dismayed after the picnic seeing Sophie and Kit happy together, and his manner, to his shame, had been a little cold towards her since. He couldn't help it - he loved her, though he knew she did not love him. She'd taken the time to learn how to communicate with him, and though her hand gestures made him laugh sometimes, he was gratified that she had even bothered to try. He liked Kit as well. He actually owed his life to him - that fact alone made Stan feel ashamed at his poor behaviour towards them both. Kit had saved him from drowning nine years ago when he'd caught Stan's adversaries, Jowan Treloar and George Blewett, dangling him in the river by a rope tied to his feet. Stan never knew what repercussions Blewett and Treloar had faced. All he knew was that he was never bothered by either of them again.

He glanced over towards where Sophie lived. He was glad Jowan Treloar had drowned - at least it had set lovely Sophie free from his clutches. He never could understand how she had ever married such a man. But now Sophie had a taking for Kit and that was that. Suddenly his attention was on something else in the boatyard. He narrowed his eyes, as he watched a finely dressed woman with red hair walking arm in arm with Kit! As Kit helped the woman aboard his cart, it was obvious that she was enjoying his company. They rode out of the boatyard and Stan moved his attention to Sophie, who was stood quite still at the top of the steps watching them leave. He didn't like the look of this. He didn't want Kit to have Sophie, but he didn't want him to hurt her either. Something was amiss. He stood up, perhaps he would walk to meet her half way and escort her to work.

Chapter 25

Eric Williams released the cow he'd been milking and glanced, not for the first time that morning, at Sophie. Normally one to sing melodically while she milked, Sophie had been notably quiet for a couple of days now.

He stood up and picked up his pail of milk. 'Are you all right, maid?' he asked wiping his hands down his smock. 'You're not your usual perky self.'

It took a moment for Sophie to register that she was being spoken to, so lost in her sorrow was she. She lifted her head, releasing the cow's tail from where she had pinioned it. 'Sorry?'

Eric pushed his finger under his hat to satisfy an itch on his head. 'I don't believe I've heard you sing these last two days! What's amiss?'

'Oh, my throat is a little dry,' she said sorrowfully.

'Well, I hope you'll be all right for tonight's supper? Here, have a sip of this.' He held his pail up to Sophie and she dutifully took a sip of the warm milk. He noted as she lifted her eyes to meet his, that hers were bloodshot. 'Are you ailing something? I can get Lydia to make you a hot toddy, though it's strange to have caught a chill in this heat.'

Sophie pulled her lips into a tight smile and shook her head. 'I'm fine, Eric, truly I am.' She returned to the job in hand.

Eric waited a moment to see if the milk had lubricated her vocal cords, but still no melodic tune emerged. Eric glanced over at Lizzy, who just shrugged her shoulders. Everyone had noted Sophie's enduring melancholy.

Charlie stood up and took his pail of milk to Ely Symonds who was waiting by the doorway. 'The cows aren't yielding much today, Pa!'

'I know. Someone's upset and it's rubbing off onto the cows,' Eric answered a little louder than necessary. 'I've seen it happen before. A cow can sense your mood, you know. If we're happy, they're happy.'

Sophie's fingers paused on the teat.

Lizzy got up to empty her pail. 'It's strange stuff, milk. I've heard an old wives' tale that butter won't turn if one of the team is in love.'

Eric roared laughing. 'Well, thank god it's an old wives' tale, otherwise our dairy would be butter free, Lizzy, especially as you spend all your time swooning over our Charlie.' Lizzy giggled. 'Nope, someone is melancholy,' Eric said. 'So, buck your ideas up - whoever it is. I want full pails from now on.'

Sophie bit down on her lip and tried to clear her mind of sad thoughts, but all she could think of was Kit and Georgie walking arm in arm to his pony and cart. She'd seen neither hide nor hair of Kit since he'd set off with Georgina two evenings ago, and was mighty heart-sore to think his affections had transferred to another woman. Why, oh, why had she not told him the real reason she could not give herself to him? She almost had the day after the picnic - maybe he would have understood and still wanted her, but she'd been frightened to lose what relationship they did have. Resting her head against the cow, she sniffed back a tear. And now it was too late. She'd lost him completely and it served her right.

*

It was with great trepidation that Sophie dressed for supper at Eric and Lydia's. Although great friends with them, socialising with people not known to her was unnerving. She'd checked her appearance several times in the mirror to see if the new dress she had made herself was fitting for such an occasion. This dress was pale blue, high necked, long sleeved and pulled in to show off her tiny waist. She'd added a ruffle running down each side of the bodice that just added a special something to the garment. The colour suited the freshness of her complexion, now tanned slightly with outdoor work. Her hair flowed in gentle curls down her back, tied up from the sides and secured with a pale blue ribbon.

The outfit was accessorised with a satin bag she'd embellished with Italian quilting. After making the cushion for Kit to see if she still remembered the skill she'd been taught, she turned her hand to making something a little more refined. She was very pleased with how it turned out – and that she hadn't lost her touch. Brushing her hands nervously down her dress, she hoped that this evening would take her mind off Kit.

Her heart faltered as she descended the granite steps - Kit's cart was back. Unable to face seeing or speaking to him to learn what she did not want to hear, she quickened her pace, only slowing down when she rounded the bridge by the Forge. George Blewett the blacksmith was leant against his door smoking when she passed. He muttered something, no doubt derogatory, when he saw her and spat on the ground. Sophie shuddered disdainfully and quickened her pace again - their dislike for each other was mutual.

As she reached the path to the farm house, she heard footsteps running along the road – she turned and her breath caught in her throat when she saw it was Kit.

'Sophie,' he called out just as she knocked on the farm door. 'Sophie, I need to… oh, my goodness,' Kit whipped his hat off and beamed a smile, 'may I say how lovely you look this evening?'

Sophie felt her heart constrict at the sight of him. He too had scrubbed up well. He was dressed in a clean shirt and his dark curls were shining in the evening sun. It was then she realised that he too had been invited. Caught off guard now, she knew not what to do or say, but was saved when Lydia opened the door.

'Oh, lovely, there you both are.' Lydia grinned mischievously when she saw them together.

Sophie shot Lydia a disparaging look when she realised Lydia was trying to match make – a look which Lydia chose to ignore.

'Come in, come in. The others are here already. They're in the front parlour.' Lydia put her hand to Sophie's back and pushed her forward.

Although the evening was warm, the farmhouse was often ten degrees cooler, so a small fire was burning in the hearth.

'Hello, Kit, my friend.' Guy Blackthorn stood up from where he was playing with two small children. He shook Kit's hand and raised an eyebrow at him before turning to Sophie. 'And you're, if I remember correctly, Sophie Treloar.'

'I am yes.' Sophie blushed and cleared her throat. 'I'm sorry, but you seem to have the advantage over me.'

Kit stepped in to make the introductions. 'Sophie, this is Guy and Ellie Blackthorn - from Poldhu.'

'Oh! I see. I'm very pleased to meet you both.' Sophie's eyes fell on Ellie's swollen stomach, and then she quickly averted them. 'You're the thatcher then, I believe.'

'I am.' Guy smiled. 'Forgive me, but I understand that your husband, Jowan came to an untimely end?'

'He did yes,' she answered flatly.

Only out of respect, and not for any regard, he said, 'I'm sorry for your loss.'

Sophie's eyelids fluttered slightly - it took all her resolve not to answer that she wasn't. Instead, she just smiled and nodded.

'Oh, my, dear!' Ellie looked crestfallen. 'I'm so sorry for you.'

'It's fine. I'm fine,' Sophie said gently and then changed the subject. 'And who are these two?' She nodded to the children.

Ellie gave a smile that only a mother could. 'This is Agnes.' She pulled her into her arms and brushed the child's hair out of her face. 'Agnes is four, and this is Zack, he's three.' She pointed to the boy sitting quietly playing with a toy on the hearth rug.

'They're adorable.' Sophie bent down to Agnes's

height.

'Not always,' Ellie joked. 'So, are you and Kit walking out together?' Ellie asked innocently.

'No!' Sophie said more abruptly than she meant to. This evening was going to be *so* awkward.

'Oh!' Ellie bit her lip and laughed lightly. 'Do forgive me. It's just that you arrived together and look like a couple - don't they Guy?' She glanced at her husband. 'Perhaps they should be.' She laughed.

Guy glanced at Kit who had the ghost of a smile on his lips, a gesture that did not go unnoticed by Sophie. *Oh, how could he stand there so innocently enjoying her embarrassment?*

Guy apologised when he saw the consternation on Sophie's face. 'You'll have to forgive my, Ellie. She's an incurable romantic and an unstoppable matchmaker.'

'Yes, so is Lydia,' Sophie muttered.

'Pardon?' Guy asked.

Sophie shook her head - she felt as though she was dying inside.

Eric entered the front room with drinks in hand. 'Lydia says supper will be in half an hour.'

'Is there anything I can do?' Sophie asked, desperate to escape.

'No, you know Lydia - she's got everything under control. But she did ask if you could show Ellie up to Pa's old room so the little ones can be put to bed.'

'Of course, I will.'

'Thank you, Sophie,' Ellie said. 'You could help me to put these two to bed if you like?'

Sophie agreed instantly. 'I'd love to.'

As the two women settled the children in bed, Sophie watched as Ellie stood up and stretched her back out and rubbed her swollen tummy. Sophie's eyes fluttered briefly - the sight of any woman carrying a baby always cut deep into her own heart.

'When are you due?'

'Another three weeks! I fear I shall be the size of a

mountain by then.' She grinned. 'Were you blessed with children, Sophie?' Ellie asked, watching Agnes fall asleep with her thumb in her mouth.

'No - I miscarried four times.' She swallowed the lump which had formed in her throat.

'That's awful, I'm so sorry, Sophie.' Ellie gently laid her hand on her sleeve.

'Well, it's perhaps for the best that it did not happen. My husband would not have made a good father, of that I do know. He was a bad-tempered individual at the best of times. Although,' she sighed. 'a babe would have been something for me to love.'

'So, you didn't love your husband?'

'Perhaps I did once, when I first met him. He was a good-looking man, who was very attentive to me at first. He offered me a life away from gutting fish - I thought my ship had come in.' She grimaced. 'He was often away from home on fishing trips, and I was left to cope with his domineering mother, who would not let me see anyone or go anywhere. Life quickly turned very sour, especially when Jowan realised I could not hold onto a baby.'

'Gosh how terrible.' Ellie squeezed Sophie's hand sympathetically. 'Well, that's all in the past now, Sophie. It's time to look to the future. You never know, perhaps you'll marry again soon and your next husband will love you dearly, and there may be children in the future.'

'No! There will be no husband or children.' Sophie answered sadly.

Ellie frowned. 'Don't let a bad relationship put you off, Sophie. I felt like that once, but then Guy came into my life and everything changed. I mean, Kit seems like a nice man,' she said lightly.

'Kit *is* a very nice man, but he's only an acquaintance - a friend, nothing more,' her voice trailed.

Ellie nodded, she knew when to keep her counsel, but she had seen the way Kit had looked at Sophie – she knew it was more than just friendship he felt for her.

*

As the late afternoon sun set long shadows over the vast Bochym Estate, Georgina locked her workshop, stripped off her clothes, pinned her fiery red hair into a loose chignon and stepped into the tin bath. With a jug of cool water, she doused herself, running her hands sensually over her soft body. After patting herself dry she gently massaged glycerine and rosewater into her skin, shrugged on a negligee and poured herself a whisky. Settling down in her thick cushioned wicker chair by the window, she rested her feet on the windowsill and sat back, feeling very pleased with herself.

'Chin, chin, darling, Kit.' She raised her glass to the empty chair. Soon *he* would occupy it - of that she had no doubt. *Oh, it was all falling into place,* she mused, confident that her plans would come to fruition. I mean, why the hell would Kit want to continue making coffins for a living in that smelly port, when he could be here, making his lovely seahorse furniture with her? The trip to Gweek had been a gamble of course, but it had paid dividends, even though he'd brought her straight back – "to preserve her reputation" he'd said, but thankfully before he'd done that, he'd shown her his beautiful furniture. Once she'd seen it, the seed was planted in her mind to install him back here, under the Bochym Arts and Crafts Association umbrella. She was certain that once her ladyship saw his furniture, she would welcome him into the fold - she just needed to get him to bring a sample of it for her ladyship to see. She pouted her lips. There was of course an ulterior motive to get him here. From the first moment she'd laid eyes on Kit, her determination to make him her own was fierce and all consuming. There had been lots of men in her life, but the sight of Kit lit within her a fire that could not be extinguished. No one had made her feel like this before. For some reason though, Kit seemed to be a little reluctant to take the bait. She'd tried relentlessly to engage with him these last two days, but he just continued to apologise, stating that he was busy for his lordship, doing some joist alterations or something. She flung her head back, perhaps she had been a little over demonstrative with him, but she simply could not help it - he was *the one*.

She twisted her lips in annoyance. He'd been elusive when not working for his lordship as well, and therefore she hadn't had time to tell him her plans for him. She should have sought him out and left him in no doubt how ardently she loved him! It vexed her that he'd left before she had a chance to say goodbye. What could be so important in Gweek to not say goodbye to her? Perhaps she would make another visit to him, perhaps he enjoyed the chase! Nevertheless, she'd poured her heart out into a letter for him. Fortunately for her, Guy Blackthorn had dropped into the estate, en route to Gweek so she'd given it to him to deliver. She smiled knowing that it would have been delivered straight into his hand. Once he'd read her note, he would be left in no doubt about how passionately she was in love with him. The letter would open up so many possibilities of a new life that he would abandon his dingy little house and workshop, and his intrusive neighbour, to come here and live a blissful life in the lap of luxury.

Chapter 26

Sophie left Ellie to say a private goodnight to her children and headed back down the stairs to join the others. As she turned into the hall, she stopped short on hearing Guy and Kit talking.

'I hear you had a visit from Georgie, Kit!' Guy's voice was not without mirth.

'I did, yes! She came all this way by wagon, bold as brass, expecting to stay the night! I mean, what on earth was she thinking?'

'I know exactly what she was thinking, and so do you. If you give that girl an inch, she'll take a mile. What did you do?'

'I had to take her back to Bochym that evening. I couldn't let her stay, obviously. How do *you* know she came to see me anyway?'

'I called in at Bochym, en-route to here - in fact I think I just missed you. Georgie caught me just before I left, and told me about the visit. She also gave me this letter to give to you. I didn't want to give it to you while the others were here, just in case - you know.'

Sophie heard Kit sigh.

'It seems she's pining for you already.'

'Why, what did she say?'

'Well, when she handed me this letter for you, she said, and I quote, "give this to the darling man who is going to father my children." You are in *big* trouble, Kit. That woman is totally smitten with you, and when Georgie gets a bee in her bonnet about something, there is no holding her back.'

Quickly dropping back into the shadows of the hall, Sophie felt her throat constrict. Clasping her hands to her mouth to stifle a sob, she knew then that all her fears had come true.

The clock in the hall struck seven and the glorious smell of home cooking wafted through the farmhouse. In a blind panic, Sophie glanced around looking for an escape - she could not possibly sit down to supper with Kit after hearing this.

'Sophie? Are you all right there?' The sound of Ellie's voice made her jump, and simultaneously halted the conversation between Guy and Kit in the next room.

Sophie dragged a smile from somewhere and turned to greet Ellie. 'Yes, I was just about to join the others,' she said, reluctantly abandoning all thoughts of escape.

'Come on then.' Ellie fell into step with Sophie.

As they walked into the front room to join Kit and Guy, Sophie studiously averted her eyes from them, wishing the ground would open up and swallow her.

They must have seen her anguish, because Guy cleared his throat uncomfortably and stepped forward to kiss his wife. 'All settled?'

'Like bugs in a rug,' Ellie grinned. 'You both look really sheepish - what have you been up to?'

Guy laughed nervously and changed the subject. 'Here, Eric brought some drinks in for you.' He offered a glass to each of the women.

'No, thank you!' Sophie said stiffly. 'I'm just going to check if Lydia needs any help.'

As she rushed from the room, Kit thrust his own glass into Guy's hand and followed her.

'Sophie!' He touched her shoulder lightly. 'Wait a moment - I need to speak to you.'

She took a deep breath and reluctantly turned to face him. His guilty face betrayed that he was aware she'd heard every word of his conversation with Guy.

'I need to explain - about Georgie.'

He took a step nearer, but she halted him with her hand. 'No, Kit. I'd rather not hear any more about her.' She was aware that her face was betraying her sorrow.

His eyes, full of pain and honesty, burned with intensity. 'I know you heard what was being said in there, Sophie!'

'It's really none of my business.' She turned to leave, but he stepped in front of her.

'Of course, it's your business! What you witnessed the other day when she came, and what you've just heard is all nonsense. It's just part of a ridiculous notion that Georgie has dreamt up in her silly little head that there is something between us. That woman is *nothing* to me, *nothing!*' He grasped her by the arms and shook her gently to bring it home. 'You have to believe me. *You,* my love, are *everything* to me.'

Sophie's eyes blurred and she blinked away unwelcome tears.

'Sophie, my Sophie,' he said gently. 'Guy will vouch for what I've just told you. He knows the struggle I've had trying to keep that woman at bay. He warned me that she was a predator, and I swear I've never encouraged her, but still she persists. I love *you*, Sophie. I told you the other day, that I shall never want another.' He lifted her chin gently. 'I only want you.' He brushed his lips tenderly against hers. 'Just you,' he whispered.

A small cry escaped her throat as the kiss, albeit fleeting, made her shiver with delight, but before anything else could be said, the door from the kitchen opened.

'Supper is ready.' Lydia stopped when she saw them. 'Oh!' She raised her eyebrows gleefully.

Kit dropped his hands to his sides, while Sophie furiously wiped her tears away. When Guy and Ellie filed past them with curious looks, Lydia just waved them briskly through into her kitchen.

Alone again, Kit turned back to Sophie and gave her a smile that almost broke her heart. 'Dry your tears, my love - all will be well. Let's go and enjoy the lovely supper Lydia has made for us.'

*

To Sophie's delight, she found that Amelia Pascoe had joined them.

'Are you all right, Sophie, you look - a little distressed?'

Amelia whispered as they embraced warmly.

'I'm absolutely fine, Amelia. Just a sneezing fit made my eyes water,' she lied, averting her eyes from Kit.

'Come on, sit yourselves down. I've made a rabbit pie with potatoes and vegetables, and I've an Eve's pudding baking in the range. We'll have that with some custard or cream afterwards.'

'Or both!' Eric chuckled.

'It all sounds delicious, Lydia, thank you,' Amelia said, and there was a collective agreement as they tucked in.

The talk around the table was cheerful and lively which helped Sophie relax. Every time she looked at Kit he was smiling back - how wrong she had been to doubt him.

Amelia was clearly rejoicing in the fact that her sister and husband had finally vacated her house to settle into their rented cottage at Gunwalloe. 'I love her dearly,' she said. 'But it's nice to have my home to myself again. Having said that, I'll be going over there to help them clean and settle in soon.'

'Will you be gone long?' Lydia said, doling out seconds of the rabbit pie.

'A week or so, perhaps.'

'But what will all your expectant mothers do without you?'

'Fortunately, Lydia, there is no one about to birth imminently, except perhaps you, Ellie, by the look of you.' Amelia grinned.

Ellie laughed and patted her swollen tummy. 'No, I've three weeks to go.'

Amelia gave her a knowing look. 'Well, just remember I'll be at Gunwalloe should you need me.'

Lydia laughed. 'If Amelia thinks you'll be earlier, Ellie, I'd be prepared if I were you. She predicted our Charlie's birth almost to the day.'

'Ah, well, I've had a lot of practice.' Amelia said and then realised that all this talk of babies was probably a little difficult for Sophie, so she changed the subject. 'I hear you've been working at Bochym Manor, Kit?'

Kit seemed lost for a moment - his blue eyes gazing lovingly at Sophie. Ellie who was sat next to him had to nudge him.

'What, sorry?' He glanced at everyone grinning at him.

'You were in a dream there,' Amelia laughed. 'I asked about your work at Bochym.'

'Oh, yes!' He cleared his throat self-consciously. 'I've been restoring the boats for their small lake there. It's a magnificent place to work, though perhaps a little strange sometimes.'

'Oh!' Ellie grinned curiously. 'In what way?' Having lived on the Estate herself when she was little, she had a fairly good idea of what he was about to say.

Kit frowned. 'I don't know what it is, but I can feel something odd there. I can't put my finger on it, but there is something strange about the place. In fact, I can't walk past the front of the house without thinking I'm being watched - even when the family are from home!'

Ellie clasped her hands together. 'Well, it *is* haunted you know.'

Kit shook his head. 'I'm afraid I don't believe in ghosts.'

'I'm sure you're sceptical, most people are, but believe it or not, Bochym Manor has a few wandering around their vast corridors. I should know - I've seen enough of them there.'

Despite the heat of the evening, goose pimples covered Sophie's arms. 'Oh, please tell me you're joking, Ellie.'

'No! It's as true as I'm sat here. They are a friendly lot - although one caused a little bit of an upheaval a few years back,' she added nonchalantly.

Guy coughed and almost choked on his food. 'Hardly a *little* upheaval - it damn near got you killed!'

Sophie's mouth dropped. 'Why? What on earth happened?'

Ellie ignored Guy's warning look. 'Well, it's a long

story, but one of the ghosts, a maid called Pearl who came to an untimely end, came to me to ask for help - she was stuck here, and needed to go onto the next life.'

Intrigued and alarmed in equal measure. Sophie stopped eating and held her knife and fork aloft in anticipation.

'Pearl needed closure on what had happened to her – you know, justice. I had indirectly witnessed the incident when I was a child - although being so young I didn't really understand what I'd seen at the time, and in fact I'd forgotten all about it, until her spirit appeared before me and jogged my memory. Anyway, to cut a long story short, the perpetrator, who was still in employment at the manor, tried to stop me from telling the police what I knew!'

'Yes, by slitting her throat!' Guy said grimly.

Sophie's knife dropped, clattering onto her plate. She'd seen the mark, still visible on Ellie's neck. 'That's *dreadful!* Is it safe for you to be there, Kit?'

He nodded. Her concern delighted him.

'Don't worry, Sophie. It is quite safe now,' Ellie said cheerfully. 'The perpetrator was hanged for his crimes and all the other ghosts seem happy enough in situ. I could tell you such stories about them.'

'Oh, no, don't,' Sophie clutched her heart, 'I'll not sleep tonight.'

'Yes, Ellie, stop it now,' Guy scolded. 'I really don't want to be reminded of that time.'

Ellie laid her hand on his. 'All's well that ends well though.'

Guy raised his eyebrows.

'Well,' Kit said, 'I'm finished there now - though I had to do a little adjustment on a joist yesterday. It was a little too proud and it took a while to ease it properly into its position. I shouldn't think I will be going back though.' He glanced in Sophie's direction - her relief was palpable.

'I understand there is a thriving Arts and Craft group at the manor, Kit?' Lydia asked. 'Sophie was telling me about it when we went shopping the other day.'

Sophie's eyes flickered up at Kit making him hesitate before answering. 'There is, yes,' he said simply.

Guy took up the thread of the conversation, realising Kit's reluctance to speak of it, and explained to Lydia about the association. 'Ellie too sells her handmade lace through them, don't you, my love?'

'I do. Are you skilled in a craft, Sophie?' she enquired.

'Not really, I can Italian quilt - I suppose you can call that a craft.'

'Sophie is selling herself short there,' Lydia chipped in. 'She's a beautiful seamstress, she makes all my dresses and look at this,' she reached over for Sophie's quilted bag which was hung on the back of the chair and held it aloft, 'If this isn't a skilled craft, I don't know what is.'

'Oh!' Ellie's eyes widened. 'Do you mind if I take a closer look, Sophie?' She reached her slender fingers out.

'Be my guest.' Sophie felt a blush rise.

Ellie's eyes swept approvingly over the workmanship. 'I've seen cushions at Bochym that are quilted like this. Sarah says they're as old as the hills and she'd like some more, but can't find anyone who can do it now. I'll have to introduce you to the Countess. She'd be thrilled to meet you.'

An anxious flutter curled in Sophie's stomach at the thought of going to Bochym. 'Oh, I don't know. I wouldn't know what to say to her ladyship.'

'Don't worry.' Ellie laughed. 'Sarah is lovely. We've been friends for years now. She's no different to us you know? She just lives in a manor house - even the servants love her! I'll talk to her about you, if you don't mind.'

Sophie bit down on her lip. 'Well, all right then, Ellie. Thank you.'

*

After a nightcap, the evening came to a close, and all were in agreement that a good night had been had by all.

'It's been lovely meeting you, Sophie,' Ellie said, 'I

hope we meet again soon.'

'I've enjoyed meeting you both too. It's the first time I've ever been out for supper and the company has been lovely.'

'You should come over to Poldhu Cove and see us. It's only five miles away. Kit would bring you. Wouldn't you, Kit?'

'Anytime.' He beamed.

'I must say that would be nice. I haven't seen the sea since my late husband brought me home from Newlyn eight years ago. I miss it so much, but I don't want to put Kit to any trouble.'

Kit's eyes glistened. 'It will be no trouble, Sophie.'

'Why not come next Sunday afternoon. We close the tea room at two. The weather seems settled so hopefully you will see the cove at its best. Oh, do say you'll come, Sophie, Kit?' She appealed to them both expectantly.

'It sounds good to me,' Kit said.

Sophie looked to Eric for guidance.

'As long as you do the morning milk, you can take the rest of Sunday off.' He winked, happy that Sophie had cheered up at last.

Chapter 27

Sophie and Kit bade Amelia goodnight at the bridge and walked into the boatyard under a great vault of stars. They were both quiet – a little shy of each other and lost in their own thoughts about the past couple of days. At the bottom of the steps to the sail loft they stopped.

'I'm so sorry that I caused you any distress, Sophie.' Kit's hand caressed her face.

'And I'm sorry I doubted you.'

'May I kiss you goodnight?' he asked tentatively.

'Yes, please.' She felt a frisson in her body as he leant closer. Very gently he pushed a wisp of hair away from her face and his lips brushed hers. Soft and tender was his kiss, as she savoured the taste of brandy still on his lips. His body moved slightly into the contours of hers, it felt so good to be so close, but the proximity of their bodies caused the rustle of the envelope in his pocket. A curl of unease unwound in her stomach – he'd clearly taken Georgie's letter from Guy! She pulled away sharply and ran up the steps.

'Sophie?' Kit's voice pleaded as he stepped up to follow her.

She turned slowly and the moon, a quarter full, bathed his face in a mellow light. 'It's late, Kit, goodnight.' A flicker of confused disappointment washed over his face – but it couldn't even begin to match how she felt.

'Goodnight then, I'll see you tomorrow,' he called out feebly.

She closed the door on him and a chill crept into her heart. *Go, go and read Georgie's love letter and leave me be.*

*

Gilbert Penvear slumped in his deep cushioned leather chair in his library. Dressed in his silk smoking jacket and little else, the material stuck uncomfortably to his sweat-drenched skin as he waited for his heart rate to settle back into a steady beat.

The library smelt of newly polished leather and cigar smoke. A glass of brandy was warming in his hot palm. His appetite sated for now, he raised a silent toast to the mental image of Sophie.

Gilbert had had a difficult time of late and this had been the first opportunity he'd had to relax. On hearing that Ian Crocker, the Custom Officer at Gweek, had been arrested by the C&E officers following the discovery of several barrels of unaccounted brandy in his warehouse, Gilbert had been ready for the repercussions that would undoubtedly follow.

He'd been questioned by the C&E officers. Firstly, as to why the brandy barrel he had reported to them, bore his name on the bottom of it? It was a stupid oversight on his part, an error which he blamed on his manservant, Jeremy Nancarrow. His job had been to erase his name from the barrels as soon as he acquired them illegally from Ian Crocker – something he had clearly been negligent about. Secondly, he'd been questioned as to why the brandy barrel bearing his name was on the river bank and why he had claimed to see someone placing it there. Gilbert congratulated himself on his rehearsed answer to them - 'Is it not clear what has happened?' he'd said authoritatively. 'I ordered three barrels, but changed my mind and only wanted two, of which I might add, I paid my taxes on! It is quite clear to anyone that Ian Crocker, who, I believe has been arrested for dealing with contraband goods, found another outlet for the barrel I did not want. It was probably him who sailed up the river with it in the dead of night,' he added, confident that Crocker would not be able to refute his claims from his prison cell. When asked for receipts of the brandy to support his claim of paying taxes, Gilbert, who prided himself on his steady and regularly used forgery skills, produced the forged receipts bearing the tax paid on the brandy.

As he drew on his cigar, the anger returned at his manservant's incompetence. It had caused Gilbert's well laid plans to rid himself of Trevellick to backfire. It had also indirectly caused Ian Crocker to be arrested, which meant he was now without a reliable source of contraband. Nancarrow would be docked a month's wage as a consequence. The only silver lining to this cloud was that he could finally get some rent on Crocker's cottage, now that he no longer needed it - Crocker's young family could go to hell.

As his bed beckoned, he downed the last drop of brandy from his glass. He had no doubt the next barrel he would purchase, tax and all, would not taste quite as mellow.

Gilbert was restless in bed – a lifelong insomniac, he was lucky to snatch two maybe three hours a night. Tonight, it being high summer didn't help matters. The night was hot and there was little breeze blowing through the open window. Pushing the sheets from his legs, he got up, pulled on his breeches, buttoned up his shirt and shrugged on his jacket. A walk would settle him, and no one would see him if he was not properly dressed.

Studiously avoiding the boatyard area for chance of meeting Constable Treen, he took the path up mill lane, crossing the stile and followed the dry mud track to the fields beyond.

*

Sophie laid abed - her mind a whirl of mixed emotions. The room felt hot and stuffy and an overwhelming feeling of suffocation swept over her. At two-thirty she gave up and got dressed. She needed some fresh air to think.

Stepping out into the night air, she took a deep breath. At this time of night there would be no one else about, so she set off up Chapel Hill to sit on her favourite stile. With the moon lighting her way she climbed the gate into Farmer Ferris's field. The air was saturated with the sweet smell of cut grass. Cuckoo spit stained her skirt in the long meadow grass, untouched by the scythe at the edge of the field, and snails were in abundance - some crushing underfoot, making her grimace. Climbing the stile at the top of the field she sat down and sighed at the moonlit shimmering view of the river. The tide was advancing, swelling in size with every minute. Sounds could be heard from the wood yard. There was no rest when the tide was up. Hitching her shawl around her shoulders, she pulled her knees to her chest and encircled them with her arms – not a very ladylike stance she knew, but she enjoyed the freedom to do whatever she wanted. The coolness of the night air settled her mind a little. She needed this time to deal with the mixed emotions she was experiencing. She felt utterly drained, having spent the last two days in a wretched quandary. When Kit declared his love for her after the picnic, she knew she should have responded more positively, but her heart yearned for just a little more time to heal physically and psychologically. And then Georgie's appearance two days ago had changed everything. The thought of losing Kit to Georgie because of her reticence had been unbearable, until Kit's tender kisses and words of love, only a few hours ago, had righted everything that had gone off kilter. They had clearly been hollow words and sentiments to appease her though, because he'd kept the letter Georgie had sent!

She shuddered. The thought of him reading Georgie's words cut her to the very core, for it must contain a declaration of love for him – hadn't she overheard the conversation between Guy and Kit? Georgie had told Guy to, "Give this to the darling man who is going to father my children!"

She dropped her head in her hands. She could not trust a man who kept secrets, and perhaps it was for the best - she could never have given Kit the gift of fatherhood.

*

As Gilbert skirted the top edge of the high meadow, the moonlit views of Gweek gave him no joy - he was just walking the frustration out of his limbs. Every single waking moment, Sophie dominated his thoughts. The image of her lithe body seared through his veins with such intensity - she was *his* prize, *his,* and it angered him to think that she had slipped his net. He was no longer offering a respectable position to her – the fact that the wench had moved in with Trevellick proved her to be loose in morals. No, his time would come, everyone would become complacent in looking out for her and she would step, quite unexpectedly, right into his trap. The thought excited him and he stopped walking for a moment to savour the feeling - it was then he saw her - sitting atop of the stile! He was almost upon her - barely thirty feet away from where he stood. There was no doubt it was her, by the way the moonlight illuminated her hair. He exhaled slowly as he rubbed his fingers together expectantly. Disbelief that his chance to own her had presented itself preceded the lust searing in his veins. *Think, think quick Gilbert how am I going to do this? Grab her from behind, yes from behind is best.* He knew he must keep her quiet - her shawl would do the trick. He'd flip it over her head so she'd never know who her attacker had been. He rubbed himself, unable to contain his excitement. *I'll take her like the whore that she is.*

*

A rustle in the hedgerow made Sophie look up. A wily fox trotted out in front of her. It stopped short, sniffed the air and scarpered to the middle of the field. Sophie remembered an old omen – 'To see one fox alone is a lucky symbol.' She sighed, little hope of any luck! The fox stopped and barked, sending a cold shiver down her spine - a fox barking was a warning of danger. Maybe it was time she headed down the meadow to her bed, but before she could move off the stile, a movement nearby made the hairs on the nape of her neck rise.

*

Kit had sat quietly at his open window looking out onto the riverbank, cursing that the letter in his pocket had so spoilt their tender goodnight kiss and brought their lovely evening to an abrupt end. Even when Georgie was safely ensconced back at Bochym, that woman still managed to cause trouble. He'd forgotten he had the damn thing. Guy had thrust the letter onto him realising that Sophie was within ear shot of their conversation, and he in turn had stuffed it into his pocket, promptly forgetting about it. Kit lifted his eyes upwards when he heard Sophie moving about – her footsteps sounded agitated. What would she be thinking – that he'd kept the letter to read in private? He hoped not! He should burn the damn thing, but he had a better idea which would make things right in the morning once and for all. With that decision, his mind settled as he thought back to what had happened immediately prior to the supper. The hollow look in Sophie's eyes when she believed that Georgie had taken his affection from her, confirmed that she was finally ready to fully accept him into her life. And then that kiss - their first kiss! He closed his eyes remembering how soft and yielding her lovely lips had been on his. He'd waited years for that moment. He closed his eyes - that would be the first of so many kisses to come. His heart sang with joy as he stripped off and climbed into bed.

Footsteps upstairs and a door closing woke him at two-thirty. Alert now he sat up on hearing Sophie's shoes pattering down the steps – *was she coming to him?* He jumped from the bed and dragged his shirt on to cover his nakedness, but she did not come to his door. Struggling to drag his breeches on, he pushed his bare feet into his boots and was out of the door before he'd buttoned up his shirt. Where on earth was she going in the dead of night? It wasn't safe for a woman to be abroad alone. At the crossroads he looked up towards Chapel Hill and then towards the Corn Mill, but he could not see her. Choosing the former road, he quickened his pace.

*

The attack happened so suddenly - Sophie had neither time nor voice to call out. Her head was covered with her own shawl and was pulled tight against her throat and she was dragged backwards off the stile. A glancing blow from off the stone steps stunned her for an instant, but hands grabbed her and she was thrown forward onto the ground and pinned down into the cowpats by an arm across her shoulders. Panic ensued. Realising what was about to happen, she struggled and kicked in vain, but her attacker's hands were already working their way up her skirt. Every fibre of her body screamed in alarm as fingernails scratched their way down her flesh as her underclothes were torn away. Exposed to the air, her skin crawled in disgust as his hand probed where they should not. Animal grunts rang in her ear accompanied by the weight of a knee pushing her legs apart. The supper she had so enjoyed earlier came back in her throat. Suffocating in her own vomit, she struggled and managed to unseat her attacker from where he straddled her, but her face was pushed into the ground until she believed she would die of asphyxiation. 'You bitch, bitch, bitch, bitch!' She heard her assailant's voice, low and filled with the bitterest contempt as she felt his naked skin on hers. Great sobs of anguish shuddered through her body as he fought to keep her legs apart and then she heard it - a voice in the distance shouting, 'Sophie, Sophie where are you?' Her assailant too must have heard, for he stopped his assault, thumped her hard in the back rendering her too winded to scream, before scrambling away into the night.

*

When Kit reached the field, he'd seen Sophie's shape sitting on the stile, but now he got there, she'd vanished. He climbed to the top, stopped and swayed while he caught his breath and then he saw her and his blood ran cold - she was prostrate on the ground, her clothes askew and her flesh exposed. He jumped down and circled her in disbelief and then fell to his knees. As soon as he touched her, she squealed in panic and began to crawl away through the cow dung.

'Sophie, it's me Kit. It's all right, my love, you're safe, I'm here,' his voice trailed to nothing as he gathered her trembling body into his arms to cradle her.

'Oh, Kit, thank god!' Her broken-hearted sobs brought angry tears to his eyes as she clung to him as though her life depended on it.

'Who did this to you?' His eyes scanned the darkness around him.

'I don't know,' she cried. 'I don't know.'

'Oh, my love.' He rocked back and forth. Hardly daring to know the truth he asked, 'How badly hurt are you?'

She shook her head and sobbed. 'Please, just take me home, Kit - take me home.'

Supporting her trembling body, they walked slowly down the field to home. She whimpered like an injured kitten and the sound almost choked him as terrible thoughts whirled around in his mind. *Who could have done this to her? And what exactly had he done?*

In his room, he sat her down carefully before putting several pans and kettles of water to boil.

'My love?' He curled his fingers around her filthy hands as he knelt before her. 'Are you, hurt? Do I need to get you a doctor?'

'No!' Her eyes widened. 'I don't want anyone to know.'

'But if you're hurt, if he…' The words caught in his throat.

'No!' She lifted her tragic face to him. 'It's all right. You came in time.' Her face crumpled as tears streamed down her vomit-streaked face. She dropped her head in her hands as great violent sobs wracked her body. 'Thank god you came in time to stop him.'

Kit sent up a private prayer of thanks, as he pulled his handkerchief out of his pocket and pushed it into her hands. 'I'm going to get the bath, Sophie. We need to get you cleaned up.'

When he returned with the tin bath, Sophie had undressed and was stood in her shredded underclothes, shivering despite the heat of the night. Laying a towel in the bath, he quickly filled it with lukewarm water and then taking her gently by the hand helped her step in. 'There are more towels there. I'll leave you to bathe. Call if you need me.'

'Thank you,' she sobbed pitifully as she sank down submerging herself fully in the water.

Kit waited a moment, wondering if she was going to drown herself, but when she emerged with a sob, he left her to her misery and took himself off to sit outside for half-an-hour. He could hear her crying and it broke his heart. Eventually silence ensued and he ventured back in. He found her ruined underclothes still in the bath water, and Sophie wrapped in the towel fast asleep on his bed.

*

At Quay House, Gilbert shed his soiled clothes which reeked of cow muck. Fastidious as ever, he washed himself thoroughly and grabbed his pen knife to scrape the blood and skin from under his fingernails. His breathing had slowed after the initial burst of energy it had taken for him to run from the scene. Damn, Trevellick for his meddling – he'd stopped him from very nearly claiming his prize. He shivered with pleasure remembering the soft skin on the insides of Sophie's thighs - like silk on his manhood. Just a few more minutes and the pleasure would have been all his and then, well, then he would have killed her! Strangling was always the best policy for women who threw his attentions back in his face.

'I'm not done with you yet, Sophie Treloar,' he said, throwing his wet towel onto the pile of clothes. 'I *will* have you.'

Chapter 28

In the cold light of dawn, Kit eased himself from the chair he'd sat in vigil over Sophie and stretched his stiff limbs.

By the soft whimpers and cries of distress, Sophie's dreams must have been punctuated with the horrors of what had happened. Several times he'd moved to her side and gently soothed her back to sleep with soft words of love.

Being as quiet as possible, he fished her underclothes out of the bath water and put them in the sink. They were her private things, so he'd leave them for her to do as she wished when she felt a little better - though he suspected they would be burned. The bath he would leave for now, fearing the noise of moving it would wake her.

With his spare key he let himself into Sophie's room to source some clean clothes for her. He'd not been in this room since the days she moved in, and marvelled how homely she'd made it. He felt awkward searching through her personal things, but she could not be seen leaving his accommodation in disarray.

Placing the assortment of clothes he'd collected on the bed near her feet, he glanced at the clock. It was time to go and see Eric at the farm.

The mist from the night still lay entwined within the branches of the trees that overhung the river. Kit stood at the gate while Eric and Stan brought the cows down the field. Stan was the first to pass him. Kit nodded a greeting, but Stan returned a curt nod. As the herd lumbered slowly past, heavy with milk, Eric grinned at him.

'Kit! What brings you here so bright and early? Have you walked Sophie to work?'

'It's about Sophie that I've come. She's really quite unwell this morning.'

'Oh! Eric pushed his finger up into his hat to scratch his head. 'To be fair she's been a little out of sorts for a couple of days, but seemed to rally a little last night –

though I admit her eyes looked quite bloodshot. Tell her
to rest, we'll manage fine.'

*

At Quay House, Jeremy Nancarrow picked up the
discarded clothes from his master's dressing room that
morning, appalled at the filthy state of them. He was used
to cleaning Penvear's disgusting habits out of his clothes,
but this, he screwed his nose in distaste, what had the dirty
little man been up to now?

*

Back home, Kit put a kettle on to boil – he tried to be
quiet but the noise brought Sophie to wakefulness. He
brought her a drink of water and sat on the bed as she
rubbed her swollen eyes with her fists. She looked
tragically beautiful with her hair spread against his pillow.

'Hello.' He smiled.

'Oh, Kit.' Her eyes filled with more tears.

'Shhh,' he whispered and with the corner of his sheet
he gently dabbed her tears away. 'You said you hadn't been
last night, but I ask again now, did he hurt you?'

Her lip quivered. 'I believe I have scratches down the
back of my legs, but,.oh, god, Kit, if you hadn't come
when you did…..'

'I know, my love. I just thank the lord that I heard you
leave.' With a feather like touch, he brushed the back of
his fingers down her cheek. 'Have you any idea who it
was? There was no one there when I reached you.'

'No! It happened so quickly. I heard something behind
me and the next I knew I felt something tighten around
my neck as I was pulled backwards. It was awful.' She
shivered. 'Just, awful! Jowan was often rough with me -
violently so sometimes, but that, that was the most
terrifying thing ever.'

Kit's lip curled with disdain at the mention of Jowan.
Was it any wonder Sophie was wary of men. 'The attacker
last night, did he speak at all?'

She nodded, her lips moved trying to form the words

and then she shuddered. 'He kept saying "bitch" over and over,' she sobbed. 'But I didn't recognise the voice.'

'My poor love.' Kit lifted her hand and kissed it tenderly, as he gazed deep into her eyes.

'Hold me, Kit will you? I need to be held.'

In a heartbeat he'd gathered her into his arms, aware of his hands resting on her naked back, but heartened that she did not flinch at being touched so intimately. He held her for what felt like an age, gently kissing her hair and murmuring sweet nothings, until she suddenly gasped and pulled sharply back.

'What is it?' he said in alarm.

'Look at the time. I should be at work!' She gathered the sheets up to hide her modesty.

'Sophie, you can't possibly work today. I've been to see Eric.'

Wide-eyed she took a sharp intake of breath. 'You didn't tell him, did you?'

'No, don't worry. He thinks you're just under the weather that's all.'

Flaking back into the pillow, she said, 'Thank god. I don't want anyone to know - I feel so ashamed.'

'Sophie, *you* have *nothing* to be ashamed of, but I do think we should report this.'

'No! Kit, please. I'll be questioned about why I was out so late.'

'Well to be honest, it's puzzling me too.'

'Oh, no,' she covered her eyes with the palms of her hands, 'I feel so stupid now telling you why I was there.'

'Look, let me make us some tea and then *if* you feel up to it, you can tell me. You're very welcome to rest there for the rest of the day, but if you feel you want to get up, I've brought you some clean clothes. Just pull the curtains across while you dress.'

*

Though her limbs ached alarmingly from the struggle, Sophie dressed quickly in the strange array of clothes he'd brought, flinching as her drawers touched her tender scratched skin. He'd brought her a dress but no chemise or petticoat, but she'd forgive him that. A woman's underclothes consisted of many garments layered over each other and were probably a puzzling mystery to men as to how they were worn.

'Would you like some bread and jam with the tea?' Kit called out.

Placing her hand on her stomach, which was still upset, she said, 'Perhaps I'll try a bite.' Her most immediate need before she broke her fast was to relieve herself. As much as her relationship with Kit had progressed, she was not yet prepared to pee in earshot of him. She pulled the curtain open and smiled weakly. 'I just need to run up to my place for a moment.' She saw his face fall and smiled. 'I'll be back within five minutes - I promise.'

Back in her room she splashed cold water on her face and pulled a brush though the tangle of curls then quickly re-dressed properly and arrived back in Kit's room as he was making the bed. 'I fear I have ruined your feather pillow with my wet hair. I have a spare one if you need it. If you leave the bed, I'll strip it and wash everything later.'

He gathered the sheets up protectively as though he wanted to preserve the sheets she'd slept on. 'It'll be fine Sophie - I'll deal with it.'

*

After they'd shared a simple breakfast together, Sophie folded her hands on her lap and said, 'I should never have gone out into the night. It was a stupid thing to do I know!'

Kit moistened his lips, not really knowing how to ask the next question. 'Did you just feel like a walk?'

'No! Yes! Oh, Kit! I just couldn't settle.'

He curled his hand over hers. 'Was it because I kissed you? You know I would never rush you to do anything more.'

'No!' She gently touched his unshaven face. 'It was not

215

because of the kiss.'

'Then *why*, my love? It's not safe for a woman to be out alone at night. There are vagrants and travellers about working the land and living free.'

'I know, I didn't think of the consequences. I always think I can sort things out better outdoors,' her voice trailed. 'I needed to think about what to do about Georgie you see.'

'Do?' He sat back aghast.

'That letter she sent you, it was in your pocket when we kissed. I….it,' she took a deep emotional breath, 'she obviously cares for you to want to have children with you. I kept thinking of you reading her letter after you left me.'

Damn that bloody letter. 'But Sophie, I…'

'I know what you said to me last night, but when I knew you'd kept it….'

He grabbed both her hands and kissed them. 'Christ, I'll never forgive myself that you were attacked over that bloody letter.' He pulled the unopened envelope from his pocket and handed it to her. 'I wasn't going to open it. Whatever misguided words of love it may contain, they mean nothing to me. *She* means nothing to me. I want *you* to open it.'

She felt her breath catch and then she pushed the unopened letter back towards him. 'No, it's a private letter to you.'

He pushed it back. 'I want no secrets between us. Whatever she's put in this letter I want *you* to read. I want you to open it to show you that I have nothing to hide.'

'Kit, I believe you. This is really not necessary.'

'I think it is!' he said seriously. 'Nothing has happened between Georgie and I. Whatever she's written in this letter will, I am sure, be a fantasised view of our relationship.'

Sophie took the letter gratefully. 'We'll read it together, then.'

Kit, darling,

You have been like a breath of fresh air in my life, and I know now that my world without you would be intolerable. I know we have only known each other for a short while, but my attraction to you was instant and passionate. I believe with all my heart that you must feel the same, even though you tease me by your neutrality – you naughty boy.

I have big, big plans for you - plans that will shoot you into the stratosphere regarding selling your fabulous furniture.

I am going to arrange a meeting with the Countess de Bochym so that you can work here with me, where you will have opportunities beyond your wildest dreams to become the master carpenter you deserve to be.

Now I don't want you to feel uncomfortable about this, I know you are very reserved, but it is time someone took you in hand to show you what a wonderful team, in work and in play we can be. You are simply too divine to be a bachelor all your life.

Drop everything, my darling, bring that little stool you've made and meet me at Bochym on Wednesday the 17th at eleven. We can start to plan the rest of our lives together and oh, what a life that will be.

Until then my love, Au revoir. À bientôt.

Georgie x

They both stared open-mouthed at each other.

'The woman is mad,' Kit said, screwing the letter into a tight ball.

'Madly in love by the sounds of it!'

Kit stood up and paced the room with indignation. He raked his fingers through his hair. 'What is she thinking? I've never given that woman an ounce of encouragement, and here she is, bold as brass, plotting my life out for me. And that line, *"even though you tease me by your neutrality,"* I was bloody ignoring her. She's such a flirt, Sophie. I've never come across anyone like her. I honestly didn't know how to deal with her. I thought if I just paid no heed to her suggestions then she would just give up. Even when I took her back home the other night, she did nothing but fawn all over me. Poor old Willow had never been trotted so fast - I was so eager to get her back to Bochym. It was only the fact that I encountered his lordship that I felt obliged to stay over to fix the sticking joists. I'll tell you for sure, I kept my door securely locked while I was there!'

Sophie allowed a smile to creep on her lips.

'It's nothing to laugh about,' Kit said frowning.

'Well, I can see the attraction she has for you, but…' She stood up and slipped her hand into his. 'I do believe you belong to me, so she can't have you.'

Kit's eyes glistened. 'So, you *do* love me?'

She brushed her lips on his, and whispered, 'With all my heart.'

Very tentatively his arms encircled her. Weightless and giddy with desire he kissed her passionately. When they parted breathlessly, they stood gazing at each other in wonder. 'Goodness, Sophie. Is this really happening?'

She laced her fingers with his. 'I rather think it is,' she said softly.

He cupped her face with his hands and kissed every part of her face, but when he pulled away, he saw her faltering a little. 'Sorry, I got a little carried away there.'

'No don't apologise. You make me very happy, it's just…'

Kit frowned feeling his elation ebb. 'It's just what?'

'It's just….'

He watched as she flushed up to the roots of her hair. 'Sophie, the suspense is killing me,' he tried to joke, but could see she was struggling to say something. *Oh, please don't change your mind now.*

She lowered her head and spoke inaudibly.

He lifted her chin gently. 'I can't hear what you're saying, my love.'

'I'm diseased,' she blurted out. 'Down there, I'm diseased.'

Kit felt his world still. 'But, I thought he didn't - I thought I got there in time.'

'I'm not talking about last night, Kit. I'm talking about

the disease Jowan gave me!' She could barely look at him for embarrassment. 'Every time he came home from his fishing trips, I ended up with yet another filthy infection - down there. I think that perhaps that was why I kept miscarrying.'

Kit felt his mouth go dry. He rubbed his hands over his chin stubble.

'You see, we can, we can never be intimate and I'll never have your children,' she whispered. 'It's why I have been so reluctant and now I feel awful for giving you hope when really there is none.'

He picked up her hands and asked softly, 'Are you in pain?'

'No, no pain. It burned for a long time, but not now.'

He felt his heart would break for her. 'Sophie, my Sophie, I'm so sorry for you.' He brought her hands to his lips. 'But this changes nothing. I love you and I need you in my life always. I want to go to sleep looking at your face and to wake up every morning doing the same. I will cherish you until the day I die, and if we can only kiss and hold each other, well, my love, it is more than I ever hoped for.'

Chapter 29

Sophie retired early that night, dizzy with the myriad of emotions coursing through her mind. It was still early as she pulled the covers over her shoulders, even the birds hadn't settled for the evening, but the events of the day had taken their toll – she was exhausted.

Kit had been her constant until this moment, offering morsels of food to tempt her to eat, though she had no stomach to do so, and being ready with an embrace when the horrors of the attack made her tremble like a leaf. There was no doubt, Kit was a man like no other. Instead of being devastated at the consequences of a life of celibacy, when she'd revealed her problem, his first thought was to ask if she was in pain. His thoughtfulness almost broke her, but most of all his enduring love was the impulse she needed to move forward from this day.

Despite Kit's protests, she was determined to be up early to go to work. It wouldn't do to hide away from what had happened. The sooner she could get things back to normal, then the sooner her life could get back on an even keel. Unfortunately, despite her exhaustion, sleep proved to be seriously problematic. No sooner had she fallen asleep, she woke as if dragged from the depths of a black void. Sitting up, she clutched her fist to her chest in panic as her heart raced and her breath laboured. Her eyelashes were wet and she was soaked in perspiration as she struggled to light her candle to ward away the terrors engulfing her. For a long time. she let her eyes settle on the comfort of familiar things in her room, until eventually her panic subsided and her eyelids drooped. Tentatively she lay back on her pillow, but within ten minutes she was sat up again clutching her heart. Again and again, the same pattern occurred, until she feared she would die of heart failure. In the small hours she lit a fire to brew some tea - too frightened to try and sleep again.

*

Sleep had evaded Kit too. He could hear Sophie walking about in the middle of the night, he hated that she was so unsettled. He got up with the lark and waited to beckon her into his house just as she was setting off for work.

Shocked to see the dark circles under her eyes, he kissed her tenderly, his hand stroking her hair. 'Could you not sleep, my love? I heard you moving about – I wanted to come to you.'

Sophie sighed with fatigue and rested her head on his chest as she breathed in the familiar smell of wood and linseed oil on his shirt. 'I'm so sorry if I disturbed you. I've had a terrible night – such dreadful terrors plagued me - I've never known the like.'

'Please let me tell Eric you're not well enough to work. You need more time.' But he could see she had real determination in her eyes.

'Honestly, I'll be fine once I've had a walk in the fresh air. I need to go to work for my own self-preservation. I need to do everything that I normally do. I will not let what happened define me!'

'Does that include your afternoon walk?' he asked tentatively.

'Even that, yes!' She was consciously aware of the slight tremor in her voice. 'I don't want to feel restricted again.'

He held her close as though his life depended on it. 'Believe me that would be the last thing I want for you too - I just want you to stay safe! Promise me you'll take your afternoon walk on the Williams's land.'

She teased her fingers through his dark glossy hair, smiling when she made it stand on end. 'I promise, Kit. I promise.'

*

Outside, the sky was a sparkling blue which dazzled Sophie when she looked up at it. She took a deep breath and walked with an air of confidence, though her heart thumped with anxiety. When she arrived at the milking parlour, Eric shot her a dubious look.

'It's good to have you back, Sophie, but you don't look yourself. In fact, you look quite peaky.'

'I'll be fine Eric. I'm a little tired that's all.'

By the time she'd tethered her fourth cow, the warmth of the parlour and tiredness took its toll. Her eyes pricking with sleep, she began to feel faint and lightheaded. It was only when her fingers loosened their grip on the teat, making her cow moo loudly, did she realise she'd fallen asleep.

Eric was up and at her side before she had a chance to grasp the teat again. 'Everything all right there?'

'Yes, sorry, I just lost my grip,' she lied.

Eric narrowed his eyes unconvinced.

'I'm fine, honestly.' When he returned to his cow, she settled her head into her cow's side. She was not fine, not fine at all. Sleep was what she needed, but she was fearful that the night terrors would be waiting again for her when she did.

*

Stan too had noticed Sophie's malaise and it worried him - to be truthful his emotions were all over the place. He loved Sophie, but after the midsummer picnic he knew when he'd seen her dance with Kit where her heart was destined. He felt angry - angry with Kit for being handsome, but mostly with himself - for looking and sounding different. With his wild orange hair and lack of speech, he knew he was no match for Kit. He'd felt desolate since that midsummer, until he'd seen Kit with that red-haired woman getting into his cart the other day. It was clear to him that Sophie's melancholy was down to Kit's behaviour, and he felt he must do something.

As always, he and Sophie fed the pigs before breakfast. The pails of whey were no heavier than normal, but when he saw Sophie struggling with hers, he offered to take the bucket from her. She accepted his help gratefully.

As he tipped the whey into the troughs, he could feel his heart thumping in his chest - it was now or never. He tugged on Sophie's sleeve, and when she turned wearily towards him, he signed. 'I want you to know something.'

'What?' She smiled warmly.

He held his palm up and whilst holding his middle and third finger down. 'I love you,' he mouthed

Shocked she pushed his hand away. 'No!'

'I do!' he signed and stamped his foot.

When she realised he was in earnest, she quickly signed, 'Please, don't.'

Distraught to see her eyes fill with frustrated tears, he watched desolately as she picked up the empty pail and rushed away. It was then he saw that Dora had witnessed it all. She looked as crestfallen as he felt.

*

Lydia glanced curiously at everyone as they assembled around the breakfast table. Stan, Dora and Sophie looked as though they wanted to be anywhere but here.

'All right, Eric.' Lydia thumped her fists into her sides. 'What have you done to upset this lot?'

Eric, just about to take a mouthful of bacon, looked up in amazement. 'Eh?'

'This lot, look at them. They look as though they've been looking forward to a party only to find there was no food or drink when they got there!'

Eric looked around the table at the sheepish faces and shrugged.

'Don't look at us we're fine, aren't we.' Charlie nudged Lizzy who giggled and snuggled closer to him.

'Well, something is amiss!' Lydia spooned some scrambled egg onto her toast crossly.

When they all cleared their plates and began to leave, Lydia said, 'Well, thank you all for the riveting conversation around my table. I'll just say this now, if anyone is in a miserable mood tomorrow, they can go and find somewhere else to eat breakfast!'

Dora lowered her head and ran outside crying, with Stan in hasty pursuit.

'Sophie,' Lydia said sternly. 'Wait a moment I need to speak to you.' She waited until everyone had gone. 'Right, what's happened?'

'Nothing,' Sophie said wringing her hands.

'I said, *what's* happened?'

Sitting down heavily on the chair, Sophie dropped her head in her hands. 'Oh, Lydia!' she cried.

'Is it Kit? Have you argued? You seemed to be…. well, on the verge of something wonderful the other night.'

Lifting her head, she smiled weakly. 'No! Everything is fine with Kit, now, it's…..'

'What?' Lydia folded her arms.

Sophie knew she could not keep it from her, so taking a deep breath she began to tell her about Georgie and the letter, the dreadful attack that Kit had saved her from and the strange declaration of love from Stan. 'So, as you see, my head is all over the place. I can't think straight.'

Shocked to the core, Lydia slumped down beside her. 'I'm grieved for you,' she breathed, 'I'm grieved indeed. An attack like this is unheard of around here. You're in no fit state to work, you must know that? You need some time to get over this. I know you probably want everything to return to normal, but things like this take time.'

She nodded. 'That's what Kit said.'

'Then take heed and go home. Take the rest of the week off, get some sleep and spend some time with Kit. You've a good man there who will see you through this. I'll sort everything out here, *including* Stan – god knows what's got into him! You have a lovely trip to Poldhu to look forward to at the weekend, so focus on that. Then if, and only if, you feel able, we'll welcome you back into our dairy family on Monday. All right?'

Sophie nodded thankfully. 'What will you tell Eric?'

'I shall have to tell him what's happened to you - but I promise he'll not breathe a word to anyone.'

*

The relief on Kit's face was palpable when she told him

she'd shared the horrors of her ordeal with Lydia, and that she'd been ordered home to rest. She also told him about Stan's strange declaration.

Kit laughed and said, 'I didn't realise I had a love rival.'

'You haven't and don't laugh,' she hit him playfully, 'the poor lad was in earnest.'

He grinned. 'I'm glad you decided to tell Lydia though. She's a good friend to you. Now listen to me, your *other* good friend, and do as Lydia says and *go* and rest - you look dead on your feet.'

'All right, I'm going.' As she turned to leave, she asked nervously, 'Did you reply to Georgie's letter, Kit? Wasn't she expecting you tomorrow?'

'She was, and I did reply, yes. I've left her in no doubt that I'm not interested in *anything* she has to offer me. I don't think she'll be writing to me again.'

Sophie felt the tension in her shoulders lift instantaneously. 'I can't help thinking though that it would have been a wonderful opportunity for you to have become part of the association!'

He shook his head. 'The negatives far outweigh the positives in that matter. Besides, another wonderful opportunity has come my way.' He cupped her face and kissed her tenderly. 'Anyway, we can set up our own little workshop somewhere. You, making your fine quilting and me my furniture, we'll be like Guy and Ellie.'

Sophie's eyes fluttered with regret.

'What is it, you look troubled again.' He searched her face for an answer.

'We'll be like Guy and Ellie without the children,' she whispered.

'Sophie, listen to me.' He pulled her into an embrace. 'I don't need children to make my life complete. *You* do that. I decided long ago that fatherhood was not going to happen, because all I wanted in life was you, and I didn't think that would be possible.'

'Will it be enough though? I mean everything went

wrong with my marriage to Jowan because I couldn't give him a baby.'

'I'm *not* Jowan, Sophie.' He squeezed her arms to reiterate his point. 'This is me and all I want is you. You must start to believe that. Now, go and rest.'

*

When she entered her room, she found Kit had filled it with jars of lavender. Sophie took off her cap and apron and looked towards her neat bed. It looked so inviting, but a thread of fear coiled around her heart that if she lay down, the terrors that plagued her would return. Instead, she sat at the window and picked up her sewing. It would be nice, she decided, to make an eiderdown embellished with two seahorses for when she and Kit found a home together. The thought of life with Kit settled her mind like nothing else could. They'd spoken at length yesterday about their future, deciding to keep their relationship secret, aware of eyes watching constantly. For now, they would just share secret kisses whilst companionably holding hands, and falling more in love as each day past.

After half-an-hour sewing, she began to feel hot with fatigue - her head swam and her vision blurred. Swilling her face with cold water, the action of drying herself with the towel made her unsteady on her feet - she could not fight sleep any longer. Sitting down on the bed, it occurred to her that if she didn't undress then she could trick her mind into thinking she wasn't there to sleep. Unlacing her boots, she propped herself up with pillows and listened to the familiar noise of people going about their everyday tasks. A large schooner had docked that morning and people were shouting as barrels and packages were being unloaded. Below her window, the gentle tap, tap of Kit in his workshop lulled her to close her eyes. Soon sleep pulled her into a deep cavern, and this time she stayed there.

Chapter 30

Sophie woke, hot and disorientated and for a moment knew not why she was on her bed fully clothed. Easing herself up onto her elbows she looked down at her ruffled skirt and glanced at the clock as it chimed nine. From the window, the evening sky had turned fiery red as the summer sun was setting. She got up, adjusted her stays which were digging into her sides, swilled her face, brushed her teeth and tidied her hair. For the first time in hours, she felt a sharp hunger pang.

She found Kit on his bench. He'd not seen her, for his eyes were closed and his head thrown back as the soft shifting light pattered shadows on his face. When he became aware of her presence, the sudden intensity in his eyes flooded her heart with love for him.

He patted the seat beside him and she sat, comforted by his presence.

'Are you all right?' he asked anxiously.

She nodded then took a deep breath. 'Except for,' she watched his forehead crease with concern, 'I'm absolutely starving.'

Kit grinned widely. 'That is music to my ears. Let me get you some supper.'

*

The trouble with sleeping all day was that when it came to bed time, Sophie couldn't drop off again. Consequently, she was as tired as ever the next day. Unaccustomed to this life of leisure, she was determined to be productive by making bread – it would go with the pot of rabbit stew she'd made to share with Kit later that evening.

As she approached Moyles Shop to buy flour, she had the great misfortune to meet with Ria bustling out of the shop.

Ria was the last person Sophie needed to see right now, but resigned herself that whenever their paths crossed, which they inevitably would in such a small village, she would always be courteous to her. She smiled. 'Good morning, Ria. I trust you are well? You look well.' In truth Sophie had never seen Ria look better. She'd obviously lost a deal of weight in the five months since she'd left her. Perhaps hard work was the making of her.

Ria snorted derisively, pulled herself up to her full size and frowned. 'I seem to be faring better than you, by the look of it. Are you ill?'

Shocked momentarily at Ria's unprecedented concern, for she had never asked after her health in all the eight years she had lived with her, Sophie's face softened. 'No, I'm not ill, Ria, I'm fine, but I thank you for asking.'

'Well, you don't look fine. Perhaps your wicked ways are taking their toll?'

Sophie sighed wearily - this she could do without. 'Ria, if you can't say anything nice, then perhaps it's best not to say anything at all. Good day to you.' As Sophie swept past her, she was sure she caught a hint of regret in Ria's face.

*

Ria set off home at a quickened pace, as if putting some distance between her and Sophie would repeal what she'd just said to her, for she felt no victory in her verbal assault - in fact the episode had left her feeling a little hollow. As far as she was aware Sophie had done nothing untoward. There had been talk of course when Sophie had moved in above Kit Trevellick, but no one had seen them do anything improper. Her prejudice stemmed from Jowan of course - he knew that his beautiful wife was coveted by Kit, and this was what she found hard to face. Jowan would be so angry that Sophie was now living with Kit, albeit as a lodger.

She knew she should let it be, life for her had changed beyond recognition. She felt better in herself now she was making her own money. The only thing she lacked was friends. People were as courteous as ever and would pass the time of day, but the Treloar's had always kept themselves to themselves, and when Jowan was alive, Ria had needed no one else. She knew her conduct towards Sophie brought her no favours and was shamed at how she'd bullied her relentlessly. Her penance was loneliness, and she now appreciated how Sophie must have felt. Was it all too late for her to change her ways? Could a leopard change its spots?

*

At Bochym, Georgie spent the morning cleaning her house. She'd put fresh sheets on the bed and selected a bottle of the finest champagne from her cold room. As the clock ticked past midday, she began to pace the room. Twice she checked her workshop for any sign of Kit, thinking perhaps he was waiting there for her. Where on earth could he be? She'd arranged a meeting with Sarah at one that afternoon to showcase his skills. At quarter-past-one she sought out Sarah to make her apologies before storming over to where Guy was working. At the bottom of the thatching ladder, she folded her arms and shouted stridently up to the roof, 'Guy Blackthorn. A word, if you please.'

Guy stopped what he was doing and looked down at her.

Silas raised an eyebrow. 'Oh, dear, what have you done to upset *her*?'

'Nothing, as far as I know.' He secured a willow spur in the thatch and moved over to the ladder.

Without greeting or niceties she demanded, 'Did you or did you not give Kit my letter?'

'I did,' he answered mirroring her tone.

'Well, did he read it?'

'Not in my presence, no.' Against his better judgment he asked, 'Why what's the problem?'

'The problem is, among other things in the letter I offered to speak to her ladyship on Kit's behalf about working here at Bochym. I had a meeting set up with her this afternoon!'

Guy narrowed his eyes. 'And is that something he

229

asked you to do?' he said flatly.

'No! But someone needs to take him in hand to show him there is more to life than making coffins in that smelly little village.'

Guy folded his arms to match Georgie's stance. 'Has it not occurred to you that perhaps Kit enjoys his life in that 'smelly little village'? After all, he has everything a man could need to make him happy there!'

'Except me, of course!' she said with a flourish.

Enraged at her conceit, he retaliated, 'Now, why would he want you, when he has Sophie, whom I might add, he loves dearly?' His words had the expected effect as Georgie visibly shrunk back from him.

'What?' She scowled. 'You mean that *mouse* of a woman who lives above him?'

'That's a rather derogatory description of her, especially as Sophie is a very beautiful woman inside and out - a concept perhaps *you* wouldn't appreciate. Now, if you don't mind I've a roof to thatch.' He turned his back on her and climbed the ladder, congratulating himself that he'd rather taken the wind out of her sails. Her cottage door had slammed before he had positioned himself back on the roof.

'That little minx,' Georgie shouted at the vase of flowers. *Not once did she indicate that she and Kit were lovers when I visited! Unless - she realised that I'd set my cap at Kit! Yes, that was it - she must have thrown* herself *at him when he'd got back from here.* 'Well little mouse, you have a battle on your hands, because Kit is mine!' She swiped the vase off the table, shattering the glass and scattering petals everywhere.

A knock on the door brought Georgie's rage to a halt. Kit! Quickly tidying her hair, she kicked the remnants of the vase under the table. Taking a deep controlled breath she shouted gaily, 'I'm coming, Kit.' Beaming a wide smile, she opened the door with a flourish only to find the postman there with a letter in his hand. Snatching it from him, she slammed the door in his face and ripped the envelope open.

Madam,

Regarding your recent letter. May I be crystal clear in this matter? Your ongoing, unwelcome pursuit of me, coupled with your offers and appointment making on my behalf, are totally and utterly misguided and quite frankly embarrassing. This must stop forthwith. I trust I shall not hear from you again on any of these matters.

Kit Trevellick.

She began to tremble with bitter contempt. A moment later the sideboard was cleared of its contents with one swipe of her hand.

*

Sophie was working on Kit's table, finishing the last knead of bread when Lydia called in bearing gifts of scones, jam and fresh clotted cream. She smiled at the sight of domesticity. Sophie had flour up her arms and a dusting of it on her nose. 'You look very much at home in here!' she quipped.

'Only because it's easier to make and prove the bread here, being near the range you see.'

Lydia smiled knowingly. 'Well, you look a lot perkier than yesterday, I must say, though still a little tired. How are you?'

Sophie eyed up the goodies in Lydia's basket. 'How can I be anything other than thrilled, when I see you here, bearing all the makings of a cream tea?' She grinned. 'Let me put this in the oven and then I'll put the kettle on the stove.'

'Are you all right though?' Lydia put her hand on Sophie's shoulder.

'I am yes, though I have some quite deep gouges on the back of my legs.' She lifted her skirts and petticoats for Lydia to see.

'Good god - those scratches look angry.'

'Whoever grabbed me had long nails!' She grimaced. 'I've been bathing them with boiled water and vinegar. I think that's what Amelia would tell me to do if she was here.'

'You might want to put some honey on them at night – it's a bit sticky but it has healing properties. I'd let Amelia look at them when she gets back at the weekend - you know you can depend on her discretion. But apart from that, you're all right?'

Sophie straightened her clothes and nodded. 'I slept well yesterday. I think that is what I needed. Another good night's sleep and I'll be as right as rain again. I could have done without the encounter with Ria this morning at Moyles shop though.'

'Oh, dear, I trust she was her usual delightful self?'

Sophie nodded. 'She was quick to remark that my wan appearance must be to do with my wicked ways.'

Lydia clicked her tongue. 'That woman's tongue is her own worst enemy. Ignore her, everyone else does now.'

'So how are things at the farm? I feel awful leaving it to everyone else.'

'Don't worry about us. Eric understands. He was shocked to hear what had happened. God help whoever attacked you, if his identity ever comes to light. Eric will kill him with his bare hands.'

Sophie felt heartened at this, as she popped the loaf in the oven and picked up the kettle.

'Stan is suitably embarrassed about his love declaration, and Dora has washed her hands of him!'

'Oh, dear! Whatever prompted him to do such a thing?'

'Well, it took me ages to get it out of him. When he's upset, his signing is all over the place, but I think I got to the bottom of it. The poor lad could see you were out of sorts and believed that Kit had upset you. He said he'd seen Kit with another woman!'

Sophie rolled her eyes in annoyance. 'That was Georgie - the one I told you about. Stan must have seen her getting into Kit's cart.'

'Well, bless him he didn't like to see you unhappy. He was worried and wanted you to know that you were loved, but I think it all came out wrong, although he is sweet on you, you do know that?'

'Goodness, I feel awful now, especially the way I reacted to what he said, and poor Dora! I'll have to apologize.'

'Well, be careful what you say, Stan has a tendency to see more into the friendship than there is, and I'll have his mother Edith Mumford on my case again.'

'I shudder at the thought. Lydia, I know you have given me the week off but I intend to come back to work tomorrow, if that's okay. Being idle doesn't suit me.'

'Well, whatever you feel is right for you. We'll certainly be glad to have you back.'

Just as they sat down to tea, Kit came in and grinned. 'Don't mind me, I just live here,' he joked.

'And I'm afraid we've turned your house into a tea room, Kit,' Lydia countered.

'That's fine by me, as long as I get one of those delicious looking scones.'

As Sophie piled the jam and cream on one for him, Lydia watched the exchange of tender looks between them. Lydia's heart sang joyfully that at last something was happening between them.

*

Sophie was welcomed back to the farm with a big hug from Eric and a tentative smile from Stan. Dora, it seemed, would take a little longer to come around. With the milking finally done and before she fed the pigs, Sophie helped Ely carry the last two pails of milk to the dairy.

'Stop right there, Sophie.' Lydia stopped churning the butter and held out her hand.

Frowning, Sophie glanced at Ely who was allowed to enter the room. She put her pail down and wiped her hands on her apron. 'Why can't I come in?'

'I'm churning butter, that's why,' Lydia said firmly.

Ely shrugged, not knowing what was going on. He

picked up Sophie's pail, deposited it next to Lydia and walked out of the dairy.

Waiting a moment to make sure Ely was out of earshot she said, 'If you step over the threshold my butter won't turn!'

'What?'

'Don't look so innocent. I saw the looks passing between you and Kit yesterday.'

'Looks?' Sophie felt herself blush.

'Aye, looks! You two are clearly in love! And you know as well as I do that butter won't turn if someone's in love, and there's a fact! So, you're not to come within an inch of this butter until it's done.'

Sophie protested whilst trying not to smile. 'That's an old wives' tale and you know it! Anyway….' She folded her arms, 'Lizzy comes in here all the time when you're churning the butter and she is madly in love with your Charlie!'

'Bah! That's only calf love. Cupid's arrow hasn't stabbed her arse yet - not like it's done with you - and don't deny it.' She nodded knowingly.

Sophie could hold her smile back no longer.

Lydia stopped churning and smiled. 'So, it's true then?'

Sophie threw her head back and laughed. 'All I will say is that I better not come in then.'

'Sophie, my dear, I'm so happy for you both.'

'It's very early days, Lydia. We're keeping it to ourselves at the moment.'

'My lips are sealed. Though I suspect you'll be planning to leave us shortly?'

Sophie nodded sadly. 'I'm sorry, but we can't stay here.'

'Don't feel bad, Sophie, this is a new start for you. I'll not mention anything to Eric yet.' She winked.

When Sophie had gone Lydia smiled - her mission was accomplished. As she turned her butter churn it ceased its squishing and slopping. *Thank goodness it is an old wives' tale,* she thought as she got her butter pats ready.

Chapter 31

On the day of their much-anticipated visit to Poldhu, Sophie decided that to avoid them being seen leaving together, she'd walk half a mile up Gweek road and wait for Kit to pick her up with the pony and cart.

Dressed in a new cornflower blue dress, she carried a large wide-brimmed white hat to keep the sun from her face, but was fanning herself furiously with it when Kit arrived.

He was dressed casually in light brown breeches and matching waistcoat, covering a fresh white shirt open at the collar. A red scarf was tied at his neck, but his jacket had been discarded for now. He jumped down to help her up onto the seat.

'Goodness, Kit it's so warm today.'

Once settled Kit joined her, picked up the reins and leant over to kiss her tenderly on the cheek. 'You look lovely, Sophie.'

'So do you.' She marvelled at the sun catching the copper lights in his hair.

As they set off up the hill, they both noted a slight tinge of yellowing to the fields surrounding Gweek, as a soft breeze moved the crops like waves on the sea.

'I hate to say this, Sophie, but we need a little bit of rain soon for a good harvest this year.'

'Yes, I've just spoken to Farmer Ferris about it. He says there is a deep depression coming in tonight. So, I think we've chosen the best day to visit Poldhu.'

Kit chuckled. 'I don't know how Farmer Ferris does it, but he can predict the weather as accurately as anyone else I know. If he says it'll rain, it'll rain!'

'Lydia can do it as well. She was complaining all morning that her bunions were telling her it was going to rain.'

They both looked up towards the vast, cloudless, cobalt blue sky - it certainly didn't look like rain.

When they finally rounded Poldhu Hill, the spectacular view of the cove came into sight.

Sophie gasped. 'Stop, Kit, stop!'

The shimmering sea greeted them with mesmeric beauty. They both gazed at the immense vista leading out to the horizon where sea and sky melted into each other. The sound of seabirds echoed from the dark cliffs flanking the golden beach, while sand martins swooped and dived to feed their young in the sandstone rocks.

Kit put his arm around her shoulders. 'It's a fine sight, isn't it? Look you can see the tea room nestled down there in the dunes.'

'I've never seen anything like it,' she breathed. 'I never thought I'd see paradise until the day I died! What a place to live.'

They dismounted at the entrance of the beach and noted a fine white horse tethered to the fence. Feeling a little apprehensive, Sophie whispered, 'Perhaps they have company! Perhaps they've forgotten we were coming?'

Kit shook his head and smiled - he'd recognised the horse.

'Kit, Sophie!' Guy called, as he and Ellie greeted them with a warm embrace. 'We're so glad to see you. Come up, Ellie has the tea ready,' he said, dodging Agnes as she raced across the veranda.

Ellie linked her arm in Sophie's. 'Your dress is beautiful, Sophie, I can't wait to get back into something that doesn't resemble a tent.' She grinned. 'Here we go. The day is so beautiful we've set the table on the veranda.'

Guy held out a chair for Sophie and once settled she sighed in delight at the view before her. 'You're so lucky to live somewhere like this.'

'On a day like this, and because it's a Sunday and quiet on the beach - yes I agree,' Guy said, 'But when it's busy or when a storm hits, it's not so good. One storm completely destroyed the tea room five years ago, you know?'

'It was a storm with a silver lining though, wasn't it Guy? It brought us back together. He came to fix the roof and my broken heart,' Ellie said happily.

Sophie watched the loving looks Guy and Ellie exchanged.

'Anyway, Sophie.' Ellie clasped her hands together. 'We have a surprise for you. Sarah - the Countess de Bochym is joining us for tea. She so wanted to meet you, after I told her about your quilting. She's at my cottage freshening up, she won't be long.'

Sophie glanced nervously at Kit for moral support and he smiled and winked.

'Ah good, here's Sarah now!' Ellie said putting the tea tray down.

'Do forgive me for holding up the tea party.' Sarah picked up the skirt of her riding habit to walk up the veranda steps.

Kit and Sophie stood in her presence.

'Oh, no!' Sarah flapped her hand. 'Please sit down. We don't stand on ceremony here, do we Elise?'

'No Sarah. Now let me do the introductions. Sarah, this is Sophie Treloar, and of course you know Kit.'

'Yes, hello again, Kit. And Sophie, I'm very happy to meet you, and may I say, your outfit is lovely, that colour matches your eyes beautifully. Tell me, who made your dress?'

'I made it. I make all my own clothes,' Sophie answered shyly.

Sarah leant forward to inspect it closer. 'Well, credit to you. You're a wonderful seamstress. I know some society ladies who would be envious of such a gown.'

Sophie, in awe of Sarah's natural beauty and friendliness, said, 'Thank you, my lady.'

'Oh!' She gave a wave of dismissal. 'Please, just plain Sarah will do.'

Sophie grinned - Sarah was anything but plain. 'Mrs Tonkin's haberdashery in Helston has patterns sent down from London, I just follow them.'

'Well, you have real skill - it looks professionally made.'

Sophie felt herself swell with pride.

'Now, Sophie.' Sarah unfolded a linen napkin and placed it on her lap. 'Elise tells me that you can Italian quilt. I would so like to see what you do.'

'Well,' she said nervously as she unhooked the bag from the back of her chair, 'I've made this.' She handed it over. 'As you can see it isn't on the finest satin, but it was all I could source at the time.'

Sarah ran appreciative fingers over the needlework. 'You have still managed to make a work of art. You were right, Elise! This *is* exquisite work! Workmanship such as yours, Sophie, is rarely found in the provinces, and of course we have Kit here who is a master boat builder as well. You are a talented couple, aren't you?'

'Kit also makes the most exquisite furniture on which he carves a beautiful small seahorse. Don't you?' she smiled affectionately at him.

'Do you really, Kit?' Sarah's interest was piqued by this. 'Seahorses, how fascinating, what made you choose such an unusual creature?'

Kit laughed softly. 'You'll think me odd if I tell you, Sarah.'

Splaying her hand across her chest, she answered, 'Hand on heart I will not, I'm intrigued.'

'So am I,' said Ellie trying to make herself more comfortable.

'Very well, I think they are romantic little creatures. They court for several days, during which time they may change colour as they swim side by side holding tails. When it's time to mate, the female deposits hundreds to thousands of eggs into the male's brood pouch and her body slims while his swells. She visits him daily for morning greetings as he carries the eggs through the gestation period, which is about two to four weeks, until the young are ready to swim free. What a wonderful thing to ease the burden for his mate, don't you think? I just think they are really fascinating.'

If Sophie was in any doubt about her love for this man - this beautiful statement would settle it once and for all.

'Gosh Kit, I would give anything for Guy to take my burden just for a day!' Ellie patted her swollen tummy.

Guy reached for her hand. 'I'd do it in a heartbeat if I could, my darling girl.'

Sarah smiled. 'Kit, that is a lovely story and yes, it *is* romantic. I would dearly love to see your work one day. Why not come to the manor for dinner? You can bring a sample of your work with you. Elise and Guy must come too.'

To the manor for dinner! Sophie cast a worried glance at Kit, but he reached over and squeezed her hand.

'That would be lovely, Sarah. We'd like that.'

'Splendid. Let's say Friday week. Would that be convenient for you all?'

They nodded in agreement.

'Excellent. Do you have any other pieces of work to show me, Sophie?'

'Only the cushion I made for Kit at the moment.'

'Could you bring that as well?

'Of course, if Kit doesn't mind me borrowing it?'

'Be my guest.'

'Tell me, Sophie, what do you know about the Arts & Crafts Movement?' Sarah said dabbing her mouth with her napkin.

'To tell the honest truth, I knew nothing until Kit told me about William Morris, setting up his company in 1861.'

'You never mentioned that you were interested in the movement, Kit, when I showed you the workshops?' Sarah said.

'Well, I didn't like to be too forward, but I do share their belief in craftsmanship - the inherent beauty of the material and the importance of nature as inspiration.'

Sarah smiled. 'You mirror my beliefs, Kit. So, our little

community at Bochym must interest you?' He nodded. 'And Sophie, I take it he told you about what we do?'

'Yes, he did, it all sounds wonderful.'

'I know you've seen it all before, Kit, but when you come to us we'll take Sophie around to meet everyone. And I'd rather like the members to see the work you both do, if you don't mind?'

Kit and Sophie smiled politely, trying to hide the fact that neither of them really wanted to meet with Georgie again.

Although Sarah was blissfully unaware of their reticence, Guy detected it - but said nothing.

*

After a very pleasant afternoon, Sarah bade them goodbye and they all parted good friends. While Sophie helped Ellie to wash up, Guy encouraged Kit to sit with him.

'You and Sophie seemed pensive when Sarah spoke of the workshops.'

'Only on account of Georgie!' He proceeded to tell him about the contents of the letter.

'Ah! No wonder she was so livid that day,' Guy grinned. 'Apparently, she smashed everything she could get her hands on when you didn't turn up!'

Kit groaned. 'You know Sophie overheard our conversation about the letter?'

Guy grimaced. 'I feared she had done. I could have bitten my tongue off that night at the Williams's.'

'No matter.' Without telling Guy that incident had put Sophie in danger that night, he said, 'Among other things, the letter sparked a shift in our relationship - for the better. I realised how distraught she was, when she thought Georgie had set her sights on me, and it gave me hope that she was ready to build a relationship with me.'

'Well, I can clearly see by the way you are with each other that something has happened between you.'

'Yes, but we're taking things very slowly at the moment. Legally she's still married to Jowan, so we will have to find somewhere else to live where we can pretend to be married until we actually can be. It means we must leave Gweek, but I can't tell you how happy I am.'

'That's good news, though I suspect that will be difficult for you, having your carpentry shop established there.'

'I know, it's been in my family for generations, but I'll do anything to enable us to be together.'

'Sarah might ask you to join the association at Bochym you know.'

'It's a nice idea, but I'm afraid Georgie would just cause trouble for us.'

'Sarah would *not* allow that to happen, Kit. Georgie has been on thin ice for a while - due to her unchecked behaviour. Nevertheless, if joining the association isn't an option for you, I'll keep a look out for vacant cottages. You've waited a long time for Sophie, the sooner we get you two together the better.'

*

With the tea dishes washed, Kit and Sophie took a walk down the beach, while Ellie took the weight off her feet. She felt exhausted.

Guy lowered the newspaper he was reading. 'Are you well, my love,' he asked, 'You look a little flushed.'

She wrinkled her nose. 'As well as anyone in the last couple of weeks of her third pregnancy,' she mused. 'It's this humidity.' She pulled her blouse away from her body. 'What I'd give for a cool breeze. My shift is sticking to me.'

'A change is on its way. Look,' Guy nodded skywards. Although it was still sunny, the clear blue sky, so prominent these past few weeks, had turned hazy. High up in the atmosphere, mare's tails and a mackerel sky were building from the west, warning of high winds and a cool front.

Ellie undid the buttons on her blouse and fanned herself furiously. She watched with delight as Kit and Sophie walked along the water's edge. 'It seems my tea party matchmaking skills were not needed after all. Kit and Sophie seem to be taking tentative steps towards being together.'

Guy grinned. *If love was in the air, Ellie would detect it.* 'I think they're finding their way now, yes.'

'Oooh, what do you know?' she said clasping her hands in anticipation.

'There's a shift in their relationship, yes. I don't think it's a secret otherwise Kit would not have told me. I'm surprised Sophie didn't say anything to you!'

'Well, perhaps our friendship is a little too new for her to confide in me.'

'You're right. Sophie is very shy. I suspect she's still feeling her way with us all in this new life. They have many hurdles to negotiate, but their immediate intention is to move away from Gweek. Living together there unmarried will not sit easy with some of the villagers.' He reached out and sought her hand. 'I intend to assist them in every way possible to enable their happy ever after.'

'Perhaps Sarah will ask them to join the association at Bochym. That might solve the problem of finding somewhere to live away from Gweek. They're very bohemian in their thinking up there! No one will give a fig if they're not married.'

Guy drummed his fingers on the table. 'Kit and I have just been talking about that, but it might add to their problems. Georgie Blake has set her hat at Kit!'

'Oh, no! But surely Kit isn't the slightest bit interested in her.'

'He isn't, but she's not a woman who takes no for an answer. Kit thinks she will try to make things uncomfortable for them.'

Ellie folded her arms indignantly 'Oh, that woman is a predator!' And then she shifted uncomfortably - her back felt suddenly terribly painful.

'Are you all right, my love?' he said, seeing her grimace with pain.

'Ooof!' A sudden pain made Ellie stand. 'No, I'm not. I think Amelia Pascoe was right - the baby *is* coming early.' And then her waters broke!

'Oh, Christ!' Suddenly feeling lightheaded, Guy jumped up and raked his fingers through his hair. 'I'll go for the doctor!'

'No, you need to watch the little ones. Good god, where's Jessie when I need her!'

'She won't be back for ages. Look, I'll go and get Sophie to help. Perhaps Kit will look after the little ones, while I go for the doctor!'

'Yes, yes, go, hurry! I think you're about to meet your new son or daughter very soon.'

Chapter 32

At the tide line, Kit and Sophie stopped to gaze out at the clear turquoise sea. His hand slipped into hers as they shared this romantic moment. She turned, and looked up at him, her beautiful smile made his heart sing. Every time he looked upon her face, her beauty struck him afresh.

'This is so lovely, Kit. Thank you for bringing me here.'

He squeezed her hand. 'We'll see lots of lovely places like this together, I promise.'

'It's very different from the sea I remember in Newlyn harbour. The water was mostly slicked with oil, and stank of gutted fish, but this, my goodness, this really is paradise.'

'You know, I've often wondered how Jowan came to meet you down there. Newlyn is a long way from Gweek!'

Sophie snuffled a humourless laugh. 'By my great misfortune.' she quipped. 'He worked for a time on the fishing boats out of Newlyn - he could make more money there. Once we were married, he joined Jack Tehidy's boat and fished out of Gweek. It meant he wasn't away from home for long - probably so he could keep an eye on me,' she said flatly.

'Hey,' he brought her hand up to his lips and kissed it. 'I'm sorry I mentioned him. That was insensitive of me - especially when we're having such a lovely day.'

'Kit.' She reached up to touch his face. 'You don't have an insensitive bone in your body. At least we're speaking about him in the past tense. He can't control me anymore!'

'No, he can't.' He reached to cup her hand in his - his skin tingling where her fingers lay and exhaled a deep breath. 'You can have no idea the effect your touch has on me.'

'Oh, I think I do!' She laughed softly.

The last few visitors to the beach had packed up and gone with it being late afternoon - perhaps seeing the change in the weather. They were completely alone, and lost in each other, when they heard their names called in earnest.

*

Within half an hour, Guy arrived back from Mullion with news that the doctor was out on another call, but his housekeeper would send the midwife down. Kit was entertaining the children in the front room, while Ellie and Sophie had gone up to the bedroom.

Ellie's labour had progressed enough to realise that Sophie might have to deliver this baby for her. By the look on Sophie's face, a myriad of emotions were going through her head. Ellie felt for her, but there was no time to dwell and fortunately for her, Sophie was managing to hold herself together.

As with her other deliveries, Ellie felt more comfortable on all fours. Sophie, bless her, crawled around after her, massaging her lower back, wiping the perspiration from her face and offering up sips of water when necessary.

'Do I need to tell you to breathe or something?' Sophie asked her.

Ellie could hear the panic in Sophie's voice and shook her head. 'I'm fine, I know what to do. I just need you to be here.'

'Don't worry,' she said seriously. 'I won't leave you.'

Ellie tried in vain to silence her squeals when the pain got too much, but every now and then the contraction was so severe she could not suppress her cries.

'Sophie, can you tell Guy to take the children away. I don't want to frighten them.'

'But….'

'I'm all right for a moment, please go and tell him.'

Within seconds Sophie was back and took up her position next to her again.

'Kit's taken them onto the beach, but Guy wanted to stay close.'

Ellie managed a thin smile and then felt another

contraction building. She grabbed Sophie's hand and squeezed it until she saw Sophie wince but she did not let go.

'Oh, Christ! You'd think I'd be used to this after already having two before, but bloody hell - this hurts!' She glanced at Sophie whose hair had come down from its pins. 'You look as dishevelled as I feel.' She began to laugh hysterically. 'I'm so sorry - this is not the tea party I had planned for you.'

'Goodness, don't worry about me. I just don't know what to do to help you!'

'You're doing fine, but I suggest you take that lovely dress of yours off.'

'Why?'

'Because I think,' her lips pursed, 'I think you're going to have to…' She gritted her teeth, 'Ow!' She lowered her head into her arms again and began to pant. 'I think, yes, I think you're going to have to deliver this baby.'

Sophie quickly unbuttoned her blouse and dropped her skirt to the floor and then in her petticoats and stays she moved back to Sophie, dragging as many towels as she could pull from the chair.

'Oh, my god, it's coming….'

*

Ellie's shriek reverberated around the room and the next thing Sophie knew, she was holding a hot wet baby's head in her hands.

Stunned into silence for what seemed like an age, Ellie began to moan loudly and a moment later she was holding a very sticky, wet, cross looking baby girl in her arms. Through blurred eyes she grabbed a towel and wiped the mucus from the baby's mouth until the child emitted a thin cry. The sound opened a floodgate of tears - she had never before held a new-born baby in her arms. 'You have another daughter, Ellie,' her voice cracked with emotion.

Ellie smiled and then flopped exhausted on the floor. The baby cried again, louder this time and the bedroom door flew open and Guy dropped to his knees to cradle Ellie in his arms.

For a moment, Sophie was lost in a world of her own, before she realised that they were waiting for her to hand the baby over.

*

After a celebratory drink with the midwife, who had arrived five minutes after the birth, Kit and Sophie said their last goodbyes to mother and baby, before setting off home. The predicted rain started as they turned the corner out of Poldhu. It would get a lot worse before the journey was over, but nothing could dampen their spirits. The baby had been named after Sophie and they had both been bestowed the honour of becoming the child's godparents.

*

By the time they had reached the crossroads for the Gweek road, the storm had broken and pelting rain rolled in from the sea. They considered pulling in for a while as Kit's pony, Willow, flinched with every crack of thunder.

'I think we'll just push on,' Kit suggested. 'The sooner we're home, the sooner I can get her safely stabled from this.'

It was eight-forty by the time Kit and Sophie rode into Gweek. Although they had snuggled up close with their heads and laps covered with tarpaulin, the deluge of rain had drenched them both.

Regardless of being seen, they pulled into the boatyard where great pools of muddy water had accumulated on the ground. It would be high tide at five in the morning and if the storm continued there would be flooding in the village.

Sophie gathered their bags and jumped down trying to avoid the puddles while Kit walked Willow back to her field to feed, water and stable her.

After putting the kettle to boil on the range, Sophie ran up to her quarters to change out of her wet clothes. When Kit returned, she'd cut some bread and cheese for supper and had a steaming hot drink waiting for him.

Quickly retreating behind his bedroom curtain to shed his own wet clothes, he marvelled at his recent good fortune and the domestic bliss awaiting him.

*

After supper, they shared a goodnight kiss, Sophie. thanked Kit profusely for the trip and ran up to her quarters, trying, but not succeeding, to dodge the torrential rain. She put on her nightgown and brushed her hair. Today had been so special – meeting Sarah, a lovely tea, a walk on the beach with Kit, and then the privilege of watching a new baby being born into the world. She closed her eyes remembering the feel and smell of the new life wriggling in her arms. The thought caught her breath, knowing she would never hold her own baby. Sniffing back a sorrowful tear she climbed into bed with her arms wrapped about herself.

*

Once Sophie had gone up to bed, Kit glanced out into the wild night. The rain was falling almost horizontally and great gusts of wind were shaking the leaves from the trees. A storm in summer was not good. With the trees being in full leaf there was always a chance of them being uprooted. He had a feeling this storm was going to cause havoc. He pulled on his wet clothes again, shuddering at the clamminess on his skin, lit a storm lamp and stepped out into the night. With the storm raging and the wind pushing up the Helford, Kit knew the high tide would flood the village. Before doing anything else he checked that Amelia had shored up her front door. With her house situated almost at river level it was an annual occurrence for her house to witness some degree of flooding, so she always kept a heap of sand sacks to use when necessary. The floods normally happened in the autumn/winter period, sometimes with the combination of high spring tides, but as it was summertime Amelia might not have seen the warning signs of this storm.

As with the rest of the village, it looked like Amelia had

taken herself to bed, so Kit quickly set to work to move the sand sacks from where they sat at the side of the cottage and began to build a dam with them against her door. Despite the coolness of the rain, sweat trickled down his back from the exertion. By the time he'd laid the last sack, the muscles in his arms were burning with the strain. With the job done he battled his way against the wind, flinching as sheet lightning lit the night sky. Thunder followed swiftly, the sound reverberating around the centre of the village. Another flash illuminated his boat making him frown - the tarpaulin was flapping loose at one corner. He knew he'd secured the ropes before he'd left for Poldhu earlier that day.

'Damn it!' That could only mean that someone had been on or near his boat. He wrenched the tarpaulin back and stilled - a large dark figure appeared before him.

Kit jumped back in shock. 'What the devil?' The figure moved again and groaned as if in pain. Stepping closer, Kit lifted his lamp – he knew this man - he'd made a coffin last year for him when his young wife had died in childbirth! 'Jeremiah Rowe? What are *you* doing here?'

His coat was draped over his shoulders and his boots were undone and when Jeremiah lifted his head, his face was streaming with anguished tears.

'Christ, man! Are you all right?'

'No,' Jeremiah moaned. 'I'm not!'

'Come inside then, you're soaked through.' He tried to pull him from where he stood, but Jeremiah cried out in pain. 'I can't move, Kit. It's my back,' he moaned, clasping his hands to where the pain was most severe. 'I've not been able to walk properly for days!'

'So, what are you doing here?' he asked dubiously. 'In fact, *how* have you got here?'

Jeremiah hung his head low. 'I've been evicted, for non-payment on my rent!' His body shook with great wracking sobs until he yelped again in pain.

'Oh, Christ man!' Kit put a comforting arm around his

shoulders.

'I can't work you see.' Jeremiah lifted his head as tears of pain streamed down his face. 'Rick Bray, the rent collector came this morning and because I couldn't pay, I received a note from Penvear an hour later giving me half a day's notice before he had me thrown out.'

Kit snorted in disgust. 'Has that man no conscience? Look, don't worry, my friend. We'll sort something out for you. Come on, gently does it. ' He patted his arm. 'You made it this far, a few more steps and we can get you inside. Have you anything with you?'

'Just a sack with some of my clothes in it - it's over there.' He pointed to a small mound on Kit's work table. 'I've had to leave everything, my furniture, the lot. I couldn't move it you see – it's locked in the house now. Penvear said if I didn't move it today, it would become his property to use when he rents it out again.'

'Like hell it will,' Kit muttered. 'We'll get your things back, Jeremiah. You mark my words.'

With a great deal of difficulty Jeremiah managed to put one foot in front of the other while Kit held him tightly around his shoulders – his body shaking so much it reverberated through Kit's arm. Slowly they made their way to Kit's house. The step up to the front door was the most problematic, but after several deep breaths Jeremiah managed to lift his foot and with a little help from Kit they were finally inside. Once in the room, Kit stripped him of his wet shirt and lowered his breeches to the floor and then moved him towards his bed.

'Oh, god, Kit, I don't think I can lie down.'

'Just take some deep breaths, try to relax and I'll lower you down.'

'Aargh!' Jeremiah grasped Kit by the arms, his fingernails almost drawing blood, but Kit held on and slowly laid him down. He lifted his feet up, eased off his boots and breeches and then stood back as Jeremiah whimpered pitifully.

Eventually he said, 'I'm so sorry for the fuss, Kit.' Jeremiah rubbed the perspiration from his face. 'But oh, Christ, it's so bloody painful!'

'It looks it. How did you do it?'

'Penvear has had me doing the work of two men, shifting sacks. I could feel it was a strain on my back, and then all I did was to bend down to tie my boot laces and I felt an almighty thwack in my back. That was it, I fell to my knees and I've been crawling around my bedroom on them for the last four days.'

'Did no one call?'

'Aye, Penvear did, two days after it happened, to tell me I was sacked for no show at work. I asked him to tell one of the lads I work with to come and help me, and you know what he said?' his voice tapered off. 'He said he'd do no such thing. He said if I wanted help, I could get off my lazy backside and ask for it myself.'

Kit shook his head in dismay. 'Have you had anything to eat or drink then?'

'I had a mug of water that was by my bed and a bit of cheese from the mousetrap, and that's it.'

Kit poured him a mug of ale and tore a chunk of bread and cheese and watched as he ate hungrily.

'Was it Rick Bray who evicted you?'

Jeremiah stopped chewing and flared his nostrils. 'No, it was Penvear himself, and very pleased he looked in the process. The bastard dragged me down the stairs! I swear when I'm back on my feet again, I'll bloody do for him,' he snarled, as he tore hungrily into the bread.

'I'll get Dr Eddy out in the morning. He might be able to give you something to ease the pain. Why did you not come straight here? Even if I'm not in, you know my door is always open!'

'Well, I do know you have Mrs Treloar lodging here now, so I knew you wouldn't have the room for me.'

Kit pulled a tight smile as his heart went out to this man. 'Mrs Treloar lives upstairs in the sail loft, yes, but I would always make room for a friend in need.'

'You're a good man, Kit - the best. Thank you. I fear I have relegated you to the chair with me being here.'

'It's no hardship, Jeremiah. I'll be up and out at dawn anyway. I fear there will be flooding on the high tide.' Another clap of thunder almost shook the tiles off the roof. 'Try and sleep if you can.'

Chapter 33

As the storm raged, Sophie feared she would never sleep. There was such crashing and banging going on outside. She even thought she heard voices downstairs, but dismissed it. Kit never kept late company - it was just another of his wonderful traits. Jowan would often bring men home after The Black Swan closed its doors. They would play cards, shout, swear and break wind with hilarity while they shared a bottle of contraband brandy long into the night. The thought made her shudder - it was those nights she feared the most. Jowan would eventually come to bed, drunk as a lord and clumsily force himself onto her, often falling asleep during the act. If she struggled to push him away, he woke angrily and tried unsuccessfully to molest her again, blaming her coldness for his lack of ardour. She gave thanks every day that those days were gone now. Over the last week she'd known more love from Kit than Jowan had ever bestowed on her. Kit's kind, gentle manner had helped her to trust again.

She must have finally dropped off because she woke suddenly with a start at dawn by the sound of shouting outside. She pulled her shawl about her shoulders to ward off the morning chill and stood at the window. The tide was full and still pushing upwards - the boatyard awash with floating wood and barrels. Small fishing vessels that had been tied alongside the river bank were listing alarmingly, not having enough rope to accommodate the unusually high tide. Kit was standing in the pouring rain, up to his ankles in muddy water, helping the other boatyard hands to slacken the sheets on the moored boats so they would not sink with the rising tide.

Pushing the sash window up, she called out to him, but her words were caught in the gale. Fortunately, he caught something of them and ran over. 'Can I help?'

'It might be best if you stay indoors for the time being. Eric shouted over from the other side of the river earlier.

He said to tell you that Stan would bring the pony and cart round for you. The water is knee deep on the other side of the bridge. I'll be busy here until the tide ebbs.'

She dressed quickly and pulled on her gumboots. If she could do no more, she'd make Kit a warm drink and put some porridge on the range ready for him when he came in later.

The water thankfully hadn't yet breached Kit's front door due to a pile of sand bags. Sophie stepped over them, shook the rain drops from her hood and as she pushed it back, she screamed when she saw a man in Kit's bed.

Jeremiah jumped. 'Christ! What's happening?' and then began to howl in pain.

'Who are you?' Sophie said, backing out towards the door.

'Jeremiah Rowe, Madam. I'm sorry to have startled you.' He raked his fingers through his hair as his face contorted in pain.

Sophie stepped closer. 'Wh…Why are you in Kit's bed?'

'He kindly offered me safe haven last night when I was in need. Forgive me, if I don't stand up, I can't. My back is paining me badly.'

'I see.' Sophie swallowed. 'Well, can I get you anything?'

He smacked his lips. 'Aye, a glass of water, please - I'm as parched as an autumn leaf. And a pot, I need to pee desperately.'

'Oh, right.' Unsure for a moment as how to help him with this request, she crouched down to reach for the chamber pot, but it had been used. She needed something else and spotted the vase of flowers she'd put on Kit's table two days ago. Yanking the flowers from the vessel, she threw the water outside and presented it triumphantly to Jeremiah.

He grabbed it thankfully and pushed it under the covers. He fiddled about for a moment and then when all was in position he glanced at Sophie with an arched eyebrow.

'Oh, sorry!' She flushed with embarrassment, realising she was staring at him, and turned away to the tinkling sound of water followed by a satisfied sigh.

Jeremiah cleared his throat for Sophie to turn around to find herself presented with a vase of strong smelling, warm, brown urine.

'Sorry,' he said sympathetically. 'I can't bend.'

Unable to chuck the contents until the river had started to ebb, she took it from him and placed it next to the chamber pot. With a quick rinse of her hands at the sink she primly filled the kettle, put it to boil on the range, handed him a glass of water and then proceeded to make the porridge.

Conscious that Jeremiah was watching her, she realised it must look very strange, her being so at home working at Kit's range.

'We only have one range between us, so I have to cook down here when Kit is out of the room,' she tried to explain.

Jeremiah nodded, but didn't look convinced.

As the kettle began to sing and the porridge cooked, Jeremiah's stomach rumbled so loudly it made Sophie smile. 'I'm cooking it as fast as I can.' She made three cups of tea and spooned a ladle of porridge into two bowls and set them aside. 'I'll just let that cool a moment,' she said walking out of the room with one of the cups of tea. At the door, she shouted to Kit to come over and drink something warm. As he walked towards her, he made a bow wave, which stirred up the silt and faeces in the water - it stank to high heaven.

'I see you have a visitor?' she said holding a handkerchief to her nose as she handed the steaming cup to him.

He took it gratefully. 'Another of Penvear's eviction victims, I'm afraid. He's also in a great deal of pain in his back.'

'I can see that. I've made him some breakfast. There's enough porridge in the pot for us all, if you want some?'

'I'll just take this for now, thank you. I'll get something when the tide ebbs.'

Returning to Jeremiah, she took a blanket out of the cupboard and tucked it behind his head. 'There.' She handed him the bowl of porridge. 'Hopefully you'll be able to eat in that position.'

The warm aroma of oats made his stomach rumble again. 'Thank you for your kindness, Mrs Treloar.'

She smiled sympathetically. 'Well, we victims of Penvear have to stick together. Now, I must get ready for work. I'll bring another vase down, just in case.'

*

Fortunately, Stan managed to draw the cart right up to the granite steps, so Sophie could jump from them to the cart's seat. She was wearing gumboots and an old oil-skin coat of Kit's. It was two sizes too big for her but at least she would stay dry. As they turned out of the boatyard, Sophie pulled on Stan's arm for him to stop the cart - Amelia's cottage was flooded up to half the height of the door! After surveying the scene, she knew there was no way she could wade through the flood, so instead shouted Amelia's name at the top of her voice.

Amelia's very dishevelled face appeared out of the upstairs window.

'What can I do, Amelia?' Sophie called up to her.

'There's not a lot to do at the moment.' Amelia leaned forward to inspect the lake of water still lapping up at her door. 'It looks like someone was kind enough to put the sand sacks at my door, but the tide was so high it's breached them. Once the water has receded, I'll come downstairs and start to sweep it out. It came from nowhere at five this morning. This damn rain didn't help.'

'I'll have to go to work now, but I'll be back to help as soon as I've finished at the farm. Will you be all right until then?'

'I'll be fine, but I'd appreciate your help later, thank you.'

As they rode through the deepest part of the flood, Sophie could see that both the post office and the Black Swan had been breached. She was heartened to find that Alpha Cottage had been saved from the flood - otherwise she'd have felt duty bound to help Ria clear up as well - despite Ria's continual unpleasantness towards her.

*

After all her farming chores, the tide had abated, so Sophie forfeited breakfast to go back and help Amelia. She'd have dearly loved to have told Lydia about her trip to Poldhu yesterday, but that would have to wait. Amelia had rescued her once - it was her chance to return the compliment.

The rain was still pouring, so with her skirts tucked into her waistband Sophie had to negotiate ankle deep silt, and twice nearly slipped on her backside.

Amelia's door was wide open and all the water had drained away but the stench of faeces, mud and mould attacked Sophie's nostrils and she was horrified as she surveyed the scene of destruction before her. The floor, furniture and half way up the walls were covered with a thick coating of slippery mud - which was almost impossible to walk on. 'Where do you start to clean this up, Amelia?'

Amelia was stood with her hands on her hips. 'I just start from the top of the mud line and swill and scrub until it's gone, but it takes a deal of bloody hard work and it'll take days to get it all out. If this damn rain continues though, it'll flood again at teatime!'

After filling two pails of water at the water pump, they started their huge clean-up operation. River debris had got everywhere. Even the bottom cupboard of the dresser contained three inches of mud and underneath it they raked out two tiny crabs, a grey mullet and a frog.

'This is terrible,' Sophie said as she scrubbed the walls

with more vigour.

'Well, it's not the first time it's flooded, and it certainly won't be the last,' Amelia said resignedly. 'I swear though, this house will be the death of me one day. We shouldn't have built here, being on a level with the river, but the land was cheap.'

Sophie stopped scrubbing. '*You* built this house?'

'Yes, with my husband, Jimmy.' Amelia's face clouded with a memory.

Sophie wiped a stray hair from her face. 'I've never heard you speak about your husband before. Was he local?'

'Yes, Mawgan. I fell in love with Jimmy when I was seventeen. He was a builder and I was a young midwife, having just taken over from my mother when she'd become too stiff with rheumatism. Jimmy and I courted for three years. I'd have married him in a heartbeat and lived in a field I was so enamoured with him, but he was determined to have a roof over our heads that was ours. When we weren't doing our other jobs we worked together building this cottage. I learned how to glaze a window and hang a door while Jimmy built the walls, fireplaces and roof. We were married the week after it was completed. He carried me over this threshold on my twentieth birthday - the walls still damp as they are now - only then it was with whitewash. That was twenty-five years ago.'

Sophie smiled at the story. 'How long were you married for?'

'Two months and then he was struck down with tuberculosis - I miscarried a week later,' she said mournfully.

'Oh, Amelia, I'm so sorry for you.'

'Well, it's no worse than you, you're widowed and *you* lost three babies.' She started to scrub again.

'Yes, but yours was a real love story. My circumstances were very different. I didn't love Jowan. Tell me, did you never wish to marry again,' she said tentatively.

Amelia stopped scrubbing. 'No! I chose my independence. For me to marry again, this house would have immediately passed to my new husband, and if he ever tired of me, he could have thrown me out on my heel. We have few rights as women! My Jimmy and I worked hard to build this cottage so that we'd have a roof over our heads that no one could take from us. I wasn't going to throw that away. Jimmy was the true love of my life, I never needed another. And there is where we *do* differ. You are yet to find the love of your life – or perhaps,' she arched an eyebrow, 'you've already found him!' She watched as Sophie flushed, then smiled. 'I thought something was afoot between you and Kit when we had supper at Lydia's the other night.'

Sophie smiled evasively. 'Let's just say we are thinking on it,' she said, returning to scrub the walls again.

'Stop thinking and start living. You'll get no better man than Kit. Oops! Talk of the devil.' Kit stepped into the kitchen and Amelia watched Sophie's face light up.

'Need any help?' he offered. 'Oh!' He smiled warmly at Sophie. 'I see you have some already.'

'Yes, I do, but many hands make light work. Here,' she pushed a couple of buckets into his hands, 'I'd appreciate it if you can you fetch us some more water, please?'

'I certainly can, and then I'll bring some more sand sacks over. The ones I put there last night obviously weren't enough. I'll do a proper job this afternoon, just in case.'

Amelia turned to Sophie. 'As I was saying, there is no better man than Kit.'

*

After bringing more sand sacks, Kit turned his attention to retrieving Jeremiah's belongings from his cottage. He went in search of Eric, who was incensed to hear of Jeremiah's plight. Without a thought for the consequences of damaging a property, they drove Eric's cart to his cottage, fully intending to break in, but by their good fortune, their friend John Rogers the locksmith was at the premises changing the lock.

'Hello, Kit, Eric.' John scratched an itch under his ear. 'What brings you to Jeremiah's door with your cart?'

Kit took a deep breath unsure of what to say. John had been friends with Kit and Jeremiah since their school days. 'We're here to collect Jeremiah's furniture from the cottage, John.'

'Oh! Why, where's he going?' John asked in all innocence.

Kit exchanged a glance with Eric. 'Do you not know?'

'Know what?' he swigged some water out of his flask thirstily.

Kit chewed his bottom lip. 'I thought because you were changing the locks, Penvear might have told you?'

He pulled a face and shook his head. 'I just got a message to go and change the locks. I assumed Jeremiah had lost the key!'

'He has - Penvear has evicted him!'

'He's done *what*?'

Kit proceeded to tell him the whole story. 'So, you see, because Jeremiah couldn't move his things, Penvear has commandeered it.'

John bristled indignantly. 'He bloody well hasn't!' he said.

Kit relaxed, knowing John was on their side.

'Come on then.' John downed his tools. 'Let's get his stuff on the cart.'

An hour later, John changed the lock of the door while Kit and Eric moved Jeremiah's furniture into Eric's barn for safe keeping. As they shut the barn door, Kit and Eric shook hands. This small victory for the honest working man felt so good.

Chapter 34

Thankfully the rain ceased and the wind died down so the tide did not breach Amelia's cottage again at teatime, but by the time Sophie had to leave her to go back to work it had become clear that Amelia could not stay in her cottage until it had fully dried out.

'I'll be fine,' Amelia protested, when Sophie offered to put her up.

'Tell her, Dr Eddy,' Sophie pleaded to the doctor, who had just called in to see them en route from administering a dose of laudanum to Jeremiah.

'Sophie is right, Amelia.' The doctor shook his head at the destruction of the house. 'There is a real risk of disease to the lungs from the spores left by the filthy water. In fact,' he warned, 'you should both wear something around your noses while you're cleaning this lot up.'

Sophie smiled at the doctor gratefully. 'I'll put a makeshift bed up for myself in my quarters, Amelia, you can have my bed.'

Amelia sighed heavily. 'I can see I have no choice now that you're both ganging up on me. So, thank you, Sophie, I appreciate it - though you'll not look so pleased with yourself, when you hear me snoring!'

*

When Guy Blackthorn returned home from work that day, he found waiting for him, not only the sheer domestic bliss of his growing family and his supper cooking, but an unexpected telegram from Kit.

JEREMIAH EVICTED BY PENVEAR STOP PERMISSION TO ASK BERT LAITY FOR A ROOM STOP KIT

Ellie watched Guy's face darken. 'Not bad news I hope?'

He looked up at her with the new-born suckling at her breast and marvelled at the beautiful scene before him.

'Just another 'rich against the poor' problem, I'm

afraid,' he said putting the telegram in his pocket. Ellie frowned. 'It's Kit asking for help for someone.'

'Oh!' she smiled genially. 'Can you help?'

'Thankfully, yes, but I need to go and send a telegram.' He bent to kiss the heads of his wife and new daughter.

'Goodness, you both smell delicious.'

*

Kit smiled with relief when he received the 'go ahead' telegram from Guy, and set off to see Bert Laity. When he stepped back out of Bert's cottage into the leafy lane, he was heartened and thankful that Bert was willing to share his house with a fellow ex-employee from the mill. He'd reside there rent free until he could get back working. Kit knew Jeremiah was a proud man and would not take charity easily, so just as soon as Jeremiah was able to get about better, which hopefully would be soon with the help of laudanum, he'd help him to move in and put his mind to finding him some sort of honest work.

The walk down Mill Lane, flanked by a canopy of self-seeded ash and oak trees, always made Kit feel at one with nature. Gweek was a fertile sheltered vale, flanked on all sides by lush green fields. Two streams fed into the great Helford River and one of them ran along Mill Lane. Although the weather had settled down to a calmer, albeit much cooler temperature than before the storm, the stream was still fast flowing due to the recent rain. On the edges of the stream, patches of foam had gathered in between the rogue branches with piles of still green leaves brought down by the wind. The air smelt mossy and dank, but it wasn't at all unpleasant. He stood a while on the flat bridge, remembering watching Sophic standing in the self-same place, the day she learned of Jowan's death. She'd loosened her hair and run her fingers freely through her golden locks, free at last from the shackles of her marriage. Kit smiled at the memory - she had never looked more beautiful. Soon they would be together and his fingers would be free to run through her lovely hair for always.

Against all odds, she'd taken a chance on him and learned to trust again. He was determined that he would never, ever, make her feel like her wings had been clipped again.

With that thought he checked his fob watch and set off back to his carpentry shop, but as he passed the mill, he had the strangest feeling that he was being watched. He was not wrong - when he looked up, he found Gilbert Penvear looking down on him from one of the windows. Kit shook his head in dismay and walked on, wondering to himself how that man slept easy at night.

*

The sight of Kit made Gilbert seethe. He'd found out that Jeremiah was lodging with him, and was absolutely sure Kit had something to do with the removal of the furniture from Jeremiah's cottage, although no one admitted to having seen it being removed. This fact he found hard to believe, as the cottage was situated in the dead centre of the village. He'd been incensed earlier that day after negotiating a very good rent with a family from out of the village on what should have been a furnished cottage, only to find it stark empty when he showed them around. Of course, Penvear interrogated John Rogers the locksmith about the matter, but the damn man had just shrugged and said the house was empty when he changed the locks. Someone, somewhere had made him look foolish, and he had a bloody good idea it was Kit Trevellick. Gilbert narrowed his eyes as he watched Kit insolently shake his head at him, determined more than ever to destroy him one day.

*

It was eleven days after the storm before everyone finally got their lives back to some sort of normality. The sun had returned to Cornwall and all was peaceful. Farmer Ferris had suffered some damage to his crops, but was confident that they would come through. He'd fared better than some farmers up country. The newspapers had been full of reports that the entire country had experienced devastating floods which had severely damaged standing crops. Apparently, trees had been stripped of their leaves and bark by unusually large hail stones. It was hard to imagine now.

Gweek as a village had mopped up after the deluge. Amelia's house was habitable again, thanks to the many hours she and Sophie had spent scrubbing the place, and Jeremiah had finally moved in with Bert. For the moment he'd been tasked with making spurs with Bert for Guy to thatch with, but Kit had other plans for Jeremiah. While he'd been recuperating, Jeremiah had spent a little time in Kit's carpentry shop as he was tentatively beginning to move around. He would hold the sides of the coffins while Kit nailed them together and was handy with the wood planer and a chisel – this gave Kit an idea about what to do with his carpentry shop, but he kept his thoughts under his hat until their plans had been sorted.

*

Sophie hung up one of the dresses she'd been making and stood back to inspect it. The other was packed in her small trunk ready to go onto the cart the next day for their journey to Bochym. As she started to clear her sewing away, she saw Kit walking down the gangplank from his boat. He stood and looked at it with his arms folded. He'd been attaching the name plate *Harvest Moon* onto her hull that morning and had pulled the tarpaulin off. That could only mean one thing! She was by his side a moment later. 'Is she finished then?'

'She is!' He nodded his head proudly. 'I want you to be the first to come aboard and take a look around her.'

'Oh!' She clapped her hands. 'I'm honoured.'

He walked the gangplank first and then held out a helping hand for her to step over onto the deck.

'Well, what do you think? Do you like her?'

Sophie was in awe of the beautiful features of the boat. 'She's lovely,' she breathed. Everything was spick and span, polished, and sanded to perfection. She walked a few steps running her hand over the smooth wood and then looked down into the cabin and smiled.

'Go down and take a look, but you must turn around and go down backwards because the galley steps are steep.'

At the bottom of the steps, there was a square area lined with fire bricks and covered with an iron plate with two holes for cooking. Though not a large boat, Sophie found the living quarters quite roomy.

'It's big enough to sleep two people comfortably. I can put a board down the middle so we can sleep together.'

Sophie felt her cheeks pink a little at this suggestion.

'Only when you feel ready, of course,' he added. 'I feel she should be called Sophie, but then our secret love would be no secret anymore, and of course it's bad luck to change the name of a boat.'

'No, Kit, *Harvest Moon* is a perfect name for her.' She looked around at all the hard work he had lovingly put in. 'You've waited a long time for this day, are you sad not to be sailing off into the sunset with her?'

He circled his arms around her waist and kissed her. 'How can I be sad about anything, now I have you in my arms?'

'But all this work, Kit!'

'It won't go to waste. We'll take her out on occasions. We'll see where we settle and then I'll bring her round to the closest port.'

They fell silent with their own thoughts about leaving Gweek – it was going to be a wrench for both of them. Sophie, sad to leave such good friends and the job she loved and Kit troubled because he had an established business here.

Kit broke the silence. 'How are your sea legs anyway?'

Sophie laughed gently. 'I'm not sure I have any. I've never been on a boat before. I've only ever stood at the side of one while the fish was unloaded. Gosh that seems like a lifetime ago.'

'And now we're embarking on a new life.' He kissed

her tenderly. 'Are you ready for our trip to Bochym tomorrow?'

'I am. I've just finished the two dresses I was making. I do hope they are appropriate clothes for polite society.'

'Sophie, stop worrying. Sarah and Peter do not stand on ceremony. I've met and drank with Peter several times, and you know how lovely Sarah is. Just remember how Sarah admired your dressmaking skills.'

'I know but, what if I say something silly over dinner?'

'I've not known you ever say anything silly. Just be your lovely self, and all will be well.'

*

Only three other people knew of their trip to Bochym - Lydia, Eric and Amelia. Sophie had dithered and worried about broaching the subject to Lydia and Eric about their plans to try and move away. The Williams had been so kind to her when she was in need and she felt like she was part of their family. In the end it was Lydia and Eric who broached the subject. They'd seen the developing relationship between them and gave their blessing to whatever they decided to do. They knew it was going to be a wrench for them all, but needs must if they wanted to live as man and wife.

Because the invite to Bochym now included an overnight stay, Eric had very kindly given her time off until Sunday, so that they didn't have to rush home, but she had one last call to make before they set off. Amelia had asked Sophie to pop in just before they left, as she was just finishing off a present for Ellie and Guy's new baby.

'There you go.' Amelia handed a parcel wrapped in brown paper. 'I've knitted a little coat and hat for the babe. It's just a little something. I must say I'm looking forward to the day I can knit for *your* little ones.'

Sophie blanched and held the parcel to her chest.

Amelia frowned. 'What's the matter, doesn't Kit want children?'

'I'm sure he does, but it will never happen!'

'Just because you lost Jowan's babies doesn't mean that will happen with Kit you know. You were deeply unhappy with Jowan.'

'But I can't,' she lowered her eyes, 'we can't ever...'

'What?'

Sophie swallowed hard and felt her head swim alarmingly having to have this conversation again. 'We can't ever be intimate,' she whispered.

'Why ever not? Oh, Sophie, do not let the way Jowan treated you put you off being with Kit. He is a very, very different man!'

'I know that, but we can't.'

Amelia threw her hands in the air. 'Why then?'

'Because of what Jowan gave me, you know down there - the disease.'

Amelia stood back aghast. 'Are you telling me you're still suffering?'

'Not suffering, no.'

'Does it still burn?'

'No.' Sophie wanted the ground to swallow her whole.

'Have you any lumps or sores then?'

Sophie's eyes blurred. 'I don't know, I don't think so.'

Amelia grabbed her by the arms. 'Why didn't you come and see me if you were worried.'

'What is the point? I know I'm afflicted with something awful. The last time I confronted Jowan when he brought another bout of his filth home, he said, "What the hell does it matter if I have the clap and you catch it, there is only me going there and it'll keep anyone from queering my pitch."'

'Jesus,' Amelia looked skyward. 'If anyone deserved to drown, that bugger did. Look Sophie, as far as I'm aware they were just infections he kept giving you. I can't be sure until you've had a proper examination. Dr Eddy can do that when you come back.'

'Amelia, no!' she said appalled. 'I can't let him look!'

'He's a doctor, Sophie. He's seen hundreds of

women…down there. Look,' she grabbed her again. 'I'll speak to Dr Eddy and if you're not comfortable with him looking, he'll tell *me* what to look for. Now, I want you to stop worrying about this. I am sure all will be well, and you and Kit will have a whole brood of children around your feet before you know it.' She hoped with all her heart that she was right and that Sophie didn't have gonorrhoea, because the mercury treatment for it was worse than the disease.

Chapter 35

Once again Sophie set off up Gweek hill a half hour before Kit - preoccupied with the conversation she'd just had with Amelia.

When Kit joined her and kissed her tenderly, he noted her reticence. 'Are you all right? You look pensive!'

She nodded. 'A little anxious about dinner, perhaps.'

'There is nothing to worry about, my love - I promise.'

*

They arrived at Bochym Manor at three. As the footman unloaded their trunks, Kit automatically made to walk his pony and cart away.

'Thank you, sir, I'll see to everything,' a groomsman said. 'Mr Treen the butler is waiting at the door for you.'

Kit grinned and reached for Sophie's hand as they walked up to the front door – they felt like royalty.

'Good afternoon, Mr Trevellick, Mrs Treloar.' The butler gestured them through the great oak door.

Sophie glanced nervously around the hall, until they heard Sarah call out to them. She was making her way up from the gardens, elegant as ever, even in her plain cream dress and long brown apron. Her hair was tucked into a wide brimmed straw hat and she carried a wicker basket in her gloved hand.

'Goodness, I had completely misjudged the time, do forgive me,' Sarah said pulling off her gardening gloves. 'I get so involved with the garden - time just flies by. Welcome to Bochym Manor, my dears, I do hope you had a good journey?'

'Thank you, yes,' they said in unison.

'I trust you would like to freshen up after your journey?' She looked up as a maid and a footman appeared behind the butler. 'We'll take tea in the French drawing room at half past three. Betsy, please could you look after Mrs Treloar? Thomas, please assist Mr Trevellick with whatever he needs.'

'Thank you, my la…I mean Sarah.' Kit grinned.

*

They followed the maid through the library towards a long corridor and then up the magnificent staircase, grinning at each other with every step they took.

'Mrs Treloar, you're in the Blue Room.' Betsy stood back so that Sophie could enter. 'Thomas will bring your bags shortly. Mr Trevellick you're next door.' She walked him to his room.

Sophie stood in awe of her surroundings. She felt like a princess in a fairy story. The room overlooked the front lawn. It was beautifully furnished with chairs upholstered with blue brocade to match the drapes. The bed, Sophie realised when she sat upon it, was made of feathers and dressed in crisp white embroidered linen. She could not resist laying her head on the pillow - it embraced her like a cloud!

A knock at the door made her scramble to her feet and she stood to attention as Betsy entered the room.

'Begging your pardon, Ma'am.' Betsy dropped a curtsy as a footman followed her in with her case. He bowed his head slightly in greeting.

'The countess asked me to help you unpack and press any of your gowns if needed,' Betsy said as she began to open the old battered trunk that Lydia had lent her.

Sophie felt her cheeks pink - the case looked so out of place within the opulence of the room.

 Sophie had brought with her an ivory day dress which she would wear to tea. She had also spent her last few shillings on some satin material so she could make a dress that looked presentable enough for her to dine at Bochym. It was a mint green, square necked creation that Lydia had said when shown, was beautiful and simply elegant.

Betsy shook her garments and after a small deliberation, they decided between them that no pressing was required and they were hung in the wardrobe.

'Would you like me to help you to change, Ma'am?'

Sophie smiled shyly. 'No, thank you, Betsy, I can manage. I do however require a chamber pot. I can't seem to see one in the room.'

'I beg your pardon, Ma'am, I should have shown you. Follow me.' She led Sophie into another room. 'This is your water closet.'

Sophie stood stock still – she'd never been in a room like it. There was a large roll top cast iron bath with ornate white and blue taps. It stood on four sturdy claw feet, and the most exquisite white fluffy towels were draped over the side. There was a washbasin, and hung above it one of the largest mirrors Sophie had ever seen. The pièce de résistance was a beautiful ornate blue and white lavatory. She took a step forward and wrapped her arms around herself as she looked down into the highly decorated pan. Without thinking she said, 'Goodness, it looks too nice to use.' She glanced at Betsy who giggled.

'We all thought the same, Ma'am when we saw it for the first time. Her ladyship says it's called Delftware.'

The two women grinned at each other.

'Well, too nice or not, I shall have to use it,' Sophie laughed. 'How do I work it exactly?'

'Just pull the handle on the chain after use, Ma'am,' Betsy said, leaving her to her ablutions.

*

When they came downstairs, they were shown into the French drawing room by the butler. It was the most wonderful room, embellished with huge mirrors and gold leaf plaster. It was also tastefully furnished with the finest French furniture, which Sophie noted by the look on Kit's face, he clearly appreciated.

They must have both looked terrified when they entered the room for tea, because Sarah could hardly keep the amusement from her face.

'Hello, come and sit down.' She held her hand out to Sophie to draw her into the room, gesturing to the table and chairs flanking the unlit fireplace. 'Goodness, Sophie, your hand is frozen. We couldn't decide whether to light the fire or not today and now you've decided for me. Although it's summer, these old houses never quite warm up. Mr Treen, would you ask someone if they could light the fire, please?'

'Yes, my lady.' The butler bowed.

'Gosh no, Sarah, please don't do that on my account. The temperature is fine, my hands are always cold,' Sophie protested.

Sarah smiled and nodded. 'You can get someone to light it before dinner tonight, Mr Treen. So now, we'll have tea for three, please, I am sure Mrs Blair has a wonderful array of delicious cake and sandwiches for us today.'

'Yes, my lady.' He bowed again and left the room.

'Now, Peter sends his apologies, but he's dealing with some urgent business on the estate, it keeps him so busy. So, it's just us for tea.'

Sophie glanced around the room noting the colourful marks the stained-glass windows threw across the large Turkish rug. 'This is a truly beautiful room, Sarah. I don't believe I have ever seen a room like it.'

'It is quite magnificent, isn't it? There are so many beautiful rooms in this house, I feel very privileged to live here. We'll go back into the library after tea. You may have noted, Kit, it has the finest hand-carved Italian walnut linenfold panelling you will ever see. It was carved in Bond Street, London in the 1840's by the same firm who undertook similar panelling in the Houses of Parliament. They shipped it from Tilbury to Falmouth docks and transported it by cart to Bochym, accompanied by two craftsmen. Do you know, it took them seventy-two days to install it and they only took two days off in that period! I should think you will appreciate the workmanship very much.'

'I admit I gave it an admiring glance when we walked through earlier - such beautiful workmanship!' Kit said.

'Talking of which, I trust you've both brought samples

of your work?'

'We've left them with your footman,' Kit said.   '

'Splendid. We'll take a look after tea.' Treen arrived back with a tea tray and placed it on the table but Sarah dismissed him with a smile and began to pour the tea herself. 'Do help yourself.' She gestured to the plate of finely cut sandwiches and cake. 'I've been in the garden all morning, so I am in much need of sustenance. We'll take a walk around the garden after the tour of the workshops if you wish, Sophie. Kit has seen it before, haven't you?'

'Yes, in the spring time. It'll be lovely to see it again in full bloom.'

'Then that is what we will do.' Within a few minutes, the conversation became less stilted and they were all chatting as though they'd been friends forever.

*

With tea over, they set off to the workshops located at the back of the manor.

'Sorry if I am repeating the tour I gave you a few weeks ago, Kit!'

'Don't bother about me,' he said, 'I'm looking forward to seeing everyone again.' *Except perhaps for Georgie,* he mused.

'We set the association up after an idea grown from speaking to Elise. She makes handmade quality lace, I don't know if she's shown you, Sophie.'

'No, not yet.'

'It's exquisite, but she was priced out of the market by manufactured lace. It worried me that eventually a specialist craft such as Elise's would inevitably die out and I simply wasn't prepared to let that happen. Peter and I had several empty cottages on the estate in need of repair, so we decided to offer them to specialist crafts people. We repaired all the structural problems, and of course Guy is re-thatching them. We charge only a peppercorn rent and in return the tenants keep their cottages in a good state of repair. They are also required to do a task a day on the estate - that could be helping with the milking, bringing in the harvest, tending the kitchen garden or mowing the lawns. Everyone who works here has the freedom to enjoy the grounds at Bochym, and we enjoy picnics by the lake, and boating, now that Kit so kindly repaired the boats for us. Oh!' She stopped at one of the workshops. 'It seems Georgina Blake is not in, so we can't look at her work.'

Both Kit and Sophie exchanged relieved glances.

'Georgina makes intricate filigree oil lamps, but I suspect you will see them before you go home. Now, this is Mr John Paul Cooper's workshop. John, these are my friends, Sophie Treloar and I believe you know Kit.'

Mr Cooper, a tall, darkly handsome man, sporting a long drooping moustache bowed a greeting, and kissed the back of Sophie's hand. 'Enchanted, Ma'am.'

Sarah and Sophie both smiled at his gesture.

'John normally works in Kent, but he is down for the summer to take in the clean Cornish air. As you see, John works in silver, metalwork and jewellery. His approach to decoration is, you will agree, magnificent and unusual. He uses materials such as coconut shell, ostrich eggs and would you believe, shark's skin, in combination with gold, silver, copper and semi-precious stones. Am I right, Mr Cooper?'

'You are indeed, my lady, I like to make intricate, fanciful pieces inspired by natural forms, medieval architecture, myths and ancient symbols,' he said with a flourish.

Sophie moved closer to inspect what he was working on. 'This is beautiful, how did you make it?' she asked.

'This is a cedar wood box,' he answered proudly. 'I covered it with linen cloth, before painting and then gilding it with gesso. The linen helps the gesso to adhere you see. Normally my darling wife, Clarisse helps to decorate the boxes, but as she isn't here, this is all my own work.'

Sophie smiled at his passion.

'Thank you for your time, John,' Sarah said as they moved on to the next workshop.

Sophie was in awe of all she saw. There was a young man called Chris making cane furniture, while his artist wife, Lesley was making beautiful screen-printed silk scarves.

'Lesley is also a very fine portrait artist,' Sarah said. 'Robert Floyd, in the next workshop is also a figurative artist and jeweller. He creates the most wonderful enamel hand painted brooches and rings, and in this workshop, we have Lucy, she makes the beautiful pottery you can see here.'

When they approached the carpenter in the last workshop, they heard him cursing slightly under his breath.

Kit smiled to himself - it must be a trait for carpenters to curse.

'This is Glenn Nedham. Is something amiss, Glenn?' Sarah asked.

'Oh! Begging your pardon for cursing, my lady, I didn't see you there. I'd just about finished this headboard ready for collection, in,' he checked his fob watch, 'a couple of hours, and I've accidently knocked one of the ornate spindles off it. It's sheared off completely. It'll not be ready in time now. I still have the last of the waxing to do.'

Kit stepped forward. 'May I be of some assistance?'

One carpenter eyed the other. 'So, you know your way around a wood lathe then?'

'Of course,' Kit laughed. 'Let me help. Take off the other spindle from the other side and I'll make a perfect match for you.'

Glenn Nedham turned his suggestion around for a moment - he had nothing to lose. 'Very well, there's a piece of oak over there,' he said with a tremble in his voice.

The ladies watched as Kit put his foot on the treadle of the wood lathe and got to work on the ornate spindle.

'Let's go and see if Mrs Blair has some lemonade for us in the kitchen while the boys get on with their carpentry,' Sarah suggested.

When they returned an hour later, they found Glenn and Kit bent over the headboard, kindred spirits together, attaching the perfectly turned piece of oak Kit had made.

*

Georgie watched from her bedroom window, as Sarah, Kit and his 'little mouse' toured the workshops. She was determined not to meet her love rival until she was ready to face her on *her* terms.

Chapter 36

After a walk around the garden, Kit and Sophie took their leave to dress for pre-dinner drinks, giving Sarah an opportunity to call a meeting of the association members to take a look at the samples Kit and Sophie had brought.

There was a collective agreement that the footstool Kit had brought was a craft that would fit in very well at Bochym. The standard of the carving of the seahorse was second to none and of course the spindle he had made earlier settled Sarah's mind of how good a carpenter he was. But when Sarah showed Sophie's Italian quilted bag, whereas everyone else thought it superb, Georgie was very dismissive about her work.

'Oh, no, Sarah.' Georgie held the bag in between her fingers as though it was dirty. 'This is so amateurish,' she said, screwing her nose in distaste. 'I have a friend up in London who can do this so much better – her work is far superior. She would love to come here and work, if you're looking for someone to do this.'

Disheartened, but determined, Sarah held up the cushion Sophie had brought to show everyone. The rest of the group inspected the workmanship with appreciative eyes again except for Georgie.

'Oh, no! It's simply awful.' Georgie dismissed it with a flick of her hand. 'This is not what we want here.'

Although Sarah had set up the association, there had been firm rules that all who worked there had to approve of the others working alongside them, so she was deeply disappointed in Georgie's response. It seemed her plan to have Kit and Sophie working here would not come to fruition. However, Sarah was determined not to give up on Kit and Sophie joining the association, and was curious to see why Georgina was so against Sophie. She decided to invite them all to an impromptu drinks party before dinner – it was an opportunity to watch Georgie like a hawk to find out.

*

Never had Sophie dreamed that she would be invited to such a palatial house to socialise with the gentry, and in truth she was quaking in her new shoes.

A quiet knock came on her door. 'Sophie,' Kit said softly. 'Are you ready to go down?'

Sophie could hear the nervousness in his voice too.

'Yes, don't go without me.' When she opened the door, Kit stood back and gave an appreciative smile.

'Gosh, you look beautiful.'

'Thank you.' She saw that Kit too had made a special effort with his clothes. He wore a new shirt with a loose tie and his best jacket and breeches had been brushed and pressed. The invitation for dinner was to be a casual affair, but they both wanted to make a good impression.

'I wish Ellie and Guy were here,' she whispered as they descended the oak staircase.

'They'll be here soon,' Kit said, squeezing her hand a little. 'They're due at six. I think Ellie wanted to feed and settle the baby before she left her with Jessie.'

They were met by the butler at the bottom of the stairs. 'His lord and ladyship are expecting you in the drawing room, if you would care to follow me.'

Kit and Sophie glanced nervously at each other as they stepped through to join a small gathering there.

It was a large room surrounded with moulded walnut panelling, which drew Kit's eyes immediately. The ornate ceiling sported a beautiful oval roll-moulded central feature and was edged with an equally ornate moulded cornice. A large, highly polished grand piano stood in the bay window and the three chesterfield sofas which flanked the granite fireplace were occupied by several people they had met today in the workshops. They gratefully took a glass of champagne from the tray offered to them.

'Ah there you are,' Sarah said. 'Come and join us. We thought we would have a little impromptu drinks party before dinner. I thought it would be nice to meet everyone you saw this afternoon, in a more social environment.'

Both Kit and Sophie spotted Georgie as soon as they'd entered the room and Kit felt Sophie stiffen when Georgie made a beeline for them.

'Darling, Kit,' she said totally ignoring Sophie. 'You naughty, naughty boy. Where have you been?' She slapped him playfully. 'I've been waiting for you to return to me, but,' she pouted, 'I'll forgive you for keeping me waiting, and now you're here we can have such fun again.' She reached out and pawed Kit's shirt front and he batted her hand away in annoyance. Georgie's eyes flashed angrily. 'Come, come, Kit that is no way to treat me after all the lovely times we've spent together!'

Sophie saw Georgie glance in her direction obviously to see her reaction, but Sophie had turned her head away. The nauseating smell of Georgie's perfume was almost enough to put her off roses for life. She hoped that Sarah would come to the rescue, but as she searched the group for her, she realised that Sarah was engaged with someone else. Turning back to face Georgie, she saw her take an unhurried look at Sophie's gown and curl her lip. She had in her hand a glass of claret and it was clear from her manner that it was not the first she'd partaken in that day.

'Kit, darling, come with me, I'm sure we can find some more interesting drinks guest over here.' As she spoke, she flourished her glass, causing the contents to splatter down the front of Sophie's dress.

Sophie shrieked and jumped back as she watched the great red stain grow with every second.

Georgie pulled a face and giggled. 'Oh, dear, silly me, I didn't see you there. Never mind, I'm sure the dress wasn't expensive,' she said pawing the damp patch with her hand.

'For Christ's sake, Georgie - you did that on purpose!' Kit grabbed her hand and pulled it away from Sophie.

She shot her hand to her heart and gave a pained look. 'On purpose, moi! What a notion.'

Everyone in the room had fallen quiet - they had all

seen Georgie drunk before, but were shocked at what she had just done.

Sarah was at their side in an instant. Sophie saw her narrow her eyes at Georgie as she placed her hand on Sophie's elbow. 'Come, my dear. Let me help. We won't be long, Kit.' At the bottom of the stairs she addressed Betsy. 'Run and fetch Lowenna, we have a little clothing problem. We'll be in my dressing room.'

'Yes, my lady.'

'Kit thought that was deliberate, Sophie. Was it?' Sarah asked, as she led her up the stairs.

'I don't know, Sarah,' Sophie lied, feeling her cheeks burning. She felt so embarrassed to have been the centre of attention downstairs.

Within a minute, Sarah's lady's maid knocked and entered the room. 'Lowenna, please find something beautiful for Mrs Treloar to wear.' She turned to Sophie and smiled gently. 'Fortunately, we are about the same size.'

'I think this will look beautiful on Mrs Treloar, my lady.' The maid produced from the wardrobe the most exquisite gold silk and lace dress Sophie had ever seen.

'Perfect. Now, Sophie, I will leave you in Lowenna's capable hands. She will help you slip out of your damp dress and get you ready for dinner. I just need to see to something. I'll be back shortly.'

*

Sarah was about to call Georgie out of the drawing room when she saw Guy and Ellie walking along the corridor.

They listened in dismay when Sarah told them about the incident with Sophie's dress, and Ellie ran upstairs to see if all was well.

'Honestly, Guy,' Sarah said, 'I cannot believe Georgie's behaviour. I mean what on earth got into her?'

Guy smiled gently. 'Come, Sarah, let me enlighten you on a letter she sent to Kit. I think that will explain everything,' he said, walking with her into the library.

*

Kit was having great difficulty suppressing his anger. He knew Sophie had spent long hours getting her lovely dress ready for this occasion, only for it to be ruined by Georgie. It was unforgivable. 'That was a disgraceful thing to do, Georgie. You should be ashamed of yourself.'

'Oh, Kit, don't be angry with silly little me.' She moved towards him, but he put his hand out to stop her. 'I just wanted to get you on your own, without *her* listening to all I need to say to you.'

Kit took a deep angry breath. 'I thought I'd made it very clear to you that I have no desire to hear any more of your fantasies about you and me. Why can't you understand that?'

Georgie turned the sides of her mouth downwards. 'But you don't understand. My life is nothing without you. I love you, and I know you love me really.'

'Then you are very much mistaken,' he snapped.

Mr Treen the butler approached and the conversation halted.

'Miss Blake. Your presence is requested in the library.'

'What now?' Georgie gave an exasperated sigh. 'Don't go away, Kit darling. Your little Georgie will be back in a tic.'

'I sincerely hope not,' Kit uttered under his breath.

She giggled and slapped him playfully. 'I know you don't mean that.' With a flutter of her eyelashes and a wave of her fingers, she followed the butler out of the door.

*

When Georgie entered the library, she found Sarah waiting for her. She looked around the room as though to find someone else there and then settled her gaze on Sarah.

'You wanted to see me?' she said petulantly.

'Yes, I did.' Sarah smiled. She had been looking for an excuse to do this for a long time.

*

281

Sophie felt like a real lady dressed in Sarah's silk gown, and by the time she and Ellie walked back down the stairs, the drinks party guests had dispersed to carry on their social soirée elsewhere, except for Georgina Blake. She had rapidly sobered up and was sat in her cottage contemplating her future, having been given leave to quit Bochym by the end of the following day.

'Do I look all right, Ellie?' Sophie stopped to look at herself in the mirror at the bottom of the stairs.

'You look beautiful, Sophie.'

Sophie ran her hands nervously down the dress and then lifted them away, frightened she would soil it. 'Thank you. I've never worn anything like it. It feels as though I am wearing a cloud - I feel naked!' she whispered.

'Well, you look sensational and don't worry about your other dress. I know for a fact that Izzy the laundry maid can get any stain out of any garment.' She grinned. 'Now come on, or we'll be late for dinner.'

Chapter 37

If Kit and Sophie had been impressed with the French drawing room earlier, the sight before them now almost took their breath away. The golden room was warmed by a glowing fire, and though the evening sun shone low through the stained-glass windows a beautiful candelabra sparkled over the table, which glistened with glass and fine white linen.

As the evening was informal, everyone broke with protocol and sat beside their respective partners.

Dinner started with smoked salmon, dill & lemon paté on a plate of delicate leaves with small triangles of toasted bread. Roast goose was followed by apple turnover with cream. The dress Sarah had leant Sophie felt a little tight around the waist by the time she'd savoured the last morsel of dessert. This was no surprise - Sarah's tall willowy figure sported the tiniest of waists and Lowenna had had to tighten Sophie's stays a little more than she would have liked. Never mind, she felt wonderful in the dress, and it was the first time she'd ever worn anything made by a professional dressmaker. She was determined to examine the construction of the garment when she took it off later that night.

'Well,' Peter smiled at Ellie and Guy. 'This is the first time we have all been together since the birth of your new baby! So, let's raise a glass and toast the little one. I trust she is thriving?'

'She is,' Ellie said as she chinked glasses with everyone. 'We've arranged the christening for the last Sunday in September. There will be a cream tea afterwards in the tea room. I do hope you can both join us. Sophie and Kit are of course obliged, as they are to be little Sophie's godparents.' She smiled at them both.

'Well, I can't wait for another cuddle of my namesake,' Sophie said.

'So, Sophie, how do you like our little group of

craftsmen?' Peter asked.

'I think everyone is wonderful,' she said shyly. 'It seems a lovely place to live and work.'

'Sarah and I were impressed with the samples of your quilting, as were the rest of the group.'

'Thank you,' she said quietly.

'You too, Kit, outstanding workmanship. You're not just a talented boat builder then?'

Kit nodded appreciably.

'And at the moment you both live in the house attached to your carpentry shop, is that correct?' Peter asked without a suggestion of disapproval.

Sophie cleared her throat. 'We do live in the same house, yes, but not together,' she looked askance at Kit, 'yet! Kit very kindly let me move into his sail loft when Gilbert Penvear started to make life difficult for me.'

'Gilbert Penvear?' Peter asked curiously.

'Yes,' Sophie said nervously. 'Do you know him?'

'I do,' Peter answered cautiously.

'Please forgive me if I've offended you. I was unaware he was a friend of yours.' Sophie silently berated herself for speaking so freely.

'Do not be uneasy. You have not offended me, Sophie, only caused some concern. Penvear is not a friend - I employ him as manager of the Gweek Corn Mill, you see.'

Kit accidently dropped his pudding spoon making it clatter on his dish and blurted, 'Penvear is *only* the manager there?'

'You seem surprised, Kit?'

'I am surprised,' he breathed. 'He's led everyone in Gweek, *and* who works for him at the mill, to believe that he owns the place.'

Peter's eyes narrowed. 'Has he now? Well, I can assure you - the mill belongs to me!'

'You!' Kit and Guy exchanged astonished looks.

Peter shifted uncomfortably.

'Yes. Goldsworthy decided to sell me their shares in the

mill two-years ago - the Bochym Estate already owned a forty per cent share in the mill, secured on the marriage of my sister Carole to their son, Philip Goldsworthy. Old Goldsworthy wanted a clean break from Gweek after his son, Philip, made an attempt on Guy's life and absconded.'

Guy nodded and said, 'Go on.'

'Well, when they moved away from Gweek five years ago, old Goldsworthy put one of his key workers, Bert Laity in as a temporary manager, and only visited the mill every quarter to oversee things. It was not an ideal situation, so when we were having one of our shareholders meetings in London a couple of years ago, he begged me to buy his sixty percent share so they could sever ties with the mill once and for all.' He paused to take a sip of claret. 'As you can imagine this estate takes up a great deal of my time. The last thing I needed was a mill to run, but I could see it was a sound investment. It was Goldsworthy who recommended Penvear to me. Apparently, he'd managed a cotton mill in the north for several years, but was keen to move back down south. I only met the man once in London, and though he was a little peculiar in his appearance…..'

'Peculiar?' Kit interrupted. *That's an understatement!*

'Yes, there was something strange about him - I remember he had unusually long fingernails for a man,' Peter said with a grimace.

Sophie's scalp began to prickle with a horrible thought - she still bore the scars of the gouges on the back of her legs.

Kit must have noticed her concern because he asked, 'Are you all right, Sophie?'

She nodded tentatively.

'Yes, Peter!' Sarah berated him. 'What a horrible thing to mention at dinner.'

'Please accept my apologies, Sophie. Anyway,' he carried on, 'apart from his peculiarities Penvear seemed an ideal candidate to run the mill without me having to have too much input, and so I employed him. I let him rent Goldsworthy's old house as well.'

Kit's mouth visibly dropped. 'Penvear *rents* Quay House?'

Peter looked up sharply. 'He does, yes!'

'Well!' Kit snorted. 'You're telling me something that will interest a great many people in Gweek!'

'I am?' Peter looked both intrigued and concerned.

'Everyone thinks he owns Quay House. He lords it up there and even keeps a manservant and a housekeeper.'

'What?' Peter sat back in astonishment. 'As far as I understand, Penvear has no capital of his own and I wouldn't think he can keep servants on the wage I pay him!'

'Well,' Kit flourished his glass, 'He must have found the money from somewhere – he owns half a dozen cottages in the village and charges his tenants a very high rent.'

Everyone watched as Peter visibly blanched.

'Perhaps he's been fleecing the mill accounts!' Kit said dryly.

A great hush had fallen over the dinner table now as Peter folded his arms and said defensively, 'Penvear has access to money for the upkeep of the mill and the men's wages, it's true, but any additional spend has to be agreed with me.'

With the bit between his teeth now, Kit said, 'I don't mean to be rude, but do you question every additional spend? Because I wouldn't trust Penvear as far as I could throw him!'

Everyone shifted uneasily as they glanced between Kit and Peter.

Peter pursed his mouth as a shadow of doubt fell over his face. 'As you can appreciate, I am very busy with the Bochym Estate. Being a mill owner was not really on my agenda. One expects to trust a manager to keep a business running smoothly. I've had no issues with Penvear running the mill, according to reports the mill is doing well financially.'

Sophie watched as Kit's nostrils flared, he looked fit to burst.

'I'm not surprised.' Kit threw his napkin on the table. 'It's running on at least four workers less than it should! So, is profit *all* you're interested in? Do you care nothing for the welfare of your workers?'

Ellie and Sarah gasped in unison and Sophie watched as Guy shot a warning look to Kit, but inside she felt her heart swell - she had never been so proud of him. She slipped her fingers into his hand to give him some moral support, realising that there was a very high chance they'd be asked to pack their bags and leave.

Peter saw Sophie's gesture to Kit, and mistakenly said, 'No don't berate Kit, Sophie. He obviously needs to get something off his chest.'

Sophie lifted her chin. 'I've no intention of berating him. I agree with everything he says.' She felt Kit squeeze her hand.

'I see.' Peter cleared his throat. The tension in the room was palpable.

Without doubt, Sophie felt a pang of regret that she wouldn't be sleeping in the comfortable feather bed after all, but there it was. What had been said could not be unsaid.

Everyone watched as Peter drummed his fingers on the table. 'I looked over the ledger only yesterday. There has been no reduction in the number of wages drawn,' his voice tapered off slightly as though he realised Penvear might have fleeced him. 'As you see from my response, I was not aware that the workforce had reduced.' His mouth twitched angrily. 'Perhaps you would be kind enough to tell me what has been happening, Kit.'

'With pleasure!' Kit sat forward. 'According to the mill workers, Penvear rules that mill with a rod of iron - he is a tyrant! People are sacked if they take a day off to bury their friends and loved ones.'

Peter's eyes widened. 'I beg your pardon?'

'It's true. Sam Pearce died of a heart attack last December. I heard say that he was forced to carry double the amount of flour sacks, day after day, until his heart gave out. When he dropped down dead, no one was allowed to pay their respects to his widow at his burial. The only people there were a few women from the village, Dr Eddy, Amelia Pascoe, the Williams and myself.'

Peter paled. 'Go on.'

'Jake Lush took the day off to bury two of his children only to be given his marching orders the next day. And you mentioned Bert Laity - the man who was deemed good enough to run the mill in the absence of the owner. Well, Penvear obviously thought nothing of him, so when Bert ignored Penvear's refusal to let him take the day off to bury his wife, Mabel, he too was sacked the very next day and consequently evicted from his cottage at the end of that month. Bert had given his whole life to working at that mill. He and Jake would have starved to death if not for the kindness of their neighbours.'

A deep blush crept up Peter's neck. 'I am grieved - grieved indeed at what you tell me, and ashamed to admit I knew nothing of this. I certainly would not have let *that* happen.'

Guy leant forward. 'If only *I'd* known that you owned the mill, Peter, I'd have informed you in a heartbeat! Bert has been living in my cottage in Gweek, rent free since his eviction. The only work he has is to make spurs for me to thatch with, but it's no job for a man of his standing. And only this week, Jeremiah Rowe has moved in with Bert after being sacked and evicted for taking time off work after injuring his back from carrying too many sacks. Isn't that right, Kit?'

'It's true, yes. Everyone who rents one of Penvear's cottages in the village is fearful of his ruling tactics. In fact the reason Sophie lives in my sail loft is because he evicted her when she wouldn't 'call' on him.'

All eyes fell on Sophie and for a split second she willed the ground to open up and swallow her.

'Forgive me, Sophie,' Kit said seeing her reaction. 'It pains me too to bring it up, but it must be said.' He turned back to Peter. 'He had me arrested the other week on a false charge of smuggling, because I gave her a room to live in when he'd made her homeless.'

'Oh, my goodness, Peter.' Sarah's hand shot to her mouth. 'You have to do something about him!'

Peter looked suddenly nauseous, as though the salmon paté was not agreeing with him. He exhaled a slow, measured breath and placed his hand on Sarah's. 'I intend to, Sarah, believe me. Kit, you have every right to be angry over this - you too Sophie and Guy. I've been negligent and obviously misguided to expect my business ventures to prosper under Penvear.' He shook his head shamefully. 'I've been so busy here, I had no idea, and I know,' he held his hand up, 'that is no excuse, but the first thing I shall do is see to it that Bert and Jeremiah are reinstated.'

Suddenly Peter looked like he was struck with an unpleasant thought. 'Forgive me, Kit, if I haven't made this connection before, but are you the same Trevellick on the invoices for repairs to the waterwheel at the mill?'

'I am yes, though I've done no repairs to the waterwheel since I overhauled the wooden buckets in 1902. Why do you ask?'

'Would you excuse me for a moment?' He pushed his chair back so fast he almost upended it.

'Peter, where are you going?' Sarah asked, as he disappeared through the door.

Everyone around the table fell silent until Peter returned almost immediately clutching a handful of paperwork.

'Are these not from you, Kit?'

Kit took the paperwork and scanned the invoices and the dates – they were all generated during the last eighteen months. Each one stated the same work done on the waterwheel with an accompanying signature and at a grossly inflated price. Kit handed them back to Peter. 'These are copies of past invoices I sent to the Goldsworthy's. They look like mine, but they're not written by my hand. Someone has forged these, along with the dates and my signature – the amount is far above what I would charge! As I said, I haven't needed to do any work on the waterwheel, and in theory it should be sound for many years to come.'

'Well,' Peter said sitting back in his seat, 'I can see I have well and truly been duped. Penvear has probably used the money generated from these false invoices to buy his first property in Gweek. Subsequently the revenue from the rent has allowed him to purchase more properties, and *that* is an offence!'

'You mean he'll go to prison?' Kit and Sophie asked in unison.

'It's very likely. I shall have my notary look over the accounts. If he's done this with your invoices, Kit, the chances are he's done it with other tradesmen.'

'If Penvear goes to prison, what will happen to the people renting from him?' Kit asked anxiously.

Peter leant forward and steepled his fingers. 'Let me deal with Penvear first, but rest assured, Kit, no one will be homeless. You have my word. Now, shall we retire to the drawing room?'

Chapter 38

When everyone settled down to after dinner drinks in the drawing room, Sarah played for them for a while on the grand piano while everyone relaxed after what had been quite an eventful meal.

After playing several wonderful short pieces, Sarah joined them on the sofa to a round of applause. 'I do hope you two are not rushing off tomorrow. As the weather is so settled again, we are having a picnic lunch down at the boating lake at noon. We were hoping you could join us, weren't we Peter?'

Peter nodded, but looked quite preoccupied.

Both Kit and Sophie knew that would mean another altercation with Georgie.

Picking up on their reticence, Sarah added, 'If you are worried about encountering Georgina Blake, please don't. Miss Blake will not be joining us tomorrow. Let's just say she is moving on to pastures new in the very near future.'

Sophie and Kit exchanged glances.

'We don't hold with unpleasantness here, you see. It's not what our little association is about. We are a community, and it's important that we all get on together. Isn't that right Peter?'

'Absolutely.' Peter raised his brandy glass and smiled amiably at them.

With the tension settled, the altercation behind them now, Kit visibly relaxed. 'Then we'll be very happy to accept your invitation to the picnic.'

'Guy, Ellie, will you join us too?' Sarah asked.

'It sounds delightful, but I must open the tea room tomorrow. I can't leave Jessie to run it on a Saturday, it's just too busy,' Ellie answered.

'That is a shame, but we fully understand.'

'And, on that note,' Ellie said, 'we must take our leave. I'll need to go and feed the baby.'

'Yes, thank you for a lovely, albeit lively, evening.' Guy

grinned at both Peter and Kit.

With the goodbyes said, Kit and Sophie retired to bed.

In the sifted glow of the gaslight at the top of the stairs, Kit took Sophie's hands in his and kissed them. 'I can't tell you how relieved I was when you supported me at dinner. I fear I could have had us thrown out into the night!'

'I was well aware of that, but I can't tell you how proud I am of you, that you are prepared to stand up for what you believe in.' She broke into a broad smile. 'I was prepared to sleep in the cart, because I too believe in the rights of the people.'

'I truly believe that I've found my soulmate in you, Sophie, and I long for the day we can be together.'

As he kissed her, she put her hands up to smooth his hair. 'It's what I long for too.'

They stood in a warm embrace, neither wanted to say goodbye. 'At least it seems that Penvear will get his comeuppance now,' Kit said softly.

'And not a moment too soon.'

Kit felt her shiver. He looked down and regarded her for a moment. 'When Peter was speaking about Penvear's nails…'

'Yes,' she answered pensively.

'I've never seen him without gloves! Have you?'

'No!' She took a deep breath. 'Perhaps he only takes them off when he attacks defenceless women in the dead of the night!' she blurted.

He held her at arm's length. 'Oh, Christ, Sophie!' he breathed. 'You don't think….?'

Sophie's eyes flickered. 'I don't know - but it's a real possibility.'

'Oh, sweet Jesus!' He gathered her back into the safety of his arms. 'I'm telling you now, if Penvear doesn't go to prison, *I* bloody will, for murdering him!'

Sophie settled into his embrace. 'You're always my knight in shining armour, aren't you?'

He smiled down at her. 'And I always will be. I'd do

anything for you, you know that. '

They melted into a kiss, until footsteps on the stairs parted them.

'Oh, begging your pardon,' Betsy said on seeing them. 'I'll come back in a few minutes to help you out of your dress, Ma'am.' She descended the staircase.

They grinned up at each other. 'I'd better bid you goodnight, Sophie before we evoke gossip.' He kissed her again. 'I'll see you in the morning, my love.'

Sophie walked to her room, still feeling where his arms had held her – she felt as though she was lit from inside.

*

She'd taken off her beautiful dress by the time Betsy knocked on her bedroom door. She had hoped that she could take a closer look at how the dress was made - but had neither time nor good enough light to inspect the intricate seam work before Betsy whisked it away from whence it came.

After the thrilling experience of carrying out her ablutions in the opulent water closet, Sophie put on her nightdress and climbed into the softest bed she had ever laid on. In a cloud of feathers, she was sound asleep in no time at all.

*

It was nothing more than the gentle touch of a hand at first – tracing the length of her arm to settle on her ring finger. Sophie turned on her side, snuggled into the pillow, resting her hand beside her face. In her slumber she dreamt Kit was beside her, until, she was aware, of a real hand resting on hers. Her eyes snapped open as her body froze in shock. The room was eerily illuminating a young girl who stood before her dressed in pink silk, pointing an icy finger to where Sophie's wedding ring had once been.

Sophie heard a scream, not realising it had come from her own throat, and the door to her bedroom burst open.

Kit, dressed only in his shirttails, ran to her side, swiftly wrapping his arms around her, but nothing could stop the tremble running through her body. 'Sophie, shush, what is it?' he soothed. 'Have you had a bad dream - Penvear perhaps?'

'No, no! There was someone here in the room! Standing right where you are now,' the words caught in her throat.

'Let me light the lamp a moment and all will be well.' He twisted to find the flint, and the room illuminated. 'There see, there is no one here, only me. Perhaps it was just a bad dream.'

Sophie watched wild-eyed as the shadows danced eerily across the walls. 'Don't leave me, Kit. It wasn't a dream. Someone was here, I know it.'

He closed his hand over hers and squeezed it reassuringly.

'Let me go and close the bedroom doors, just in case we've woken the household.'

'Come straight back, won't you?' she panicked.

'I will - I'll just go and get a blanket from my bedroom and I'll stay here with you. I'll be back in a moment.'

Sophie sat up against the pillows, her eyes searching wildly around the room for the girl. She looked down at her hand, still feeling where the icy finger had traced the small indent where her wedding band had once sat. Cradling her hand under her armpit, her mind was working overtime. What did it mean? Even if it was a dream, what was the significance of the gesture?

Kit returned within the minute, dragging a blanket in his wake. 'I'll sleep on the chaise longue,' he announced.

'No, Kit, please come here.' She patted the mattress beside her.

He hesitated. 'Are you sure?'

'Yes, I need you near me, if, if you don't mind.' She patted the mattress again with more urgency.

In a heartbeat he'd climbed up beside her, but lay on top of the bedclothes. The blanket was settled over his legs and he pulled Sophie into an embrace.

'That frightened me, Kit!' She snuggled up close to him feeling her heart pump furiously. 'Didn't Ellie say that this place was haunted?' she whispered.

'Shush, now. Nothing can hurt you. I'm right here by your side.'

With the lamp burning and the warmth from Kit's body, Sophie's ragged nerves settled. She listened as he murmured reassuring words of love until eventually her eyelids drooped and she drifted off to sleep.

*

When Sophie woke at first light, she revelled in the warm, safe proximity of Kit's body. Sometime during the night, he must have snuggled down to cup his body against hers. His arm draped lazily over the side of her body, his hand softly cupping her tummy, while his breath, deep and peaceful, rose and fell tickling the back of her neck. Although he still lay on top of the bed covers, there was a perfectly lovely intimacy about their close confinement. Once she believed the intimate closeness of another man would alarm her, but Kit as always, had treated her with the utmost respect.

She stilled when Kit's breathing altered - he was waking. He gently pulled his arm from where it lay and then she felt the bed move. A little shy that they'd spent the night together, she closed her eyes feigning sleep, listening to the soft pad of his bare feet on the floor until they stopped beside her.

Very softly he whispered, 'I love you,' and then left.

She opened her eyes, turned on her back and smiled - the terrors of the night swallowed up with the dawn of a sunny day.

Betsy knocked softly and came in within moments of Kit leaving.

'Good morning, Ma'am,' she said, opening the curtains. If Betsy had seen Kit leave, there was no judgment on her face. Over her arm she held the dress Georgie had ruined last night.

'I'm drawing a bath for you, Ma'am,' she said, opening the wardrobe door to pick out a hanger. 'Her ladyship tells me that you will be attending the picnic luncheon. I trust you'll be wearing the dress you wore for tea yesterday?'

Sophie smiled. Betsy was obviously trying to tell her that was the correct attire to wear for a picnic. 'Thank you, Betsy.'

'It's pressed and ready in the wardrobe, and here is your lovely dress from last night. Izzy has done a fine job at removing the stain.' She held the dress up for Sophie to inspect.

She had indeed done a fine job! Sophie fretted that the dress would be fit for nothing, but here it was, pristine. 'Goodness, Betsy, please convey my utmost gratitude to Izzy – she's a miracle worker.'

Betsy grinned. 'I'll tell her Ma'am, she'll like that. Your bath will be ready now.'

*

Sophie indulged herself in a deep fragrant bath – certain in the fact that she would never have the opportunity to do this again. Bath time at home consisted of dragging the tin bath, normally used to do the washing in, to sit beside the fire, and then boiling several pans and kettles of water to fill it. Afterwards the tiresome act of bailing the water out by the bucket load would defeat the object of a bath. She sighed blissfully as the silky water washed over her. How she would love a room like this, and oh, how she would love to start every morning like this one! She knew now, without a single doubt in her mind, that she wanted Kit beside her forever.

*

While Sophie lounged in the bath, Georgie was gathering the last of her belongings together. She was seething at the turn of events, and it was all Sophie Treloar's fault. Georgie had requested a meeting with Sarah first thing that morning, to try and smooth things over with her, but received a firm note of refusal and that she was no longer welcome at any social events within the estate. Humiliated at her banishment, Georgie requested and was granted one thing - a carriage to take her where she needed to go. The mighty Bonython Estate, a couple of miles up the road, would welcome her, of that, she was sure. Without a doubt she'd miss her life here, but apparently, she'd gone *too far* last night. Bah! It was only a little spillage and the dress was clearly homespun. She glanced regretfully around the cottage she'd occupied for the last two years - the scene of many parties and, she thought with a wry smile, a few trysts. So yes, she'd go, if she had to, but this wasn't the end of it. If that 'little mouse' thought she was going to sail away with Kit into the sunset, she had another think coming!

*

Very reluctantly Sophie stepped out of the bath. She dried herself with the softest of towels and then shivered as if the room had suddenly chilled. With an unnerving feeling of being watched, she clutched her towel to her breast and spun around, her eyes scanning the room for someone. It was then she was aware that once again an icy finger was touching where her wedding ring had once been.

She fled from the room, colliding with Betsy, who was standing waiting outside the door, causing them to end up in an untidy heap on the corridor floor.

'Oh!' Betsy squeaked in alarm and scrambled to her feet ready to help Sophie up. 'Are you all right, Ma'am?'

'I'm so sorry, Betsy, I didn't see you there.' Sophie struggled to regain her composure. 'Please forgive me. I err, it's just that….' She could see Betsy was waiting for her to explain her sudden exit, but she couldn't get the words out.

'Perhaps… you had a funny turn in there?' Betsy offered cautiously. 'Sometimes a hot bath does that!'

'Yes.' Sophie looked warily back into the room. 'I think perhaps you're right.'

'Well, no harm done.' Betsy brushed down her apron.

'Let me help you dress. Mr Trevellick is in the French drawing room with my lord and ladyshop, if you care to join them for breakfast.'

'Thank you,' Sophie said shakily.

Chapter 39

Aware that she had luxuriated in the bath a tad longer than she should have, Sophie took her seat at the breakfast table and bid everyone a good morning, apologising for her lateness.

'No apologies necessary, Sophie.' Sarah smiled. 'We are taking breakfast a little sooner than normal. Did you sleep well? It's just that we thought we heard something last night. I got up to see if all was well, but your bedroom door was closed and all was quiet.'

'Yes, thank you,' she hesitated.

'Sophie had a bad dream, didn't you?' Kit prompted. 'I heard her call out, but she settled again shortly after I investigated.'

'Oh! I am sorry. What was it about, can you remember?'

Sophie smiled. 'It was the strangest thing - I don't think it was a dream. I woke and thought I saw a woman in a pink dress.'

'Pink dress?' Kit said, holding his toast aloft. 'You didn't tell me that!'

Sophie glanced warily at him. 'Yes, why is that significant?'

'Well perhaps it really wasn't a dream,' he said cagily. 'It's just that I spoke to a girl dressed in a pink dress in the gardens a few weeks ago. It was next to the Holy Well and she asked me if I was here to help her father. I assumed she was your daughter, Peter, although she looked a little old to be so, but I told her that yes, I was here to help you, and that I was mending the boats. She then did the strangest thing, she stamped her foot and said, "So you're not a lawyer!" and stomped off.'

Peter glanced at his wife to explain.

'She is definitely not our daughter - our daughter Emma is only two-years-old. I do believe you have both met one of our resident ghosts,' Sarah said nonchalantly.

'Peter doesn't believe! But that is only because he has never seen them! The father, the pink lady was referring to, is the gentleman who died in a duel on the front lawn. We…'

Peter cleared his voice.

Sarah gave him a smile. 'Sorry, *I* believe she cannot settle until justice is done and the man who killed him is brought to task. I'm afraid there is nothing any of us can do for the girl, but she does have a tendency to ask people for help.'

Sophie felt her appetite diminish. 'But why did she visit *me* last night?'

'I don't know, Sophie. What did she say?'

'Nothing, she just touched my hand, where my wedding band used to sit!'

This time Sarah and Peter exchanged a worried glance.

'It's rare that she does anything to help anyone. She's normally the one asking for help,' Sarah said seriously. 'I've only known her to do that once before.' She took a sip of tea and continued 'She came to me one evening, doing much the same thing, pointing at my wedding ring. It turned out that Peter's carriage was held up by robbers at gun point and he was made to give over all his valuables.'

'Oh, my goodness - were you all right, Peter?' Sophie asked.

'A bit shaken to say the least, but as Sarah said - and I hate to admit this, Sarah knew something had happened to me en route home, before I had a chance to tell her.'

'So,' Sarah added, 'what I'm saying, is that she normally only does something like that if the recipient has to be wary of something - a cautionary visit perhaps?'

Sophie glanced at Kit. 'Well, she's a little late in telling me that my husband is in danger! He drowned in March!'

'Perhaps she was telling you that you might get news soon that they have found his body!' Peter said.

'That would certainly solve all our problems, wouldn't it?' She reached out to Kit.

'Well, let's hope that is what it is,' Sarah smiled, gently masking her doubts.

'Do you have many ghosts then?' Sophie asked cautiously, not really wanting to know.

'A few.' She grinned at Peter. 'The pink lady's father is here too. Now he is a sight to behold. He is dressed in a full 17th century outfit and has a tendency to brush past you on the staircase.'

Sophie blanched. As much as she enjoyed the opulence of this house, she was glad she wasn't spending another night in it!

'Don't worry, Sophie, he doesn't appear until four in the afternoon.'

'What? *Every day!*'

'No, not every day.' Sarah smiled at Peter who just shook his head at Kit.

'You may mock, Peter,' Sarah said. 'The duel has been witnessed by many people over the years.'

'Have you seen it happen, Sarah?'

'No, but I believe it does.'

'Gosh. Don't you feel unnerved by everything?' Sophie asked.

Sarah laughed. 'They can't harm you. We just have to learn to live with them. After all, they live here too. We are just the next generation to walk these rooms.'

'Well, talking of lawyers,' Peter said throwing his napkin onto the table. 'If you will all excuse me, I need to take the carriage up to Helston to see mine.' He gave Kit a knowing look. 'Forgive me if I'm late for the picnic, darling. I'm not sure how long I will be.' He kissed Sarah on the cheek. 'I hope to see you before you leave, Kit, Sophie.'

*

Gilbert Penvear rose as usual that Saturday morning, quite unaware that an extraordinary meeting had been called in Helston between his banker, the Earl de Bochym and his lawyer. Gilbert sipped his tea and buttered his toast as he took a leisurely breakfast. He'd not venture to the mill until after midday - he liked to keep his workers on their toes. If they were unsure when he would turn up, they would not try to skive, as he knew some of them did. He had his eye on one or two of the older employees. They were forever coughing and slacking while shifting the bags of flour. If they were old and useless, they were no good to him and they would have to go.

*

Just after lunch, Jeremy Nancarrow was helping Gilbert on with his jacket when two horse-drawn vehicles drew up outside Quay House. Gilbert took an unhurried look out of the window to find a covered horse drawn cart alongside a fine carriage. When the knock came to the door Gilbert waved Jeremy away with the flick of his wrist to see who it was. 'Whoever it is tell them I am busy and to make an appointment.'

Jeremy returned to the dressing room slightly flustered.

'Now what?' Gilbert asked impatiently. 'What is it man?'

'Three gentlemen are waiting in the library, sir. The Earl de Bochym, Mr Coad, who I understand is the earl's lawyer and Mr Kernow your bank manager.'

Gilbert felt a sudden pang of panic. *Did they know something, surely not! He'd been meticulous in covering his tracks.* There must be another reason for their visit. With that thought he pulled his jacket straight, eased the stiffness out of his collar with his finger and set off downstairs with an air of authority. He walked into the library buttoning his gloves.

'Gentlemen, to what pray do I owe the honour of this visit?' he said lifting his chin in the air. 'I was just about to go out.'

'Perhaps you would care to take a seat, Mr Penvear,' Mr Coad said.

Gilbert paused for a moment and then moved to sit behind his desk, aware there was no pleasantry in the lawyer's voice.

Peter flipped the back of his jacket enabling him to sit opposite Penvear. 'It has come to my attention that you have abused your position as manager of the Gweek Corn Mill.'

Penvear narrowed his eyes. 'Now look here,' he said defensively, shifting uneasily in his seat.

Peter stopped him. 'Do not speak until I have finished. You have fraudulently used money allocated to the running of the mill and its workforce, to substantially feather your own nest.'

Penvear pinched his lips together. The mention of fraud caused a clawing sensation in his stomach.

'You have also fraudulently obtained money by forging invoices for work that has not been carried out, and used that money to purchase properties within the village.'

Gilbert frantically searched his mind for the names of the invoices he had forged – one of them had been for Kit Trevellick. 'Oh, I see!' Gilbert sat back steepling his fingers. 'This is Trevellick's doing, isn't it? I heard he was working down that way – didn't realise it was with you at Bochym Manor. Well, I can tell you now that whatever he has told you, it's a pack of lies. I'm surprised at you, my lord, to take such heed of a wastrel such as him, especially as he's been back and forth pretending to mend the waterwheel these past eighteen months. I was beginning to question the invoices myself! Perhaps you should look into *his* finances. He has already slipped the net on a smuggling charge.'

Peter was beginning to lose his patience. 'Enough, Penvear! Messers Coad, Kernow and myself have spent the morning going over the mill accounts with a fine-tooth comb and the evidence speaks for itself. You have put good men out of work and continued to draw their wages from the bank, causing untold, unnecessary suffering to the good people of this village. You are a despicable individual and you will be severely punished for your misdemeanours.'

'Now just you wait a minute.' Gilbert stood up as though to dismiss them.

'I said, *enough,* Penvear. Now sit down and be quiet. Mr Coad would you be kind enough to ask Sergeant Wallis and his colleague to step in - their prisoner is ready.'

'Prisoner! What the devil are you talking about?'

'*You* will be going to prison for a very long time.'

*

Kit and Sophie had spent the morning walking the gardens before taking the trail through the vast arboretum. Hand in hand they walked in glorious companionship, stopping several times to watch the wildlife in the series of ponds, lakes and streams edging the pathway. They walked as far as the Dower Lodge, before retracing their steps back, until they came to an ornate wrought iron gate. Resting their arms atop of the gate, they took in the delights of the soft, lush green hills this glorious estate settled in.

At midday they changed for the picnic lunch and joined the others by the lake. Shoes and stockings had been shed with abandon and Lucy and Sarah were dipping their feet in the water. Sketch pad in hand, Robert drew the scene before him, while John and Glenn lay on the blankets soaking up the summer sunshine.

Sophie and Kit settled on a blanket on the perimeter of the party, shy and reticent at first amongst their new bohemian friends. The champagne had already been opened which accounted for everyone's languidness. Glenn stood up and thrust two glasses of champagne in their hands and the picnic baskets were open, spilling over with fruit, scones, bread and cheeses. A gramophone had been brought down to the lake and soft melodic music drifted along in the warm breeze, while cheerful, relaxed chatter filled the air.

Eventually the champagne relaxed Kit and he lay back on a cushion with a sigh. His tie discarded, and his shirt open revealing dark hairs at his chest, while Sophie happily watched an abundance of butterflies flitting from flower to flower - ethereal in the sunshine. Georgie wasn't mentioned once so it seemed no one was too concerned at her departure.

One of the boats bumped against the mud bank, followed by shrieks of laughter.

Chris jumped from the boat and pulled Lesley to the safety of the bank. 'Here you go, Kit, take her for a row. It's thanks to you we have boats this year, for they were in a sorry mess after last year's season.'

Kit sat up. 'I don't mind if I do! Sophie?' He stood up and held his hand out to her and she took it eagerly.

The boat was steadied while Sophie was helped in. There were blankets and cushions strewn everywhere, onto which Sophie sat. The boat wobbled slightly when Kit stepped aboard but settled as he sat and picked up the oars.

Though the lake was small, the murmurings from the bank were swallowed up by the gentle swish and dip of the oar in the water, and the cacophony of buzzing bees and bird songs. The gentle thump, thump of the ram which pumped the water into the lake from the Poldhu River seemed to synchronise with Sophie's heartbeat.

She lay back, luxuriating in comfort whilst trailing her hand delicately in the cool water. Occasionally her fingers would gently bump against the water lilies, rising up from the muddy depths to open their faces in the sun. The warm August air was sweet and heady with the scent of tuberose, lilies and honeysuckle adding to the sublime afternoon.

Kit stopped rowing for a moment, letting the oar drip and the boat drift for a while. 'I love you,' Kit whispered to her. 'Isn't this the most perfect moment in time?'

'It is. I cannot believe this is me, sitting here with you. I fear I shall wake up from this dream one day. I don't want it to end, Kit.'

'This is just the beginning, my love.'

Back on dry land, their glasses were filled once again.

The bubbles tickled Sophie's throat and her head swam pleasantly. This time when Kit lay down, Sophie leant her head on his lap, and her little finger curled around his. 'Together like seahorses,' she whispered.

*

As the afternoon drew on and with no sign of Peter returning from his business meeting, Sarah watched Kit and Sophie blend with this gathering – she knew it was time to speak. 'What do you both think of our little group then?'

Kit and Sophie sat up and smiled.

'I think I can speak for both of us,' Kit said. 'It's wonderful what happens here, the work, the social scene, everything.'

Sarah looked around, everyone had stopped what they were doing, waiting with anticipation for her to speak again. 'That is gratifying to hear. We are all in agreement that you could both bring something very different to our little community, *if* you would like to join us.'

'Us?' Sophie's mouth dropped open and looked to Kit for his reaction.

'You could take over Glenn's cottage, when he sadly leaves us on September 21st. It's yours if you want it.' Sarah watched as they digested the news. 'It's a lot to take in, so go home and think about it. I suspect you'll have a lot to sort out with your current business, Kit, if you do decide to join us, but if you can let us know either way before the end of this month - we would appreciate it.'

Kit shook his head - he couldn't believe his ears. This life was theirs for the taking - somewhere to start again and be with Sophie. He clasped Sophie by the hand and she smiled. 'Well, thank you, we don't know what to say.'

Sarah gave a deep sigh. They were clearly not expecting this news, which in itself was heartening. Several people had come to Bochym thinking that just because they could craft something they had some sort of right to be there. This couple were different. From the moment she'd met them at Poldhu, she knew they were not the type to expect the privilege of being asked to join the association. They came here yesterday with no other expectations than to have dinner – that made a very refreshing change.

Chapter 40

Jeremy Nancarrow sat at the bar in the Black Swan nursing his second stiff whisky, still undecided whether to drown his sorrows or drink to celebrate now that Penvear had been arrested and he was unemployed. The Earl de Bochym had apologised to him for the turn of events, and told him he could stay on in Quay House until he found new employment. He wrote him a very generous severance pay cheque and offered a reference should he need one. The housekeeper too was given a cheque which would see her right for a long time. After the third whisky, Jeremy decided this *was* a celebration. Penvear had got his comeuppance at last and oh, but the look on his face when he was carted off in the police wagon was a sight to behold, he would savour that sight for years to come.

*

There were celebrations all round in Gweek that day, as word of Penvear's arrest swept through the village like wild fire.

Bert Laity walked back into the Corn Mill that afternoon as the newly appointed Mill Manager. He was greeted with cheers of relief and welcoming back-slaps - quite unable to believe the turn of events in the last hour, when he'd opened his front door to three gentlemen, one of which was the Earl de Bochym.

As for Jeremiah, his back injury clearly rendered it impossible to return to his job lugging heavy sacks of flour all day long. The earl promised that he would be found appropriate work as soon as he was fit and able. For now, though, he'd been tasked to visit every cottage the earl now owned, to make sure his tenants were happy and living in accommodation fit for use. He was also to tell them to expect a letter informing them that their rent would be reduced significantly from this day forward.

*

Oblivious to what was going on in the village, Stan lay on

the grassy riverbank to ease the stiffness from his back. With Sophie away today, they'd all had extra cows to milk. He had a damn good idea that wherever Sophie had gone yesterday, she'd gone with Kit, because Kit's pony and cart had been gone all night, and that made his heart heavy. He sat up and glanced at the *Harvest Moon,* wondering if they would sail off in her. He'd been down to take a look at her that morning and could see it was finished now. He felt so confused, he knew Sophie wasn't interested in him and he wanted Sophie to be happy, of course he did - Jowan had been awful to her - he just didn't want Sophie to leave Gweek.

He yawned and stretched. It was teatime so there wasn't a soul about - either that or people were keeping cool indoors as it had been a hot day. The tide was just starting to flow in, it was time for him to move - the cowshed still needed sweeping and swilling. He got up and dusted the grass from the seat of his pants, but as he turned, he noted someone un-harnessing a pony from a cart at the top edge of the cow field – the figure looked vaguely familiar. It was only when he began to walk back to the farm that it registered who it was, and he felt a deep sense of foreboding. God may have decided not to give him hearing or speech, but his eyesight was as keen as mustard. He ran back down to where he'd stood a moment earlier, but the figure had gone. Being a hundred percent sure of what he'd seen, his eyes scanned around the village. It was then he spotted something equally disturbing - a figure running out of the boatyard! He narrowed his eyes, struggling to decipher what exactly was going on, and then he saw the smoke and took a sharp intake of breath.

*

Kit and Sophie were quiet as they made their way home to Gweek - each lost in their own thoughts about the offer. It was a truly wonderful opportunity and they were both thrilled if not a little anxious for their own reasons.

'I'll..'

'It'll..'

They laughed when they both spoke in unison.

'You first,' Kit said.

'I was going to say that I'll miss Gweek. You'd think all the unhappy years I spent there that I would be glad to leave it behind, but,' she gazed at Kit, smiling at his sunburnt nose, 'you changed all that. These last few weeks have been some of the happiest I have known.'

He reached over and squeezed her hand affectionately.

'I love my job and my farming family too. Lydia, Eric and Amelia have been such good friends to me - it makes me a little sad to think I have to leave them all.'

'I know what you mean.' His broken sigh spoke volumes. 'My carpentry shop has been in our family for generations. I grew up here, where all my friends are.'

Sophie felt her throat thicken. 'I'm sorry that my circumstances mean that you have to leave everything.'

Kit frowned. 'You've nothing to be sorry about. I've waited eight long years for you. I'd go to the ends of the world so that I could be with you every day. I want to wake up with you every morning like we did this morning – warm, safe and happy. You're my world and it's time for us to build a new life together. Gweek was just the start of our journey - our friends will always be there. As for the carpentry shop - I have a mind to offer it to Jeremiah. He knows his way around a piece of wood. If he's interested, I'm sure it'll be in good hands. This opportunity for us at Bochym Manor is more than we ever hoped for. I say we should grab this chance with both hands.' He pulled his pony to a halt. 'Come, get down from the cart a moment.'

'Why?' she laughed.

'Come.' He lifted her down and knelt on one knee. 'I know we cannot marry, but would you do me the honour of being betrothed to me until we can?' He took her finger and slipped on the beautiful gold ring, embellished with an enamelled heart, that he'd purchased that morning from

Robert Floyd, the jeweller.

'Oh, Kit!' Sophie clasped her hand on her heart – she'd never been given a proper piece of jewellery before. Her wedding ring had been brass, which constantly tarnished her finger. 'Kit, it's beautiful.' She splayed her fingers to admire it.

'I hope you don't mind a seven-year engagement,' he said.

'You may have grown tired of me in seven-years,' she teased.

'I shall grow tired of you, the future Mrs Trevellick, the day it snows red ink!' He cupped her face in his hands and kissed her tenderly. 'We may not be sailing off in the *Harvest Moon,* but if we take this opportunity at Bochym, we'll be together when the harvest moon rises this year.'

'I can hardly wait,' she breathed.

*

It was almost six-forty-five when they joined the road to Gweek. The evening was warm and the sun was setting among the accumulating clouds in the far west of the county. The sky turned pale blue and pink and was a sight to behold.

'I don't believe there is a more pleasant sight than this drive down to Gweek, do you not think so, Kit?'

'I agree. I never tire to look at this green fertile land, though it looks a little misty down in the village.' Kit looked into the far distance. 'In fact, it looks more like smoke to me!'

They both fell silent, hoping that all was well in their community. As they neared the Corn Mill, the acrid air began to sting their nostrils - something terrible was happening. Kit flicked the reins to make Willow move faster and as they neared the centre of the village - it became clear the fire was down by the river. Kit pulled the pony to a halt. 'Can you see to Willow, Sophie? I'm going to help.'

He'd only run a few yards when he stopped dead in his

tracks. Everywhere was chaos. Villagers were running to and from the river, all trying to put the fire out on *his* boat.

Stunned momentarily, he snatched a bucket from a child's hand, scooped a gallon of river water into it and ran to the *Harvest Moon*.

'Oh, Christ, Kit!' Eric shouted when he saw him. 'We can't save her. She's completely ablaze. We've been battling for nearly an hour now.'

Aware there were tears streaming down his face, he shouted back, 'What the hell happened, Eric?'

'I've no idea. We'd just finished milking when Stan alerted us to the flames leaping from the boat.'

*

With Willow fed, Sophie ran down to see what was happening, but was caught by Amelia and pulled to one side.

'There is nothing you can do, Sophie. There isn't a spare bucket in the village.'

So, they watched helplessly as everyone battled in vain for another hour, but eventually everyone stepped back defeated – their faces blackened with soot. There was a stunned silence, except for parched throats being cleared from the smoke.

Kit dropped to his knees in desperation having watched all those years of work, gone, in the space of two hours. He felt the weight of Eric's arm around his shoulders and was aware that Sophie now stood silently and tearfully by his side.

Constable Treen stepped forward, his face and shirt blackened with soot. 'Have you any idea how this might have happened, Kit?'

'God knows!' He felt the muscles along his jaw line tighten as he threw his head back in despair. 'There was nothing, *nothing*, on that boat that could have spontaneously combusted. I cleared away all the tools and materials, because she was finished,' the last word caught in his throat.

Eric wiped the black sweat from his forehead. 'I think it was deliberate!'

Both Kit and the constable looked up at him curiously.

'Stan here alerted us to the fire, and there was a strong smell of kerosene oil when I got here.'

The constable addressed the crowd. 'Did anyone here see anyone acting suspiciously near the boat?'

'I saw Stan cross the river and look around the boat this morning,' a small boy chipped in.

'Did you now!' Constable Treen beckoned Stan over. He pointed at Stan's chest, then at his own eyes and then at the burned wreckage of the boat.

Stan nodded anxiously. He moved towards Sophie, reached for her arm and pointed at her ring finger.

Sophie pulled her hand away from his grasp before anyone could see the ring Kit had just given her. 'What are you doing?' she mouthed crossly.

'I reckon the mute did it,' George Blewett shouted from the crowd.

'Don't call him that!' Eric shouted him down.

'Just a moment, Eric,' Constable Treen said, and then turned to Blewett, 'What are you trying to say?'

'Everyone knows the mute is soft on the widow Treloar – he watches her often enough.' He grinned. 'I reckon he was worried Trevellick was going to sail away with her, now that boat was finished.'

Suddenly all eyes were on Kit, Sophie and Stan.

Stan looked puzzled as to why everyone was staring at them. He turned and glanced at the angry faces of Kit and Sophie and then felt Treen grasp him roughly by the arm. In a panic he pulled free and ran to Sophie, and stuck his ring finger in the air.

Sophie gasped in disbelief at his rudeness.

Constable Treen yanked him away from Sophie, but Stan stamped his foot in frustration and then pointed at where a ring would go on his finger and then at Sophie.

'Told you,' Blewett guffawed. '*He* wanted to marry the

widow himself.'

Kit's anger knew no bounds then as he lurched towards Stan. 'God damn it, you had better not have done this! Christ, I saved your bloody life once. Is this how you repay me?'

Stan reeled back from Kit's angry face.

Sophie pulled on Kit's sleeve. 'He doesn't understand what you're saying.'

Sheer frustration got the better of Kit. 'Get him out of my sight, before I make him understand then!'

Constable Treen stepped in-between Stan and Kit. 'We'll get to the bottom of it, Kit, you mark my words.' But as Stan was escorted away, he struggled frantically, and broke free. Running back towards Sophie he pointed at his ring finger and cast an imaginary fishing rod.

Blewett roared with laughter, 'See, the daft lad wants to reel the widow in for himself!'

Stan felt his shoulder being grasped again, but made a last-ditch attempt at being understood. He pointed at Kit, made the shape of a woman with his hands, and then pointed at Sophie making the gesture of tears running down his cheeks.

Blewett who had moved closer shouted, 'Seems the lad was worried you were going to use her and leave her, by the look of it, Trevellick.'

'Shut it, Blewett,' Eric shouted, 'You're not helping matters.'

Kit glowered at Stan. 'What the hell - for Christ's sake, someone get him out of my sight.'

As the Constable dragged Stan away from Kit, Eric growled at him not to be rough with the lad. He turned to Kit to try and sooth his temper. 'You know Stan would never do such a thing! There must be a rational explanation for all this.'

'Must there, Eric? All I know is somebody did it and Stan seems to know something about it!' He couldn't listen anymore. He threw his hands in the air, and walked off, dismissing Eric's pleas.

*

When the crowd dispersed, Kit sat down by the smouldering hull in silent despair. Sophie joined him, but Kit's mind was so far away, it seemed even her presence could not ease his sorrow.

She reached out to his stricken face, blackened and streaked with sweat and tears. 'I'm so sorry for you, Kit,' she whispered. 'Come on home, now.'

He shook his head. 'Leave me be, Sophie. I need to be alone for a while.'

*

The cell attached to Constable Treen's house was just a room with a lock. There Stan sat, head in hands, mucus and tears dripping down his face, confused as to why he was here, and truly frightened he'd been unable to make them all understand.

His ma had been equally distressed and angry, which in turn had upset him ten-fold, rendering him too flustered to sign properly to explain himself. Edith Mumford had screamed and bared her fists at Constable Treen, demanding her son's release, claiming that he was not capable of such a crime, but Treen stated that they'd have to wait until the morning when Stan had calmed down and they could get to the bottom of this. For the moment though, all evidence pointed at Stan and he couldn't be released. Arson was a serious offence – a crime, that if found guilty, would result in hanging.

Chapter 41

When darkness began to loosen its grip, Kit rose wearily from his sleepless night. With no appetite for breakfast, he dressed quickly and stepped out into the chill of the morning. The river valley hung heavy with acrid smoke, mingled with a blanket of fog. When the sight of the charred remains of his boat swirled into view, he felt a pain so deep in his heart it almost stopped his breath.

Stooping down to pick up the name plaque, which was all that remained of the *Harvest Moon*, he wiped his hand over the sooty words as his eyes blurred. His sorrow was interrupted by the sound of Sophie's footsteps descending the granite steps. Jumping down onto the dry river bed, he hid from sight. He heard her call out to him, but he leant against the river wall, squeezing his eyes tight shut, praying that she would not come over. If she came to him she'd wrap her sympathetic arms around him, and that, he was afraid, would open the floodgates and he couldn't bear that. He needed time to himself, time to process what had happened, and time to put his feelings into some sort of perspective.

He reached out to run his fingers along the blackened hull, sick to the heart about the wasted hours he'd spent lovingly restoring it. There wasn't a person in this village who didn't know what this boat meant to him! How could anyone take it on themselves to destroy it, and why? This question had kept his sleep at bay, and several theories had surfaced. Stan wasn't the only person unhappy at his relationship with Sophie. Gilbert Penvear had reason. His constant vendetta against him showed that, and of course hadn't Kit just brought about Penvear's downfall? And then there was Georgie! Hadn't she been banished from Bochym because of them? But to torch a boat - would she do that? No, he couldn't believe that of her, even though she was a woman scorned. He sighed resignedly. Unfortunately, all the evidence pointed to Stan, though he'd have been the last person Kit would have thought responsible for such an act. The only way to settle this was to go and see Stan Mumford in his cell.

*

After knocking at Kit's and receiving no answer, Sophie glanced towards the river which was obscured by fog.

'Kit?' she called out softly. No answer. He must have gone off somewhere, away from the smouldering hull. Her heart ached for him. His anguish was hers too, and she felt it keenly today.

Shivering, she pulled her shawl closer to ward against the damp chill of the morning and set off into the swirling fog to work. Oh, why does life have to throw up these awful scenarios? Everything was so perfect yesterday! She patted the ring Kit had given her - it was looped on a ribbon around her neck and tucked away in her bodice for safe keeping. She may as well have worn it on her finger though after Blewett's proclamation of her relationship with Kit last evening. Damn the man for his loose tongue! Sophie was not ashamed of the inference - she just didn't want people to know yet. A jab of pain pierced her temple, a symptom of anguish due to the lack of sleep. Amongst other things she'd worried about all night, was Stan - alone and frightened in a cell. Despite his erratic behaviour towards her last night, she simply would not believe him capable of such an act of destruction – she'd go and see him after milking.

The fog was denser on top of the bridge and the dampness penetrated her shawl making her wish that she'd put a coat on. After the sunshine of yesterday, August, it seemed, felt like it was being pulled in by the chilly claws of autumn. Although the changing colours of the leaves were a lovely sight to see, autumn was Sophie's least favourite time of the year - spring would always hold that trophy. Spring was about renewal, as indeed this spring had been for her. Without doubt she had been reborn especially with the help of Kit. *Oh, lord please let him find his*

317

way through this catastrophe, so we can continue our journey together.

Turning back onto the riverbank, the fog was clearing in patches, but the breeze carried an overwhelming acrid smell and there were remnants of the smoke lying low on the riverbank. She made to cover her nose with her shawl when a shuffling noise caught her attention. Barely a second later she fell to the floor doubled over - something had hit her! Her head swam nauseously as she grasped at the searing pain in her stomach. Groping in the dirt, saliva dribbled down her chin as she gasped for breath. She opened her mouth to scream, horrified when she found she could make no other noises but a terrible choking and wheezing sound. In the next instant something was thrown over her head and she was being dragged along the road.

*

There was a strained atmosphere in the milking parlour that morning, causing the cows to not yield properly. Eric, normally a placid man, was angry. First that Stan was locked up in a cell and that people thought ill of him, and secondly, Sophie hadn't bothered to turn up for work!

'It's no good, Charlie.' He threw his cap on the floor. 'I know Kit has had this setback, but that does not merit Sophie not coming to work. I'm off to get her.'

Stomping down the river bank, he could see Kit through the clearing mist, moving bits of blackened wood around with his foot.

'Kit,' he yelled angrily.

Kit looked up in alarm.

'I know you've a lot on your plate, but can you tell Sophie to hurry up and come to work, we need her.'

Kit frowned. 'But I saw her set off for work three quarters of an hour ago!'

Eric turned to look towards the village. 'Well, she's not turned up for milking, and what with Stan locked up, I'm short-handed. It's not like her to be late!'

'Leave it with me, Eric, I'll go and see if she's fallen or

something.' Forgetting his despair momentarily, he ran towards the centre of the village, but Sophie was nowhere in sight. Would she have gone to see Stan? Dismissing that thought because of the early hour, and like Eric said, she would never be late for work. He walked a little further until he passed the water pump and stopped dead in his tracks. Sophie's milking headscarf was laid at the side of the road. He grabbed it and looked around for her. A menacing feeling of dread began to creep into his belly.

'Are you all right, Kit?' Amelia said, emerging from the mist to fetch water from the pump.

'You haven't seen Sophie, have you?'

Amelia shook her head, put down her bucket and walked towards him.

'She set off for work nearly an hour ago and I've just found her milking headscarf on the grass verge.' He held it up to show her.

'Look at this.' She pointed out the scuff marks in the dirt. 'It looks as though she fell or something. Come on, stop fretting, we'll go and see Dr Eddy. If she's hurt herself, she'll have made her way there.' Leaving the bucket by the pump she linked her arm in Kit's and led him across the bridge.

*

Disappointed to not find her there, Kit and Amelia stepped out of Dr Eddy's surgery.

Kit felt a great sense of foreboding. 'I don't like this, Amelia, something has happened to her - I just feel it in my bones. I'm going to see Penvear, I have an awful feeling that he's behind this.'

Amelia caught his arm. 'He can't have, Kit.'

Kit's eyes blazed. 'He can, and with good reason! We spoke to the Earl de Bochym yesterday about Penvear and told him what he'd done to Sophie and all the other misdemeanours. We learnt things about that man that would make your eyes water.'

'I know, Kit but ....'

'His lordship was going to look into it, don't you see? He's taken his revenge - he's got Sophie! It wouldn't surprise me if it was him who torched my boat! I'm going to see him.' He began to run up the road towards Quay House.

'Kit, stop!' Amelia shouted. 'Penvear can't have done what you say.'

Kit slowed and turned. 'Why not?'

'Because he was arrested for embezzlement early yesterday afternoon!'

Kit put his hands on his head and walked back towards her. 'Where is she then?'

'I don't know, Kit, but we'll find her. Someone must have seen something. Look, you go and gather together as many people as you can and so will I, we'll call a meeting at The Black Swan.'

*

People piled into The Black Swan, some hoping that the landlord would open the bar early and some just to gossip about what had happened in the last twelve hours. Nothing like this had ever happened in the village and there was an excited buzz in the air.

Kit pulled a chair up and stood on it to get everyone's attention. He was going to try and arrange a search party, when Minnie Drago, the landlord's spinster sister, walked into the bar to see what was happening.

She grinned gleefully when she saw everyone. Minnie always liked to be the first one to share a bit of juicy gossip.

'You'll never guess who I saw last night?' she said pushing her way through the crowded bar.

Kit glanced over at the village busybody. 'Not Sophie by any chance?' he asked hopefully.

'No!' She bared her rotten teeth. 'But it's a close guess.'

Kit felt a frown form. 'What do you mean?'

'It was her so called dead husband - Jowan!' she said with a nod.

A collective gasp rippled through the crowd.

'Jowan!' Kit suddenly felt nauseous.

'As I live and breathe,' said Minnie enjoying the attention.

'Where?'

'Well, the first time I saw him, he was hobbling a horse and cart on the rough land behind my house, near the Williams's cow field.'

Kit had to grab something to stop his knees from giving under him. 'When?' he asked, aware his voice was quivering.

Minnie's eyes sparkled. 'Twas last night about six-o-clock! In truth, I couldn't really believe my eyes, so I shouted over to him, but he was being his normal ignorant self and ignored me, then I blinked and he was gone.'

'Why didn't you say anything? It's not like you to keep gossip to yourself!' John Drago sneered.

'Because, dear brother, I wasn't sure, and I like to get my facts right,' she said haughtily.

'That's never stopped you before,' someone piped up.

Minnie pursed her lips. 'I did wonder if I was seeing things, you know, his ghost or something. I thought that again when he appeared out of the fog over there by the chestnut tree at about six this morning. His hair was long and he had a full beard, but it was definitely him, I could tell by the build of him.'

Kit hardly dared ask the next question. 'What was he doing?'

Minnie shrugged. 'He was just stood there. I watched him for a while, but my porridge started to burn, when I looked again, he'd gone.'

Amelia locked eyes with Kit. They both knew now that wherever Sophie was, Jowan had something to do with it. A moment later, Amelia, Kit and Eric made a bee line for Alpha Cottage, only to find it deserted.

'Oh, god, Kit, look!' Amelia grasped Kit's sleeve to steady herself. There was blood splattered on the walls near where the furniture lay broken and upended.

The hairs rose on the back of Kit's neck at the sight before him.

*

Sophie drifted in and out of consciousness to a series of violent flashbacks. She remembered being thrown across the room of Alpha Cottage, landing hands first into the hot ashes of the fire. Her hair had been torn at the roots as she'd been yanked back to be sent hurtling towards the granite wall - a chair had splintered, breaking her fall, and going by the dreadful pain in her side, had broken her ribs also. The memory made her breath restrict to short, shallow gasps and then she slipped back into a huge black vortex.

A while later the rolling motion of a vehicle dragged her back into consciousness again. This time the sight of Jowan baring his teeth burned into her brain. The remembrance of his huge hands squeezed around her throat as he pinioned her to the wall, made her physically flinch again as he growled, "What sort of widow doesn't shed a tear for her husband's passing, eh?" He'd pulled her from the wall and slammed her back with teeth shattering force. "Shacked up with the Trevellick afore I was cold in my grave, you were!"

His foul saliva ran down her face as he spat his venom at her. Great rough hands clamped her face in a vice like grip, while his filthy thumb pulled at the side of her mouth until her lip burst and filled her mouth with a hot metallic taste.

Try as she might, she could not will herself to slither back into the safety of her black void, to stop her mind from reliving the struggle and fight she'd put up against his overwhelming strength. She had pitted her pleading eyes against his unforgiving anger. Her body trembled, slicked with perspiration at the memory of him drawing his fist back and returning it with such force, her world turned red. "That's for leaving my mother to fend for herself."

A pulsating throb emerged from the stars bursting in her head with frightening intensity as her skull rattled, and gristle and bone cracked. His next words were punctuated with his fist. "And. For. Being. A. Whore."

Although dazed and almost senseless, she remembered sliding down the wall, aware of two things before she lost consciousness - Ria pleading with Jowan to stop, and the second - the second, sounded like a baby crying!

Disorientated and nauseously dizzy, the motion of the moving vehicle brought Sophie to full wakefulness. Though her eyes remained agonisingly shut, she knew she was shrouded in rough sacking. A hot prickly sweat drenched her broken body as she became acutely aware of every single pain. A stifled moan mounted in her throat and she choked on the rag across her tongue. Fearing suffocation, she gasped for air, prising her lips open, ripping the tender skin from where they were stuck fast to the material. Terrified tears formed, but when bubbling mucus built up behind her blocked nose and trickled down the back of her throat, she choked again. Blind panic ensued realising she was drowning in her own mucus. With an almighty effort she tried to bring her hands to her mouth, but they were bound tightly behind her back. With suffocation moments away, she snorted hard to release the clotted blood from her nostrils. The pain almost made her faint but one cleared and began to bleed profusely - the other remained thoroughly blocked. She sniffed a small, albeit disgusting stench of fishy air, but for the moment her panic abated. Focusing again on her hands, she realised the one she was laying on was numbly swollen. Tentatively she brought her fingertips together, wincing at the touch of burnt skin. After a silent mental check on all her injuries, she knew she was in desperate need of medical help, but who would help her? Not Dr Eddy, for they'd so obviously left Gweek! Realising her most pressing concern at the moment was that she was desperate to pee, she tried to move to ease the pressure on her bladder but could not shift and the effort made her face burn like a furnace. Apart from the rough sacking covering her head, the stifling heat suggested that she was also wrapped in tarpaulin. Perhaps Jowan meant to suffocate her! Jowan! How the hell had her hateful husband come back from the dead? Her body began to tremble, adding to her misery. *Stay calm, Sophie, stay calm. Panicking will make things worse. Think of nice things, flowers, clean sheets, sunshine, Kit! Oh, god, Kit!* She longed for his loving arms to reach out and save her. Where the hell were they going and how on earth would Kit ever find her?

Chapter 42

Shocked to the core, Kit stumbled blindly out of Alpha Cottage where Eric grabbed him by the arms to steady him.

'Christ, Eric,' Kit shuddered uncontrollably, 'I think Jowan has killed her!'

'Come on, Kit, keep your chin up,' Eric said and then shouted, 'Can someone fetch Constable Treen. He needs to see this.'

Everyone reconvened in the bar - clearly shocked by what they'd seen.

John Drago glanced at the emerging crowd feeling very disgruntled – first because his bar was full to capacity and he couldn't sell a single drink this early in the day, and second, if by what he'd heard, Ria had gone missing too - his laundry wouldn't get done! He thought it best to keep his discontentment under wraps for now though - he could see there was a more serious problem afoot.

Kit slumped down on the nearest chair as dismayed voices around him intensified. His eyes blurred and then cleared when Amelia put a comforting hand on his shoulder.

'I have to find her, Amelia.' He dropped his head in despair. 'Oh, Christ! I just hope she's still alive, but seeing all that blood - I fear she's been gravely injured.'

'Hold it together, Kit,' Amelia said firmly. 'Sophie needs you to stay strong. Come on, stand up. Look, Constable Treen is here now. He'll help us rally everyone and get a search party organised.'

Kit nodded. Amelia was always one to keep a steady head in any situation.

Constable Treen glanced gravely at Kit as he took off his helmet and addressed the crowd. 'Right, I've seen what has happened. I know this is a domestic matter, but Treloar has clearly overstepped the mark. I think you'll all be in agreement that Sophie needs to be found quickly - to make sure she's all right. I don't hold with wife beating.'

George Blewett, who had joined the crowd, hoping for an early glass of ale, pulled a face. 'I reckon a husband is allowed to thump his wife if she's committed adultery!'

Kit felt a red mist fall before his eyes and he flew at Blewett. 'Keep your filthy lies to yourself - Sophie has *not* committed adultery.'

Eric grabbed Kit and held him back. 'Don't waste your breath on him.'

Blewett laughed and Kit lurched forward again, but Eric held tight.

'Enough, Blewett, or *I'll* bloody thump you,' Eric snarled.

'Now settle down everyone,' Treen said.

Shrugging Eric off, Kit glowered at Blewett, before turning back to Constable Treen. 'You need to release Stan. I am fairly certain now that Jowan torched my boat – probably revenge because Sophie was living in my house.'

'Not just living - I'll wager,' Blewett sneered.

'Shut it, Blewett. If you've nothing constructive to say then bugger off,' Constable Treen snapped.

After a few muttered expletives Blewett stomped out of the door. No sooner had he left, than the Black Swan door crashed open again and a stranger marched in. Everyone stopped and stared at the stranger in astonishment - the man looked wild and unkempt and his bloodshot eyes darted back and forth glaring at everyone in sight.

'All right, where is the bastard?' the man growled.

John Drago puffed his chest out. 'Hey, and who the hell are you when you're at home?'

The man bared a set of broken, crooked teeth. 'Never mind who I am. I want to know where he is.'

'Where *who* is?' John threw his hands in the air.

'Jowan Treloar! Tell me where he lives. I'm going to rip his bloody head off.'

*

Another hour into the desperately uncomfortable journey, Sophie added to her misery when she could no longer hold her bladder. When the vehicle finally stopped, she was dragged unceremoniously across the rough boards of the wagon and she heard Jowan snort in distaste.

'You dirty bitch - you've pissed yourself,' he spat.

Sophie had never felt so wretched in all her life. With the sack still covering her head, and her wet underclothes flapping about her legs, she was dragged a few yards and was made to step up into a building. She heard a door being kicked open a moment before being dumped on the ground. It was then she heard Ria's voice, and she felt her scalp prickle. If Ria was here too, they must have planned this together. It was no wonder she had tried to keep her from leaving - she must have known Jowan was coming back!

'We're not staying here!' Ria protested.

'Oh, yes we are, Ma,' Jowan snarled. 'It'll not be for long, and then we'll be on the road again.'

So terrified was she, Sophie could almost hear her heartbeat thrashing in her ears, intensifying the ache in her head. She flinched as the sack was pulled from her head, and then panicked, realising she could not see through her swollen eyelids. The filthy rag at her mouth was untied and removed. She yelped as the corners of her lips ripped as it was pulled away. Trying desperately to swallow down the disgusting metallic taste, she realised how dreadfully sore her mouth was. A sizable bite had been taken out of her tongue – nevertheless, she used it to painfully probe into the many wounds to her gum and lips. As far as she was aware though, none of her teeth were missing – small mercies.

Without warning she was pulled forward again and her wrists were untied, but she struggled to move them, so leaden were they from being bound so tightly. As the blood flooded back into her hands, horrendous pins and needles ran up her arms and then the searing heat from her burnt hands almost made her faint. Realising her breathing had become erratic, she forced herself to sit still. *Mind over matter, Sophie - block out the pain, think, think. You must think only of how you're going to escape?* And then suddenly there it was again - the sound of a baby crying and her thoughts were stilled.

*

A hush had fallen over the crowd at the bar at The Black Swan and all eyes were on the stranger.

Kit was the first to step forward. 'Hello, Mr....'

'Rutter, Harry Rutter. Who the hell are you?'

'Kit Trevellick.' He held his hand out in welcome but it was ignored. Unperturbed Kit said, 'We're looking for him too. What's he done to you?'

'The bastard got my sister in the family way nine months back, buggered off when she told him and then turned up again in March, out of the blue. After a beating he promised to marry our Vera if she gave birth to a living baby. But it was all a bloody ploy, wasn't it? Our Vera gave birth yesterday and the next thing we knew, puff, he'd gone, taken my horse and cart and buggered off with the babe. Our Vera is distraught. I only found out when I got back from my fishing trip this morning!'

'He's got a baby with him!' Amelia said incredulously. She turned to Kit. 'That's why he's taken Sophie then, and if that's the case, Sophie will still be alive.'

Rutter's eyes darted between them. 'Who the hell is Sophie?'

'Sophie is Jowan's wife!'

Rutter looked fit to explode. 'So, that's his plan then, is it? He told me his wife was dead. Were they in this together? I'll bloody murder them both!'

'Whoa there!' Kit said, 'Sophie has not gone willingly. She's been taken by violent force, judging by the amount of blood on their cottage wall. We believed Jowan had drowned in March, and Sophie was glad of the fact - she hated him!'

'Where have they bloody gone to then? I want that babe back with its rightful mother!'

Kit gave a long tremulous breath. 'We don't rightly know - that's why we're all here. The last time Sophie was seen was at five-thirty this morning.' He glanced at his fob watch. 'They've probably been on the road four hours already. They could even be at Truro now!'

'Where have you come from today, Mr Rutter?' Constable Treen asked

'Coverack, by horseback.'

'Coverack!' Kit was astounded. 'You mean to tell me Jowan's been living in Coverack since March? But that's not ten miles from here! I can't believe he hasn't been seen.'

'Ah well, we live remote, we're farmers mostly – I occasionally fish out of Coverack, but Treloar's been working on the farm the whole time. Doted on our Vera - wouldn't let her out of his sight. He stopped her from working as a barmaid at *The Paris Inn* and didn't even go down there himself - though he drank enough homebrew at home,' he added scornfully.

Kit scratched his chin and glanced at Treen. 'I should think he'll have gone well away from the Lizard now.'

'I agree, but it won't harm to search the surrounding area. If any of you can spare an hour or so to go on a search, that would be appreciated,' Constable Treen asked the crowd and several local men nodded. 'I'll ride up Pemboa way to Helston and alert my colleagues there to keep a look out.'

'Good man,' Kit said. 'Eric, can I saddle one of your horses and Mr Rutter and I will go looking further afield? They can't have got far by horse and cart, and we'll cover more ground than them if we are on horseback.'

'Of course, you can. I'll saddle one myself and join you. But I need Stan released now - they'll need him on the farm in my absence.'

Constable Treen nodded. 'I've just had a thought

though,' he said cautiously. 'If Jowan is the rightful father of that babe, the police have no jurisdiction to recover the child to its mother you know.'

'Yeah!' Rutter snarled. 'Well, we'll see about that, won't we?'

*

The baby was screaming now and the sound pierced through Sophie's sore head.

'What are you doing, Jowan? Give her back to me,' Ria protested.

The plea ignored - Sophie gasped when she felt the weight of the warm, smelly bundle settle into her deadened arms. Instinct made her close her hands protectively around the baby, but the burns made it impossible to hold it properly. Despite herself she did her best to jiggle the fractious baby to stop it crying.

'Whoth it thith baby,' Sophie lisped.

'It's yours!' Jowan snarled in her ear. 'I was sick to death of watching your barren body reject my children, so I went and found someone who could bear my child,' he hissed. 'So, you'd better look after it, and make a better job than the way you've looked after my widowed Ma.'

Sophie trembled as she turned away from the smell of his foul breath. Thankfully he moved away from her, but not before kicking her on the ankle bone. She retracted her foot with a yelp, and the sudden movement made the baby scream again. Unable to see through her swollen eyelids, she panicked – she'd never felt so totally helpless.

'Give the babe back to me, Jowan, Sophie is in no fit state to see to it!' Ria pleaded.

'No! She'll just have to manage. It's hers now! I'm going for some wood to make a fire. See that *she* behaves, Ma.' He slammed the door shut behind him.

As soon as he'd gone, Ria came over and lifted the squirming, screaming baby from Sophie's arms.

'Shush, now,' Ria's voice seemed to sooth the baby.

Sophie looked in the direction of Ria's voice. 'Whath

the hell ith going on?' she asked.

'He's back, that's what!' she replied flatly.

Sophie frowned - from the tone of Ria's voice she surmised that she was none too happy at the prospect either.

'Whoths baby ith it?'

'I don't know. I believe its mother is dead. Oh, I wish Jowan would hurry up with that fire wood though, this baby needs feeding.'

'It needth changing too.'

'I'm well aware of that. You don't smell too sweet either,' Ria snapped.

Sophie cringed. 'Are you thuprised?'

An uneasy silence fell between the women. The baby began to cry again, and a moment later Sophie could hear Ria ripping fabric.

'John Drago will go mad when he realises I've pinched his sheets to make napkins for the child,' she was muttered.

'Where hath thowan been all thith time?'

'I don't know.'

'Dith you know he wath still alive?'

'No! Of course not!' she snapped. 'It's as much a surprise for me as it is you.'

Sophie didn't know whether to believe her or not. 'Where the hell are we going, Ria?'

'I don't *know*!' she answered shortly.

*

Ria cradled the baby, her little finger in its cupid bow mouth to sooth it as she glanced around at the dirty cottage with its mud floor and rising damp. She was as much put out as Sophie was about all this. She'd carved a life out for herself back in Gweek, learned how to fend for herself and make her own money – she was almost glad that Sophie had walked out on her. No one had been more surprised than her when Jowan burst through her door last evening - the shock almost caused her heart to stop, thinking his ghost had come to bestow penance on her for letting Sophie slip the net.

Ria glanced anxiously towards Sophie, appalled at the violence Jowan had inflicted on her. She was ashamed to call Jowan her son, and heartily ashamed of herself, for it was her fault Sophie was in this state. Ria had been so frightened of Jowan's rage when he found Sophie missing, that she'd inferred that Sophie and Kit were living together as lovers - even though there was no evidence of such a claim. She thought perhaps Jowan would direct his anger at Kit. When all was said and done, Sophie was still his wife, and Jowan had a right to reclaim her, but she'd never believed he'd be so violent with Sophie.

*

It was almost nine before Kit, Harry and Eric set off towards the main coach road, four miles outside Gweek. The day was lowering and thunder rumbled in the far west of the county. It looked like they were in for an uncomfortably wet ride.

Amelia's eyes filled with hopeful tears as she waved them off in a blaze of dust. 'Godspeed,' she shouted.

Stan stood red-eyed and distraught by her side. *This is all my fault*, he thought. *If only I could have made them understand the warning I tried to give them last night, this would never have happened to Sophie.*

Chapter 43

Once they'd reached the main Falmouth to Helston road, the three men pulled to a halt. Their horses, lathered and snorting, whinnied and sidestepped in the dust, eager to set off again. Kit turned his strained and sweaty face towards the dark, ominous clouds gathering from the west, as great dollops of rain splattered on the dusty road.

'We'll split up here,' Kit said breathlessly. 'We might all be on a false trail, but we'll have to give it a try. I'll take the Truro road, if you, Harry, can set off towards Helston and Penzance. Eric, you take the Stithians road. If we all travel for fifteen miles in our different directions, asking en route, we might be able to find them. We'll return via a different route so we can cover quite a lot of ground. The fact that they're travelling in a horse and cart, means they will have to keep to the main coach roads - otherwise they'll certainly lose a wheel.'

*

Jowan, anticipating being followed, had driven off road only six miles from Gweek to make camp at Hallvasso. He'd known about this abandoned cottage they'd made camp in, from sheltering here one stormy winter night en route from a trip to Stithians. He planned to stay put for three days, hoping any attempt to follow them would be well and truly thwarted. From here they would travel on, via the King Harry Ferry, to St Just-in-the-Roseland to settle in Porthscatho where nobody would know them. He'd heard tell there was a small fishing community there and would find work easily. He had no qualms that he could silence Sophie with his fist should she attempt to escape or bring attention to herself. He'd been her master before and would be again. Distracted by the gathering storm and thoughts of his wayward wife lying with Trevellick, he misjudged his aim while chopping a log, causing a large sharp splinter of wood to pierce right through the skin between his thumb and finger. A barrage of cursing and a copious amount of blood followed as he pulled the splinter out from the wound. 'Damn that bitch of a wife,' he muttered, binding the rag he'd used to gag Sophie, around the bleeding wound.

*

Minnie Drago was in her element. For once everyone in Gweek wanted to hear what she had to say. 'Back from the dead, Jowan is,' she told her attentive audience. 'I saw him with my own eyes. He came home with a babe stolen from its rightful mother, kidnapped Ria and rode away with her, but not before he beat that wayward wife of his to death! They are out now looking for her body,' she proclaimed with a nod.

It was Amelia who put a stop to her tittle-tattle, when she realised Minnie was encouraging a macabre interest in peering through the window of Alpha Cottage to see the blood splattered wall.

'If there is misfortune to be enjoyed, we can always count on you to relish in it, Minnie Drago,' Amelia said angrily. And then she took it on herself to go in and close the curtains in Alpha Cottage.

*

The storm broke overhead, rattling the windows of the cottage in Halvasso. A torrent of rain filled the gutters to overflowing, splattering noisily above the baby's screams.

Sophie lay motionless in the corner of the room where Jowan had left her, trying to disconnect her mind from the terrible pain engulfing her body, and her all-encompassing misery.

When Jowan burst through the door, Sophie sobbed in panic. Logs were thrown down and the smell of damp oilskin filled the room. She flinched as the weight of his boot pressed on her thigh.

'*You*,' he said brutally. 'Get up off your lazy arse and nurse that screaming baby like I told you to.'

He kicked her with such force her body moved a good foot from where she'd been laying. White hot pain shot up her leg and for an agonising moment, all other injuries were forgotten.

'Jowan! Leave her be - she's hurt enough,' Ria intervened.

'I aint bloody finished with her yet. That baby needs mothering. If she thinks she's going to lay there feeling sorry for herself, she's another think coming.'

'Jowan! She's in no fit state, thanks to you,' Ria retaliated. 'Please light the fire so I can warm some milk up and feed this baby.'

'We don't *need* any milk warming! *She'll* feed it!'

Sophie shrieked as Jowan's great hands grabbed her. She was pulled into a sitting position, and gasped in horror when he ripped open her bodice to expose her breasts.

'What's this then?'

She felt the tug of the ribbon holding Kit's ring as it was torn from her neck.

'Where did you get this ring?' he snarled at her. 'Trevellick, I bet.'

From the tiny slit in her swollen eyelids, she watched him bite it to test its authenticity.

'I'll take this as compensation – for the unlawful use of my *wife*.'

Sophie whimpered fearfully as she tried to cover herself, but he dragged her arms away and dumped the screaming baby at her breast.

'For goodness' sake, stop it Jowan,' Ria shouted. 'Sophie can't breastfeed a child!'

'Yes she bloody can! Lots of women feed other women's children. I've seen it with my own eyes.'

'They're wet nurses! They've given birth to their own recently, you fool.'

'Watch it Ma, unless you want a black eye too.'

Ria took a sharp intake of breath. 'If your father heard you speak to me like that,' she warned.

'Father is dead! And by god there'll be another death soon if someone doesn't shut that baby up!'

'Then light a fire so I can warm some milk up, but as I warned you last night that babe will get diarrhoea if we keep giving it cow's milk, and then we'll never stop him screaming.'

'So, what do you expect me to do for Christ's sake?'

'The child needs a mother's milk to thrive, failing that, formula milk or condensed will do, if I water it down. So, you'll have to go and get some from somewhere and we need a feeding bottle - I can't feed it from the spout of a milk jug forever.'

Jowan looked outside at the weather and then again at the baby. He knew the nearest shop was a mile away. He looked at the deep cut across his hand. 'Oh, for Christ's sake, bandage this then before I bleed to death.'

Ria inspected the gash. 'Jesus, Jowan, what the hell have you done?'

'Just bloody wrap it woman.'

Ria ripped a ribbon of material from one of the sheets. 'You need to wash that first,' she said.

'Get on with it,' he yelled and the baby screamed louder.

Ria pursed her lips. 'It'll go septic,' she warned.

Jowan pulled his hand from hers. 'I'm off out. Light the bloody fire yourself.'

*

Curled into a ball on the filthy floor, Sophie felt the warmth of the fire on her back - though it brought no comfort. If anything, it intensified the pain of her burnt hands. With her palms outstretched towards the granite wall to cool them down, silent tears trickled down her cheeks. Everything was lost - her liberty, her dignity, her new life with Kit and now his ring. Denied these things now, and with little chance of escaping this hell, then she might as well.......she gave a long, low sigh, she might as well die.

The rain had eased, though the thunder rumbled in the distance. The baby was now mollified with a full tummy, so the only other sound was the fire. After a gentle baby belch Sophie heard Ria singing.

Hush, little baby, don't say a word. Papa's gonna buy you a mockingbird. And if that mockingbird won't sing, Papa's gonna buy you a diamond ring....... The singing stopped and a few minutes later Ria moved up beside Sophie.

'Here, sit up and take a drink,' she said pressing a cup to her mouth.

Parting her lips lined with dried blood she sipped the water. 'Thank you.'

'I have your shawl here - let me put it around your shoulders.' Sophie leant forward as Ria crossed the shawl across her chest to hide her exposed flesh, before tucking it into her skirt. 'Lift your bottom and I'll take your underclothes off to soak.'

Overwhelmed at these small uncharacteristic acts of kindness from Ria, Sophie clutched her arms to her stomach and wept as she allowed Ria to remove her wet underclothes. Ria lifted one of her hands and turned it over. After a click of her tongue, she moved away, water was poured and then she shuffled back to her side.

'I've a pan of cold water here.' Ria guided her hands to the water. 'It'll soothe them a little.'

Sophie sighed heavily as the water eased her pain. Thinking she might have an ally in Ria, she said weakly, 'I want to go home, Ria.'

'Shush, you'll wake the baby.'

Sophie slumped back into her despair, albeit a little more dignified now free of her urine-soaked drawers. She listened as Ria swished her clothes in water, wrung them out and then dragged over a chair to drape and dry them by the fire. There were sounds of peeling and chopping and a pan hissing on the fire as Ria made a soup to eat. Eventually the room fell quiet, but for Ria gently snoring. Without the luxury of sight, escape was out of the question, and with that thought, dark feelings engulfed her again.

*

Acutely aware of pain, but so desperately tired, Sophie dozed with the heat of the room, only to be brought to wakefulness by the sound of Jowan returning. She forced the slit of her eyelid to open and watched in trepidation as Jowan emptied his bag by Ria's side, whilst glancing at the sleeping baby.

'I needn't have bothered going for this lot or getting bloody soaked doing it,' he hissed, as he took off his coat and shook it over everyone. 'It looks like the cow's milk sufficed.'

Ria yawned noisily, cross at being roused from her slumber. 'I've no doubt it'll go straight through him,' she hissed.

'Huh! What have you made to eat, Ma, I'm bloody starving.'

'I've made what I can from the vegetables we brought but we need some proper supplies.'

Sophie held her breath as Jowan leered at Ria's face. 'You should have told me, before I went to the shop.'

'What chance did I have? You were in such a temper when you stormed out,' Ria argued.

'Oh, stop your moaning, woman and feed me.'

No sooner had Jowan sat down to eat the meagre soup, the baby woke on cue and filled the room with the most horrendous smell - even Sophie baulked at the stench.

'Jesus Christ!' Jowan threw his meal to the floor and clasped his hand to his face as Ria began to take the soiled nappy off the baby.

'I'll need a fresh pail of water fetching, Jowan. I think I'm going to have a lot of washing to do,' Ria said.

'She should be bloody doing this!' He kicked Sophie hard on the thigh again. The agony was too much to endure and Sophie turned and retched, vomiting bile and blood.

'*She* can't see to do anything because of you, so stop bleating and fetch me some water,' Ria snapped.

Returning with the pail of water, Jowan swore profusely and shook his bandaged hand.

'Is your hand bothering you, son?' Ria asked with motherly concern.

'No,' he said dismissively, plunging his hand into his pocket. 'I'm going out to fetch some more wood. Hopefully the stink will have gone by then.'

'Before you go, Jowan, I need to know when we're leaving this god forsaken place. We need to settle somewhere where I can have running water if we are to have a baby in the family!'

'We're staying here until I know it's safe to move.'

'Safe! From what?'

'Safe from being found - I have no doubt Trevellick will be out looking for my wife, and *he's* had enough pleasure with her.'

Sophie's sharp intake of breath at the mention of Kit's name did not go unnoticed and Jowan knelt at her side. 'You're *my* pleasure, not *his*,' he hissed, breathing his foul breath on her face. 'And now you're the mother of that baby.' He jabbed his fingers into her side and her corset dug deeper against her broken ribs. Sweat drenched her body as she coughed and retched again at the agonizing pain. 'And you *will* conform.' He jabbed her again, and white stars danced before her eyes. 'I'll tell you this - *wife of mine*. If that bastard Trevellick comes anywhere near you again, I will tear him limb from bloody limb.'

Chapter 44

Eric and Harry returned to Gweek at seven that evening, via a different road they had taken out. Sore in heart and saddle from their long, unfruitful task, they gingerly sat in Lydia's kitchen. Kit arrived back some three hours later, soaked and exhausted. He too slumped dejectedly down in the kitchen. The others had already eaten a dish of hearty stew to warm their bones, which in normal circumstances would have cheered the saddest soul. Lydia doled out a dish for Kit, but he had no appetite.

'I've failed her, Lydia.' He lifted his weary eyes.

Sitting beside him Lydia said, 'No you haven't, Kit.'

He drew a deep breath. 'I have! I vowed to look after her - to keep her safe.'

She caught his hand. 'You were not to know. None of us could have envisaged this would happen.'

'Oh, God.' A single tear ran down his cheek. 'I'm so frightened for her.' He wiped his face with his sleeve. 'She must be badly injured. She could die before we find her.'

'Listen to me, Kit. Have faith that you *will* find her alive, and you *will* bring her back.' She watched him for a moment - her statement seemed to be problematic judging by the serious furrow on his brow. 'What else is troubling you?'

Kit wrung his hands. 'It's something that's been going over and over in my mind while I've been riding. If I do find her, I *will* bring her back, of course I will, but Jowan will hound us forever, because by law, Sophie isn't mine, is she?' He blinked furiously to clear his vision. 'Nor is that baby Harry's to bring back, for that matter,' he dropped his voice to a whisper.

Lydia drummed her fingers thoughtfully on her lap. Constable Treen had been to see her earlier to tell her that the police were looking out for them, but had reiterated that because Jowan was legally the child's father, their hands were tied - the law would not act on a father kidnapping his own child. Lydia had decided to keep that to herself, confident that Harry Rutter would take the law into his own hands on that matter. She leaned forward and whispered, 'I think, Kit, you'll have to take Harry's "we'll see about that," stance, on that matter. That baby belongs with its mother, and Sophie belongs with you.' She patted him on the shoulder. 'As for Jowan – you will have to go where he cannot find you! Just remember, love will always find a way. Now try to eat something. I'll bring you some dry clothes and then you can join the others in the front room.'

The brandy was brought out but Kit felt no relief from the liquor as it settled in his empty stomach. They had done the best they could for the day and had left details and descriptions in every village en route, in a hope someone would recognise the travellers and send word back to Gweek. All they could hope for was that someone would see them eventually. Jowan was a fisherman, not a farmer by choice, and sooner or later he'd have to work. They would put word out with Jack Tehidy and his crew to ask the local fishermen to keep a look out for him. Jowan was a mountain of a man so he should, in theory, be easy enough to locate.

Silence fell on the small gathering. All three men were dead on their feet, but no one wanted to take to their bed. Fuelled by brandy, they settled in Lydia's front room with a mug of tea each and dozed uncomfortably in front of a roaring fire. Their search would resume the next morning.

*

As darkness fell, a great fire roared in the grate and peace prevailed in the cottage at Hallvasso. Ria cradled the sleeping child and watched Jowan drain the remains of what looked like a bottle of homemade whisky. It wasn't long before he was fast asleep and snoring loudly. She put the baby gently down and poured some of the thin soup in a mug and took it over to Sophie.

'Here.' She pressed the cup to her lips. 'I know you

didn't want any earlier, but you need something in your belly.'

Sophie felt her stomach groan painfully at the smell of food. She tentatively took a sip of the soup, but the hot liquid stung the cuts in her mouth. She shook her head. 'It huth too muth.'

'Try and get some sleep, then,' Ria replied resignedly.

*

Sophie curled into a ball on the damp, filthy floor - her palms outstretched to keep them cool as she willed herself to sleep. It must have come to a point when her body could take no more pain, because blackness fell and she slipped into an exhausted sleep. *The soft comforting feather bed at Bochym encompassed her, and once again the girl in pink stood over her touching her ring finger. The girl's face was pained with the expression - I tried to warn you! Sophie felt the warmth of a body behind her, an arm winding its way over to cup her tummy. Oh, Kit, my Kit. She turned to face him - his heart so full of love for her. The soft curve of his mouth gave the smile that he kept just for her. His lips soft and warm kissed her gently on the cheek.*

Catapulted to wakefulness, she was back on the filthy floor and a great rough hand was grasping at her breast. Her throat, raw with grief, emitted a muffled scream, when through the tiny slit of her swollen eyelids she saw Jowan's great hairy arm and bandaged hand groping at her. He pulled her onto her back and straddled her. His face, lit by the firelight was angry and sweaty. He leant one arm against her chest making her gasp for breath while the other hand fumbled behind him, dragging her skirts up her legs. His hand moved to her mouth stifling her scream, though they continued noisily in her head. In a blind panic she braced herself, clenching her teeth, willing her mind to block what was happening as he took her, but a few moments later he collapsed like a dead weight - before he'd finished the act! His hand fell away from her mouth and he relaxed, so with all the strength she could muster, she pushed his bulk off her. He rolled onto his back grunting and groaning like a pig.

Needing to rid herself of his filth, she scrambled towards where she'd heard Ria use the chamber pot earlier on. With limited vision she located the pot, accidently putting her fingers into the disgusting contents. She sat against the wall after relieving herself and looked up at the window - it was still dark. Both Ria and the baby had slept through the commotion and Jowan was still groaning for some reason. The fire had burned down to a flicker, but the room was hot and stank of dirty bodies and faeces. Now she could see just a fraction more, this was her chance to escape, but to where? She had no idea where she was and it was dark outside. If she could just get out of the door, she could follow the road, for there must have been a decent road for the horse and cart to drive on. She pulled herself to her feet and slowly ran her fingers along the wall until she came to a door. Her burnt fingers located the handle and she held her breath. Very slowly and painfully she turned it until the catch gave. Tentatively she pulled it open and it creaked on movement. Sophie grimaced, wincing at the pain the movement evoked.

'Ma, wake up,' Jowan's voice boomed.

Sophie pulled the door open and fled out of the room, but found herself inside another room of which she could find no exit.

'Wha...what is it? Ria whined.

'Grab her - she's escaping.'

Sophie heard Ria's footsteps shuffling across the floor as she frantically tried to find the way out, but it was too late, Ria grabbed her by the arm and led her back to her corner.

'What's wrong with your own legs,' Ria berated Jowan, but he just groaned back at her. She lit a candle and held it over her son. He was covered in perspiration.

'What's amiss with you? You look hot!'

'I'm cold!' He shivered.

'Sophie, get beside him and warm him up,' Ria ordered.

'I will not!' she lisped indignantly.

'You're his wife, you should comfort him.'

'After what he'th done to me?'

The noise woke the baby and it began to scream.

'Shut that bloody child up someone,' Jowan yelled.

Ria huffed noisily. 'Here.' She plonked the screaming child in Sophie's arms. 'If you're well enough to escape, you're well enough to feed that baby.' She thrust a bottle into her burnt hand. 'The bottle's been by the fire, the milk should be warm.'

Having no other option, Sophie settled the screaming baby in the crook of her arm. She'd never fed a baby before, but instinct told her to test the temperature first. Her hands felt as though they were on fire, so she hitched her skirt up and tested the milk on the skin of her thigh. As the child suckled, Sophie's mind wandered back to less than two short weeks ago when she'd helped deliver Ellie's baby - it felt like a lifetime ago. Her swollen lips quivered, knowing she would never be that child's godmother now - everything that had been good had gone from her life.

Ria had built the fire up and soon it became stiflingly hot in the room, but the warmth settled the baby and soon he slept peacefully in Sophie's arms.

Ria stood over them. 'You're a natural with that babe,' she whispered.

Sophie ignored her. *How the hell can I be a natural with someone else's baby in my arms?* With the heat of the room and the weariness of her situation, Sophie felt her head droop. She shuffled herself down and snuggled the sleeping baby into the crook of her arm and drifted off this time into a dreamless sleep.

It was daylight when she felt the child squirm and cry in her arms, and then the smell of his soiled nappy almost overpowered her. Sophie prised her sticky eyelids open as far as she could, to find Ria standing over her.

'Give the babe here, he needs changing by the smell of him.'

They both looked towards Jowan as he laid moaning and groaning in his own sweat.

A few minutes later, Ria thrust the baby back into her arms. 'Here, I've warmed another bottle for him. I'm going out. I'll be back shortly.'

Jowan roused and his groaning deepened. 'Where are you going, Ma,' he growled when he heard the door open.

'You need some medicine, you're not well. I'll try and get a fever powder.'

'Get back here. I need nothing!' He tried to lift his head but flopped back down and moaned again. 'Lock the bloody door after you then,' he said resignedly.

With Ria gone, Sophie watched in trepidation as Jowan turned his attention on her. 'I need to pee. Bring me the pot.'

Sophie sat stock still while the baby suckled the bottle.

'I said bring it *now*!' He slammed his hand flat on the floor.

Sophie pulled the teat from the baby's mouth, pressed the child to her own chest and scrambled towards the pot. Thankfully, Ria had emptied it. As she moved closer to Jowan, she could hear his rasping breath had become quite rapid. Through the slit in her eyelid, she noted that his weather-beaten face was pale and dotted with red patches. His breeches were still half way down his legs from where he'd tried to claim his marital rights last night, so he had no problem peeing straight into the pot. Thankfully, the effort seemed to exhaust him and he was soon fast asleep again. For the first time since her capture, Sophie felt a curl of optimism. Jowan might be dying!

*

Peter Dunstan was at Gweek Corn Mill bright and early, attempting to right the wrongs Gilbert Penvear had done, when he heard talk of what had happened in the village. He listened, horrified to learn that Kit's boat had been set on fire, but more worryingly, that Sophie's husband had returned from the dead and after a violent scuffle, absconded with her and someone else's baby.

'How do I find Kit?' Peter asked Bert Laity. 'I feel I must do something to help, but I know not what.'

'Well, my lord, by all accounts he stayed at the Williams's Farm with Mr Rutter, the missing baby's uncle, last night. I think they're setting off again this morning to resume their search.'

'Could you show me where the Williams's Farm is?'

'Yes, my lord.'

*

Lydia turned from cooking the breakfast and her mouth dropped open when she saw the fine carriage pull into the farmyard. Wiping her hands down her apron, she opened the door to greet the gentleman emerging from it, closely followed by Bert Laity.

'His lordship would like to see Kit, Lydia,' Bert said.

'Oh!' Lydia attempted a rather clumsy curtsy and mentally cursed herself that she hadn't tidied her kitchen that morning.

*

Ria had been walking for twenty minutes, but had no idea where the shop Jowan had visited last night was. All she knew was that she was going in the right direction to get to the main road. It was imperative that she needed to get help for Jowan. The last time she'd seen symptoms like that, was when her husband had died of blood poisoning. It was that damn cut to that hand of his – hadn't she told him it would turn nasty. It was a long walk for her, not being used to physical activity, but it gave Ria a lot of time to think. She missed her cottage in Gweek, with her china and rugs and home comforts. She would miss her little job doing the laundry too. Having her beloved son back from the dead had not turned out to be as pleasant as one would have expected. It pained and appalled her at the way Jowan had treated Sophie. She certainly didn't deserve that beating or his anger. And then there was that baby he'd brought home - *that* did not sit easy with her. She hadn't told Sophie but she knew where it had come from and how. Taking a baby from its real mother was an unforgivable act, and she did not know how she would live with herself knowing the true facts. When she finally reached the road, the shop was clearly in sight. When she reached the door, she found that it was also a Post Office – that's when she made a monumental decision. Jowan wouldn't like what she was about to do, but she needed to get some help for him - the consequences of which she would have to deal with later.

*

Polly Jenkins from the Gweek post office could hardly believe her eyes when the telegram came through.

'Watch the shop for a moment, will you,' she asked a customer, who was just about to buy a loaf of bread.

'Wait a minute,' the customer shouted, but Polly had rushed out of the door.

Lydia had just popped into the dairy for more milk after making a cup of tea for the earl in one of her best china cups. She'd left the men arranging another search, happy knowing that his lordship was also to join them this morning. She was deeply worried about every moment poor Sophie was with that hateful man, Jowan, and had sent a myriad of prayers up to whoever would be listening for her safe and swift return.

Lydia clutched the jug of milk to her chest when she saw Polly Jenkins from the Post Office running across the yard towards her.

'Goodness, Polly, whatever has happened?'

Flushed and breathless, Polly grasped the door jamb of the dairy to catch her breath, waving the telegram at Lydia.

Lydia grabbed it, read it, and set off as fast as her legs would carry her with a gasping Polly following in hot pursuit. Lydia burst through the kitchen door and into the best room making every one jump.

'Eric, look!' She pushed the telegram under his nose.

HALLVASSO STOP BRING DOCTOR STOP RIA.

Chapter 45

Jowan woke when Ria returned to the cottage and shot her a baleful glance.

'Where the hell have you been? You've been gone near on two hours!'

'You know where I've been!' Ria said indignantly.

Sophie watched with interest as Ria knelt beside Jowan - her manner and movements seemed edgy.

'I've managed to get you a fever powder, and some ointment to put on that wound of yours,' she said, her voice wavering slightly. 'It's gone nasty by the look of your skin.'

Jowan narrowed his eyes. 'You better not have told anyone where we are!'

Ria kept her eyes averted while she mixed the fever powder in a mug of water.

'You have, haven't you?' Jowan glowered as he lifted his head from the pillow.

Sophie held her breath. *Oh, please god let her have told someone.*

'Come on, spit it out, woman.' Jowan grabbed and twisted her arm until she yelped.

'You need help, Jowan,' she cried. 'Your father died of blood poisoning - I'll not let you die the same way.'

'You bloody stupid woman.' He tried to get up, but fell back groaning. 'Help me up, Ma. We need to get out of here!'

'Jowan, please, you're very ill.'

'Ill am I?' he said savagely, 'I'm not too bloody ill to give you a good hiding.' He heaved himself up and punched Ria full in the face, before collapsing with a groan, weakened by the effort.

Through the narrow aperture of her eyelids, Sophie watched in horrified silence as Ria huddled in the corner, dabbing her split lip with her apron, while Jowan tried to get to his feet. His great bulk staggered and fell onto the hearth, scattering the logs across the floor. The noise woke the baby in Sophie's arms. His little limbs stiffened and he began to cry.

'Get up, both of you, get up and get packing.' But both Sophie and Ria sat stock still.

Sophie could feel her heart hammering inside her chest as she tried to comfort the screaming child. Jowan was flailing on the floor, sweating profusely – he was clearly too ill to pack up and leave before help came.

'Help me up, Ma,' he said through gritted teeth.

'No!' Ria shouted adamantly.

Amidst the ensuing chaos, Sophie thought she heard horse's hooves! Holding the baby as tight as she could, she got to her feet just as the door burst open.

'Kit!' she cried. He was by her side in a heartbeat, cupping her swollen face. 'My god, Sophie! What the hell has he don…. Argh.!'

Sophie's joyous tears turned to disbelief as Kit's eyes widened and he collapsed at her feet. 'Kit?' she wailed, and then she saw Jowan wielding a knife.

A moment later, the room seemed full of people. A man Sophie didn't recognise, flew at Jowan, disarming him before pinning him to the wall by his throat.

'I'll bloody kill you for taking that baby,' he yelled at Jowan, but before he could strike a blow, Jowan buckled unconscious from his grip.

Kit was moaning incoherently on the floor and Sophie fell to her knees beside him. A moment later, Dr Eddy joined her, and Peter, who had also crouched beside her, put his arm protectively around her shoulders.

Harry Rutter was stood over Jowan who was out cold. 'I didn't get a chance to bloody hit him,' he bemoaned, as Ria cradled her son in her arms, keening like a wild animal.

Despite the chaos of the room and the screaming baby in her arms, all Sophie could focus on was Kit's desperate gasps for breath.

Dr Eddy had turned Kit over and ripped his shirt open.

'What happened to him, Doctor?'

'I think the knife has punctured his lung - he's struggling to breathe.' He turned momentarily towards her and saw the extent of her injuries, 'My god, Sophie!'

'I'm all right. Pleaths thee to Kit. Don't let him die.'

'Can someone pass that medical bag to me?' Sophie struggled to get up off her knees, but Peter had already fetched it.

Settling back on her haunches she watched with bated breath as the doctor treated Kit, until she became aware of the man who had disarmed Jowan, standing over her.

'Give the baby to me,' Harry said gruffly. 'His mother is frantic for him.'

Sophie gasped and looked to Dr Eddy for guidance.

Dr Eddy explained, 'This is the child's uncle, Sophie. Jowan took the baby from its mother.'

'Oh!' Sophie looked down at the poor little mite.

'Harry, leave the baby with Sophie - he'll come to no harm. I'll need your help in a moment,' Dr Eddy said and then turned to Peter. 'My lord, could I impose on you a while longer? We need to get Kit to hospital as quickly as possible and your carriage has four horses.'

'Certainly. I'll fetch my coachmen to help carry Kit,' Peter said. 'Where are we taking him?'

'The Royal Cornwall Infirmary at Truro, otherwise he'll not survive an injury like this.'

Once Kit was put aboard and made comfortable on the sumptuous leather seating, Harry returned and once again demanded the baby from Sophie. Tentatively she handed the warm bundle to its rightful owner, shocked at how she felt to part with him. Where the baby had lain all these hours in her arms, a cold empty feeling filled the void.

'I hope heth all right. We did our best to look after him.' She glanced at Ria, who was crying over Jowan. 'I'm so very thorry he was taken away from hith mother. It mutht hath been dreadful for your thithter,' Sophie said her voice cracking with emotion.

'Yeah well - I'll tell her what you said,' he grunted.

'Come on, Sophie,' Peter walked her out of the gloom of the cottage into the bright sunlight. Although deeply embarrassed that she smelt appalling and her clothes were torn and soaked in sweat and blood, she felt relieved to be safe in his arms. At the door of the coach, a blanket was draped over her shoulders before she boarded.

Dr Eddy watched as the carriage set off at high speed. He knew there was nothing more he could do for Kit - they just needed to get to hospital as soon as possible.

'Doctor?' Ria grabbed his sleeve. 'What about Jowan?'

Dr Eddy knew Jowan was clearly in the last stages of blood poisoning - it would be a miracle if he survived. 'Harry, can you help me put Jowan on the wagon so we can take him to Helston Hospital?'

'I aint taking that bastard anywhere,' Harry growled, nursing the fractious baby in his arms.

Pulling Harry to one side, Dr Eddy whispered, 'You'll need to take the baby to hospital too, just to check it over. The chances are Jowan will die en route anyway, but even if he doesn't, with arson and an attempted murder charge pending, he'll hang and justice will be done. Either way Ria will lose her son. Please, Harry, do this for her. I believe Ria was an innocent in this too.'

Reluctantly Jowan was loaded on the wagon. While Harry took the reins, Dr Eddy rode alongside.

Ria sat beside Jowan, cradling the baby for the duration of the journey. In her heart Ria knew Jowan would die and she'd never see this baby again after today, so she relished this short time she'd have with her one and only grandchild.

*

Sophie sat quietly at the hospital with Peter by her side, waiting for news of Kit. A nurse attended to Sophie's bruised and bloody face and had released her from her stays, which eased the pain in her cracked ribs. Her hands had been cleaned and bandaged. The application of warm clean water on her eyelids had eased them open so she could see more easily. A doctor had stitched the cut in her gum, but her tongue, she was told, would have to heal on its own, so she was saddled with the lisp for a while longer. All this paled into insignificance, knowing how seriously ill Kit was.

It was almost four in the afternoon when a doctor came out to update them on Kit's progress. They'd operated and inserted a long flexible tube of India gum rubber into Kit's ruptured lung to drain the excess fluid from it. He was not out of the woods by any stretch of the imagination, but he was in a clean environment now and would have all the care he needed.

Thanking the doctor, Peter sat down again with Sophie. 'You need to go home and rest,' he said seriously. 'You've been through a terrible ordeal. There is nothing else you can do for Kit that isn't being done. I know you don't want to leave him, but he's in good hands.'

Very reluctantly Sophie nodded. 'I'd like to thee him before I go.'

Five minutes later, Sophie was dressed in a white gown and led into a private room which Peter had kindly paid for. Kit looked terrible. His face was deathly white and his breathing was laboured.

The nurse smiled and explained that Kit had been given laudanum and a sleeping draft in order to keep him quiet and still while the tube did its job.

Sophie glanced at the bottle on the floor collecting watery blood. 'How long will hith tube be in?' She winced in pain - so great was the effort to speak.

'It'll drain one to two ounces of pus daily and we'll continue until the patient's condition improves – usually about two weeks.'

'He'll be fine though, won't he?' Peter asked on Sophie's behalf.

'He's a strong young man,' the nurse said and then smiled at Sophie. 'I'm sure he will fight his way back to you.'

Sophie reached over, placed her bandaged hand on his and sent up a silent prayer for him.

*

When the Bochym carriage pulled in at the Williams's farm, Lydia was first out of the house swiftly followed by Eric.

'Oh, my poor, poor girl,' Lydia cried as she hugged Sophie and then jumped back in shock when she yelped. 'Oh, goodness, I'm so sorry.'

'Along with everything else, Sophie has a couple of broken ribs,' Peter explained.

Lydia's face crumpled. 'Come on, let's get you inside. You'll stay here so I can look after you.'

After a few tentative spoonfuls of soup, in the safety of the warm farm kitchen, Lydia took her upstairs, bathed her gently and washed the blood from her hair. Dressed in one of Lydia's voluminous nightgowns, she was tucked up in bed and with heartfelt thanks, fell into a deep exhausted sleep.

*

Once Peter had arrived back at Bochym Manor, the shocking news of what had happened to Kit and Sophie soon spread around the Arts and Crafts Association members. There was talk of nothing else in the Wheel Inn that evening.

Georgie, who had decamped to Bonython Manor some two miles away, was not the sort to just fade into the background, therefore continued to socialise at The Wheel Inn. She listened with great interest, if not a little concern, at the news buzzing around the bar.

'According to his lordship,' Glenn Nedham said to his engrossed audience, 'first this Jowan Treloar fellow, who had pretended to be dead, kidnapped a baby he'd fathered, leaving its mother in terrible distress, and then came to Gweek to claim back Sophie, his wife! The scoundrel torched Kit's boat, and then beat poor Sophie senseless and drove her away into the night dragging his mother along with him. A search party found them, but Kit was injured and is seriously ill in hospital in Truro. The chances are they won't be taking over from me in September, now.'

Georgie lifted her whisky – and toasted fate. *So, Sophie's estranged husband torched the boat, eh?* She tapped her perfectly manicured fingernails on her lip. If Sophie's husband was back on the scene, that would inevitably pathe the way for her to re-establish her acquaintance with Kit – she just needed him to make a swift and full recovery. She lit a cigarette. Life was looking up.

Chapter 46

Ribbons of autumnal mist encircled Sophie's bare feet as she stood on the damp, lush grass of the riverbank. All was still and quiet but for the sound of her heartbeat. Kit was waving from the charred remains of his boat as it drifted aimlessly down the swollen river, his handsome face fading into the distance. Cradling the babe in her arms, she cried out for him to wait - but no sound came. Heartbroken, her silent tears fell into her now empty hands - everything good had slipped through her fingers.

'Sophie, Sophie.' Lydia woke her from her dream.

The pain and agony, suppressed by slumber, flooded back into every fibre of her being, and she moaned as reality prevailed. Unconsciously she touched her face with her bandaged hands, gasped in pain and dropped them back on the eiderdown.

'You were crying out in your sleep, Sophie, you've slept for nigh on twelve hours,' Lydia said, stroking her hair back from her forehead.

Disorientated for a moment, she forced her eyes open and turned to the familiar voice.

'I brought you some porridge. Do you think you can manage to eat some?'

Suddenly panic ensued, as the horrors of the last couple of days began to dawn on her. 'Kit!' She tried to get up.

'Sophie, please stay calm.' Lydia put her arms around her. 'Don't try to speak.'

Swallowing hard to moisten her paper dry mouth, she cried, 'I need to go to Kit!'

'Sophie, with the best will in the world you're in no fit state to go anywhere today.'

'I don't care what I look like! I have to thee if Kit is all right.'

Lydia held fast. 'I know you're worried, sweetheart - we all are, but it's too far for you to travel back and forth.' Lydia dug out her handkerchief to dab Sophie's frustrated tears away. 'He's in the best hands and *will* come through this, I'm sure of it. I'll go and see Dr Eddy after breakfast. He might be able to get some news wired down from the hospital. All right?'

Sophie lay back in resignation.

'Come on, dry your eyes and try to eat something and then I'll help you get dressed. I took the liberty of fetching some clean clothes from your room. I'm afraid the clothes you had on yesterday were in a terrible mess. I've had to wash them.'

With an uneasy truce, Sophie managed a few mouthfuls of porridge and then Lydia helped her to dress warmly, albeit without a stay.

'It's a good thing you have the figure to be able to go without your stays. If I left mine off, I'd look like a fruit stall.' She grinned.

Sophie smiled at Lydia's joke, regretting it when it made her lip burst open again.

'Oh, bless your poor face!' Lydia dabbed the blood trickling down her chin. 'Let me bring some salt water for you to rinse your mouth with – it heals all ills you know!'

Never had Sophie been so grateful for Lydia's friendship. Alone in her room now, she inspected her battered face in the mirror in horror – ashamed at her vanity when Kit was fighting for his life.

*

Lydia's kitchen embraced Sophie with its warm, inviting, cosy domesticity. Prudy the cat stretched its paws languidly towards the fire and Rosie the hen clucked on the cushion of one of Lydia's kitchen chairs, no doubt laying an egg for some unsuspecting person to sit on.

'Sit yourself down. I'm just brewing some tea before I go to the dairy.' A knock on the door halted the conversation and Amelia popped her head around the door.

'Mind if I join you. Oh, my!'

Sophie was getting used to the look of horror when anyone looked at her. Amelia put her bag down on the table and moved to inspect Sophie's face. She clicked her tongue in annoyance. 'Nothing makes my blood boil as much as the battered face of a beaten wife.'

'I'm all right, Amelia, honethly. I'm just thore.'

'Why do some men think this is acceptable behaviour? I've just seen Ria stepping off the Helston wagon. She's sporting a swollen blackened eye too. Did Jowan do that?'

Sophie nodded. 'When he found out Ria had called for help.'

'Well, thank goodness she did!'

'Amen to that' Lydia replied, pouring the tea.

'Jowan?' Sophie asked tentatively.

Amelia grimaced. 'He made it through the night, but his condition is still critical – he has blood poisoning.'

Sophie emitted a small strangled cry.

'Now, Sophie, don't fret. He's not coming back here again. With an attempted murder charge and arson, he'll very likely hang.'

Lydia cleared her throat. 'Not arson!' Both women looked at Lydia questioningly. 'It wasn't Jowan who torched the boat! Once Stan had calmed down after being released from jail, he told me what he'd seen. Yes, he saw Jowan, but he was up in the top meadow with a horse and cart. He said it was a woman who did it! He saw her running away from Kit's boat moments before he saw the smoke.'

'A woman!' Sophie winced regretting the sudden exclamation. 'Ria?'

Lydia shook her head. 'Stan said the woman was known to Kit. He described her as wanton, with red hair.'

'Georgie!'

Lydia glanced at Sophie. 'From Bochym?'

'Yes.'

'You need to speak to Constable Treen then. As for Stan, bless him, the lad was distraught that he couldn't make you both understand what he was trying to say to you. He blames himself for what happened to you,

Sophie.'

'Poor, lad, I'll thpeek to him.'

They all looked up when Dr Eddy knocked and popped his head around the kitchen door.

'May I come in?' He put his bag down. 'Now then, how is my patient faring this morning?' He inspected Sophie's face and then the inside of her mouth and smiled. 'Mmm, I can see they did a good job at patching you up. How sore is your nose?' He touched the bridge gently and Sophie squeaked. 'Sorry. I'm afraid it's broken. Fortunately, it has set itself in the correct position. 'You might look like you've done a couple of rounds with the boxer Bob FitzSimmons at the moment, but there will be no permanent disfiguration.'

Sophie smiled at his joke and then winced when her lip split again.

Gently taking the bandages from her hands, he muttered inaudibly and then smiled. 'If you can leave them uncovered, they'll heal better with air around them.'

'Thank you,' she whispered.

'We're all worried about Kit,' Lydia said.

'Well, let me put your mind at rest on that score. I've had word from the Hospital this morning. Kit's doing well.' He picked his bag off the table. 'I'll bid you ladies good day then.'

'Docthor,' Sophie said haltingly.

'Yes, my dear.'

'Nothing…ith nothing, thank you.'

Amelia narrowed her eyes, gesturing a 'leave it with me' nod to Dr Eddy.

'I must be going too,' Lydia said, pulling off her breakfast apron. 'I'm late opening the dairy.'

When they'd all gone, Amelia asked, 'What couldn't you tell Dr Eddy?'

Sophie's lip trembled in distaste. 'Jowan forced himself on me.'

'Did he now?' Her lip curled with distaste. 'Well, I

think we need to give you a quick check then.'

*

Kit was propped up in bed trying his damnedest not to breathe too deeply - if he did, a pain shot through him like a bolt of lightning.

'Now Kit,' a pretty nurse berated him. 'I can see you. You're holding your breath and it's not good for you! Dr Waite told you to breathe deeply.'

'He hasn't got a bloody tube in the side of his chest!'

'Hey! No profanity now. Think of my delicate ears.'

'Sorry, but this treatment is far worse than the injury,' he moaned.

'But absolutely necessary until your lungs are clear. Now we need deep, measured breaths to keep your lungs clear. Come on, do it now with me. Deep breath through your nose, good, and exhale.'

Reluctantly, he did as he was told, giving an agonising groan on his exhale.

'That's better,' the nurse said tidying his bed covers.

'For whom?' he grimaced.

'You'll thank me for it in a few days.' She pushed a thermometer in his mouth to stop his protest, and then proceeded to ask him a question. 'Do you need anything?'

He pulled the thermometer from his mouth. 'The train fare home!'

She shook her head, took the thermometer from his hand and put it back in his mouth. 'In a fortnight, we might consider it, but, *only* if you continue with your breathing exercises. The sooner you do as you're told, the sooner you'll go home.' She smiled warmly.

When she'd gone, Kit glanced at his surroundings, truly grateful for Peter's generosity at paying for this room and his treatment. To do all this for him when they had only been acquaintances for a few days - Kit would be forever in his debt. For now, Sophie was his main worry. He desperately needed to know how she was faring - the image of her poor battered face haunted him. When he'd burst into that filthy cottage, he'd seen nothing else but her. The shock, mixed with euphoria at finding her alive, had made him a sitting target for Jowan's attack. More than anything, he wanted to see her, but knew she was in no fit state to make the journey back to Truro.

His idle fingers itched for something to do - the sedentary life was not what he was accustomed too. Normally he'd either be working in the carpentry shed or on his boat. Oh - but his heart was sore for the loss of his boat – the thought of all that work gone up in smoke. If Jowan didn't hang for his misdemeanours, he would damn well kill him himself - if he ever got out of this place!

The nurse popped her head around the door.

'Yes, I'm breathing,' he joked.

'Good!' She grinned. 'There is a visitor for you.'

Sophie? His heart lifted, until the waft of familiar rose perfume preceded the very last person he wanted to see - Georgie.

'Oh, Kit darling. You poor, poor thing.' She planted a fragrant kiss on his cheek.

Kit scowled as he frantically looked for a nurse to help. 'What are *you* doing here?'

'Oh!' She pouted pulling off her gloves. 'Come now, what sort of welcome is that, after Georgie came all this way to visit you?'

'I don't want you here,' he hissed.

'But you're all alone, darling. There is nobody else here looking out for you now is there? Not now your lady friend's husband has returned. That's just too bad. Never mind, you can rely on Georgie to look after you. I, my darling, don't have an errant husband lurking in the background.'

'I said I *don't* want *you* here!'

'Of course, you do, darling. Don't be silly now.' She walked around the bed and pulled up the chair and sat down. Noticing the bottle of bloody water on the floor by his bed, she said, 'Ugh! That's vile!' With a swift kick she sent it flying under the bed out of sight, yanking out the tube inserted into the cavity of his chest.

Kit, convinced she'd stabbed him, due to the horrendous pain searing through his body, emitted an almighty howl, akin to a large animal caught in a trap.

Georgie reeled back in shock. She saw the tube on the floor and the gaping hole in Kit's side and realising what she'd done, grabbed the tube from the floor, blew on it and attempted to push it back into the wound. 'Kit, I'm so sorry. Keep still, I can't get it back in!' she wailed.

'Get the hell away from me,' he yelled, trying to swipe her hands away. The commotion brought the nurse and the matron running into the room.

'Stay calm, Mr Trevellick,' the matron said, but the pain was so intense, Kit could not refrain from crying out. She saw the large patch of dark red blood growing by the second on the sheet, made a swift assessment of the situation, dragged the tube from Georgie's hand and knocked her sideways. 'Nurse, go and fetch Dr Waite,' she ordered, and then turned to Georgie who had pushed herself into the corner. 'What on earth happened here?'

'I really don't know,' Georgie pleaded innocent.

'She bloody kicked the bottle out of the way. Get her out of here. Argh!'

'Kit darling,' she pouted, as she stepped out from the corner. 'Sorry, silly Georgie didn't realise it was important.'

'Get out!' he shouted, 'Argh!' He began to pant wildly as the pain came in sweat drenched shock waves.

The doctor appeared, checked the open wound and ordered the curtains be drawn around him. As the matron pulled the curtains, she glared at Georgie. 'You, go!'

'And don't let her back in here!' Kit cried as a film of sweat slicked his body. The pain - this agony was far worse than the actual knife wound.

'Mr Trevellick, try to stay calm.' He turned to the matron. What's happened?'

'Mr Trevellick's visitor had the tube in her hand and

was trying to push it back in! She's probably contaminated the wound.'

'I was trying to *help*!' Georgie shouted irritably.

The doctor and Kit exchanged an incredulous glance. 'Nurse, bring hot salt water and swabs, quickly. Matron, remove *that* woman!' he hissed.

Cupping Georgie's elbow, matron said curtly, '*You* must leave, *now*!'

'*No!*' Georgie said sullenly. 'I want to stay and help.'

'*Madam,* you've done enough damage!'

'How *dare* you speak to your betters like that?' Georgie said indignantly, but matron grabbed her arm and marched her out of the room. 'Unhand me at once!'

At the end of the ward, matron handed Georgie over to a rather burly looking orderly. 'Escort this woman off the premises, and *don't* let her back in,' she said, dusting her hands briskly.

'I'm going to give you a shot of Laudanum for the pain, Mr Trevellick,' the doctor said calmly, 'but I'm afraid I'm going to have to operate again to put the tube back in.' He glanced at matron – they both knew there was a very high chance of a serious infection now.

Chapter 47

In order to stop all the horrified gasps, stares and sympathy, Sophie presented herself in the dairy shed after milking the next morning, believing that the sooner everyone at the farm had seen her injured face the better. Stan had been the most emotional - dropping to his knees to beg her forgiveness. It took her a good five minutes and some frantic hand gestures to tell him it was all right, and it wasn't his fault.

*

When she returned to the kitchen, and despite Lydia's protests, Sophie was determined to set the table for breakfast. Using her wrists to carry things to the table, she managed the task with a satisfied smile. After assuring Sophie that she was not carrying any awful disease, Amelia had given her aloe vera to put on her burns - the cooling gel had eased the pain significantly. The salt solution was also helping to heal her mouth, enough to reduce the swelling of her tongue, making her lisp a little less defined that morning - though words with the letter s in them were a little problematic. She was still sore but felt so much better.

Just as the table was set, they both looked up when a clatter of hooves and the rumble of a carriage came into the yard. Lydia glanced at Sophie, holding her spatula aloft. 'Now who can that be at breakfast time?'

Sophie moved the net curtains and gasped as the de Bochym's carriage came to a halt. 'It's the countess!'

'Oh, blooming eck!' Lydia dropped the spatula, pulled the frying pan off the heat and kicked the pile of shoes lying about the kitchen floor into the broom cupboard. 'If I'd known I was going to be entertaining posh society I'd have had a spring clean!'

The knock came at the door before Lydia had chance to do anything else. She scanned the kitchen and threw her hands in the air. 'Well countess or not, she'll have to take us how we are.' She wiped her hands down her apron and opened the door.

'Good morning. Mrs Williams I believe?' Sarah smiled. 'Do forgive this early hour visit, but I'd rather like to see Sophie, if that is possible. I believe she is residing with you.'

Lydia bobbed a clumsy curtsy and stood back to let her fine visitor in - for once she was speechless.

Sophie braced herself for the familiar look of horror when Sarah saw her, but it did not come.

'Sophie.' Sarah hugged her gently. 'Bless you, what a dreadful thing to have happened to you. What can I do for you? I feel so helpless.'

'I'm fine. Lydia is looking after me.'

Sarah smiled warmly at Lydia. 'Well thank goodness Sophie has a good friend in you. May I?' She gestured to a seat.

'Yes of course.' Lydia pulled out the chair only to find a hen egg on the cushion. 'That bloody hen!' She clamped her hands to her mouth. 'Beg your pardon, my lady, but I've a wayward hen that drops her eggs everywhere. There isn't a person in this household who hasn't sat on one!' She quickly brushed the cat hairs off the cushion and gestured for Sarah to sit. 'May I offer you a cup of tea?' she said glancing nervously at the clock

Sophie could see Lydia was clearly fretting, and said, 'We're just about to serve breakfast to everyone.'

'Oh, forgive me. I'll not keep you then,' Sarah said getting up.

'No, stay there. You're very welcome to join us, my lady,' Lydia said.

'Well perhaps I'll take some tea and toast with you, thank you.'

When Eric breezed into the kitchen, he said, 'Bloody hell, whose is that carriage outside - is the king here? Oh!' He swiftly pulled his cap off. 'Begging your pardon, my lady.'

'Her ladyship is taking breakfast with us,' Lydia said proudly.

'Oh!' he answered incredulously, 'good.'

As the rest of the dairy folk filtered through into the kitchen, a stunned silence fell on the room.

'Come on you lot, sit down. We have company, so watch your manners,' Eric said.

Everyone sat silent and wide-eyed at their grand visitor.

'So, what do we owe this pleasant and quite unexpected pleasure, my lady?' Eric asked, tucking into a plate of bacon and eggs.

'I came to enquire on Sophie's health, but I can see she is in good hands here. I also wanted to know if there is anything I can do for you, Sophie.'

'She wants to see her Kit, that's what she wants,' Lydia said, placing a bowl of porridge in front of Sophie. 'Don't you, maid?'

'More than anything,' Sophie sighed.

'Of course, you do. Well, that is easily rectified - we'll go after breakfast if you please. I have the carriage all day, so perhaps I'll do a little shopping in Truro while we are there. How would you like that, Sophie?'

'Very much, thank you,' she said with a grateful smile.

Just as everyone finished breakfast, Amelia popped her head around the kitchen door. 'Hello, it's only me!'

'Goodness, you are a busy household,' Sarah said.

'My door is always open,' Lydia said proudly.

Amelia's eyes fell on Sarah and for a moment couldn't place where she'd seen the woman before.

'Come in Amelia, her ladyship is just having breakfast with us,' Lydia said brightly.

Amelia's eyes widened.

Sarah stood. 'Mrs Pascoe, isn't it? We met at Ellie and Guy's wedding some five years ago now, didn't we. It's lovely to see you again.'

Amelia was heartened that she remembered her. 'It's nice to meet you again too. I'm sorry to disturb you all, but

I just wanted a quiet word with Sophie, if I could?'

Intrigued, Sophie got up and followed Amelia out of the door.

'I've spoken to Ria, she's just home from the hospital. I thought you should know - Jowan passed away in the early hours.'

'I see.' Relief washed over her momentarily. 'Is Ria all right?'

Amelia smiled. Only Sophie would think of others before herself. 'She's holding up. For all his faults, and there were many, Jowan *was* her son. She's bound to feel the loss deeply, especially as she's lost him twice this year now.'

Sophie nodded.

'I've been doing the laundry for her from The Black Swan. At least she will still have her job when she feels able.'

'You're a good friend to everyone, Amelia.'

'Well, we all have to pull together. I must say, I was surprised to see her ladyship in there.'

'Not as thurprised as Lydia!' Sophie grinned.

'I bet.'

'Sarah has very kindly offered to take me to see Kit.'

'That's good news. It'll do you both good to see each other and…of course you're free to make plans to be together now Jowan has gone.'

As Amelia was about to take her leave, Lydia and Sarah stepped out into the yard.

'I'm just going to show her ladyship the cheese in the dairy, Sophie, before you set off to hospital.'

'In that case, I might just go and see Ria. Amelia has just told me that Jowan died last night.' Both Lydia and Amelia raised their eyebrows, but Sophie justified her visit by adding, 'I wouldn't be free if it wasn't for Ria.'

*

Sophie knocked tentatively on the door of Alpha Cottage, but when there was no response, she turned the handle and stepped through. So many unpleasant, unhappy memories came rushing at her, none more so than when she saw the blood - *her* blood splattered across the wall. The cottage felt cold and uninviting, splinters of the chair Sophie had fallen against still lay broken on the floor. Ria sat at the table, her hands folded on her lap, her complexion grey from a night sat in vigil. She looked up at Sophie, quite unperturbed by her visit.

'May I come in?'

Ria remained silent.

'I've just heard about Jowan.'

Ria smiled tightly and gestured for Sophie to sit. Without asking, she reached for another cup from the dresser and poured some tea for her. 'Sorry, there's no milk,' she said flatly, pushing the cup towards Sophie.

'I'm so sorry for your loss, Ria,' she said slowly, trying not to lisp

Ria nodded in acknowledgment, and turned her gaze downwards. 'It's strange, I'm not grieving for Jowan - perhaps because I've already grieved for him.' She lifted her eyes. 'The loss I feel is for that baby - my grandchild - my only grandchild.' Her eyes fluttered with emotion and Sophie knew it was not said with any malice. 'Harry snatched the babe from my arms without a by-your-leave when we reached the hospital - understandable of course, but I can still feel his presence in my arms.'

Sophie reached over and put her hand on Ria's. 'I understand that feeling too. Ria, thank you for calling for help. I'm deeply indebted to you.'

Ria gave a short humourless laugh. 'It wasn't a purely selfless act. Jowan taking that baby from its mother, did not sit easy with me, but most of all I wanted my freedom back, my life, my home, my job.'

Sophie shot her a sharp look.

'Yes, you have every right to look indignant. I know now how trapped you must have felt here, so I want to take this opportunity to apologise for how both of us treated you. You were so young and lovely when you came here. Jowan knew how coveted you were with the men of the village – how Kit looked at you!' She arched an eyebrow. 'He didn't like it, you were his, and he wanted to keep it that way, but he didn't do right by you and you did not deserve that beating.'

'No, I didn't!' she said firmly. 'I may live in the same house as Kit, but we haven't...'

Ria frowned when she heard the regret in Sophie's voice. 'Will Kit recover?'

'I sincerely hope so,' she whispered.

'I hope so too - for both your sakes. Here, I found this in Jowan's pocket.' She presented the ring Jowan had snatched from her neck and placed it gently on Sophie's burnt hand. 'I think Kit must love you very much to give you such a beautiful ring.'

Sophie nodded as her eyes blurred. 'Thank you, Ria.'

*

Sophie dressed formally in a dark blue dress and jacket for the journey to Truro. She knew her face was a terrible mess and had borrowed Lydia's 'best black funeral hat', which was the only one she had with a net to cover her face.

'Oh, God! Kit will think he's dying if I turn up at his bedside with this on!' Sophie joked.

'At least you're wearing it to visit him, not to bury him.'

Sophie sighed. 'God willing.'

*

They chatted amiably during the long journey to Truro, Sophie glad of the comfort of the padded leather seats, because her ribs hurt terribly. Sophie was heartened that their decision to join the association would be deferred until they had both made a full recovery. Sophie wondered whether to tell Sarah about Georgie being responsible for burning Kit's boat. It was a dilemma - but Kit should know first. It was his call to bring her to justice or not.

They were almost at Truro when Sarah said, 'Sophie, I

was unsure whether to say this or not, but as it was the topic of discussion at our dinner table the other night, I thought you should know.' She cleared her throat. 'Peter was very misled about Penvear's character. After his arrest, enquiries were made at his last place of work – a cotton mill in Yorkshire. It seems he embezzled money there too, but the most awful thing,' Sarah wrung her hands, 'he was also wanted by the Yorkshire police for the rape and murder of two young women! He's notoriously known as the Hooded Claw – something to do with what he does to his victims.'

Sophie exhaled, shivering at the memory of his nails tearing her skin.

'Forgive me, Sophie, I've upset you.'

'No! I'm just so relieved now that we brought him to your attention.' She shivered again.

*

Dr Eddy called in at the Post Office en route back from offering his condolences to Ria. As he emerged with his morning telegram update from the hospital, he bumped into Amelia.

'You looked troubled,' she said, noting the frown on his face.

'Yes, I need to go and see Sophie.'

'That sounds ominous, but you've just missed her. She set off to the hospital with the Countess de Bochym half an hour ago.'

He drew a deep breath. 'She hasn't, has she?'

'Yes, why?'

*

Sophie could hardly wait to see Kit, and was in such a rush Sarah had to quicken her step to keep up. 'I think he is down here,' she said, making for the room she had last seen him in. She was stopped at the door by a nurse.

'Oh, hello,' Sophie said breathlessly. 'I'm here to see Kit Trevellick.'

'I'm so sorry, but no one is to be admitted into this

369

room,' she said sternly.

'But.' Sophie looked to Sarah for guidance.

'It's all right.' Sarah placed her gloved hand on Sophie's shoulder. 'Good day to you, I am the Countess de Bochym, my husband arranged for Mr Trevellick's treatment - this is Sophie Treloar, his fiancée.'

'Oh!' A flicker of concern shadowed the nurse's face. 'Well, in that case. Would you mind taking a seat - I think Dr Waite would like to see you first.'

Sarah and Sophie exchanged worried glances but no sooner had they sat down, Sophie stood up again and began to pace. A sense of dread was building. 'Something has happened - I just know it!'

'Let's just wait and see,' Sarah answered, with more conviction than she felt.

'Dr Waite will see you now.' The nurse ushered them into a tiny, starkly furnished white office. 'The Countess de Bochym and Miss Treloar, doctor.'

'Thank you, nurse.' The doctor put down his pen. 'Please, take a seat.'

Sophie glanced around the room - the walls bare but for an amateur looking painting of a tin mine behind the doctor's desk. A clock ticked away the seconds, rather too loudly for Sophie's liking - she had an inordinate dislike for clocks. Though they were a necessity if one was to be on time for things, they reminded her of the silent hours she spent in Alpha Cottage with only the grandfather clock ticking her life away. The doctor wore a strained look as he leant forward and steepled his fingers. Panic rose in Sophie's throat - something *had* happened, she felt it in every fibre of her being. Sarah too must have felt the same impending doom, because she reached out and closed her soft hand over hers.

'Your ladyship, Ms Treloar,' the doctor took a slow measured breath, 'there is no easy way to tell you this…..'

Chapter 48

Peter Dunstan watched from his study window as his wife's carriage drove into view. He glanced at the clock as it struck five - she was very late, considering she'd arranged a charity dinner that evening. He pulled on his jacket to meet her at the door, but the moment he saw her face, he knew that something was wrong.

'Oh, Peter,' she placed her gloved hands in his, 'the most awful thing has happened.'

*

After an enlightening conversation with his coachman, Peter set off up the long drive towards The Wheel Inn. He needed a little time to himself to deal with what he'd just learned, first from Sarah and then from his coachman. Having several 'ladies of worth' gathering in his French drawing room for a charity dinner was not the place to be at the moment. In light of Sarah's shocking news, Peter had offered to send out notes to the ladies to cancel their event, but Sarah, ever the perfect host, insisted that it go ahead, even though she was deeply distressed by the events of the day.

*

Peter heard Georgie's laughter well before he entered the hostelry - it grated on his nerves like never before.

Dressed in her finery, she held a whisky in one hand, a cigarette in the other, and was holding court over anyone who would listen. 'Oh, hello, my lord,' she gushed, when she saw Peter. 'I was just telling everyone about my jolly little jaunt to Truro to visit Kit in hospital.'

Peter's eyes narrowed. '*Were* you now?'

Georgie's laughter faltered at the tone of his voice.

'And pray tell, have you explained the consequences of your *jolly little jaunt* and your thoughtless act of carelessness?'

With her hand to her chest she gasped, 'Moi? It was hardly my fault if that silly nurse left something on the floor to be knocked over. And what do you mean consequences?' Her laugh tinkled around the room. 'Kit was fine when I left - a bit overwrought perhaps.'

'I should think he *was* overwrought! You carelessly kicked the tube, that was draining Kit's lung, out of position!'

Georgie flinched at his vehemence. 'It was an absolute accident.'

A stunned hush had fallen on the crowd in the bar - no one had ever seen Peter so angry.

'And was it an accident that you picked it from the dirty floor and tried to insert it back into the wound?'

Georgie fell silent.

'Good god woman, what the hell were you thinking? Have you no sense in that silly air head of yours? Have you not given one single thought to the seriousness of the secondary infection you gave to Kit - a man already fighting for his life from a stab wound?'

Georgie's lip trembled. 'It was an accident, I tell you!' She put down her glass and made to leave.

'One more thing, Madam,' Peter said, halting her exit. 'Was burning Kit's boat an accident too?' This brought a collective gasp of horror from around the bar.

She regarded him reproachfully. 'I don't know what you're talking about.'

'That is strange, because my coachman verifies that he took you to Gweek the day you left us - even though you were to reside at Bonython! He said he was made to make the ten-mile round trip so that you could deliver something, and you did, didn't you?'

She lifted her chin. 'It was a present for Kit, that's all!'

'Whatever it was, it had a strong smell of Kerosene, according to my coachman.'

'I'd made him a lamp!' she said arrogantly, 'that is what I do!'

'A lamp that you lit before you left it on the boat. There was a witness who saw you running from Kit's boat, moments before smoke was seen coming from it.'

Georgie stumbled slightly, she reached out for someone to catch her, but found there was no help forthcoming. She grasped hold of the bar. 'How *dare* you accuse me of such a crime?' she said crisply.

'The evidence speaks for itself! Mark my words, Madam, even if Kit is unable to bring charges against you, I will personally have you held accountable for the arson attack.'

*

At the hospital, Dr Waite had explained to Sophie and Sarah that Kit had undergone an emergency operation to reattach the tube which was draining his lung, but despite every effort to flush the wound with saline, Kit had developed a high temperature due to an infection. It was very likely this had stemmed from the contaminated tube which Georgie had tampered with. He'd left them in no doubt that Kit might not survive.

That settled it, Sophie decided she would not leave Kit's side and had to practically force Sarah to leave without her. so determined was she to stay with him.

Gone now was her hat with the net hiding her bruised face. What did it matter what she looked like? Kit was fighting for his life.

Although Kit was in an induced sleep to keep him still, he was clearly agitated and extremely hot. Every few seconds his skin would glisten with perspiration and then he'd shiver uncontrollably. All Sophie could do, was watch helplessly.

At eight that evening a kind nurse came in to check on Kit. She brought a cup of tea for Sophie, which she received gratefully.

The nurse smiled sympathetically. 'I'll just see to Kit and then I'll take a look at your hands in a moment to see how your burns are faring. We need to look after you as well. It seems that you've both been through the mill recently.'

'I'm fine, really.' Sophie took a sip of tea. 'Nurse, give me something to do please - I can't just sit here.'

She assessed Sophie's blistered hands. 'You could perhaps bathe him with a cool flannel if you're up to it. It might even help your hands to heal. Here.' She passed the bowl of water over to her. 'See how you get on. Shout me if you need me to take over.'

Relieved to be doing something, Sophie rolled up her sleeves and for the next few hours bathed his body with cool cloths when necessary. It was an intimacy they should have shared for the first time in the privacy of their home, not here in hospital while Kit fought for his life. Throughout the night she watched with mounting concern as his condition worsened, fearful at seeing the same high spots of fever on his face that she'd seen on Jowan - and he'd died! Having no idea if Kit knew she was there or not, she constantly whispered words of love and encouragement, as she bathed his fevered brow. His response was an incoherent string of mumbles and moans.

Every hour, the nurse flushed the wound with saline. 'Germs have a funny way of hiding and multiplying. If we can get rid of the germs, we'll get rid of Kit's fever. So don't give up hope. Kit has his age and strength in his favour,' she'd told her.

Throughout the night, Dr Waite or his colleague visited Kit's bedside. Each time she would sit up hoping for some good news, but none came.

At eight the next morning, Glynis the nurse Sophie was now on first name terms with, popped her head around the door. 'I'm going off duty now, but you have an early visitor.'

Relieved tears formed as Guy walked falteringly into the room.

'Hello, Sophie. I thought you might need a little moral support.' He held his arms out to her.

Despite their brief acquaintance, Sophie flew to him. If nothing else, there was a common bond between them – a shared love for Kit.

'Peter told me what had happened. Once his horses had rested, he kindly lent me his carriage to come here. Neither of us wanted you to be alone at this time. If you'll permit me to stay with you, I'll send the carriage back.'

'Thank you. You don't know how much I would appreciate your company.'

'How is our boy?' Guy moved to Kit's side.

'Very, very ill. I'm terribly frightened for him.'

Guy picked up Kit's hand. 'Come on, my friend. It's not your time to go yet. You've a lot of living to do. If you can hear me, you bloody fight this, okay?'

Kit's eyes flickered open in recognition, and then closed again as though the light hurt him.

*

Kit was acutely aware of people around him, but confused as to where he was. Ghostly apparitions speaking, cold damp cloths touching his skin, fingers probing - all these things added to his nightmare. It was disconcerting to be prostrate and clearly injured, but unable to do anything to help himself. He fancied that he must still be in that filthy hovel, because occasionally Sophie's poor battered face came into his vision and then would fade from view - nothing felt real. He felt a sharp stab in his side and shrank back. Had he been stabbed again? If so, Jowan must still be in the room.

'Stay calm, Kit, the doctor is just taking a look at your wound.'

Sophie's voice came from far away and Kit panicked – Sophie must get away from here - away from Jowan!

'The wound still smells clean, that's a good thing,' the doctor said, 'Try to keep him cool, Sophie, you're doing a good job.'

Kit shrank from the cold cloth on his skin and began to shiver uncontrollably - concerned that he was naked in front of all these people. He tried to speak, but no words formed.

'It's all right, my love, I'm just cooling your body.'

He opened his eyes momentarily – it was Sophie's voice, but he could not recognise her face. He shrank back again.

'Don't be alarmed, my love. It's just me, Sophie.'

He was mortified, to think that he *was* naked in front of Sophie! His hands flailed, trying to grasp something to cover himself with, and then the pain seared through his side once more. Had Jowan stabbed him again? He knew he must get dressed and kill him. Otherwise, Jowan would kill *him*, and if he died, who would save Sophie from him then? She'll be trapped again, trapped back in her loveless marriage.

'He's getting very agitated. Can you hold him still, Guy? I'm going to fetch the doctor back.'

Kit was confused. *Why was Guy here? It's not safe for his new-born to be here. Jowan will snatch his baby too. He must take the baby away to safety and take Sophie with him.* He opened his eyes as Guy's face came into focus briefly. 'Help Sophie,' he rasped.

'Sophie is fine,' Guy assured him.

He shook his head. 'No, save her from Jowan.'

'She's with me now,' Guy said.

Kit's wild eyes locked on Guy, but then his face changed and Jowan stared down at him. Kit shrunk back in horror. "She's with *me* now," Jowan growled. Many shadows were around him again leaning and peering over him.

'He's been trying to speak, Sophie. He thinks Jowan still has you,' Guy told her.

'Kit, darling, I'm here.' Sophie stroked his damp forehead. 'I'm safe. Jowan is dead.'

He looked fearfully at her. 'No, he's not dead, he's here! He's come back for you.'

Sophie looked up at the doctor. 'He's very confused.'

Kit glanced wildly at the man in the white coat and then flinched - something was sticking in his side! He reached down to move the offending object, but the man grabbed his hand and held him tight.

'I think we need to secure his arms until he calms down a little,' Dr Waite said.

Kit pulled his hand free, twisting and turning, fighting the demons around him as they tied him down. *Let me loose. How can I fight Jowan like this?*

'How much longer will he be like this doctor?' Guy asked.

'It's hard to say - a couple of days perhaps.'

Kit panicked. *A couple of days! Jowan would be miles away with Sophie in a couple of days!*

'I'm going to give him some more laudanum, to settle him,' the doctor said.

Kit's head began to spin alarmingly as the room fell suddenly silent, and very slowly he began to slip back into oblivion.

*

Once Kit settled, Sophie sat down with her head in her hands - she was utterly exhausted.

'Get some rest, Sophie. I'll watch Kit and wake you if there's any change.'

'How can I rest, I'm so worried!'

Guy knelt at her feet and picked up her hands but she flinched at the touch. He turned them over, they were red raw. 'You've been through a lot these past few days. Be kind to yourself, it's what Kit would tell you to do. Now look, he's resting. You do the same.'

She gave a quavering sigh and nodded.

*

Sophie hadn't intended to sleep and woke disorientated in a room flooded with evening sunlight. The doctor was leaning over Kit, and she shot a questioning look at Guy, who smiled gently back at her.

'He's waking up and a bit restless,' Guy said.

She watched as the doctor took his pulse and frowned as he placed his hand on Kit's forehead.

'He's not out of the woods yet, I'm afraid,' the doctor said.

*

Kit fought his way through the bright red swirling fug towards wakefulness, and could hear Sophie's voice. It seemed far, far away.

'Come and look at this,' she was saying. 'I don't remember ever seeing such a sunset. It's like the sky is on fire.'

A powerful light penetrated Kit's eyelids. *Can't you see that's not a sunset – that is a fire! My boat is on fire!* He wanted to fight the great flames licking the sides of the hull, but he was tied down. Hot splinters of wood fell against him, spearing his side with agonising pain. The heat felt unbearable as the fire engulfed him.

They both turned as Kit began groaning.

'He's broken out in a sweat again,' Guy said. 'I think we'd better close those curtains. The sun seems to be bothering him.'

He could feel splashes of water on his skin - was someone putting the fire out? He struggled to move, to escape from the flames, but his bindings held fast. *I must get away from the fire and out of this filthy cottage. I must find Sophie – I know she's hurt.*

Ghostly shadows were around him again, murmuring, muttering. Would they free him? He shivered again. The fire had been extinguished, but his skin felt raw and terribly burnt. He was tired, so very, very tired, as he felt himself falling back into the smoke.

*

Finally, after many hours, Kit seemed to settle and Sophie could return to her chair. Guy too sat pale and spent - his eyes, dark with concern, stared out into thin air. It had been a constant battle to keep Kit still and cool, and they were both exhausted.

Glynis the nurse came back on duty and smiled softly at Sophie while she checked Kit's temperature and pulse.

She sniffed the wound and then looked down at Kit.

'Kit seems very calm tonight.'

Sophie searched Glynis's face for reassurance. 'Is that a bad thing?'

'It's better for him that he's not thrashing about,' she said evasively.

Sophie glanced at Guy, but he looked away - there seemed to be a marked shift in everyone's manner and it frightened her.

She moved towards the bed. 'Kit my love,' she whispered. His dry, cracked lips were open slightly as she kissed him gently on the mouth. 'Please, don't give up on me.' As she pulled back from him, he drew breath a little deeper than normal.

*

A veil of peace ensued as Kit's world fell quiet. People moved vaporously around him, fingers touching, probing, words spoken in hushed tones. An image of Sophie floated into his mind, her soft lips brushed his and then she drifted far, far away. His fight was over, the battle lost – he'd failed to save her. A real sense of loneliness prevailed, such as he had never felt before - he was totally and utterly spent. With one last tremulous sigh, the light loosened its grip and darkness prevailed again.

*

The air was hot and the stillness of the night felt oppressive. Sophie's eyes settled on Guy, who was sound asleep in the chair opposite. He'd not left Kit's side since he'd arrived, other than to relieve himself or to get some refreshments. Sophie was so grateful for his company - she knew she could not have done this without him.

At two in the morning a doctor came to check on Kit. He took his pulse, and placed the back of his hand on his brow. He glanced at Sophie and she searched his face for reassurance, but his tight smile left her with a sick sensation.

'I'll leave you for a while now,' he said gently. 'Call for

379

me if you need me.'

Nervously she stood and laid her hand on Kit's brow. Whereas he had been burning hot previously, his skin now felt cool - cold even. The change in temperature would surely be a good thing, if not for the fact that he looked deathly pale. Fearful of what the dawn would bring, she felt an overwhelming desire to be as close to him as possible. Ignoring the pain in her fingers, she unlaced her boots and climbed gently onto the bed, settling beside him. Gently her fingers traced a path down his lovely face and she whispered, 'I'm right here, my love, I'll not leave your side, I promise.' A violent surge of grief engulfed her, she opened her mouth to a myriad of soundless sobs, and a river of hot endless tears began to fall.

*

The morning light woke Sophie from her dreamless sleep, as the sun rose on another day. Dust motes floated in the shaft of light falling across the room towards where Guy slept peacefully, albeit uncomfortably, going by the alarming angle of his head. Her arm lay languid over Kit's body and her fingers slowly curled around the sheet covering him. She took a deep breath - fearful of what she may find when she looked up at Kit.

'Sophie.' It was no more than a whisper, as soft as a breeze. She lifted her head and turned to face him, astonished to find Kit's blue eyes gazing down at her. He smiled the smile he kept only for her. 'One morning, Sophie, I'd like to wake up next to you with us *both* under the covers.'

'Oh, Kit!' Tears blurred her vision. 'We will soon, my darling, soon,' she said, curling her little finger around his.

Chapter 49

Thirteen months later

The pale morning light sifted through the great bay window of the master bedroom at Quay House. The birds were wakeful and so too was Sophie, though her eyes seemed reluctant to open, wanting to luxuriate between the sheets a while longer.

'I know you are watching me, Kit,' she whispered.

She heard him laugh softly. 'I like to watch you sleep.'

Her lips curled. 'But I'm not sleeping.'

'You were a moment ago.' He moved a fraction closer and kissed her eyelids. 'Open your eyes, so I can wish you happy anniversary.'

Sophie did, to find his face radiant and his blue eyes gazing lovingly at her. She curled her little finger around his. 'And a very happy anniversary to you too, my love - how fast a year goes.'

'And so many things have happened.' He kissed her again.

Twelve months ago, and despite still recovering from their injuries, Kit wanted to keep his promise to Sophie that they'd be together by the harvest moon. They had waited long enough for their happy-ever-after, and it had so nearly been taken away from them. So, with only a few close friends in attendance, they had married at Constantine Church on Saturday, 21st September 1907.

Unable to fashion a dress for the occasion, due to the burns on her fingers, Sophie had worn Sarah's beautiful wedding gown - an exquisite waterfall of fine ivory silk and lace. As they said their vows, Kit placed a gold wedding band on her finger, next to the ring he'd bought her previously. Later that evening, they danced together as man and wife as the harvest moon rose in the sky.

'Even after twelve months of marriage, I never tire of waking up beside you,' he said. 'Do you know you smile in your sleep?'

'I have a lot to smile about!'

His eyes wrinkled gently. 'As do I, my love.' He pushed the covers back and kissed her extended tummy through her muslin nightdress. 'How is our precious little gift today?'

'Very active,' she replied stretching luxuriously. She glanced out of the window - this really was a beautiful room to catch the early morning sun. Peter Dunstan had offered them Gilbert Penvear's old residence to rent, after Sophie and Kit declined their kind offer to join the Bochym Arts and Craft Association. Their decision came following Kit's return home from hospital. He was met with a hero's welcome and many expressions of goodwill for his future with Sophie. It seemed their love story had touched the hearts of many in the village. They knew then that Gweek, where all their friends were, was where they really belonged.

Fortunately, Peter and Sarah understood their decision, but still wanted them to be part of the Association. If Kit and Sophie had any reservations about living in Penvear's house, the positives far outweighed the negatives. Quay House was a large spacious residence, with a range of outhouses which would convert into workshops - one for Kit to make his bespoke furniture and the other for Sophie to make her quilts. This they did, which enabled them to be part of the Association via outreach workshops. It was a concept that worked well. Kit had been inundated with commissions for his furniture, and Sophie's unique quilts had been picked up by Liberty of London. As for Kit's carpentry business - Jeremiah had taken over the lease of Kit's workshop and accommodation, and was now happily making coffins. All in all, everything had turned out well.

'Thank goodness the weather is going to be fine for our anniversary party,' she said.

She'd spent the previous day with Lydia, making bread, cakes and scones. A ham had been cooked and eggs boiled, and the table had been set in the sunny front room of Quay House.

Kit stretched and yawned. 'I'll cut the grass today, so if the weather stays good, we can dance outside later this evening.'

Sophie shifted uncomfortably. 'I'm not sure I'll be doing much dancing this year.' As Sophie enjoyed the last few moments in bed with Kit, she looked up at the plaque bearing the name *Harvest Moon* hanging on the wall behind their bed. It was the only thing salvaged from the wreckage of his boat.

Kit followed her gaze. He knew what she was thinking - it angered him too that Georgie had evaded prosecution on the charge of arson. The case had been dropped due to lack of proof and very little evidence, other than Stan's sightings of a red-headed woman running from the boat, and the coachman's testimony that she had delivered a gift to Kit. Whatever she'd delivered had perished in the fire and of course, having the best lawyer money could buy, helped her case.

'I'm sorry you never got to sail her, Kit.'

'I'm sorry too, but you know Sophie, she was just a set of timbers that kept me busy while I was waiting for you.' He kissed her tenderly. 'I may have lost the *Harvest Moon* but I gained everything any reasonable man could ever want.'

She winced slightly - her back ached dreadfully today, perhaps she had done a little too much yesterday.

Kit sat up on his elbow and frowned. 'Are you unwell, my love?'

Sophie winced again as a pain tugged in her lower abdomen. 'I don't know.' Reluctantly parting from him, she swung her legs over the side of the bed and pulled a shawl around her shoulders. One of the first things they had done in the house was to install a water closet, and this was where Sophie was swiftly heading. No sooner had she entered the room, a sharp pain tore through her, and her waters broke.

'Oh, my goodness! Kit!' He was by her side in a moment – his face pale with concern. She smiled weakly and put her hand to his face. 'Don't worry, but could you fetch Amelia quickly, please? I do believe our baby is in a hurry to meet us!' Her smile turned into another grimace as she drew a deep trembling breath.

The pregnancy had been a long, worrying journey for them, waiting for, and expecting, the misery of another miscarriage. For once though, Sophie had the benefit and luxury of being able to rest during the first few months, and with all the tender care and love bestowed on her, it seemed their miracle baby was about to be born.

*

Once Amelia and Dr Eddy were in attendance, Kit paced the gardens of Quay House, hoping and praying that all would be well. So wrapped up in what was happening upstairs, Kit realised it was too late to stop their party guests from Bochym and Poldhu from coming, so when they all arrived at two, they found to their delight that Sophie and Kit had welcomed a baby daughter into the world - albeit two weeks early.

Although exhausted and sore, Sophie asked Kit to carry her downstairs to join in the celebration. Although it was mid-September, the sun still had some real warmth in it, so they had, as planned, moved the party outdoors into the garden.

In the distance, the last of the harvest was being collected and loaded onto carts high up in Farmer Ferris's fields. The harvest dance would take place on the front garden of Barnfield House in the next few hours. The band had already struck up, and along with the sound of fiddle music, the rich meaty aroma of the hog roast cooking on the spit lingered in the air - but all that was for another celebration. Here at Quay House, there was just as much food, drink, music and good company to be had. While Kit poured the champagne into the glasses for the toast, Sophie sat in a deep cushioned wicker chair, with her precious baby in her arms, enjoying a cup of tea with all the wonderful friends she had made over the past eighteen months. Amongst their guests that day was Ria. When Sophie knew she would go full term with her pregnancy, she'd asked her to be their baby's surrogate grandmother, which Ria had tearfully accepted.

With a tinkling of a spoon on a bottle to get everyone's attention, Kit raised his glass.

'Ladies and gentlemen, please join me in a toast to Sophie, my beautiful wife of one year, and our equally beautiful daughter. As you know the moon in its many forms has played a huge part in our relationship, so we have decided to name our daughter, Selene, which I believe means goddess of the moon. Ladies and Gentlemen, I give you Sophie and Selene.'

They all raised their glasses in unison.

Sophie lifted her cup and said happily, 'And may I raise a toast to you, my darling Kit. I would like to thank you with all my heart, for your love, kindness and enduring patience while you waited for us to come into your life.'

A happy cheer went up. Eric began to play a romantic tune on the fiddle and Ria took the baby from Sophie's arms, so she could dance a few steps with her husband.

The End

SS SUEVIC

On 17 March, the Suevic ran aground against the rocks of the Maenheere Reef, a quarter of a mile off Lizard Point in Cornwall. Sixty volunteer crewmen from Cadgwith, Coverack, The Lizard and Porthleven rowed back and forth for 16 hours to rescue the passengers and crew.

Their incredible courage and perseverance saved 456 lives that day, and not a single life was lost. Six of the rescuers, including two Suevic crew members, were awarded Silver Medals by the RNLI to honour their heroic actions.

BOCHYM MANOR

Please note, Bochym Manor is a private family home and the house is not open to the public. They do however have holiday cottages available via Cornwall Cottages.

Bochym Manor Events also hold various art and craft workshop throughout the year.

Take a look at Bochym Manor Events on Facebook and Instagram for more information.

If you enjoyed Waiting for the Harvest Moon, please share the love of this book by writing a short review on

Amazon. x

Printed in Great Britain
by Amazon

79793723R00226